novum **pro**

AF192408

Lee Kite

The saga of
AGNEW THE MIFFED
and the
RAKE OF HEL

novum pro

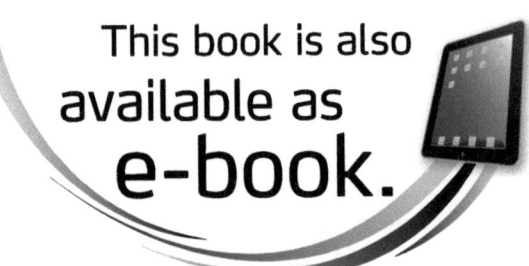

This book is also available as e-book.

© 2024 novum publishing

ISBN 978-3-99146-979-7
Editing: Charlotte Middleton
Cover photos: Lenapix,
Alla Batiuk I Dreamstime.com
Cover design, layout & typesetting:
novum publishing

www.novum-publishing.co.uk

Print product with financial
climate contribution
ClimatePartner.com/16547-2311-1001

Prologue

They came in the night. Heavily armed with murder in mind. At their head Gudrød the Hunter stood at the prow, hand clasping and unclasping the haft of his axe. The dragon boats glided silently under black sails towards the entrance to the fjord. Riding low in the water, even if anyone had been on lookout, they would have struggled to spot the sleek vessels as their forms merged with the dark sky and even darker sea, little more than vague ethereal shapes sweeping closer.

Gudrød's helmsman guided their boat towards the lights of King Harald Granraude's great hall and the settlement about. With the other boats forming a loose V behind, they entered the shelter of the fjord, the crews moving quickly to furl the sails and un-ship the oars before straining manfully against them to accelerate towards the settlement, beaching their boats upon the shingle where the fjord met the land.

The men leapt ashore, shields readied, swords, spears, and axes in hand and stormed forward with purpose. The first warning Harald's people had of the impending doom was of dogs barking. The first to fall to the invaders were those who ventured out to see what was causing the hounds' distress; unprepared, they were dispatched with ease. With malicious intent the men swarmed towards the great hall. They failed to spot one young boy who had also gone to see what had alarmed the dogs, and on spying the warband he rushed to the King's Hall to raise the alarm, but it was too little, too late.

King Harald Granraude, his son, Gyrd, and those warriors gathered in the hall grabbed what weapons they could and stood to face the onslaught. They fought hard; they died well. Their heroic stand would earn them places at the fabled hall of the fallen in Valhalla. For the women left behind, no such honour awaited them, only rape, murder, or both as Gudrød's men cut a vicious swathe through the town, until the prize they had come for was secured – Asa, daughter of King Harald.

Asa was discovered, raped, and bound but went defiantly, cursing Gudrød for his cowardly attack, and the oath breaker he was, beseeching the gods to punish him.

Most of the gods could care less, but one goddess watched the slaughter, witnessed the treachery but more than that saw the part another god played in the brutal raid, missed by all but her, and for that alone she accepted the call of vengeance, a call which would pit men against men and the goddess against the other gods.

Unaware of what he had begun, Gudrød sailed away, leaving the dead behind to rot.

1

There has been many a great heroic tale told of the good, the mad, bad, bloodthirsty, and downright psychotic warriors of the dark ages. Tales such as Beowulf have survived the centuries to delight small boys who like stories of men with swords beating up creatures like Grendel and his mum.

However, as well as the mythology the histories have also recorded the feats of real warriors, adventurers, pirates, and kings – such men as Eric Bloodaxe, Bjorn Ironside, Erik the Red, and Ivar the Boneless. Yes, he really was called Boneless. Why? Well, because he had no bones as such, hence the name, okay? Hey, I am not making this up, you know. Anyway, these men, the giants of their day, blazed a trail across the Dark Age world bringing fear, hero worship, and some unsavoury practices with monks to the rich tapestry which was life.

But there is one man who has been overlooked – a man of stature, a descendent of Siegfried himself, a pagan, a warrior, a man with exceptional hair. This is his saga, the saga of...

Agnew the Miffed

The saga starts on a storm-ravaged sea, aboard Agnew's dragon ship, a ship which is currently being bounced around like a child on a bouncy castle, leaving most of the crew wishing they had stayed home.

'Agnew, this is madness. I fear any moment the Midgard Serpent will rise from the ocean and snap us in two. Never have I seen the sea so angry. We must find land.'

Agnew, middling of height, lean, dark-haired, clean-shaven and not at all fitting the archetypal stereotype of a Viking warrior, spared a moment from his position hanging over the side of the ship, where he was diligently throwing up, to face his best friend.

'Tostig,' groaned Agnew, 'this is not a good time right... oh, by Odin's bea... heugh!'

Tostig, who by contrast was every bit the archetypal Viking warrior – big, strong, heavily bearded – watched his friend with some concern.

'Sorry, Agnew, I forgot you had a weak stomach.'

'Weak? I'm throwing it as far as I can... euuuuwh!'

'Agnew, the men can't take much more; the ship can't take much more.' Tostig's normally gruff voice broke with worry. 'This is not a way for a warrior to die.'

With a groan Agnew forced himself away from the side of the ship and stood to his full height, which along with his pasty complexion did not exactly make him look imposing.

'We can't head for land, Tostig.'

'Why not?'

'Because I don't know where the nearest land is.'

'You jest,' Tostig replied more in hope than conviction.

'No; I'm lost.'

'But how? You are a master navigator!'

'No, not really.'

'Did you not find the fabled land of Atlantis? And were you not Naddodd's navigator when he discovered Iceland?'

'Well, yes,' said Agnew, who at least had the decency to look guilty, 'but we just sort of ran into Iceland. I swear, one minute it wasn't there, just fog, then suddenly CRACK and there we were, run aground on the place. I can't really say I navigated us there.'

'And Atlantis?'

'Ah, yes, Atlantis, a good one, that. I just made it up.'

'No!'

'Yes, never existed. I was drunk. Helga, you remember Helga?'

'Blonde, buxom, eaten by a bear?'

'Yes, that was the one. Well anyway, she was saying, "Oh you never do anything great; all the other lads are off finding places and bringing back stuff. What have you ever done?" So, I said I had found Atlantis.'

'But those beads and that exotic pottery you brought back? And what about those slave girls that were all dusky and very accommodating?'

'Hispania. I had been to Hispania. The girls were just left over from a party and thought it would be cool to see Norway.'

Tostig, for once his indomitable spirit crushed by Agnew's blithe apology, slumped down into the ship, back against the bulwark, head in his hands. 'We're doomed. Your lies have doomed us.'

'Look, don't worry, these things usually have a way of sorting themselves out.'

'You can lie to the rest but not me,' sniffed Tostig. 'How long have we known each other?'

'Since the day we were old enough to get our first axe.'

'Yet knowing that you have still brought me on a fool's errand to an angry sea. I shall drown. We shall all drown, Agnew, and it's your fault,' Tostig yelled angrily over the roar of the howling tempest.

'That's a bit unfair. I can hardly be blamed for the weather,' Agnew yelled back grumpily.

'The gods are punishing you for your deceptions and are taking us with you. We should die a heroic warrior's death in battle, not be pulled to our doom by Ràn's daughters.'

'I'll be honest – I don't see how this is any worse than a warrior's death,' said Agnew with remarkable candour. 'I mean, if it's a choice between drowning or having someone shove three feet of cold iron through my guts, well, drowning doesn't sound so bad.'

'But we are warriors. It is our birthright to die gloriously in battle, where the Valkyrie will carry us to the fabled halls of Valhalla, there to sing, to quaff ale, to satiate our lusts on the buxom serving wenches during the nights, to fight during the day, ready for the final battle at the time of Ragnarök.'

'Okay, I get the point,' snapped Agnew. 'Glory in battle, wenches, honour, blah, blah, blah...' Agnew began his tirade only to look down at where his friend was slumped, and apart from wondering where Tostig had learned the word 'satiate', his mood softened. It was hard not to be touched by the fervent gleam in

Tostig's eyes when he spoke of Valhalla, especially the bit about the serving girls. In truth, the bit about the wenches was the only part of the afterlife which appealed. You could keep the fighting day in and day out for all he cared. He was also not entirely sure of the validity of the entry criteria for getting into Valhalla. It had always seemed odd to Agnew that the heroes the gods chose to represent them in the final battle against Loki's brood were those warriors who had not been good enough to survive a battle in this life. Surely the ones you want are those who survived to a ripe old age – you know, the wily, clever ones who had not got hacked to death in some random battle, but hey, who was he, Agnew, son of Grimor the Furious, to question the will of the gods, insane though they most obviously were.

Sighing slightly and still feeling a bit queasy, Agnew hunkered down by his friend. 'Cheer up, Tostig,' he said brightly. 'If it's a warrior's death you want then it is a warrior's death you shall have.'

'You swear?'

'Yes.'

'But the sea? The gods?'

'Damn them all, I'm not drowning today, and neither are you. If this ship were going to break, she would have by now, yet see how she still rides the waves.'

'Agnew, we're sat in a foot of water,' observed Tostig gloomily.

'What's a foot of water?' Agnew said strongly, his words carrying across the roar of the wind. 'We can bail. Tostig, get the men bailing, bailing for their lives, and I shall steer this ship. If they keep us afloat, I will get us to land. And then we shall quest to find you an enemy worth fighting, worthy of your warrior's soul, and should you fall, it will be celebrated by the bards till the end of time.'

As Agnew stood there damning the gods, Tostig felt his spirits lift and with a bellow of defiance he stood steadily against the roll of the ship.

'You with me?' demanded Agnew.

'I'm with you!' roared Tostig and thumped Agnew on the arm, proof of his belief.

'Then get these whoresons off their arses and start bailing.'

With a determined grimace Tostig turned away from Agnew and went from man to man, rousing them from their cold sea-sick terror to turn their hands to saving the ship. Agnew, rubbing his arm where Tostig had just thumped him, *damn, that hurt*, he thought, stumbled to the steering board, unlashed it, and took a firm grip. He had no idea where he was, no idea where he was going, but if he could steer this thing through the storm, and providing they did not sail off the edge of the world, he was confident they would hit land at some point. Providing he looked confident the men would continue to bail. At least that was the plan.

Watching the men wearily set to their task, Agnew could not help but think this was going to be a very long day.

2

When you joined us, Agnew was taking charge of his storm-ravaged ship with every intention of sailing it to safety. Now, the usual convention at this time would be to flash forward to a calm sea under an azure sky with our battered but happy vessel being rowed smoothly to the sound of raucous song, but alas this is the Dark Ages, so no such luck.

As we look down through a tumultuous sky, we see an angry sea doing everything in its power to swamp a Viking ship as it bravely battles the elements. The ship is clearly not having the best of it, and if this were set in the future you just know there would be a Scottish engineer screaming, 'She cannae take it, cap'n!' right about now.

On board, Agnew knew his actions were fruitless. He could feel the ship becoming ever heavier beneath his feet, feel it struggling to respond to his attempts at steering and all the time he felt his own hope being washed away with every cold, salty wave which broke over his head. All in all he was not having a good day.

The men, seeing him standing there seemingly unflustered, were either bailing or rowing gamely, but the hours of strain had taken their toll. Burning shoulders and blistered hands meant their efforts were becoming nothing more than a token effort. Another monstrous wave broke against the side of the ship threatening to capsize it, yet once again it righted, though now Agnew could feel it wallowing even more horribly than before.

One more like that, thought Agnew, *and we are done for.* And so, for the first time in a long time, Agnew implored the gods for help. It wasn't that he didn't believe in the gods, he did, he had been raised a good heathen, but he generally thought it best for man and gods to leave each other alone. The less they poked their noses into his affairs the better, but now, it seemed, they were his only hope. He couldn't help thinking that coming back to them, contrite and desperate, they were going to have the last laugh, but with a mixture of trepidation and not a little scepticism, Agnew pleaded for the lives of his crew to any god listening, and should any god see fit to save them they would have Agnew as their most gracious servant. In times to come Agnew would wonder if it would not have been better to have stayed quiet and let the sea have him, but the prayer yelled to the sky for any god to hear was out there and there was no taking it back. Little did Agnew and his crew know their real troubles were just about to start.

The ship heaved over as a flash of lightning split the sky accompanied by an almost instantaneous crash of thunder as another wave swept the deck. Agnew braced himself against the tiller, ready for the impact, the cold grey water hitting him with the force of a war hammer, forcing him off his feet. Desperately he reached out to grab at something, anything to stop him being swept overboard, but his hands clasped nothing but air, and with resigned dread he went over the side.

Agnew instinctively screwed up his eyes and gulped in as much air as he could, ready for when he hit the sea, which seemed to take an age, and then he hit... the floor.

What the... he thought as he realised he wasn't in the sea. Slowly, cautiously, he opened one eye and then the other, and then as his breath began to give out, he remembered to start breathing again. Agnew sat up. Not only was he not in the sea but he was also not on his ship either, which given his recent circumstances was a little bit strange. He wasn't even laying on a beach or rock with the sea crashing about him. Wherever he was, he was underground.

Agnew stood up carefully and shook the sea from his soaking hair, and if ever a man was made for a L'Oréal advert, it was him. The moment he stopped shaking his head his hair fell back into place in a style which can only be described as windswept and interesting. In years to come, Hollywood leading men would need an army of stylists to achieve the same effect. Agnew, though, being of Viking stock was completely unaware of what a model agency's dream he would have been and instead put his mind to more practical matters.

'Where in Thor's name am I?' he asked no one in particular.

'Where do you think?' said a cold voice behind him.

Startled, Agnew spun round, drawing his sword in one fluid motion only to stumble backwards in fear, his sword wavering at the terrible apparition before him.

'Lower your sword. It will do you no good here.'

'I'll be damned if I will.' Agnew's voice quavered even as he toughened his stance.

'Have it your way,' said the woman, if woman it was, for she was half ebony black and half pallid white, partially skeletal where her thin, aged, translucent white skin pulled tight across her frame, split in places with bone and sinew breaking through, with a face which was cold, hard, and devoid of compassion. She lifted a bony finger and touched it to the point of Agnew's sword, which Agnew dropped instantly with a howl as a soul-numbing cold spread down the blade into the haft, burning his hand with its intensity.

'Who... who are you?' asked Agnew, cradling his damaged hand.

The woman rolled her eyes in disbelief. 'Look at me,' she said angrily. 'Do you know of anyone else who looks even remotely like me? Your people tell stories of me; they fear me. Think, man, how many half-black half-white girls do you know?'

'Well, none, but I've never been here before. All the girls here may look like you.'

The woman's eyes narrowed dangerously 'Choose your next words carefully or they may be your last, Agnew.'

'You know me?'

'Of course.'

'But how?'

'You called for help; I answered.'

'But, I mean, I didn't expect... Then that means...'

'Go on, you almost got there,' the partly skeletal creature taunted sarcastically.

'But that would mean that you're a...'

'Are you really this stupid? Who am *I*!'

Agnew stared at the woman, at her terrifying form, took in the less-than-cheerful surroundings, and as the tales from his childhood came flooding back, he blurted, 'HEL!'

'Hurrah! Finally,' said Hel. 'How is it no one ever recognises me? I would say I'm pretty distinctive.'

'Distinctive, yes. I'm not so sure about the pretty...' began Agnew then backpedalled desperately, 'though you are a goddess, so the being pretty is not that important, I guess? I mean, you're a goddess; what does pretty even mean to a goddess? Nothing, I'm sure.'

'Carry on like that and I will throw you back in the sea, where Ràn will claim you,' the goddess of the Underworld growled tetchily.

Agnew did not move. He did not speak, though he had a lot of questions – primarily, was he dead?

'You aren't dead,' said Hel as though she had read his mind. 'I merely plucked you from your ship and brought you here. You are quite alive... for now.'

'My crew?'

'Still alive. I think they may be wondering where you have got to.'

'You have to put me back; I have to save them. Put me back now,' demanded Agnew.

Hel regarded the sopping-wet Viking coldly, but then Hel tended to regard everything coldly. Being the goddess of the Underworld did tend to colour one's judgement of humanity and life in general, and given the typical Norse propensity towards doom and gloom, her domain had done little to lighten her mood down the years.

'I could put you back...' she began.

'Good. Then do it.'

'But your ship will sink before your men pull another stroke. No Valhalla for them, for which they will hold you responsible until Ragnarök finishes us all. Or you could accept my help, and you and your men will live to fight another day.'

'What's the catch?' asked Agnew, more astutely than most would have given him credit for.

'You will owe me, but then that was the core of your prayer, was it not?'

'Err, yes, I suppose.'

'Suppose nothing. Either you accept my help and my conditions or I toss you back and leave you to Ràn's tender mercies. Your choice, but hurry up, I don't have all day, you know.'

Agnew shuddered. He knew for his proud warriors a death at sea was as bad as dying in one's sleep. As we have already determined, Agnew had wondered about the attractions an afterlife which consisted of fighting all day and drinking all night offered. He had always been less than enthusiastic with the idea of being slain in battle, as that just sounded bloody painful. So potentially being slain daily till the final battle at Ragnarök was a bit disconcerting, though the drinking all night and partying with buxom wenches did hold more allure. When put together, pain in the day and pleasure at night was a much better afterlife than was likely to be offered by Ràn, which only offered shame and misery.

'Well?' said Hel. 'What's your answer? I am quite busy; I do have an underworld to run, you know, so choose, NOW!'

'Save my crew and I will do whatever you require of me,' Agnew answered humbly.

'I was hoping you'd say that, aaaaaaaaaaahahahahhaha haaaaaaaaaaaaa...'

'Oo-kay,' said Agnew as the cackling goddess' laugh drifted away, 'could you save my crew now, please?'

'Humph.' Hel sniffed disappointedly. She had hoped for more of a reaction to her best maniacal laugh. 'It's done,' said the goddess, clicking her fingers. 'Now, let's you and I talk business.' Putting a semi-skeletal arm around his shoulders, the goddess led Agnew deeper into her realm.

3

So, as our hero is taken on a tour of Hel's abode, and a more cheerless place you could not imagine – it certainly will not be topping anyone's list as a tourist attraction any time soon, that's for sure – we should maybe go look at what is happening to his ship instead.

Let us slip back in time to the moment a certain Viking with film-star good looks was washed overboard. Take a moment to drink in the heady brew of fear, anger, consternation, and not a little disappointment at Agnew's sudden disappearance, for as the wave which spelt his doom cleared the ship, the crew were left staring at an unmanned tiller bar. For Agnew's close friend, confidant, and drinking partner, Tostig, it was almost too much to bear.

'Agnew! NOOOOOOOOOOOOOOOOOOOOOOOOOOOOOO OOOOOOO!'

For little Snorri Alfsson, it was a moment to declare in doom-laden tones what all the others had been thinking. 'That's it; we're finished. No warrior's death for us. We have been led to ignominy.'

'Ignominy? What's ignominy?'

'Dunno.'

'Maybe it's an island?'

'What, like Iceland?'

'No, then he'd have said we've been led to Iceland, not ignominy.'

'So, where is this ignominy? I can't see any island round here – it's just the sea.'

'Maybe it's only small?'

'If it's so small we can't see it, why have we come here?'

'Search me; I wasn't steering.'

This discussion could have gone on for ages. Well, when you are stuck out at sea far from land and a good pub you must make your own entertainment. Luckily for us but not so lucky for our bunch of sea-sodden Vikings, a sickening crack from the ship's hull brought their attention back to their precarious predicament.

Grim-faced, the crew turned to Tostig for guidance, which proved how desperate they were. That is probably not a fair assessment of Tostig. If you wanted guidance on how best to cleave a man in two or how to throw a screaming maid over your shoulder in one sweeping motion whilst hacking her husband's head off, then yes, Tostig's your man, but guidance on sailing? Well, that really wasn't his strong suit.

Tostig stared back at the faces staring at him and fear gripped his soul. There was not much which scared Tostig. In fact, only two things really scared Tostig. One was the thought of not dying a hero's death, a bit like now really, hence his current palpitations, and the other thing was bats. The gods alone know why a small flying rodent should reduce him to a quivering wreck, but it does. Isn't it strange how the human mind works? But enough of that. With Agnew gone and with the ship about to break apart, his fear of a less-than-heroic death led him to the only decision left open to him.

'Grab your weapons.'

Without hesitation, the Vikings, warriors to a man, drew their weapons.

With a voice which sounded like it consisted entirely of gravel, Tostig yelled above the storm, 'We are warriors; we are not meant for a watery death. We demand death by sword and axe!'

'HURGH!' his men roared.

'It's our birthright!'

'HURGH!'

'The field of battle our resting place!'

'HURGH!'

'But we have no enemies here, only the sea. The only weapons, our own.' Tostig stated the obvious

'True.'

'He has a point.'

'Bit shit really.'

'So,' Tostig took a deep breath then uttered the words that to you and me must sound like utter madness, 'we only have one option – to take each other's LIVES!'

'Er?'

'What?'

'Are you sure?'

'It's hardly death in battle, is it?'

'What, you want me to kill Audolf? But he's my best mate!'

Tostig responded to the crew's lukewarm uptake of his idea. 'Do you want to spend the afterlife in the halls of misery?'

'No.'

'Do you want to be accursed to an afterlife of shame?'

'Not really, but...'

'Or do you want to spend a glorious afterlife drinking, wenching, and fighting?'

'Yeah, but...'

'To stand shoulder-to-shoulder with Odin, Thor, and Tyr as they vanquish their foes?'

'Well, when you put it like that...'

'Enough talking. Grab your weapons, face each other, and for the sake of our warrior souls, kill the man in front of you.'

The men looked to each other uncertainly as Tostig stood bristling, and once again unenthusiastic dissent broke out.

'Will this work?'

'Buggered if I know.'

'I'm not sure it's in the spirit of the thing.'

'What if you insult me first and I insult you? Then we would have a grievance against each other, and it would count as death during a quarrel.'

'By Odin's beard, SILENCE!' Tostig roared above the howl of the wind. 'This is our only hope of reaching Valhalla. It may not be death in battle, but it is still death by sword and axe. We will all die with weapon in hand. It counts; it must count. If we don't kill each other, we will drown and be nothing more than a plaything for Ràn. Do you want that? Do YOU?'

The men looked at Tostig, carefully considering his words, and as the ship creaked and cracked and the sea started to flood in, his reasoning took hold, and death at each other's hands seemed the better option. I know to you and me it sounds stupid, but these are proud Norse warriors, and they live by a different code, and frankly drowning is simply not an option. Look, this isn't my religion. I don't make the rules. You will just have to accept it.

The crew quickly paired off, friend-to-friend, warrior-to-warrior, and, each placing a hand behind the other's neck, pressed their swords or knives against each other's chests and braced themselves, ready for the final thrust.

'Okay, on my count of three,' yelled Tostig. 'ONE, TWO, THR–'

WHOOOSH.

'ARGH!'

WHOOOOMP.

Silence fell briefly, then as the shock wore off from suddenly being in a flying spinning ship, which dived, folded, and twisted through a giant whirlpool only to be spat out the other side, the groaning started.

'What the...?'

'My ears are bleeding...'

'My head hurts. Why does my head hurt? I thought the sword was supposed to go through my chest?'

'Are we dead?'

'I don't feel dead.'

'How would you know?'

'No idea. I've never been dead before.'

'Where in Odin's realm are we? Tostig?'

Tostig was dazed, confused, and feeling like he had been turned inside out. Like the others his head was thumping, his ears were ringing, and he felt sick. This was not how he had imagined death. He was also surprised to find himself still on board the ship.

Tostig got unsteadily to his feet and stared over the side. What he saw did not fill him with glee. Instead of seeing the

Bifrost Bridge with Heimdall ready to welcome them to Asgard and send them on their way to Valhalla, instead he found himself staring at the inside of a large cavern, dim and cold. A grim, rocky shore was off to his left, which ran up to the cavern wall and with no way out other than into an even darker more foreboding cave. However, even the cave seemed inviting compared to what he saw when he looked down.

Their ship was afloat, just, though no longer on the sea but on a large underground river, which flowed past them with a strange slith, slith, slith sound.

Those watching Tostig suddenly saw his shoulders sag despondently. He slowly turned his back against the bulwark and slid down to the ship's deck.

The crew looked to one another uneasily then all rushed to the side of the ship to see what Tostig had seen. As the grim realisation of their fate struck them, their faces turned white beneath their beards. Tostig, from his crumpled position, could only murmur repeatedly, 'We were too late, too late, too late!'

4

Hel sat back on her throne and simply said 'Well?'

Agnew, seated in a less grandiose chair, stared up at the goddess with a mix of apprehension and resignation, none of which was helped by his surroundings, which even by Norse standards were miserable. Dark Age Norse habitats were not light, airy places full of IKEA furniture. Instead they tended to be dark, smoky, and heavily wooded with lots of animal skins and weaponry strewn about the place. Hel's chambers took the same basic theme but added a damp and chill atmosphere with a soundtrack of wails, moans, and much gnashing of teeth, and for good measure threw in a dash of menace coupled with a smidgen of foreboding. I suppose if Dulux did the colour scheme it would probably be called Misery with a Hint of Despair.

With Hel's question hanging heavily before him Agnew swallowed hard. With a deep sense of unease he answered, 'Yes, I will hunt down your rake and return it to you.' From the gleam which flickered in Hel's eyes he almost immediately wished he hadn't, though in truth he didn't really have much choice.

Agnew had lost track of how long he had been in the Underworld. There was no sun, no day or night by which to gauge the passing of time, just an endless gloom punctuated here and there by candlelight and the occasional fire or flaming torch. It felt like he had been here for some considerable time. His body ached, and he felt tired, though that could just be the aftereffects of the battering he had taken in the storm. Although Hel had made him walk some distance to her hall, once there she had fed him and given him ale, so although not the prettiest hostess in the world she was at least mindful of her visitor's immediate needs.

After hearing his reply, Hel stood and beckoned Agnew to do the same.

'Your answer pleases me. This will be beneficial to us both. I presume you want to get back to your ship and your men. The quest is waiting, so off with you.'

'Er?' said Agnew as he was half-coaxed half-ushered out of Hel's hall by some fawning dwarven lackey.

'Let your men know who saved them. Oh, and Agnew...'

'Yes?'

'I will be keeping a close eye on your progress. If I get any sense that you are backing out of our bargain, trust me when I say you will rather I had let you drown.' Hel finished menacingly with a smile colder than a Norwegian fjord in winter.

By contrast, and primarily because he wanted away from the goddess of death as quickly as was possible, Agnew smiled warmly and said with as much conviction as he could muster, which was not much, but given his situation it was as good as it was going to get, 'We'll get it back for you, have no fear.'

'I haven't,' replied Hel, 'but you should.'

Agnew gulped. 'Show me out, dwarf,' he said, hurriedly turning away from Hel, giving the dwarf a push.

The dwarf led Agnew out of Hel's hall and into the dark and dreary passages of the Underworld. As they walked, he caught glimpses of the dead, souls which mooched about in a state of perpetual misery and depression with nothing to do, nowhere to go, and saddled with a sense that their lot was a worthless pointless one, a bit like being from Milton Keynes but without the concrete cows.

'Tell me, dwarf, why don't the dead try to leave this place?'

'My name's Delling.'

'What?'

'My name isn't dwarf; it's Delling,' Delling said indignantly.

Agnew stopped and stared down at the dwarf. 'And?'

'There is no "and". I would just rather you call me by name than call me dwarf. I don't call you man, so you shouldn't call me dwarf.' Delling's rich baritone rumbled at the sleight.

'How about midget?'

'Sod off!'

'Haven't I seen you in one of those wandering shows that come to the village from time to time?'

'If you don't shut it...' Delling bristled.

'My, you are a tetchy little fellow,' Agnew taunted. He was miffed, on edge, and taking it out on the dwarf was making him feel better.

'I'm warning you...'

'I bet my sister would think you're cute.'

'I'm not cute.'

'Yes, you are, yes, you are, yes, you are.'

'Say one more thing, just one more, and I'll bloody have you...'

'Can I give you to my sister as a pet?'

'Right, that's it, I'll bloody kill ya!' Delling snapped and swung his battle-axe, admittedly quite a small battle-axe, well, it would have to be small – he was a dwarf – after all, no point having a... Anyway, that is not the point. The point is he hefted it into his hands and swung with all his might at Agnew.

'What are you doing?' Agnew laughed, stepping out of the way.

'Stand and fight, you piece of shit.'

Grinning, Agnew skipped out of range of Delling's clumsy attack. 'You'll never hit anyone swinging your axe like that.'

'Fight me, damn it! Why won't you fight me?'

Agnew took a step backwards, avoiding the wickedly sharp axe head as it swiped past his midriff harmlessly. Infuriated, Delling reversed his swing and lunged at the laughing Viking, who deftly kept just out of reach of the dwarf's whirling blade. Like a mad dervish Delling kept up his attack, only for his laughing tormentor to step away from each killing blow. Eventually Delling's frenzied attack slowed as his energy ran out. 'Stop... uhngh... laughing... argh... at... uurg... me!'

'I'm... hahahahahahahaha... sorry, but you... hahahahaha-hahaha... you're... aaaaahahahahahahaaaaaaaaaa... very, very... ha-ha-haaaaaa... funny!' Agnew could barely get his words out, tears of mirth streaming down his face.

'Bastard!' swore the dwarf as his attack ground to a halt. Breathing hard and sweating profusely, Delling rested wearily against his axe.

Agnew, his sides aching, tried to get his laughing under control. Looking at the despondent dwarf he felt the slightest tinge of guilt. 'I'm sorry,' he apologised, wiping the tears of laughter away from his eyes, 'but you looked ridiculous swinging that thing around. Have you ever actually fought anyone for real?'

'What? Why?'

'I've seen children with more idea of how to attack someone with an axe than that. You were all over the place.'

'So?'

'So, if I had half a mind, I could have cut you in half without blinking.'

'And if you had even just half a mind, you'd have never wound up down here beholden to Hel,' snapped Delling nastily.

Agnew stiffened at the insult but, staring down at the panting dwarf, conceded the point magnanimously. 'Fair point. I asked for that.'

'That you did.'

'Okay,' Agnew composed himself, 'how about we start again, Delling?'

Delling cocked an inquisitive head but said nothing.

'I'll not call you dwarf. I'll use your name, and you can call me Agnew. But no more of your attacking nonsense, okay?'

Delling nodded begrudgingly. 'Okay,' he said and held out a hand.

Agnew grasped Delling's forearms and shook them. Delling re-shouldered his axe and the pair set off once more.

'You never answered my question,' said Agnew.

'What question?'

'Why don't the dead try to leave here?'

'They do, but they get stopped.'

'What stops them?'

'Haven't you heard the tales?' asked Delling with a touch of surprise.

'Yes, but I never really took much notice. I was raised expecting to die in battle and go to Valhalla. What happens in the Underworld was usually skimmed over. That was considered talk for women and the old.'

Delling looked up at Agnew askance. 'You mean you have no idea what is down here or what Hel represents?'

'Should I?'

'You may have thought twice about invoking Hel's help if you had.'

'To be honest I didn't expect to be saved.'

'Then why plead to the gods if you didn't expect an answer?'

'I was out of options.'

'So, you called on Hel?' Delling sounded amazed.

'No – I threw it out there for any god to hear. I must admit I was hoping for a different god to answer.'

'Let me guess – Thor, Odin, Frey, perhaps?'

'Now you come to mention it.'

'Huh, fat chance. They don't care about anything but themselves.'

'You lie. They watch over us.'

'Bollocks. They're the biggest self-serving bunch you are ever likely to meet.'

'No!'

'Yes.'

'But they are the gods. They created us, gave us life and purpose.'

Delling gave Agnew a friendly pat on the lower back. Well, he couldn't reach Agnew's shoulder. He decided to put the fearsome warrior straight. 'It's not your fault that is what the gods have led you to believe, but it's a crock of shit. The gods are not great. Thor is not a hero; he's just an immature thug. Odin is a doddering old fool who refuses to accept change and believes nothing good has happened since 684 and as for Frey, well, they say he sleeps with his sister. Mind you, I've seen his sister and given half a chance I would sleep with her too.'

'Lies.'

'No, really, I'd be all over her like a rash.'

'I meant you lie about Odin and Thor.'

'Why would I lie?'

'Well, because, I mean, then again...'

'Exactly, I have no reason at all. The gods are, for the most part, a bunch of drunken idiots, and why wouldn't they be? They all know their days are numbered and that they are going to cop it when Ragnarök comes storming along. They have foreseen their own demise, and if that isn't enough to drive anyone loopy, then I don't know what is. If you knew exactly how and when you were going to die, wouldn't you be a bit depressed and start drinking heavily?'

'Well, I...'

'And wouldn't you go just a little bit mad, looking to find new ways to amuse yourself and have a bit of fun before it all ends in a nasty blood-soaked catastrophe? And that's exactly what the gods have done. Thor is always drunk and looking for a fight. Why do you think the weather is so bad and stormy up above in your world? It's because Thor is forever bashing folks with his hammer and brawling, and when he does that, the weather goes mental. He doesn't care who he thumps either, friend or foe alike. I tell you, if Thor turns up after having a few jars everyone does a runner – even Odin makes himself scarce. As for Odin, he gets his kicks messing with you humans. He loves nothing better than sticking his nose into your affairs, sending men off on stupid quests and having his way with your women. He's just an old letch at heart.'

'And Frey?' asked Agnew, grey-faced.

'Let's just say the less said about Frey the better.'

'Even if what you say is true...'

'Believe me, it is.'

'Okay, so even if it is, what's your point?'

'My point is that no god or goddess will come to man's aid unless there is something in it for them. I mean, why would they go to all that trouble for no good reason? Takes a lot of power to mess with the world and simply pluck people out of harm's way at a whim.'

'But the gods are all powerful.' Even as he said it, Agnew's long-standing doubts about the gods made him question himself.

'You think? Huh, even the gods have to play by certain rules, so for the most part they don't answer prayers unless they want something in return. In your case it was Hel who needed something, so here you are. To be honest, if it were me, I would have probably chosen death.'

'You'd choose death here rather than a chance to die heroically and go to Valhalla?'

'I'm a dwarf; our afterlife is different to what's saved up for you lot, but yes, if I'd have been you, I'd have taken an afterlife with Hel or Ràn, seeing as how it looked like you were about to drown, rather than go through the hell, pardon the pun, you and your men are likely to go through now. I have seen men on gods' quests before and it never ends well. Also, Valhalla is not all it's cracked up to be. Trust me, fighting and dying every single day can get a bit wearing.'

Agnew let Delling's disparaging remarks, which just confirmed what he had always feared, settle over him like a blanket of gloom. He fell silent as he contemplated what he had gotten his crew into, talking of which, where were his men? Deciding he would not like the answer, Agnew kept his question to himself and simply followed Delling further into the Underworld.

Eventually, feet throbbing, Delling brought him to a wooden jetty which reached out into a dark underground river teeming with swirling knife blades. On the edge of the jetty was a bell with a metal striker dangling from a rope attached next to it. Delling took hold of the metal striker, which had the form of a small hammer, and struck the bell sharply three times, which clanged dully. With nothing else to do Agnew sat down on the jetty, back resting against the wooden pole, and waited. Nothing happened for some time, and just as he was beginning to get bored and considered ringing the bell again, he began to hear what sounded like the steady splash of oars. As the sound of rowing grew closer, out of the gloom a low, dark shape with what looked like a mountainous misshapen blob rising from it pulling upon a pair of oars appeared. As it got closer, so the blob became a man, only three times the size of any normal man, heaving on oars twice the size you would find on any longship.

With a deft twiddle on the oars the giant raised them smoothly from the river and turned them, so the paddles rested on the ferry's deck as it came to rest gently against the jetty.

'Who rang for passage?' the giant boomed from beneath his cowl.

'I, Agnew, son of Grimor the Furious, son of Hardrada the Restless, son of –'

'I do not need to know your entire history. Agnew will suffice,' interrupted the giant. 'Why should I give you passage? You know the dead cannot leave here. On whose authority ha… oh, hello, Delling, didn't see you there. This one with you?'

'Farbauti,' the dwarf answered with a curt nod, 'yes, this one is with me. He has Hel's authority to leave.'

'Are you sure?' the giant's deep voice conveyed severe doubt. 'Because you know that's what the last one said and look what trouble that has caused. I swear I will never hear the last of it.'

'Aye, well, we all make mistakes,' replied Delling sagely, 'and he was carrying her rake, so I think I'd have thought the same, but we are where we are.'

'Alas, so, I will just have to take my punishment with dignity,' the giant grumbled unhappily.

'Surely Hel can't have been that harsh with you? You're her grandad.'

'Delling, she has me ferrying souls across the Slidr. If she had any regard for family, she would have given me something better to do eons ago.'

'True, true,' said Delling pursing his lips, 'but you're okay with this one. Agnew here is the one chosen to put right what was done.'

'Really?'

'Yes.'

'What, him?' said the giant, looking down at Agnew with a mix of surprise and contempt.

'Fraid so.'

'Hey, what do you mean, "Fraid so"?' challenged Agnew.

'Well, you'd best get him on board then,' said the ferryman, ignoring Agnew. 'Are you coming as well or are you just here to wave him off?'

'Wave him off? What in Niflheim do you think I am?'

'Hel's lackey,' the giant smirked.

'Don't you start. I've had enough with him earlier.' Delling jerked an angry thumb towards Agnew.

'Hey! I can hear you,' snapped Agnew.

'Good, then get on the ferry,' ordered Delling.

Giving Delling a dirty look which suggested he was likely to throw the dwarf into the knife-infested river at any second, Agnew hopped aboard the ferry, grumbling. Once he was on and joined by Delling, Farbauti started to row the vessel away from the jetty.

'Don't I have to pay you?' asked Agnew.

'You can if you want; I won't stop you,' answered Farbauti.

'But I thought you always collected payment?'

'Off the dead, yes, but you are not dead, or are you?'

'No, I'm alive, at least that's what Hel told me.'

'Then there is no fee. You work for Hel, and I work for Hel, so work rates.'

'Thanks,' Agnew replied dubiously. He took a seat, staring back at Farbauti.

'What?' asked the ferryman tetchily after a few minutes of staring from Agnew.

'Oh, nothing.'

'Then stop staring at me. Anyone would think you hadn't seen a giant before.'

'I haven't, but it's not that.'

Farbauti shipped his oars and stared back at Agnew, 'Then what is it which has you so interested in me?'

'Nothing.'

'Then stop staring or I'll toss you over the side.'

'Is he allowed to do that?' Agnew asked Delling.

'It's his ferry. I reckon he can do whatever he wants.'

'Oh.'

'So? What's your problem, Viking?' growled the giant.

'It's nothing really, just wondering what you do with all that money?'

'What?'

'The money the dead have to pay you to ferry them across the river. What do you do with it all?'

'Well, sometimes I need a new cowl, or I need to replace an oar. Have you any idea how much they charge for one of... anyway, why do you care what I do with the money?'

'Just curious?'

'That sort of curious will get you killed,' Farbauti replied threateningly.

'Oo-kay. You lot really are touchy down here,' said Agnew.

'Wouldn't you be if you were consigned to work in the Underworld? It's all right for those up top in Asgard – lots of wide-open spaces, sun, ice flows, mountains – ah, how I miss it. Instead, I'm stuck down here ferrying ungrateful souls across the river. You would think they would be happy for my help, but oh no, they just whine, "Oh, I'm so sad, I'm so damned, why am I down here?" Miseries; I should make them swim across and really give them something to whine about,' the giant grumbled morosely.

Rather than answer, Agnew decided it was best just to let his question go and leave the giant to his grumbling. He settled down on the ferry alongside Delling and stared out into the gloom as the River Slidr sliced by.

5

I could regale you with Agnew's ferry trip along the River Slidr, but to be honest it was hardly like sailing leisurely up the Nile, so I won't. It would only depress you. Instead, we will skip time on a bit and take you to the moment the ferry finally brought Agnew within sight of his ship.

As soon as he saw it, he instantly felt his spirits lift, which is no surprise, as his spirits had taken a bit of a battering of late, plus you must remember that by Dark Age standards a Norse longship was a thing of young boys' dreams. This was the Ferrari of its time. If they had posters back then you can bet every boy of about ten years old would have had a poster of a longship hung up in their bedrooms. Well, that or some shield maiden scratching her arse.

The longship was a thing of beauty – sleek, purposeful, and unlike a Ferrari, reliable and big enough to take all your mates out on a raid at the same time.

Slowly the longship came closer. However it did not take a genius to realise something was wrong.

'Where is everybody?' Agnew asked Delling.

'What?'

'My men – where are they?'

'They should be on board. It's not like they could have gone anywhere.'

'Then why can't I see them? Someone should be on lookout. And why are they just drifting in the middle of the river? Why haven't they rowed to the shore and moored up?'

'Search me. I'm a dwarf; boats really aren't my people's thing.'

'If Hel's done anything to them then the deal's off.'

Delling looked up at Agnew and had to admire the way his hair seemed to bristle with rage and yet still manage to look heroically coiffured at the same time. *Some folks have all the luck,* he thought as he scratched at his bald pate just under the rim of the metal helm he wore primarily to conceal his baldness.

'Where are they?' asked Agnew suspiciously.

'Dunno. Have you tried calling them? They could be sleeping?'

'Sleeping? All of them?'

'They're your men, so how should I know?'

'They know better than to all sleep at the same time. Someone should be on watch. If they are all asleep I'll have their gizzards.'

'Nice image.' Delling smiled. 'Sure, Hel will love you killing your own men and reducing your chances of success. Yep, she'll really admire that.'

With a soft bump the ferry came alongside and rested up against the hull of the longship. Barely waiting for Farbauti to steady it, Agnew reached up to the side of the ship and half-leapt half-pulled himself up and over the side onto the deck. He landed lightly then abruptly dived for cover as a spear thrust towards him from out of the gloom.

'Die, foul Hel spawn!' Tostig roared, coming from behind and hacking at the dodging Agnew, who only just avoided the whirling axe only to find another spear coming at his midriff from another quarter.

Agnew twisted sideways, feeling the spear point slice across the leather of his jerkin. Deftly he wrapped his arm up and over the spear shaft, locking it to him, and wrenched forward, pulling the unsuspecting spear man off his feet only to have to drop the spear immediately and fall backwards as Tostig's axe threatened to lop off his arm. Agnew was unable to avoid the kick Tostig planted firmly on his chest, sending him crunching onto the deck, arms flailing loosely. At Tostig's mercy, Agnew could only stare up as with a ferocious yell his friend stepped forward, chopping down at his prone body.

Just as it seemed Agnew must be cleft in two, a giant oar deflected the death stroke then swept back, upending at least three Vikings and clattering four others into the ship's mast.

The attacking Norsemen were momentarily stunned into inaction as they faced the oar-wielding giant, who loomed over them.

Breathing heavily, still on his back, Agnew scrambled to his feet praising his lucky stars, and more importantly Farbauti, for his continued existence. His crew, over their immediate shock, seasoned warriors that they were, yelled a battle cry to Odin and charged the giant. Farbauti swung his oar at the attacking Vikings, but this time they were ready and skilfully parried the giant's attack, pressing home their advantage. Before they could skewer the giant on any number of blades, Agnew swept up the spear he had dropped seconds before and struck it down where the deck met the hull to give himself a pole to swing around the giant and come in feet first into the side of the front two attacking men, bowling them over into their comrades. Reacting quicker, Agnew pulled the spear free, spinning it viciously before him, forcing the other attackers back and giving them little way through without risking being diced by the slashing spear point. Knowing he had only brought himself seconds, Agnew yelled desperately, 'TOSTIG! CALL OFF THE MEN!'

'Agnew?'

'YES.'

'AGNEW?'

'YES!'

'Is that you?'

'YES! Call off the attack, NOW!'

'How do I know it's really you and not just some foul trick?'

'Call them off, Tostig, or I'll tell them all about you, Ilse and the...'

'WHOA! EVERYONE, HALT! STOP FIGHTING!'

There was a momentary pause as all on board weighed up their next move, then slowly the Vikings backed away from Agnew's whirling spear and lowered their weapons. Only when he was convinced they were not going to chuck an axe at him did he slowly bring the weapon to a halt.

From among the clustered men watching him wearily, Tostig stepped forward, dropped his axe, and clasped Agnew in a bear hug which threatened to break his spine.

'Agnew, I thought you'd drowned.'

Desperately, Agnew patted Tostig feebly on the shoulder and gasped, 'Tostig, I... I can't breathe.'

'What?'

'I can't bre...'

Tostig dropped his friend, laughing wildly, slapping him hard on the back as Agnew tried to drag some much-needed air into his lungs.

'It's good to see you too,' croaked Agnew.

'Hey, what's going on up there?' said a voice from below the ship.

'Can someone pull him up, please?' asked Agnew, still breathing heavily.

Tostig turned to two of the men, gesturing for them to do as Agnew commanded, then turned back to Agnew and whispered quietly in his ear, 'You promised you'd never mention that time with Ilse.'

'I didn't have time to think of something else which only you and I know about.'

Tostig regarded him closely for a moment and then, with a wide grin which threatened to split his face in two, grasped Agnew in another bear hug, only this time allowing Agnew just enough air to breathe.

It took some time for calm to return to the ship, as all the crew cheered, roared, and took part in much back slapping and playful thumping of Agnew, who would swear later they had cracked a couple of his ribs and almost dislocated his shoulder. Still, no matter – these were burly warrior types and a mere battering delivered by friends wasn't about to spoil the mood.

Agnew introduced Delling and Farbauti to the men, who sheepishly apologised to the giant ferryman who, it must be said, accepted the apologies with good grace before returning to his ferry, leaving Agnew, his men, and, surprisingly to everyone else, including Agnew, Delling behind.

'Are you not leaving with Farbauti?' asked Agnew.

'No. I'm coming with you.'

'What?'

'You didn't think Hel was just going to let you wander off without someone to keep you focused on your quest, did you?'

'She sent you to spy on me?'

'I prefer to think of it more as providing a liaison between you and the goddess. Besides, you need me.'

'Really? How is that then? I've seen you fight, remember. What skills can you possibly offer us?'

'Are you always this dismissive of other folks?'

'This isn't about me,' Agnew replied sharply, 'this is about you. What do you bring to this expedition? You cannot fight, you are too small to row, come to that you can barely see over the side of the ship without standing on a box, so you aren't even going to be much of a lookout.'

'All true, but tell me, oh great Agnew, how do you propose to get out of the Underworld?'

'What?'

'I asked you how intend to leave the Underworld.'

'Well, I, we'll just... bugger!'

'Exactly,' said Delling smugly, 'you haven't a clue, have you?'

'No.'

'So, you need me. Yes?'

'Yes,' admitted Agnew peevishly.

'Good. Now that we have that sorted, we should really get going. Get your men together and follow my direction and we will be on our way.'

Agnew stared down at the smugly smiling dwarf, cursing Hel for lumbering him with him, and stomped off, calling back over his shoulder, 'You'll have to wait a bit longer, Delling. I need to talk to my men.'

'Hel doesn't want any delays.'

'We don't go until I say so. Hel will have to wait,' Agnew growled defiantly.

As Agnew gathered his men together for a quick consultation, Delling, standing on tiptoe, looked forward from beside the rising prow of the ship and along the black ribbon which was the Slidr and smiled. It had been ages since he had been allowed into the world of men and he was going to enjoy every minute of it.

From the centre of the ship Agnew addressed his men. 'Okay, first off, why did you lot attack me when I climbed on board?'

'We thought we had drowned and were cursed to a life in the Underworld, but then we got to thinking that we didn't feel dead, and nothing which happened met with the tales about what happens in the Underworld, so we opted to fight anything which boarded us so that we could still die fighting and get to Valhalla. It just happened you were the first thing to board. We didn't stop to check if it was you or not,' answered Tostig reasonably.

Agnew looked at Tostig with a new respect. 'Did you come up with that idea?'

'No,' answered Tostig honestly, 'I thought we'd drowned and were cursed to a death in the Underworld. It was Erik who decided we weren't dead.'

'Clever lad,' said Agnew, turning to Erik. 'How did you work that out?'

Erik, who had been quiet up to now and had been lurking in the background held up his left hand, which was more of a bloody stump now, missing three fingers and wrapped in a blood-soaked bandage.

'I put my hand in the river and the blades tore my hand to ribbons,' he answered sadly. 'I was bleeding too much to be dead.'

Agnew shook his head and sighed despondently. He had hoped that they had worked out they were not dead by using their heads, not by sticking their hands in knife-infested waters to see what happened, bloody idiots.

'Okay,' said Agnew, 'here's what's happened – why, why we're down here and still alive.'

His crew settled down to listen. Some time later, story finished and after quite a few questions, especially from Ragnar, who seemed a bit over-fixated on Hel for Agnew's liking, they were ready and up for the challenge, which came as a relief.

With little cajoling his men took up their oars and began to row. Stood at the steering board following Delling's directions on which way to steer to leave the Underworld, Agnew chatted quietly to Tostig.

'You okay with this?'

'Yes. I get to take part in a heroic quest for a goddess. What's not to like?'

'You do realise the goddess is Hel?'

'She's still a goddess,' replied Tostig proudly, 'so I'm happy to serve.'

'Good. I doubt I could do this without you.'

'Anyway, how hard could this be? It's only one man we have to track down and remove the rake from,' said Tostig confidently.

Yes, that's what worries me – why does she need an entire crew to bring him down, thought Agnew darkly as he steered his ship steadily through Hel's domain.

6

We will leave Agnew and the boys behind for a while and instead switch our attention to a rough drinking dive in Hel. Now, this is not Hel as in the goddess whom we have already met, nor is it the Underworld but rather a small village in Norway which just happens to be called Hel. It is still there to this day. In fact, I would love to visit and send someone a postcard from there, then they would literally get a postcard from Hel – how cool is that? No? You don't think so? Oh well, have it your own way. Some folks have no imagination.

But enough of this. Yes, we are in Hel. Now, you may think that strange or even a little weird, but it is more to do with our hero's prime protagonist in this tale, one Guthrun the Berserk, and his twisted sense of humour. Yes, even a man as crazy as Guthrun is allowed a sense of humour, who thought it would be a good way to show his contempt for the Queen of the Underworld and her supposedly inescapable abode by drinking in the place which carried her name. By coincidence it also happened to be where one of the entrances from Hel's domain came out.

You may think it a tad obvious that the entrance to the Underworld should be in a place carrying her name, but to be fair to Hel, when she named it, she had not taken into consideration human nature. By naming the place Hel she had expected it to sound so terrifying a place that no one would come anywhere near, let alone set up a village there, but then again us humans have never given dire warnings the respect they are due. If you need proof, one only need look back through history to see just how bloody stupid a species we are. To be honest it is a wonder we have made it this far. Your average guinea pig has more common sense than a human. For instance, when Samson warned Delilah not to cut his hair or there would be trouble, well, he might just as well have put the scissors in her hand himself and asked for a short back and sides. When

Howard Carter discovered the tomb of Tutankhamen with all its dire warnings of curses and imminent death to all who entered and defiled said tomb, did he back away cautiously, whistling while kicking sand back over the discovery hiding it from human sight once more? Nope, he uttered the 1920s version of cool, probably 'by Jove' or 'golly' and dove straight in, tearing the place apart. Needless to say, many of those involved with the desecration met nasty, untimely ends. Well, they cannot say they were not warned. So, as you can see, humans are basically stupid, though you could guarantee if Hel had named the place in a language a guinea pig could understand no guinea pig worth its salt would have gone anywhere near.

This is not the only place in the world called Hel, though in later years those places got hijacked by Christians and got converted to Hell, but just to prove once and for all humans are stupid, there is a thriving settlement in every one. There is one in the Grand Cayman Isles; there is a Hell in Michigan, USA; there is even a Hell in England, but the Yorkshire accent could not stop itself from mangling that simple word and so it became Hull, although Hull happens to perfectly mirror the despair and misery of Hel's actual abode, so it is well named.

But enough of this pondering on the human condition. Instead, let us take a wander inside the tavern, which is really nothing more than a glorified hut serving ale to whoever wants it. The place is dark, lit only by a fire burning in the centre of the building with much of the smoke escaping through a hole in the roof. The smoke which fails to escape is co-mingling with the smoke from various candles and burning braziers dotted around the building, giving the place an atmosphere so thick you could cut it with a spoon.

The room is noisy with lots of drunken revelry. By contrast there is a man, who despite being on his seventh ale is still stone cold sober. He is dressed in black leather with a wolf pelt over his shoulders and with a beard so thick a hawk could nest in it, and is currently sat at a bench, flagon of ale in one hand, serving wench propped on his knee with his other arm around her waist. A short while ago he was feeling happy, but with every passing drink which fails to take effect his mood is slipping towards anger. By way of introduction this is Guthrun the Berserk, and he is a monster. To be honest, he does not look much like a monster. Okay, there is a mad gleam in his eye, but he is only about five foot eight and weighs in at just over eleven stone, and even though most of that eleven stone is muscle he does not look like much. But Guthrun the Berserk is a monster, for unlike most berserker Guthrun happens to be highly intelligent, a rare combination.

Guthrun was, is, entirely suited to the lifestyle of a Norse berserker. He is fearless and loves to do nothing more than fight. If this were now, he would be the sort of man who would either end up running a street gang in one of the world's most dangerous cities, spending his life in and out of prison moving on to ever more violent and vicious crimes, or someone would have spotted his potential early on, turning him into an exceptionally good welterweight boxer or had him playing rugby – he would make a great scrum-half. Admittedly, he would spend a lot of his career in the sin bin, as his temper knows no bounds and his fuse is so short that if he were a firework, as soon as you so much as set a spark near the blue touch paper he would explode in your face. Yes, Guthrun was a perfect berserker.

By rights he should have wound up in Valhalla – most berserkers do. Well, the habit of running headfirst into the strongest part of an enemy force wearing nothing but a smile means that even the best berserk warrior eventually gets hacked down in battle, but Guthrun is smart and attacked where he could do the most damage to an enemy without ensuring his own death. For, as Guthrun would point out, if asked, what is the point of killing ten men and then getting killed, when by staying alive you can have the fun of killing thirty? Hey, I never said he was sane, just clever.

Alas, for Guthrun it would have probably been better for him if he had been a thicko, as that way he would have died in battle and gone to Valhalla, where he would have spent the afterlife indulging in his three favourite past times: fighting, drinking, and getting dirty with serving girls. Sadly, this was not the end which claimed him, for although he might be more intelligent than your average berserker, he was also a barely functioning alcoholic, and it does not matter how clever or tough you are, if you stumble out of an inn pissed as a fart on a cold Nordic winter's night and fall asleep in a ditch, hypothermia is going to get you. Suffering such an ignoble death only gets you a ticket to Hel's domain as a sad, angry, and humiliated berserk. There are rules to a Norse death, and it does not matter that he would have been a great addition to Odin's end-of-days army; if you don't die in battle then no Valhalla. The amount of paperwork required to get you transferred from the Underworld to Valhalla means it simply is not worth the bother and so no Valkyrie is going to touch you with a barge pole let alone cart you off to the feasting halls. Nope, you die of exposure, and you are on a one-way ticket to the Underworld.

So Guthrun was in the town of Hel solely to rub Hel's nose in it. He had escaped her Underworld and was alive once more. Not only that, he had stolen her rake, of which more later, and was now enjoying being alive again, even though he was struggling to get drunk, and because he was alive Hel had no jurisdiction over him and was not allowed to come after him herself, goddess or not. There are rules. You should not be surprised by the fact that this lot do things by the book. After all, in ten centuries' time they are going to be making Volvos, which are tough but hardly the mavericks of the road.

Guthrun finished his flagon, slammed it down on the bench, pushed the wench up off his knee, slapped her bum and demanded she bring him more beer.

As he watched her scurry away to get him more ale, he looked about the bar until his eyes alighted upon a man twice his size, and with an evil grin playing over his lips, Guthrun threw his empty flagon at him. The large Norseman turned around to see what looked like a smallish man with a thick beard growling obscenities at him. Angrily he got up and barged his way across the room, which took about four steps because the place was not big, with every intention of ripping the bearded whelp in the black wolf pelt in two. As he reached Guthrun, the large Viking balled his fist and threw a punch which, if it had connected, would have taken Guthrun's head off, but Guthrun was quick, and even before the punch had fully extended, Guthrun had bobbed beneath it and was on his feet. He stood to the side, throwing a flurry of punches at the now off-balance Viking's unprotected side. Bellowing angrily, the large Viking turned to face the small irritant that was Guthrun and tried to gather him up in a bear hug, but Guthrun, ever light on his feet, dodged the clumsy grasp and picking up another man's flagon, smashed it into the larger man's face, following up with a flying headbutt, flattening an oft-broken nose across the large Viking's face with a sickening crunch and shower of blood.

Behind Guthrun, the man whose ale jug Guthrun had used to smash into his first victim's face flew angrily to his feet and grabbed Guthrun by the shoulder, wrenching him back, giving Guthrun's first target a momentary chance to land a punch on Guthrun, knocking him off his feet. Both men then set about kicking Guthrun to a pulp whilst he was down.

Most men at this point would normally curl up into a ball and protect themselves from the blows raining down upon them as best they could, but not Guthrun. Taking the hits, he focused on his second opponent's foot, and as it stamped in for a third time he grabbed it and twisted violently, forcing the stamper to fall into a bench, sending more men and beer flying.

Laughing wildly, Guthrun parried another kick from the Norseman he had attacked in the first place and scrambled to his feet, grabbing a stool as he went, sweeping it around viciously to smash into the large man's knee, dropping him to the floor. Almost as soon as he hit the ground, Guthrun was on him, pummelling his face with punch after punch, and he would have continued until the man's face had been turned into nothing more than an unrecognisable mush had not another pair of hands grabbed him by the shoulder, hauled him away and thrown him across a table and into the side of the timber wall.

Guthrun landed heavily, the wind knocked out of him for a second or two, but now a full-scale brawl had developed, and the inn was complete mayhem as everyone attacked everyone else.

Catching his breath, Guthrun stood slowly and, ignoring the fight raging all about him, moved across to the place where he had rested Hel's rake. It felt cold in his hands, and he felt a strange tingle of fear run through him, only momentarily but it was enough to remind him that this was no ordinary rake. his one had power, and now he possessed it he was damn well going to use it.

Switching his grip on the rake's haft so he now held it like a staff, he launched himself into the fray, this time sweeping all before him. In less than a minute, Guthrun had reduced the inside of the drinking inn to nothing more than a room full of coughing, spluttering, bleeding antagonists, leaving him the only man standing. The rest, if not unconscious, were a retching mass on the floor.

Whistling a jaunty tune, Guthrun the Berserk stepped outside into the wind and sleet and gloried in being alive. As he walked off into the night, behind him inside the ale house the air had taken on the stinking hue of pestilence. All those left inside had turned a ghastly pallor and were rapidly succumbing to the effects of chronic dysentery. By morning all would be dead, and a curse of plague would sweep through Hel.

As he disappeared into the dark, rake swung lightly across his shoulder, Guthrun wondered if he needed to change his name. After all, Berserk was so last battle, and there were loads of berserkers around, and he was altogether something more than that now. As he wandered away a thought came to him. He rolled it across his tongue, let it play about his lips, shouted it to the night sky and liked how it sounded, and so began the bloody career of Guthrun Doombringer.

7

It had taken a lot of beer chits dished out by Delling to the various guardians and denizens of the Underworld, whose job it was to stop the dead from simply walking out, to persuade them to allow Agnew and crew passage back out into the land of the living. They had sailed the River Slidr, passed through Niflheim, traversed the roots of Yggdrasil the World Ash, and after some magical jiggery pokery, courtesy of something sent with Delling from Hel, Agnew and his men were once again afloat upon the oceans of the world.

All this of course was met with much cheering and celebration amongst Agnew's crew. Unfortunately, the celebration was short-lived. In truth, it lasted about a minute, maybe a minute and a half at a push, when a curse from their leader pulled the celebrations up short.

'Oh shit! The dozy cow never fixed the ship.' Agnew's exasperated curse rang frighteningly in the ears of his men as they noticed that the sea was pouring in from all manner of holes and rents in the side of the hull.

'Great, just bloody great. Save us from drowning, why don't you, then dump us right back in the sea in the same knackered ship as before. Perhaps I should throw myself overboard and drown properly this time. ARE YOU LISTENING, HEL? YOU BLOODY STUPID BITCH!' Agnew cursed, enraged.

'Um, perhaps you shouldn't be quite so...'

'Quite so what, Delling?'

'Er, be so dismissive of the goddess. She's got a foul temper. You really don't want to be on the wrong side of that.'

'Listen to me, Delling, if we drown because she couldn't see fit to have our ship fixed before dumping us back out here then her temper will be as nothing compared to mine!'

Delling shrunk back in the face of Agnew's fury and held up his hands in supplication.

Agnew spun on his heel, paying the dwarf no more heed and shouted, 'TOSTIG!'

'Agnew?'

'Get someone aloft. We need to find land and quick.'

'Well, I could, but...'

'But? But what?'

'But we've already sighted land. It's over there, see?' said Tostig steadily, pointing aft of the ship.

'What?'

'Yes, there, see?'

'Why didn't you say something?'

'I just did.'

'By the gods, do I have...' Agnew paused, took a deep breath, 'and count to ten: one, two, three...' he began, then barely maintaining a modicum of calm said, 'Never mind, just show me.'

Tostig took Agnew aft and pointed. Sure enough, there in the distance was the unmistakable brown smudge of land on the horizon and the promise of salvation. It was going to be a close-run thing, and Agnew wasn't about to take a bet either way as to their chances. Rubbing his chin nervously, belying his fears, nevertheless he commanded authoritatively, 'Tostig, get half the men rowing and the other half bailing.'

Tostig looked towards the smudge doubtfully. 'It's a long way to row, and with only half rowing the men will not last.'

Agnew looked skyward but he could see no cloud. The day was still, and while not having to battle an angry sea was good, especially given the state of the ship, some wind would have been a god, or in this case a goddess send, as at least they could have used the sail to spear them on.

'We have no choice,' Agnew stated with the calm of those out of options. 'The men will row till they can row no more. We swap rowers with those bailing as they tire. We let those who have just rowed rest as long as we dare then we put them to bailing. It's that or we sink.'

Tostig nodded curtly and left Agnew to carry out his orders, moving along the length of the ship barking orders as he went.

With Tostig sorting the men, Agnew called to Delling, who approached him wearily.

'You called?'

'Yes. Go grab a sea chest which is not being sat on and bring it back here.'

'May I ask why?'

'It's to stand on. More accurately, it's for you to stand on. You are going to need to be higher if you are going to be able to steer the ship for me.'

'You want me to steer the ship?'

'Well, it's either that or you row and bail.'

'I'll go get something to stand on.'

'You do that.'

With the Dwarf scuttling off to grab an unused chest to elevate him to a height where he could use the steering board, Agnew turned his attention to the horizon and tried to estimate the time it would take to row there. If they were lucky, they may just make it before the sun went down. One way or another it was going to be a long, hard row and would not allow for much rest between the rowing and bailing.

Delling returned to Agnew carrying one of the wooden chests which all Vikings carried with them on a voyage. Agnew showed him where to place it, asking Delling to stand upon it. Even then he still only just about came up to Agnew's chin, but it would have to do.

'Delling, you hold the board like so,' said Agnew, demonstrating the proper stance to manage the board.

'Okay.'

'Keep the nose of the ship pointing for the dead centre of that smudge on the horizon.'

'What happens when the smudge gets bigger and starts looking like proper land?'

'Keep us dead centre. That way it will give us more options for finding a suitable place to beach as we get closer. If you can't keep us on course, call me immediately.'

'Why? Where are you going?'

'To row and bail like my life depends upon it,' declared Agnew with a forced smile.

'You don't think we'll make it, do you?'

'Honestly?'

'Yes, honestly.'

'Honestly, I haven't a clue, but we must try. What else is there?'

'How about some form of cunning plan or amazing seamanship or running repair that will keep us afloat till landfall?' said Delling hopefully.

'If it's cunning plans or amazing seamanship you want then you're on the wrong ship. Why do you think we're in this mess in the first place? We row, we bail and see how far we get.'

'That's rubbish.'

'Hey, keep your voice down; no need for the others to know we're sailing on little more than blind faith.'

With a sickening feeling in his gut, Delling watched Agnew make his way to the centre of the ship and take up one of the oars. Delling noticed that seeing their leader was literally pulling his weight instantly gave his men a lift and they pulled strongly on their own oars. Poor fools, though Delling, they actually trust this idiot. Hel help us all.

For the rowing men, time seemed to pass all too slowly. For those bailing, if anything it was moving even slower as they battled an ever-increasing rush of water, against which despite their best efforts they were making little headway in keeping the water level down. As the first of the rowing stints finished, Agnew and the first shift lent heavily upon their oars, shoulders burning, breath coming in huge heavy gasps, yet the land still seemed beyond reach. Tostig, bare-chested and sweating like he had just spent an hour in a sauna while doing press-ups, came and crouched by Agnew. 'It's no good; we're sinking. We can't keep this up. We need to find another way.'

'What do you suggest?' replied Agnew desperately. 'There's no wind, the sail's useless, the current is against us. If we don't bail, we sink, and if we don't row we won't make land and we still sink.'

'The men are exhausted. I'm exhausted. We can't keep going,' Tostig replied gravely. 'Can't we ask the dwarf?'

'Ask him what?'

'To help.'

'He is helping; he's steering.'

'Is there nothing else?'

'He's too small to row, and as for bailing, well, he could, but then who's going to steer the ship? We're always going to be a man short.'

'Was that meant as a joke?'

'Yeah,' cringed Agnew, 'don't tell him.'

'I'll let you off.' Tostig smiled weakly. 'But the dwarf, he's Hel's minion – can't he ask her for help?'

Agnew stared at Tostig in horror. 'You can't be serious?'

'Why not? We're doing this for her. If she wants us to succeed she can't want us to drown, so why can't she help?'

'Do you really want to be in even more debt to her than we already are?'

'If it's a choice between that and drowning, I'll take it.'

'He's right,' said Snorri, who had overheard everything which had passed between them. 'Hel may not be the goddess I would have chosen to be beholden to but better that than drowning, again.'

'What do you mean, again? You didn't drown last time.'

'As good as. If Hel hadn't pulled us to the River Slidr we would have. We're already in her debt; how could more debt be any worse?'

Before Agnew could respond, the rest of the crew within earshot began to agree with Snorri and Tostig, and it is easy to see from this carry-on how credit cards caught on, isn't it? It is so much easier to take the credit and worry about the debt later. For Agnew's part, he had a horrible feeling they would come to regret that debt, but he knew they were out of options. With an impending sense of doom, he left his oar and went aft to where Delling was still guiding the ship.

'How's it going?' asked Agnew.

Delling looked up at Agnew, though for once not as far up as normal, what with being stood on a box and all, which is probably why he felt he could answer as sarcastically as he did. 'Keep the boat in a straight line, aim for the middle of the smudge, um, not that hard, really. As if I couldn't manage that? I don't see what all the fuss is about. This sailing lark is easy.'

'Yeah, well, try it in a storm sometime and then tell me there's no skill involved.'

'What do you want, Agnew?'

'Help.'

'From me? You and your men are sailors; this is your thing. You tell me what to do and I'll do it, but if you are looking to me to get you out of this, forget it,' replied the dwarf darkly.

'You heard them, didn't you?'

Delling looked straight ahead but said, 'Yes.'

'So, you can ask Hel to help?'

'Aye.'

'Well, then?'

'Trust me, you don't want that.'

'I don't see that we have a choice.'

'There are always choices, Agnew, but this isn't the one to take.'

'I'm out of ideas, Delling. We need help,' Agnew conceded.

Delling looked up at Agnew once more. 'You've met her, Agnew; they haven't. You know there will be a cost to this. They don't realise her nature – you do. Are you sure you are prepared to do this?' he asked seriously, his deep voice practically heralding doom.

'Just do it. We'll take the price.'

Delling hung his head momentarily and with a sigh replied, 'So be it. Take this bloody thing off me then. You know sailing? It's really boring.'

'What?'

'Just saying, dull. I don't know why you lot do this.'

'Delling, we don't have time for this.'

'Yeah, yeah. You won't be saying that in a bit.' Delling let go of the tiller, handing it to Agnew, and hopped off the box, shuffling unsteadily towards the centre of the ship. He grabbed his pack from where he had stowed it and brought it back aft to sit down cross-legged next to where Agnew stood. Delling rummaged inside his pack till he found what he was looking for. He held it in his hand and with his back turned to Agnew, so that the Norseman could not easily see what he was doing, Delling chalked a circle on the ship's deck then began to chant. The language Delling used sounded strange and arcane to Agnew's ears. Slowly, deeply, Delling continued the chant, the rhythm strangely hypnotic, then with ever more urgency it got louder and louder until with a mad cry he raised an arm to the sky. Fearfully, the crew watched him, mesmerised by his actions. With everyone seemingly holding their breath waiting for what was to happen next, Delling brought his arm down with a flourish, casting bones into the chalk circle, and let out a high keening wail which chilled the blood of even the bravest amongst them.

Delling stopped. A strange calm settled across the ship, as though the world were holding its breath to see what would happen next, but nothing did, except slowly and angrily the crew began to mutter. With malicious intent they began leaving their posts to stalk towards the rear of the ship and the dwarf.

'What's he done?'

'He's cursed us?'

'We're doomed.'

'Gut the bastard.'

'I knew we should ha' thrown him in the Slidr.'

'Down wi' dwarves!' Well, yes, there is always one who isn't very imaginative with his cursing and so just resorts to general bigotry, but you get the idea.

Ignoring the angry crew coming for him, Delling turned to Agnew and simply said, 'It's done.'

'What? What's done?'

'She answered, Agnew. Now pray the Norns save us all,' he said heavily and remained cross-legged on the deck, head hung despondently, seemingly oblivious to the angry ruckus heading his way.

As the first of the angry warriors reached for Delling, Agnew let go of the tiller, stepped forward, drew his sword and slapped it across the wrist of the first man reaching.

'ENOUGH!' bellowed Agnew. 'Did I command you to leave your oars? NO! Then get back. You wanted his intervention with Hel. Do not make him the scapegoat for your request.'

'How do we know he hasn't just cursed us? How do we know that he doesn't mean to kill us all?' someone shouted angrily.

'Aye!'

'What he said.'

'Arrrr!'

Again, they are not very imaginative, but that doesn't really matter, because before Agnew has a chance to answer, if you care to look over the port side of the ship, which is the left to the non-sailors amongst you, you will see what has been until now a calm sea begin to broil, bubble, swell, and heave, causing waves of ever-larger size and magnitude to surge towards the failing ship. With the exception of Agnew, who quickly took grip of the tiller to steady himself, and one other member of the crew, a Norseman by the name of Olsen, who was just ridiculously dexterous and blessed with a sense of balance which would have made him an excellent gymnast or skateboarder, who kept upright, the rest were knocked off their feet, ending up sprawled in a heap in the bottom of the ship, which unfortunately also happened to be under about two feet of water.

With cries of surprise and fear they hauled themselves up, spluttering and cursing as the ship rocked ever more violently, then suddenly it was hit with an almighty thump which caused the bow to rise alarmingly and then the whole craft shot forward as though flying.

Everyone took a grip of whatever was nearest for fear of falling over the side as the ship careened violently through the air. Agnew, the only man even vaguely on his feet, well, and Olsen, obviously, could see the smudge which had been on the horizon grow ever bigger by the second as it came towards them at a rate of knots the likes of which the ship had never sailed. Wind whistled in the rigging and a great roaring sound accompanied the men's cries of anguish and Olsen's crazy whooping. What can I say? The man's obviously a born extreme sports junkie – any minute now you just know he is going to turn round and call someone dude.

After only seconds, the land filled the entirety of the view in front of the ship. Suddenly, the forward motion became downwards as the prow dropped alarmingly. Agnew braced himself for the inevitable impact and closed his eyes, his body tensing as the sea rushed up to meet them.

There was an almighty crack, shudder, and splash as the ship hit the water, bounced, tilted alarmingly, and spun sharply as it skidded to a halt. No one, not even Olsen, had kept their feet during that. Wearily, painfully, the men began to drag themselves up, which was difficult given the strange angle the deck rested at.

Gathering himself quickly, Agnew commanded, 'Everybody, off! Head for the shore!' The men obeyed quickly, dropping themselves from the ship into the water below. The sea was about three feet deep, so the initial going was slow, and Agnew had to grab Delling by the scruff of the neck and haul him forward lest he drown, but despite the drag of the sea the crew made for shore, and that was when they heard the roar. Looming over the wrecked ship, the head of a giant serpent snaked menacingly. The men cursed and did their best to make it up the beach and to the hope of cover.

Another roar chased their flight and a shadow spread over them, blotting out the sun. Most ran but three stopped and looked up. It was their undoing, as the head of the serpent struck down and snapped up the three in its great gaping maw. The head flicked back and with a single swallow the screams of those taken were no more.

As quickly as it had appeared the serpent turned back to deeper water and disappeared beneath the waves.

'What foul demon was that?' cried Tostig angrily.

'Jörmungandr,' answered Delling bluntly as he flopped to the sand, thoroughly soaked and miserable.

'What?'

'Jörmungandr, the Midgard Serpent to you.'

'Surely not?' said Agnew.

'Seriously? You think I would make that up? How many serpents do you know that are that size?'

Agnew and Tostig both had the sense to remain silent.

'I warned you, Agnew – don't ask Hel for help.'

'She sent the serpent!' said Agnew, incredulous. 'Who in their right mind would send a giant serpent to rescue us? It ate three of us.'

'Hel would,' snapped Delling, tiring of the Viking's stupidity. 'It is her brother, after all.'

'But we wanted rescuing, not eating.'

'There is always a debt to be paid for Hel's help. You said you was willing to pay the debt; well, the debt for rescue was three souls. The serpent claimed what it was owed – it won't be back. We're safe, so you have your wish, Agnew. Hel saved you.'

'With friends like that, who needs enemies?' scowled Tostig.

'You asked; she delivered. Don't blame me if you don't like her methods. She's a goddess, and she doesn't see things the same as you.'

Tostig took an angry step forward, but Agnew placed a restraining hand against his chest. 'Leave it. He's right – we did ask. It's not like Delling didn't warn us.'

Tostig looked to say something but a look from Agnew made him hold his tongue. Agnew helped the dwarf to his feet, half-carrying half-dragging the dwarf up the beach beyond the tidal line, where exhausted they all collapsed, breathing hard. All about them the surviving crew dropped. Once he had caught his breath, Agnew took a moment to take in his surroundings and realised they were not in good shape or a good position. Agnew stood painfully and shouted, 'Okay, get yourselves up. Salvage what you can from the ship.'

'Then what?'

'Then we head inland and find out where the serpent dumped us.'

Slowly the men began to get up. Tostig, next to Agnew, barged past Delling on the way back to the ship, deliberately knocking him over.

'He doesn't like me, does he?' said Delling, picking himself up off the sand.

'No.'

'What will he do?'

'He'll kill you,' Agnew answered coldly.

'Well, that's just bloody great. Not only do I have to make sure you lot succeed, or Hel will have my hide, but there is also a chance a hulking brute of a Viking will put an axe through my head. This day just keeps getting better and better. I should have listened to my mum.'

'Why?'

'She told me not to go working for Hel, said it was a bad move and that I'd regret it. Told me I should have stayed working the mine.'

'So, why didn't you?'

'I was young, stupid, I was only a hundred and fifty-three and I was seduced by the prospect of working for a goddess – dark halls, smoky caverns, as many errant souls as I could whip – what's not to like?'

'So, go back; quit.'

'Can't.'

'Why not?'

'Pride, shame. Besides, would you fancy telling Hel you quit? Besides...'

'Besides what?'

'I'm a lousy miner, okay? And I can't stand singing about gold all the time. Is it too much to ask that we sing about something else, just once? Even about iron would do, just not sodding gold. I hate it. If I hear one more person go "Gold, Gold, Gold" I swear I'll rip their throat out.'

Agnew looked down at the visibly shaking Delling and sensing some of his own history reflected, felt his own anger subside.

'Don't worry about Tostig,' Agnew said reasonably, 'he won't touch you.'

'Really? Why not?'

'Because if anyone needs to take the blame for this mess,' Agnew sighed despondently, 'it's me.'

8

It is only right that we give Agnew and his men some time to get themselves sorted. Well, they have just lost three of their comrades, their ship is wrecked, and they are currently milling around a beach with no idea where they are, so it is not really the time to bother them. By contrast, Guthrun Doombringer is having an altogether less distressing time, so let us go bother him.

We currently find him pulling his bloodied axe from the throat of someone who had got in his way. This was not the first time this had happened since leaving the ale house where we initially found him, this last kill putting him into double figures. Guthrun had one of those personas which just attracted trouble, that, and his knack for picking a fight.

His latest victim crumpled back onto the floor, gurgling nastily from the gaping wound in his throat, dark blood rapidly spreading about his dying body. With the bored air of a man who had seen it all before, Guthrun casually wiped the blood from the blade before holstering his weapon. The question before him now was what to do next? Should he carry on wandering, bringing mayhem to the world in general or instead find a bed for the night? He was getting tired of sleeping outdoors. He wanted a proper bed, preferably with a hot, busty woman beside him. Unfortunately, his exploits tended to make him unwelcome anywhere he was known, and where he was not known he usually made himself known by picking a fight and killing someone within an hour of two of turning up, which, generally speaking, got him kicked out of the village. So, it was with some surprise, as he stood over the dead body of his latest adversary, that he heard clapping.

Guthrun did not so much turn as simply throw his head round to look at whoever was mocking him before killing them too. The fact it turned out to be a woman, an extremely attractive woman at that, for once threw Guthrun off his stride. She was dark-haired, was wearing more leather than would be considered normal – she looked like an advert for an extra in an episode of Xena or a poster girl for a sadomasochist club, but dress sense aside she was athletic, long-limbed, had a clear complexion and a wicked smile.

'That was magnificent.' She smiled. 'The way you turned his parry back on him to put him off balance and use his own stumbling momentum so he practically impaled himself was masterful. Where did you learn to fight like that?'

'Huh?' Guthrun grunted.

'I said – oh, you know what? Never mind. What are you doing in Nidaros?'

'Looking for food, drink, and a bed for the night.'

'Why did you kill him?'

'He was stopping me getting food, drink, and a bed for the night.'

'I have need of men such as you. If you will agree, hear me out about why a man of your immense talents is suited to my needs. You will have your food, drink, and bed, even if you turn me down once you have heard my offer. What do you say?'

'I'd say what's to stop me coming over there and just forcing you to give me food, drink, and a bed?'

'In truth, nothing, but my way might be more beneficial in the long run.'

Guthrun, for once putting his natural belligerence on hold, paused to properly weigh up this woman who was addressing him as an equal, which was all wrong. Oh, he had known some feisty girls in his time, but none had ever talked to him directly, as though they could offer him something he could not just take at will. He was slightly insulted but bright enough to be intrigued.

'Go on,' he said.

'Do you really want to discuss business out here beneath the cold and darkening sky?'

'You have a better idea?'

The woman laughed, deep and throaty, which was partly sexy and partly off-putting. She spun on her heel and set off down a small alley. When Guthrun did not follow, she stopped and threw him a challenging look over her shoulder. 'Are you coming or are you just going to stand in the dark?' She then continued, not looking back to see if he was following.

Guthrun paused briefly, shrugged off his mistrust, picked up the rake he had discarded when the fight had started and followed. He was aware he could be walking into a trap but was confident enough in his own abilities to get himself out of a tight corner, and pity the first man who tried to jump him, because Guthrun would make sure that the first to come at him at least would die. What happened then would be in the hands of the gods, and Guthrun could live with that.

The woman moved fast, twisting and turning as she did from alley to alley. As they walked, so the number of buildings crammed together thinned. Finally, on the outskirts of the town the woman stopped before a large, low barn situated on the brow of a small hill. Guthrun was aware that she did not look back to see if he had followed. She simply walked up to the barn door, pulled it open just enough to get through and entered. Guthrun approached cautiously, stopped to listen for a moment and, hearing nothing untoward, stepped through into the gloom, holding his axe ready, expecting to be dropped upon or shot the moment he crossed the threshold, but much to his surprise nothing happened. Even more surprising, he found himself facing the woman, who was now sat, calm and cross-legged in the centre of the barn atop some hay with a ring of similarly seated men all looking back at him.

The only light in the barn was coming from a single small oil lantern hung from one of the barn's low beams, which if anything merely enhanced the gloom casting long shadows.

'Don't just stand there,' said the woman, 'come in, sit.'

Saying nothing and with his axe still in hand, Guthrun moved deeper into the barn and with a show of total mistrust stayed standing before his seated audience.

'You have nothing to fear from us, mighty Guthrun Doombringer. Please, sit, relax. I only want to talk.'

'You know who I am?' Guthrun said, unable to keep the surprise from his voice.

'Of course; that's why I want to talk to you.'

Guthrun made no answer. Instead, he made a deliberate show of looking behind him. No one was creeping up on him. Confident that no one was behind and no one was lurking in one of the animal pens to either side of him, Guthrun sat, placing his axe down very carefully so that it remained close to hand, then did the same with the rake he carried in his other hand.

For a moment no one moved. Nothing was said, as though a final sizing up were taking place by the woman, her band of men, and Guthrun. Satisfied that neither side was about to set upon the other, well, at least not immediately, the woman broke the silence. 'You are probably wondering who I am?'

'No.'

The woman glowered at Guthrun's flippant reply but composed herself and announced, 'I am Asa, daughter of Harald Granraude, wife of Gudrød the Hunter, Skadi curse his name.'

'And I care because?'

'Because I intend to kill Gudrød, the gods willing. It will be my revenge for the deaths of my father and brother, whom Gudrød killed so he could steal my father's land and rape me.'

'So, this is...'

'Yes.'

'I did not ask...'

'The answer is still YES.'

'I don't...'

'YES, this is about revenge – cold-blooded, murderous, vile, deceitful, wilful, bitter REVENGE!' Asa screeched bitterly.

Guthrun opened his mouth to speak, paused to see if this crazy, admittedly attractive but downright loopy woman would let him get a word in edgeways, and when she did not seem like she was going to say anything, Guthrun finally asked, 'So you want me to kill this Gudrød then?'

'Not by yourself, but I want you to help me kill him,' Asa hissed viciously. 'I also want you to help me take his kingdom, where I will rule till my son is old enough to lead.'

Guthrun regarded Asa and her retinue critically, hummed a few questions to himself and asked, 'If I join you, what's in it for me?'

'Infamy.'

'What's that? Sounds like a sickness.'

'No; infamy – it's like famous, only more so.'

'Hmmmmmm, don't much care for that.'

'You don't care for revenge and murder?'

'I've no problem with that. I don't give a toss about Gudrød. I'll happily bury my axe in his face without a second thought, but infamy won't get me food, riches, and women.'

'It will, eventually.'

'I care more for the here and now.'

Asa laughed richly. 'I like you, Guthrun – you're simple.'

'Careful, wench, don't take the piss. I've killed for less.'

'I don't doubt it, but when I said simple, that wasn't a reflection on your intelligence, only your tastes. So, tell me, Guthrun Doombringer, what can I offer you which will make you embark on this quest for vengeance with me?'

'I no longer play second to any man. My days of that are done.'

'So?'

'I want command.'

'Command of what?'

'Your men. In battle they answer to me. They follow my orders, not yours.'

Asa paused to consider Guthrun's demand, even as her own men grumbled dangerously beside her. 'Done,' she said with absolute authority and turned to stare down each of her Jarls, men of high standing and rank in their own right,in turn. Despite some scowls of displeasure, none objected. 'I was led to you deliberately, Doombringer, so in battle I give my men to you to command. Anything else?'

'Aye. I want a different woman brought to my bed every night.'

'Shouldn't be a problem. What's your type?'

Guthrun's eye narrowed, and his hand strayed towards his axe. 'You agree; why? You are on a quest to revenge a rape, yet you agree to bring me women to do with as I please. What trickery is this?'

'No trickery, Guthrun. I look at it as merely feeding you. Some men want meat, others demand beer to satisfy their thirst, you hunger for women. I will struggle to achieve what I want without a warrior of your ability being my war leader, so I am willing to pay you in female flesh.'

'Even though you were raped, you are willing to give women to me?'

'Yes, I was raped. Did any woman come to my rescue? No. So damn them all; I owe them nothing. Tell me what is your type, Guthrun, and you shall have them.'

A wicked smile began to play across the face of Guthrun and a manic gleam lit in his eye. Neither was lost on Asa.

'I like you,' said Guthrun honestly, 'you tell it like it is – I can respect that. I will join you.'

'And that is all you want, field command and women? Not money? Most men would ask for plunder and riches.'

'I'll take my own plunder.'

'Fair enough. Then we have a deal, Guthrun?' asked Asa. Standing gracefully, she held out her hand. Guthrun stood less gracefully and clasped Asa's forearm as a partner and equal.

'Deal,' Guthrun agreed willingly.

9

Valhalla – the fabled hall of the slain, the place where the heroic dead go to feast, party, and fight. To the casual onlooker it is mightily impressive, designed to awe those in its presence. As you approach, the first thing you see is the golden tree, Glasir, shining beneath the wintry sun. As you get closer, and should you own a helicopter so you can look down on the impossibly high roof, you would be able to see that the roof is thatched with shields, which is no mean feat, and they are a bugger to make waterproof. Going inside the hall, you can see that the rafters holding up the roof are made from bound spear shafts. The benches upon which the fallen sit when feasting are covered in coats of mail, which I would think are quite cold and uncomfortable, but then I'm not a fallen warrior, so what would I know? This is clearly a place for fighting men to hang out.

Throughout the place, nailed to the wall are of course the regulation flaming torches, spears, swords, shields, axes, wolf pelts, bear pelts, maybe even the pelt of a badger which got too close to some marauding Norseman. In essence, it is everything a fallen hero could wish for in a drinking hall.

However, for all its glory and magnificence, right now it is daytime and that means the heroic dead are off out someplace beating the crap out of each other. Most of the serving wenches are taking a well-earned nap, leaving only a couple of staff around to serve the odd god or straggling warrior a drink. A few hounds lie curled near one of the many fires which smoulder in the grates and the whole place has the feel of an empty pub on a grey Tuesday afternoon – slightly dark, a bit over-warm and stinking of old ale and stale farts. Nice.

Now, you may wonder why you have been brought here at this time. Is it simply to look round a rather magnificent building? Well, no, not really. We are here because in a dingy corner, near one of the fires, is a gathering, not much of a gathering number-wise, but in sheer magnitude of importance this bunch takes some beating. The group are huddled together and talking animatedly in between huge gulps of ale, because when you are a god, it is never too early for a pint.

Leading the talk is a man of great stature, with a long grey beard which suggests great age and wisdom, which is a joke really, because I have met a lot of grey-haired oldies in my time and most of their collective wisdom has been pointless to say the least, but that aside, this fellow wears an eye patch, and a great spear rests by the wall next to him. In truth he did not really need to have brought the spear, but this is Odin, king of the gods, and he has an image to uphold and so the spear is here.

At the other end of the table sits a huge figure wearing a chainmail vest. An iron helm rests on the table before him, and he is casually tossing a giant war hammer into the air and deftly catching the spinning weapon as it falls back to earth.

'For the umpteenth time, what have I told you about not using that thing indoors? You'll have someone's eye out!' Odin growled at the hammer-throwing god.

Thor – well, who else did you think it would be – caught the hammer and, with the petulance of a teenager being told he had to stop playing on his Xbox and come eat his tea, placed it heavily on the table.

'Thank you,' said Odin sarcastically. 'Right, now that we don't have that distraction, let us get back to business. So, any of you know what Hel is up to?'

The various gods sat around the table looked to one another, looked to the table. Frey seemed to find something highly interesting under his nails to concentrate on, shrugged, muttered incoherently and generally failed to answer their king.

'Well, come on – are you all trying to tell me that none of you know anything?'

'Sorry.'

'No.'

'Not heard a word.'

'Why? What's she been up to now?'

'I wonder if that's a splinter?'

'You lot are useless,' snapped Odin. 'Call yourselves gods? You are supposed to be wise and all-knowing, yet not one of you has the wit to keep an eye on the Underworld and Hel's scheming. Did you learn nothing from Baldur's death?'

'Aye that we did, which is why none of us go anywhere near the narky bitch,' said Thor. 'Anyway, you gave her the Underworld to rule. It's hardly our fault if she lords it about the place like she owns it.'

'Technically she does,' chipped in Forseti, who never missed a chance to remind his fellow gods of the legalities of their thoughts and actions.

'Killjoy,' spat Thor.

'Arse!'

'Nerd!'

'Prat!'

'Wimp!'

'Be quiet! I didn't ask you here just to argue.' Odin thumped the table with such force that down on earth a small earthquake took out three whole villages somewhere just north of Copenhagen. However, it had the desired affect and both Thor and Forseti quietened down.

'So, what's up, chief?' asked Heimdall. 'I haven't heard of any trouble, certainly none caused by Hel.'

Odin hung his head in exasperation. 'What do I pay you for exactly?'

'Um, to guard the bridge, be the watchman, listen out for –'

'I KNOW what you do; it was rhetorical. By the great tree Yggdrasil, is it any wonder we're doomed? Right, listen up, you fools. I was wandering around on Midgard when a rather worrying tale was told to me. Apparently someone with something which sounds a lot like Hel's rake cursed the village of Hel with plague and pestilence. What do you have to say about that?'

'Maybe she didn't like what they'd done with the place, so she's having a clean-up.'

'Another village a few days after went the same way, and then another and another and so on.'

'So what? We all know Hel goes out and cleans out a few villages a year. It's just the usual cull – what's the problem?' asked Frey, momentarily ignoring his finger.

'What's wrong? I'll tell you what's wrong. To date, fifteen villages have been culled, as you put it, fifteen. That is about ten too many. Not only that, it is at the wrong time of year, but it's also the height of winter, and we all know Hel isn't allowed to run off plaguing places during the winter – that's not sporting. Worse still, it sounds like the rake is in the hands of a human who is doing the work for her. Now what do you say to that?'

'She's subcontracting out?'

'No; she's up to something? She's wiping out whole swathes of our worshippers, and for what?'

'No idea.'

'Maybe she's bored.'

'She hasn't met her dead quota and is doing an end-of-year catch-up?'

'You know, I really do think that's a splinter. Anyone got any tweezers?'

'I still don't see the problem,' said Thor, who was rapidly getting bored.

'Oh, don't you?' replied Odin. 'Well, let me tell you, son, just what this means. If Hel has sent someone out to lay waste to the entirety of Midgard with plague, that means the dead will go to her.'

'So?'

'Really, do I have to explain this? Don't you lot know anything of our fate? I didn't hang from Yggdrasil and lose an eye for the good of my health, you know. If Hel gets all the warriors who should come to us, then who is going to stand by us at Ragnarök? If we go into the final battle completely outnumbered, we will lose, game over, we're done.'

'But we know we're going lose. That's been foretold, by you, as you forever keep reminding us, which is a great bloody downer, Dad. Why couldn't you have kept that to yourself? Would have been much better for everyone,' Thor grumbled.

'Because if I had kept it to myself, we wouldn't have been able to build an army for the final fight, would we?'

'So what? We're going to lose. What does it matter if we have one dead warrior with us or a hundred thousand? We're still going to die.'

Odin stood and paced about, his fingers clenching agitatedly before he stopped and brought his fist down hard upon the table. 'Do you understand nothing?' Odin raged. 'If we have our army then yes, we will not win, but neither will the Jotun-Heim. It's mutual destruction all the way, which will leave the way open for a new order to rebuild a new world for all men. But if we don't have an army we will be crushed underfoot, and the Jotun-Heim will hold sway, unleashing a reign of terror on what is left of mankind, and we cannot allow that.'

'Don't see why not.'

'Do you not? So, you would rather your worshippers talk of you when you are gone as a failure, as someone defeated, a god who let them down, who let the Jotun-Heim torture them for an eternity?'

'No, course not.'

'Exactly!' Odin thumped the table again, and somewhere a farming village was taken out by an avalanche. 'I'm a warrior god,' declared Odin proudly. 'We all are, and when we go, we should go out in a blaze of glory, to be remembered by man for all time, not as some kind of laughingstock, or worse still, forgotten. Do you want our final battle to be thought of as nothing more than a skirmish, where we were brushed aside by the armies of ice, like a man swats away a fly?'

'I don't want to be thought of as a fly.'

'Me neither.'

'Bollocks to flies.'

'I think the splinter has infected my finger. It's all swollen and sore.'

'If you keep going on about your finger I'll cut it off, then you won't have to worry about it any more,' Thor growled.

'Yeah? You and whose army?'

'I don't need an army to beat you, Vana boy.'

'Then bring it, if you think you're hard enough.'

'Yeah?'

'YEAH!'

'ENOUGH!' Odin thumped the table again, and back on Midgard sudden aftershocks rippled through the devastation of the previous earthquake, killing off what few survivors were left. All except, that is, one dog, a small blonde child and two star-crossed lovers, who always seem to survive these things. Thanks to the dog's barking they would find the child and raise it as their own to live happily ever after, that is until the child grew to adulthood and in a drunken rage one night would murder his adoptive parents because they wouldn't let him go off to train to be a warrior, as they insisted he remained a farmer and help them tend the land. Just goes to show you how one good deed does not always get the rewards it deserves.

Unaware of the destruction he had just caused and with his errant audience listening to him once more, Odin continued, 'Right, you lot, I want you out there finding out what Hel's up to and who is doing her dirty work for her, and I want it stopping.'

'How are we going to do that?'

'You have worshippers down there. Give your seers and witches a vision and get them to start asking around, find out what's happening and report back.'

'Why can't we just ask Hel?'

'Oh, like she'll tell us.'

'She might not tell us, but she'd probably tell Loki,' said Thor.

At the mention of Loki there was a sharp intake of breath and the mood shifted to an uneasy silence.

'What?' said Thor. 'Why shouldn't we ask Loki? She is his daughter, after all.'

'You can't trust Loki,' answered Forseti. 'He has no respect for any law.'

'Spoken like a true lawyer,' Thor replied with undisguised disdain. 'Sod the law; we don't need that to get Loki to do some snooping for us.'

Forseti was about to protest but Odin shushed him and said, 'Go on?'

'Loki's bored.'

'How do you know that?' asked Odin. 'He's barred from Asgard.'

'Aye, well, that's as maybe, but he's still my mate and we still meet up for a drink every now and then.'

'What's the point of us barring him if you break the bloody embargo?'

'I felt sorry for him.'

'For Loki? After all the trouble he caused?'

'Aye, I did, so what? He's my mate. You want to make something of it?'

'I'm sure there is a precedent somewhere which means we could bar you too.'

'Forseti, keep the law to yourself for the moment,' ordered Odin sharply. 'I want to hear what Thor has to say.'

'Cheers, Dad. Loki is bored. He just wants back into Asgard, to hang out with the boys again. Plus, if we ask him to go snooping for us, he'll love that.'

'So, if we lift the ban he'll spy on his own daughter?'

'It'll take more than lifting the ban.'

'How much more?'

'He wants back in the weekly card game.'

'No way.'

'Yes way.'

'He can fuck off.'

'Cheating bastard still hasn't paid me what he owes me from the last time.'

'My finger's really, really sore.'

Odin sat back from the table, stroking his beard thoughtfully. The arguments against Loki raged on around him, but Odin was not the king of the gods for nothing, and he knew that sometimes you had to look at the bigger picture. 'Okay,' he said.

The argument around the table stopped abruptly and all looked to the king.

'I said OKAY.'

'You can't be serious?'

'You're mad.'

'Nothing good will come of this.'

'Maybe,' admitted Odin, 'but we have little choice. Okay, Thor, he's your friend – see if you can get him to look into his daughter and find out what she's up to.'

'And the card game?'

'I'll think about it. Information first.'

'Okay.'

The rest of the gods grimaced but said nothing. Their King had spoken and in a tone which brooked no argument. With a sense of trepidation and a fear of being conned out of their money at the card table in the weeks to come, the gods left Odin to himself.

Odin called over one of the few serving wenches who were working and ordered another beer and a steak. Come on, he was hungry – can't a god have an afternoon snack when he wants one? Really, everyone is a critic. Steak finished, Odin sat back to ponder whether his decision was all that wise. Something was afoot, and he needed to know what it was lest the foot become a booted leg which would give them all a damn good kicking.

10

In this age of satellite navigation, ordinance survey maps, and GPS tracking, it is almost impossible to ever be entirely lost. Even thrill-seeking adventurers who crash their aircraft in large track-less wastes usually have a damn good idea down to a square metre of just where their mangled aircraft lies in the world. Admittedly, if they are bleeding, their radio is dead and the mountain lion which has just strolled over to investigate has anything to do with it, knowing where one is, is not going to save one's bacon, but at least you can die with the sound knowledge that you were not lost at the time. Unfortunately, in the Dark Ages it was all too easy to be lost, and this was exactly the situation facing our dashing Viking hero and crew, which is why Agnew had sent some of his men out to try and get their bearings.

The men given the scouting task were generally happy to do so. Firstly, it got them out of salvaging all the equipment from their wrecked ship. Secondly, it took them away from the cold, windswept, spray-covered beach they had crashed upon. Thirdly, and by no means the least important reason, after what had seemed like weeks stuck on the ship it gave them a chance to stretch their legs, so it is no surprise that Ogmundr, Alfarr and Siggeirr were striding out with reckless abandon rather than creeping surreptitiously through the un-dergrowth, not that there was much in the way of undergrowth behind which to creep.

Ogmundr was tall, rangy, solidly built and just a bit clumsy, as though he were not quite sure where his extremities were. A generally cheerful sort, with a warm smile which was always ready to burst forth from behind his short, well-kept black beard, Ogmundr tended to be the calming influence of the three. Alfarr by contrast was short, stocky, barrel-chested, bow-legged, and as bald as a coot, which he made up for with an expansive sandy beard. Unlike Ogmundr, Alfarr seldom smiled and tended to always look like he expected the gods to unleash pain and destruction upon him at any given moment. And that left Siggeirr. Middling of height, skinny, with dishevelled hair, a patchy beard mottled with specks of grey and a mouth full of broken teeth, Siggeirr moved through life with a devil-may-care attitude and a cheeky grin, forever talking loudly and indulging in his favourite pastimes of sex and annoying Alfarr.

As they moved ever further inland, the three Vikings soon came to realise that wherever this place was it was a low-lying, flat, windswept, barren wasteland mainly consisting of peat bogs, tufty grass, the occasional shrub, and even less occasional tree, usually of a short, twisted, stumpy nature, and Alfarr did not like it one bit.

'This place is accursed,' spat Alfarr. 'The sooner we are away, the better.'

'How do you know it's cursed?' asked Ogmundr. 'It is just a bit bare.'

'A bit bare? Look at it. Not a tree to be seen anywhere, except for those twisted dwarf trees. It's not natural.'

'If it's not natural then where do you think we are?'

'I don't know – elf lands, perhaps.'

'Elf lands?'

'Bollocks!' said Siggeirr.

'Ha! You won't say that when some elf steals your soul,' Alfarr snapped back.

'What elf?'

'What?'

'I said, what elf? There's nothing here – no elves, no dwarves, not even a squirrel, nothing, so why would any self-respecting elf live here?'

'They are fey creatures in league with dark forest spirits,' answered Alfarr knowingly.

Siggeirr shook his head at his comrade's stupidity. 'Forest spirits?'

'Aye, them. They'll lure you down some path to kill you and devour your soul.' Alfarr was warming to his subject.

'That they may do,' said Siggeirr, 'but don't forest spirits hang out in forests?'

'Of course.'

'I thought so,' replied Siggeirr dismissively, staring across the barren landscape. 'You're talking bollocks again.'

'Piss off, Siggy. This place is cursed; you'll see.'

'Maybe, but not by elves or any other forest folk.'

'And what makes you so sure?'

'Look around – there's no forest.'

'Maybe they've just hidden it. They can play with your mind, you know.'

'You're a moron.'

'Well, don't say you haven't been warned.'

'Whatever.' Siggeirr waved off Alfarr's fears.

'Smoke!' called out Ogmundr suddenly.

'Where?' asked Siggeirr.

'Rising above that hill.' Ogmundr pointed off to their right, where a thin plume of black smoke was snaking into the winter sky from behind a hill which was nothing more than a low rise.

Instantly more alert, the three Vikings drew their weapons. Crouching low so their silhouettes would not stand out against the sky, they made their way to the hill's crest. Lying on their bellies, they peered down the other side and found themselves looking over a smallish village stretched around a small, wind-swept bay.

'Still think it's elves?' asked Siggeirr sarcastically.

'Could have been,' replied Alfarr touchily. 'We still don't know it isn't.'

'There are people down there,' observed Ogmundr.

'Oh, all right, so it's not elves, but it could have been, and it's better to be prepared and on your guard than caught unawares by some fey spirit with sharp, pointy teeth and an unquenchable thirst for human flesh, waiting to murder you in your sleep.'

Siggeirr stared at Alfarr with utter contempt then turned back to Ogmundr. 'How many do you think are down there?'

'Village that size – about fifty, give or take.'

'Can you see anyone armed?'

'No. I can see a few men, but they look more like farmers than warriors.'

'Then let's go down and have a go,' said Alfarr.

'Oh, so now it's just farmers you're suddenly brave.'

'Fuck off. I'm every bit as brave as you, Siggy.'

'Really? When was the last time you fought anyone any good?'

'I've fought.'

'Huh, sure.'

'I have.'

'What about our last battle?'

'What about it?'

'You turned up late after all the hard work had been done.'

'That wasn't my fault. Agnew had sent me off to scout behind the enemy's lines.'

'Strange how you only made it back once the fighting had stopped. Did you get lost on your way back?'

'Screw you, Siggeirr. You've no idea what I went through.'

'Coward!'

'Take that back!' hissed Alfarr dangerously, bringing his axe up, ready to strike.

Before Alfarr could lash out, Ogmundr reached out and grabbed Alfarr's axe, dragging it down, and pointed urgently to the village. 'We've been seen.'

Sure enough, looking up from the village, it was clear some of the villagers had noticed their presence on top of the hill. Suddenly, amongst the villagers there was a flurry of activity, as men appeared from every building carrying an assortment of weapons, mostly of the gardening implement type, but as anyone who has been on the receiving end of a well-handled scythe will tell you, it can be every bit as dangerous and off-putting as facing a man with a sword.

Even Alfarr could see they would be outnumbered if the entire village's menfolk chose to come up the hill and investigate. The three Vikings slipped hurriedly back down the hill and ran back towards the beach. It did not take a genius to realise the village may be less inclined to fight when confronted by their full strength rather than just the three of them. With a bit of luck and backed up by the entire crew they would be able to sweep in and take the place through fear alone.

Breathless, the three made it to the beach unimpeded, where they gave Agnew and Tostig the news. Of the two of them, Tostig was the happier.

'Great,' said Tostig gleefully. 'Should I get the men armed and ready to strike?'

'What? No,' said Agnew. 'Let's just go talk to them.'

'And then we fight them?'

'No.'

'But why not? We haven't fought anyone in ages. We will be losing our touch.'

'It takes more than a couple of weeks to lose your touch. Anyway, they sound like farmers; hardly a worthy opponent for you, Tostig.'

'It's not my fault they aren't up to much; doesn't mean we can't attack.'

'And what if one of them gets in a lucky strike? How do you think that will be greeted in the afterlife? Do you really think someone slain by an old man armed with a pitchfork will get you entry to Valhalla?'

'Um...'

'No, of course it won't.'

'Even Freya wouldn't take you, if you got killed like that,' chipped in Delling, who had been listening in.

'I didn't ask you, dwarf,' snarled Tostig.

'You should listen to him,' said Agnew. 'He works for the gods, after all. He knows what they're like.'

'You spoil all my fun.'

'Just looking out for you, mate.' Agnew gave Tostig a friendly punch on the arm. 'But you could be right – we may have to fight, so best be ready. Get everyone to kit up, full battle dress. We may as well look scary. BUT Tostig...'

'Yes?'

'Tell the men they are not to kill and rape everything in sight.'

'What if the villagers decide to attack us first?'

'Then just subdue and restrain, but no killing, clear?'

'But if they attack –'

'NO KILLING!'

'Seems a bit of a waste of an expedition if we don't get to kill anyone,' Tostig grumbled. 'This will hardly make for a great saga on our return. I cannot see the skalds queuing to tell the tale of Agnew and his non-violent adventure, with no danger, blood, or excitement.'

'Just get the men ready.'

'I'm going. But we will be a laughingstock. That's all.'

'Go,' commanded Agnew.

Unhappy, Tostig left to rally the men. Watching him go, Delling asked, 'So, why won't you let him go and kill a few folks? I thought you Norse types were all bloodthirsty warriors, whose only aim in life was to fight, kill, and die gloriously in battle.'

'We are.'

'Really? Because you do not seem to be a bloodthirsty Viking. Quite the opposite.'

'How so?'

'"Don't kill them; we only want to talk to them."' Delling imitated Agnew. 'Hardly very Viking, is it?'

'Who are you to judge me?'

'No offence, Agnew, but my mistress, and currently your boss, is looking for someone to get her rake back at all costs, no matter how much blood needs to be spilled. If she wanted someone to just politely ask for it back, she could have sent a woman's sewing circle instead.'

'So, you'd rather I just slaughter a village of farmers just to find a rake?'

'If that's what it takes. Kill half so the other half are scared and will do exactly what you want them to. Better still, they'll tell you whatever you need to know to find the rake.'

'Or they'll just tell me the first thing which comes into their heads, hoping I will believe whatever lie they spin me just so I will bugger off and leave them alone.'

'They wouldn't do that, would they?'

'Yes.'

'Even if you threatened to come back and kill them if they were lying?'

'You'd be surprised.'

'Wow, you humans must be really dumb. If someone did that to me, I'd tell them exactly what they wanted to know.' The dwarf laughed, astonished.

'Folks can be less predictable when faced with death.'

'You humans are crazy.'

'Maybe, but that's why we're just going to talk to them.'

'And what if Tostig's right? What if they do just attack?'

'Then we'll cross that bridge when we come to it.'

'Oh dear,' said Delling despondently.

'What?'

'You know that bridge you were just talking about?'

'Yes.'

'Well, it's coming for you right now.'

'What?'

Delling leant to his right and pointed behind Agnew, who turned to see a bunch of men charging towards him and his scattered crew.

'Oh, you stupid piss sacks...'

11

What is this, I hear you cry. Agnew and his men are about to be attacked, and we've cut away from the action. Are you insane? That's the best bit! Well, fear not. It takes time to set up a battle properly: lines have to be drawn, troops have to be formed into their units, logistical supply lines need setting up, rousing speeches made, plus the pre-battle team photos always take ages. With all that going on, it will be a while before the action kicks in, so we've time to kill before the off. Besides, there's an interesting meeting going on in the Underworld we really should listen in on.

As we re-enter the Underworld, we find a disturbance going on at its entrance, with Hel storming along to investigate. What she finds is rather a distressing sight for the Queen of the Dead, so our more sensitive readers may want to look away now. What? You don't want to? Oh well, don't say you were not warned.

As Hel nears the threshold to her domain, she finds Garm, her beloved hound, guardian of the Underworld, as fearsome a beast as one could hope to meet, with jaws so strong he could snap a man in two with a single bite, on his back, legs in the air, panting with delight as Loki, who as you may remember happens to be Hel's father, rubs the hound's tummy, and before you say, 'Ah, that's not scary,' trust me when I tell you the look on Hel's face is enough to chill your piss.

'What do you think you're doing?' yelled Hel as she set eyes on the sickeningly happy sight before her.

'Playing with your dog.'

'That's not a dog – it's a Hel Hound, my Hel Hound. What have you done to make him so soppy? That's no way for him to behave. You've turned him into a bloody lap dog.'

'Nothing – I just rubbed his ears, that's all.' Loki protested his innocence, switching from rubbing Garm's belly to roughly stroking Garm's head, causing the Hel Hound to wriggle and snap at Loki's hand playfully. 'There, you like that, you like dat, don't you? Who's a good dog? Who's a good dog?'

'Stop that NOW!'

'Why? He likes it.'

'He's not supposed to like it. He's supposed to stand guard and tear intruders like you limb from limb.'

'What, Garm?'

'Yes, Garm. Who else?'

'But he's a good dog.'

'He's a fearsome hound that's supposed to keep the dead in check and stop them escaping my realm. He's not meant to roll on his back and play dead.'

Loki looked at Hel then back down to Garm, who looked back up at Loki with utter devotion.

'Nah, he wouldn't hurt a fly.'

With Loki daring to stop stroking him for oh, at least a second, Garm squealed with impatience and jumped at Loki, licking his face, then dropped back, ready to chase anything the fire god wished to throw for him. From some hidden pocket Loki pulled out a stick – well, to you and me it would look like a small tree, but we are dealing with gods here and they do not do things by halves – and hurled the stick, branch, tree thing away, instantly followed by Garm, bounding off with the excited yip of a puppy to retrieve it.

'You don't play with that dog enough. When did you last take him for a proper walk? Have you seen the length of his claws?' Loki chided his daughter.

'It's no business of yours.'

'It's not healthy for the poor creature, being cooped up down here all the time. He needs a good run every day, otherwise he'll get fat.'

'How... why... I... argh, damn you, Dad, you make my blood boil!' Hel struggled to get her curse out. She didn't know why but her father always had this effect on her and that, if anything, made her even more angry.

Loki gave his daughter a disarming smile and threw an arm around her shoulders with fatherly affection. 'Well, I am a fire god,' he said with a smirk.

'I hate you.'

'Now, now, is that any way to talk to your old dad?'

'I should have you tied to a chair and then flay your skin from your body.'

'Well, you could, but you know what? A beer would be better.'

Hel flicked her father's hand from her shoulder, stepped away and with an angry huff tramped off into the gloom of her kingdom. 'Well, come on,' she called back to Loki ungraciously, 'I haven't got all day.'

Loki looked around the gloomy vista of her lands. 'Day? Huh, chance would be a fine thing,' he remarked in a barely concealed whisper.

'What was that?'

'Nothing. I just said it's a fine day for a walk.'

'Liar.'

'Naturally.'

'I really do hate you.'

'Yes, I know. Now, where's that beer you promised?'

Being gods and not mere Vikings trapped down here as had been Agnew, it didn't take them long to reach Hel's hall. It took a little longer than Hel would have liked, what with Loki stopping every now and then to throw the branch Garm kept bringing back to him, but as both Loki and Garm seemed to be enjoying the game, Hel let it pass.

Inside the hall, which unlike the drinking hall in Asgard was a cold, unwelcoming place carved out of grim, dark rock, they sat at a large table, where one of Hel's many minions served them ale. Garm bounded up to the table, dropped the branch at Loki's feet and sat panting, waiting for Loki to throw it again, only now Loki commanded the hound to sit. Obediently, the great dog sat then lay down, curled up at Loki's feet, who happily scratched the dog's ears.

'How do you get him to do that?' asked Hel. 'He doesn't do that for me.'

'You just have to know how to treat him right, that's all. He's just a dog; they're all the same. Anyone with half an idea about dogs' behaviour can do this.'

'Whatever.'

Loki took a contented swig of beer. 'Mmmmmm, this is a good brew. What's it called?'

'Does it matter?'

'No, not really. Would it be possible to take some with me?'

'If it means you won't come back in a hurry, I'll have some delivered to your place of choice.'

'Great. So, how're things? Underworld okay? Keeping busy?'

'Actually, it's been a bit cra... Hang on – why do you want to know?'

'Can't a father show some interest in his child's job?'

'Yes, he can, but you've never shown the slightest interest in anything any of your children have done, ever.'

'That's hardly fair.'

'Really? Okay, tell me when you last did anything for any of us.'

'No problem. For starters, there was, um... maybe not, but I definitely went to... oh, no, I got diverted by... but there was that time when... ah, no, that was Tyr, wasn't it, and he's not one of mi...' Loki paused. 'Okay, so I've been an errant father, but that's just me. I'm a god of fire and mischief. It's in my nature; I can't help it. You can hardly expect me to do the doting dad stuff.'

'Doting dad stuff – ha! How about just being a dad, full stop?'

'So, what would you have had me do? Take you to dance lessons? Sit through your first recitals of the runes? Maybe listen to a bad rendition of "Little Wolf's Head" on one of those damn whistle flute things they make all kids play? No, sorry. I had better, more godlike things to do.'

'I would simply have settled on you visiting occasionally when you didn't just want something.'

'I'm here now, aren't I?'

'Yes. What do you want?'

'I'm deeply hurt by that. As if I'm here for something. I came just because I wanted to see you.'

'You expect me to believe that? And stop with the sad eyes – they do not work on me.'

'Charming.'

'You bring it on yourself, with all your devious behaviour and the fact mayhem follows you around like a bad smell.'

'Sticks and stones, Hel, sticks and stones," Loki replied, his voice dripping with hurt. 'I know everyone thinks I don't care about anyone but myself, but it's simply not true. I find it very hurtful that even my own daughter has no faith in me.'

'Oh, for... Okay, okay, I take it back. You just want to see me – great, fine – it's good to see you too. Well, Garm's happy you're here. So then, now you are here, what do you want to talk about? Or are you just here for my beer and food?'

'As excellent as your beer is, and it really is,' said Loki, taking another appreciative swig, 'let's not talk about me. Let's talk about you. How're things down here?'

'I'm fine; it's fine; it's dark and dismal, so the usual, really.'

'Good, good. I like what you've done with the place. Very, erm...'

'Miserable?'

'Yes, that's the word, miserable. You've really captured that spirit of misery.'

'That's the general idea – can't have the dead being happy, now, can we?' said Hel sarcastically.

'I don't know, always seemed a bit unfair to me. The fallen warriors get all the good stuff and everyone else who just got on with making sure the everyday stuff got done get stuck with this. Doesn't seem fair. After all, someone has to be a farmer; not everyone is cut out for the warrior lifestyle.'

'If you care so much about the unheroic dead, take it up with Odin. They're his rules.'

'But you don't have to keep the Underworld so gloomy. Surely you could brighten it up a bit? Maybe a bar or two, a bevy of dancing girls dotted about the place, the occasional gambling den – the possibilities are endless.'

'Unlike my patience. What do you want, Dad? And don't insult me by telling me you care about the dead. You don't give two hoots about them. They're each just one fewer person to support Odin and his mob at the end of days.'

'When did you get so cynical?'

'The moment you abandoned me and left me at Odin's mercy.'

'I said I was sorry.'

'No, you didn't.'

'Didn't I?'

'No.'

'Mmmmmm, I really am a crap father, aren't I? Don't answer that.'

'Huh – like I need to.'

'All water under the bridge. I'm not here to argue with you, just to make sure you're doing okay, see if you were maybe dating anyone yet?'

'Dating?'

'Yes, going out with a boy, dating. How else am I going to get grandkids unless you give me some? I can hardly rely on your brothers. Fenris is a prisoner, and personally I think Jörmungandr bats for the other side, so it's all down to you.'

'Me?'

'Who else?'

'Look at me, Dad. I'm hardly a catch.'

'Nonsense – you'd make someone a great wife. After all, anyone who brews beer like this would be most men's dream.'

'I'm a half-skeletal hag. If I were a boy, even I wouldn't go near me. Have you never noticed there are no mirrors down here?'

'Can't say I have, no.'

'Well, there aren't, because even I don't want to look at me.'

'Looks aren't everything, and I should know – look at some of the monsters I've been with, which reminds me, how's your mother?'

'Leave Mum out of this.'

'Sorry, that was a bit cruel, but it does demonstrate my point – if she could get laid, so can you.'

'Mum only got laid cos you'd shag anything with a pulse – no – you'd just shag anything, pulse optional.'

'Any port in a storm.' Loki chuckled, reliving a fond memory. 'But this isn't about me, this is about you. Surely you must have some suitors?'

'Now you're just mocking me.'

'Hardly – you're just approaching this all wrong. Instead of thinking of yourself as an ugly hag who no man in his right mind would be seen dead with –'

'Thanks, thanks a lot.'

'Instead, think you are the Queen of the Underworld. You have almost as much power as Odin. You have dominion over thousands of souls. You are a rich and powerful goddess in your own right, and many a man will find that extremely attractive. I tell you, start thinking like that and your confidence will soar and before you know it, you'll have men knocking down your door to be with you.'

'Are you drunk? How strong is that beer?'

'No, why?'

'Because you're talking drunken bollocks.'

'Nope, sober as a judge, and you're wrong, daughter. Power is a great aphrodisiac; how do you think Odin lays so many chicks? It's hardly down to his looks, is it? It's all about the power and confidence which goes with that power. Trust me, power is sexy.'

'I really don't want to discuss this and especially not with my dad.'

'I'm only trying to help. You know I only have your best interests at heart.'

'What heart?'

'Unfair.'

'Maybe, but I really don't want to discuss my sex life, or lack of it, with you.'

'Suit yourself.'

'Okay?'

'No worries. If you don't want to confide in me then don't let me impose.'

'Don't start playing some guilt trip on me and make out I've hurt your feelings; we all know you don't have any.'

'You say some very hurtful things, Hel.'

'Shut up.'

'No. I came down here to see how you are, provide some fatherly advice and what do I get? Shut out, that's what, but if I'm not good enough then I might as well go if I'm not going to be of any use to you.' Loki sighed and stood slowly, drained the last of his beer and placed the flagon down gently on the table with a look of utter dejection.

'Oh, please, you don't expect me to fall for that.'

'No, don't say another word,' said Loki, holding up his hand as if to ward off any more hurtful words from Hel. 'I'll leave – wouldn't want to get in the way of your very important job.'

'Dad, stop, I didn't mean...' Hel began as she too stood.

'No, don't trouble yourself. I'll show myself out, I know the way.'

'You don't have to go...'

'I think I do. Is it all right if I take Garm with me, for the company?'

'What? Yes, I mean, stay, stay a while.'

'Really?'

Hel sighed deeply. 'Yes, really. It's good to see you.'

'And you don't mind? I wouldn't want to be a burden.'

'You're not a burden.'

'Okay, I'll stay, but only if you're sure?'

'DAD, I'm SURE. Let's just not talk about my love life.'

'I'll not mention it again.'

'Good.'

'Fine.'

'Great.'

'No problem.'

For a time, the pair of them sat quietly at Hel's table, Hel trying not to glare and Loki trying not to break the silence. Unfortunately for Hel, Loki had never been one to hold his tongue. 'So, tell me,' he said, 'is it true someone actually managed to escape from down here recently?'

12

I had planned to take you back to the fight on the beach so you could experience the clamour, the adrenaline, the stench of fear and sheer craziness of battle. I was going to take you in close so you could hear the clash of metal against metal, the splintering of bone, the roars of the victors and anguished cries of those about to die brutally. I had hoped to let you witness the showers of blood and thwack of metal against unprotected flesh, but unfortunately the battle was over rather quicker than one anticipated. In fact, we have got back just in time to witness the aftermath, and it is not a pretty sight.

Bodies, weapons, and the occasional limb lay discarded across the beach in pretty much the same way a teenage boy discards his dirty clothes across his bedroom floor. Mind you, warriors are not by nature a particularly tidy bunch, forever leaving the countryside littered with their vanquished foes.

But what of Agnew's crew? Have they survived? Are they now nothing more than a mutilated mass of corpses serving no other purpose than to feed the crows? Well, worry not, dear reader, for our Viking adventurers have survived, which is just as well, otherwise this would have been a worryingly short tale. Sure, some are nursing a few wounds here and there – a nicked thumb, a bust lip, Ogmundr has even managed to get a black eye – but all in all they have come away unscathed, unlike the men from the village, who are generally either dead, dying, or at the very least captured and sporting some nasty-looking wounds.

Unfortunately for Agnew's crew, our hero is not a happy man right now. In fact he is, as his name would suggest, rather miffed, even fuming, but the life of a leader is seldom without its problems, and Agnew's problems were mounting fast. First off, his orders to not kill anyone had been by and large ignored by his men, as the scene of slaughter on the beach will testify. The blatant disregard of his orders was the first thing to set his temper off, which was then stoked further when, on raising the issue of the crew's conduct, Tostig openly dismissed his orders as having been pointless and inherently against everything a Norse warrior holds dear. Obviously Tostig did not use words like 'inherently'. What he actually said was, and I quote, 'They were fucking stupid.'

The only thing which stopped Tostig and Agnew getting into a fight right there and then was Ogmundr stepping between them to break them up. This was also where he got his black eye as he stopped the punch thrown by Agnew with his face rather than letting it connect with Tostig. The net result was that Agnew felt bad about hitting Ogmundr, which only added more fuel to his anger, so he stomped off in a sulk, leaving Ogmundr rubbing his swelling eye, cursing the day he ever joined this ragtag crew of misfits, deviants, and idiots.

Ogmundr, as you may be starting to realise, is not your archetypal Viking warrior. His first love is cooking, followed by poetry. Ogmundr is a sensitive and creative soul, and if he were born today he would probably be trying to fashion a career as a celebrity chef whilst reciting modern verse, but this being the Dark Ages, there is little need for such a mix. The skalds tell the tales, the women do the cooking, and all the other men were expected to be men. Sensitivity was not a quality which got you very far. With that kind of peer pressure, he had basically two choices: he could either have stayed working on a farm, which simply did not win you the best girls, or he could become a bloodthirsty warrior, where he would at least get the chance to seduce a better quality of woman, and if he could pick up some exotic cooking tips while on his travels then so much the better.

Eventually tempers cooled enough, though not all the bad feeling cleared, so that our less-than-merry band could pull themselves together, gather up their prisoners – another sore point, by the way, but more of that in a bit – and head back inland towards the village first spied by Ogmundr, Siggeirr and Alfarr.

And so it is we find our angry mob cresting the small rise overlooking the village to descend upon it with terrifying fury.

Oh, what? You expected them to turn up with a welcoming smile and for everyone to greet each other as long-lost brothers? Well, forget it. These are dark and dangerous times, and where Vikings go, warm welcomes are seldom the order of the day. When Vikings turn up in a village with what is left of the town's fighting men bloody, beaten, and bound as prisoners, the remaining villagers tend to react with fear and terror, making them an unpredictable and dangerous group. Agnew had wanted to arrive without having to follow the usual marauding path of brutalising a settlement into submission, but the battle had removed that as an option, which is one reason he was bloody angry, but also, even for Agnew, it is not always easy to avoid one's own stereotype, so he sent half of his men to sweep into the settlement to instil terror and fear into the remaining populace. Any man left, mainly those who had been too old to fight or too young to hold a sword, were instantly beaten down the moment they showed any desire to resist. With the settlement's folks suitably subdued, Agnew marched into what passed as the centre of the village with a suitably disdainful sneer upon his face and regarded the cowering villagers coldly.

'Who is the leader here?' Agnew demanded harshly.

No one moved, which, let's face it, is hardly surprising. Would you put yourself forward to face some crazed nutter with a dangerous gleam in his eye who said, 'I am going to kill the first person I don't like the look of'? Well, no, neither would I, so do not judge them too unkindly.

'I said, who is the leader here?'

Again no one said anything.

'I don't think they understand you,' said Delling.

'By the...' began Agnew then paused and switched to speak in a broken Celtic tongue. 'Who is the leader here?'

Slowly, a woman detached herself from the crowd, bravely stepped forward and pointed at one of the prisoners. 'Ya already 'ave him there,' she answered slowly in Norse but with a strange accent.

Agnew stared at her dispassionately, but she remained resolute and stared right back.

'You know our language?' Agnew asked in Norse.

'Aye.'

'What's your name, woman?' asked Agnew, reverting to speaking in stunted Celtic.

'Morag,' the woman replied in her own tongue.

'Well, Morag, your man is no longer your leader. For the purposes of tonight, you speak for your village.'

'It's naw my place ta speak for tha men.'

'I see no men here,' Agnew spat contemptibly, 'only boys and those who have given up the right to be called men. When only a woman steps forward to speak then there can be no real men here. I will not deal with those too scared to talk to me. You spoke, you have courage – you speak for your village.'

The woman cast a fearful eye to the bound man whom she had indicated as leader.

'Don't look to him. Look to me, Morag.'

'I... I... sorry, I...'

'Is he your man, Morag?'

'He's naw mine.'

Agnew turned to Tostig and slipping back into Norse said coldly, 'Dispatch him,' pointing at the leader of the village.

Without a word, Tostig stepped up to the bound man and heaved his great axe above his head. Immediately the bound man let out a cry of fear, but it was not enough to save him, for in these times pity was not a commodity which carried much weight. With cold efficiency Tostig swept his axe down, the blade smashing into and through the man's head, splitting it in two down as far as the bridge of his nose.

Immediately, all the women in the village screamed, all the men cursed, and all the children cried as their leader fell dead to the floor, all, that is, except Morag, who kept her gaze steadily fixed on Agnew.

'There, he is no longer leader. You are,' declared Agnew.

'What do ye want?'

'Food, shelter for tonight, and in the morning, a ship.'

'Food and shelter are yours. I dinnae know if we have a ship you will want.'

'Then we'll worry about the ship in the morning. Tell your people that if they cause us no trouble and do as we say then we shall not harm anyone else.'

'And them?' Morag pointed at the men held prisoner.

'I will release the prisoners back to you, alive, when we leave. Tell them not to think about trying to get revenge. Any uprising will be met with extreme violence. We will kill you all. Do you understand, Morag?'

'Aye.'

'Good. Then tell them to obey my orders or by Odin's beard more blood will flow. Go!'

Quickly, Morag scampered around the townsfolk, relaying Agnew's command, who all looked past her fearfully to Agnew. Agnew turned his attention to Tostig, Delling and the rest. 'There, is that what you wanted?'

'It worked, didn't it?' replied Tostig casually.

'Yes,' conceded Agnew with a disparaging sigh, miffed that Tostig and Delling had been proven correct.

'So, what now?'

'The usual – get the woman Morag to show you to whatever passes as the main hall in this place. We'll sleep in there. Get them to bring food to us. Don't let the men kill anyone else unless they have absolutely no choice – do you understand?'

Tostig nodded.

'And no raping. I've given my word that if they behave, so will we; that includes not abusing the women.'

'Okay, no rape.'

'Good.'

'Okay.'

'Fine.'

'Sorted. Anything else?'

'Yes. Get some of the lads to look over their boats. I want to know if there is anything at all out there which might suit us.'

'Why do we need a ship?'

'I don't know where we are, but we certainly aren't in our own lands. This lot are Celts.'

'You're right there. They're a right bunch of Celts...'

'No, I mean they ARE Celts. Look at them, all red-haired and angry.'

'So?'

'So, it means we aren't home. There are no Celtic settlements back in our lands. Wherever we are now it means home is going to be across the sea.'

'Ah, I see. So we need a –'

'Ship, yes.'

'I'll get Alfarr to check it out.'

Agnew let Tostig go to send Alfarr to look at the villagers' boats and issue Agnew's orders about not raping and killing, which were greeted with the sort of enthusiasm a school kid has when faced with a lesson of double maths, but for now, at least, they followed the orders.

Delling, who for the most part had stayed out of the way, felt that they had overlooked one small problem – the prisoners. 'What do you want to do with them?' he asked, pointing at the bound men.

'What?'

'The prisoners. We can't just set them free, or they'll be slitting our throats in our sleep.'

'By Odin's beard, do I have to think of everything around here?' Agnew implored the sky.

'Well, you are the leader. You were the one who wanted prisoners. Why you didn't just kill them back on the beach is beyond me.'

'We aren't all bloodthirsty killers.'

'No? I saw how you just had their leader done in. That looked pretty bloodthirsty to me.'

'I didn't have a choice. I couldn't leave them with someone to rally to. He's dead, they're scared, now they'll do what we say.'

'Or you could have just killed them all on the beach.'

'O-KAY, YES, I could have killed them, but you know what? I don't need to. We really don't need to, and if we did then we might as well have come here and killed all the women and kids as well, because if we'd killed all the men, who would go out onto that sea and fish? Who would hunt? They would starve – is that what you would have wanted? Well? IS IT?'

Delling shrank back from the ranting Agnew, who was now quite red in the face, shrugged and said, 'I only meant we –'

'What? Only what?'

'You know what?' said Delling, who, looking at Agnew right then could have sworn he was staring into the eyes of Hel herself. 'It doesn't matter. You're the boss. We'll do it your way.'

'Thank you for your unwavering support. I'll be sure to let Hel know what a help you have been.'

'Er, yes, well, no need to sing my praises. Just doing my job, ha!' Delling laughed weakly.

'Just see that you do. We wouldn't want you to become a pointless burden slowing us down. It wouldn't be in Hel's interests to have us lagging behind because of you.' Agnew's words dripped with menace.

'You know, I think I'll go and find some place to secure the prisoners and get out of your way. You're obviously busy right now.'

'You do that.'

Quickly, Delling ordered the Vikings on prisoner detail to follow him, bringing the prisoners with them to find a place to imprison them securely. Delling cast a cautious glance back at Agnew, who remained stood in the centre of the village, directing his remaining men with an icy, dangerous calm, and for the first time Delling began to suspect that his mistress had known exactly what she was doing when she chose this angry man to do her bidding.

13

Leaving one angry man behind in Agnew, it seems only right and proper that we switch our attention to if not an angry man, then to one who is at the very least feeling a bit narked, not to mention soaked.

Who is this man, and why is he soaked? Well, all will be revealed, but first let us take a moment to drink in the beautiful vista opening out before you. It is night. The cold light of a half-moon sparkles across the snow-covered landscape. Everything glistens except for a much darker streak which cuts a swathe across the land. Looking closer it becomes obvious that the dark swathe is not land but water, the cold, icy water of a fjord, which is lapping gently against the snowy shoreline. If you allow yourself to follow the shore a short way north you will see a strange circular pattern in the snow, probably a mile round in circumference, and inside that circle there seems to be a mix of regular and irregular shapes, though the snow has helped soften their lines, making them hard to discern. The occasional flickering torch only helps to cast yet longer shadows, blurring things further.

Despite the blurring it is evident that the outer circle is a high wooden palisade, with sharpened wooden stakes built out of the wooden wall pointing down at the ground, intended to discourage anyone from trying to climb the imposing barrier. Inside there is a raised walkway which runs around the length of the wooden wall, affording the people inside a method of patrolling the palisade to keep watch over the land beyond for any unwanted visitors: peddlers, attacking warbands or Christians coming to convert you to their god. Oh yes, you think it's bad now, being harassed by a Jehovah's witness as you're about to sit down to your Sunday roast, but trust me, there is nothing more inconvenient than some wandering monk rolling into town telling you everything you are doing is wrong, especially blood sacrifice, just as you are about to cut someone open and feed their entrails to your dog just to make Odin happy. It can really put a crimp on the whole mood of your pagan sacrifice.

Ignoring the imminent threat of conversion, let's go back to the palisade. It is big, and it is strong, and it only has two openings, both of which on this night are closed tight and bolted shut, and it is quite clear it would need one hell of a battering ram to get through. More importantly, the palisade circles the entire town, almost.

Yes, almost, because the palisade spans across two rocky outcrops which jut out into the fjord with a gap beneath it just large enough to let water into the town but not a gap big enough to sail a ship through and land enough men to launch an attack. So, although the gap exists it is considered secure and the town safe, that is until now, because a man, dripping wet from having swum up the fjord and under the opening, is beginning to climb out of the water.

That man is the freezing and unhappy Guthrun Doombringer. In some ways he should be happy, because if he were not holding Hel's rake right now, he would have surely frozen to death, again, from the rather lengthy swim up the fjord, but as it is he is very much alive.

Stealthily, Guthrun climbed out onto dry, no, make that snowy and icebound land, pausing to see if anyone had noticed his presence. Sadly, his entrance had gone unnoticed. You may be wondering why Guthrun should feel sadness at not being discovered. Unfortunately, what he was about to do went against everything his warrior soul craved and believed in. He had snuck into his enemy's lair, not called them out and faced them bravely on the field of battle. Well, he had, several times if truth be told, but they had refused to bite and remained steadfastly ensconced behind their palisade.

By choosing not to fight and instead sit out the siege in their nice, cosy town while Asa and her men froze outside in their makeshift camp, which, as anyone who as ever camped in a winter environment can tell you, ceases to be a jolly experience pretty damn quickly, they had put a large spanner in the workings of Asa's campaign.

They had tried to take the town by force, twice, and each time it had ended badly. Asa had pushed to try again but Guthrun had refused. Faced with either having to retreat for the winter or bypass the town and press south, leaving a dangerous enemy to their rear, Asa came up with a new plan, a plan which only involved Guthrun, the rake he had stolen from Hel, and a bit of sneaking about, which is why, with rake in hand, he was creeping into the town like a damp death come in the night. And the reason Guthrun was feeling so narked was that he was not sure why he was doing this. He remembered Asa pointing out that he had already left a few towns plagued and arguing against it, as that had not been deliberate, as he hadn't at that time realised the power of the rake and that he needed to keep it wrapped when not wanting to use it, but he could not quite remember how Asa had persuaded him to go through with the plan to bring pestilence down upon the whole town. It seemed cowardly in the extreme and yet here he was. As he took stock of his situation, he could not help but worry that he himself wasn't the victim of some form of witchcraft fooling him into this role, and that, more than anything, was really pissing him off. Still, he was here now and determined to see the job through no matter how ill it sat with him.

For the next hour, Guthrun slunk about the town, dragging the rake behind him through the snow, around every building, barn, pig pen, and anything which resembled a place the townsfolk might gather. Come morning it would look like fourteen snails had raced around the town in perfect formation criss-crossing back and forth, this way and that, leaving no possible pathway in the town untravelled, though few in the town would ever witness the fourteen uniform lines, as most would already have succumbed to a hellish plague before the morning sun had risen, and for that hardy few who were not yet dead they would be too ill to raise themselves from their beds. By midday all inside were staring with lifeless eyes into the next world.

Job done, Guthrun slipped away back into the fjord and returned to Asa's camp. He felt wretched, tired, and deep within felt his soul shrivel just that little bit more. It was as though every time he used the rake it took a part of him. He felt almost permanently cold, unnaturally so, for even at the height of a Scandinavian winter it was still possible to get warm, but that simple pleasure seemed denied to him. As the following days passed by, his mood growing darker, Guthrun became an ever more isolated and feared figure. Asa by contrast was radiance personified. With the fall of the town to the sudden mystery plague, well, it was a mystery to all but Guthrun and Asa, there was nothing holding Asa back, and with renewed vigour she led her motley band around the stricken town and took them further south. Three days later they swept into a largish town, which wisely chose not to resist Asa's demands and allowed her and her men to take over the place.

With a proper place in which to winter, with food aplenty and enough buxom wenches and beer to keep her men amused during the nights, even so Asa charged Guthrun and her Jarls to plan the next part of her campaign. She did not intend to sit around idly for five months waiting for the snows to clear. To keep her men occupied through the day she sent them out to hunt and gather information on what lay beyond. Wisely, she began to build a picture of what confronted her to make plans to take it so that when the snows cleared she could strike immediately.

For all but Guthrun spirits were high. Guthrun on the other hand was on edge. Failing to find any comfort in beer or between the legs of a slave, he threw himself into planning the next steps of the campaign as a means of distraction from the cold gnawing away at his sanity. What he needed now was a fight, and a bloody good one. His blood was up and his mood black, and the only thing which was likely to relieve either was to bury his axe in someone's face.

Asa had taken over the town's chief's dwelling and made the chief's daughters be her servants, so when Guthrun burst in unannounced, he found Asa relaxing in an over-large barrel, with the two daughters pouring hot water from steaming skillets into the barrel.

'What are you doing?' said Guthrun gruffly.

'It's called taking a bath; you should try it sometime,' Asa scoffed playfully.

'What is wrong with diving in the fjord?'

'Well, apart from the fact the fjord is icy cold, the water is not as clean. You should try bathing with hot water. It is actually a very pleasant sensation.'

'Seems a bit of a pointless waste of time to me. A quick dip in the fjord will do the job. I see no reason to spend time just sitting in water.'

'And there speaks man,' sighed Asa. 'Why do we bother with them, girls?'

The two daughters giggled nervously and kept their eyes fixed firmly on Asa, not daring to look up at the scary man in the black wolf pelts. The women of the village were accustomed to having warrior men about the place and so were seldom fazed even by the largest and gruffest types, but something about Guthrun unsettled them.

'Send them away,' ordered Guthrun.

Asa flicked her head to the girls and both left quickly, thankful to be out of Guthrun's way.

'So, what do you want that's so important I can't even have a bath in peace?'

'I have a plan which will allow us to take Kaupangen Borgund.'

'Go on, and don't stand so far away. You won't get suddenly lazy just by being close to this, you know.'

Chuntering unhappily, Guthrun moved closer to Asa's bath, who for her part with only her shoulders, neck, and head above the line of the water sank down a bit further so even her shoulders were submerged whilst Guthrun outlined his plan.

Once he had done, Asa said nothing for a moment then slowly a mischievous grin lit up her face and she began to laugh.

'What's so funny?' Guthrun's voice dipped dangerously, and his lips tightened at the perceived sleight.

Asa pushed herself smoothly forward, rising slightly so that she could rest her arms on the lip of the barrel immediately in front of Guthrun.

'I'm not laughing at you, Guthrun Doombringer.'

'Then what? Do you like the plan or not? Can I get on with –'

Asa raised a finger and placed it lightly on Guthrun's lips. 'Ssshhh. What's the hurry?'

'What the...'

'You're always in a hurry. Sometimes you need to just kick back and relax.'

'I thought you were the one who was in a rush.'

'It's winter, it's cold, and Kaupangen Borgund isn't going any place soon. We can take it another day.'

'So, we're just supposed to sit around doing nothing till then?'

'I don't know about nothing. I can think of plenty of dis... tractions,' she purred, pushing back across the bath and under the water, so she was only visible from the shoulders up.

'A bath may distract you, but it won't keep the men happy.'

'Depends on who they're in the bath with.' Asa raised a slinky arm from her bath, letting the water run down, leaving behind skin glistening in the soft candlelight. 'Anyway, the men are fine. They have enough beer and women to keep them fat, dumb, and happy for months. No, I sense the problem is with you, my favourite monster. You are the unhappy one. Why is that? Have I not given you all that you craved – battle, command, women, even fame?'

'You had me plague a whole town. That is not a warrior's battle.'

'Are you still angry about that? Let it go, Guthrun, or the guilt will eat you up.'

'What do you know of my guilt?' asked Guthrun, suspicious, though Asa only laughed. 'Are you mocking me, woman?'

'Who? Me? No. I wouldn't dream of it. I value you too much to mock you,' she answered complicitly and smiled sweetly, noting the look of anger etched deep within his features soften slightly, 'but I do want you to be happy. So, warrior, what will bring you happiness, or at least satisfaction, if not now then later? Girls? Gold? Girls and gold? Maybe a city all your own?'

Guthrun, suddenly faced with the question of 'What do you want?' found himself for the first time in a long time entirely unsure of just what it was he craved. He thought it was glory in battle but even that now felt hollow. Riches, maybe? No, that wasn't it. Riches were just baubles; they were of little use other than a means to show off how great you were. But baubles could be bought. They didn't have to be earned with blood, sweat, or tears. A man could simply steal the trappings of fortune without ever putting his life on the line. No, he needed, wanted, bloody hell, what did he want?

Asa watched him from her bath. After letting him stare into space for a while as he contemplated the question, she said softly, 'Guthrun, are you okay?'

'What?' he said, as though coming out of a trance.

'I asked you what you wanted,' she said, concern in her voice, 'and you just seem to lose yourself in that head of yours. It was as though your body was here, but a devil had taken your soul.'

And at that moment, Guthrun knew, knew what he wanted, knew what he needed. 'My soul.'

'What?'

'You asked me what I wanted. Well, that's what I want. I want my soul back.'

'I... I'm not sure I understand,' said Asa.

'You asked what would make me happy. Well, it's my soul. I've lost it. Hel has it.'

'I'm sure you are mistaken.'

'No, she has it. I can feel it freezing in her grasp as we speak.'

'But you live, you walk, you are here now before me. You do not look like the dead walking, which is what a man with no soul would be.'

'You asked, I told you,' snarled Guthrun. 'You want me happy; you get me my soul.'

14

At about the same time as Guthrun was having his epiphany, realising what was missing in his life, Ogmundr, Alfarr, and Siggeirr were stood overlooking the little sheltered bay which protected the boats of the village they had taken as the weak winter sun began to sink beneath the horizon.

'So, what do we think?' asked Siggeirr.

Alfarr, in the manner anyone who has ever taken a car into some backstreet garage to be fixed would recognise, took a sharp intake of breath, whistling through his teeth, and replied, 'They'll never make it. We'd stand more chance swimming.'

'Even the big one?' asked Ogmundr, looking ruefully at the sorry collection of boats bobbing wretchedly in the bay.

With a practised eye, Alfarr considered the largest vessel amongst the collection, a fat bulbous cob which had seen better days, and with his usual candour said, 'Get that out on the sea and it will bounce around worse than Hilde's tits when she's fucking Siggy.'

'Fuck you.' Siggeirr reacted sharply. 'My Hilde has great tits.'

'He's right,' agreed Ogmundr.

'See? thanks, Oggi.'

'Yeah. Many a time you have been out I have gone round to your place and used Hilde's tits as earmuffs.'

'Screw you.'

'Yeah, that's what she said.'

Alfarr and Ogmundr laughed as Siggeirr fumed, 'Yeah, well, you can laugh, but my Hilde is a passionate creature and keeps me warm at night.'

'I'm not surprised. It would be like going to bed with a shaved bear.' Alfarr winked at Ogmundr. 'If that couldn't warm you, nothing could.'

'You're just jealous cos my girl has got a big appetite. Whereas your hard-bodied warrior girls just want to fight, my Hilde just wants to rut.'

'Damn right she's got a big appetite. I've seen her eat a whole hog,' said Ogmundr.

'Exactly. Just think what a girl with that kind of hunger is like in the sack when she wants you.'

'Bloody terrifying?'

'Bollocks! You don't know lust till a big girl has stared at your cock with hunger in her eyes.' Siggeirr defended his girl with a wistful gleam in his eye.

'Well, that explains a lot,' said Alfarr cryptically.

'What do you mean by that?' Siggeirr shot back suspiciously.

'I mean, you're such a skinny runt. Now I know why – your girl is sucking you dry.'

'I ain't complaining.' Siggeirr smiled.

'You don't think she's some kind of succubus, do you?' asked Ogmundr.

'By the gods, no,' Alfarr replied in terror. 'If Hilde were a succubus, she'd need to drain the entire town's men to satisfy her lust. None of us would be safe.'

'Yeah, well, fuck you,' snapped Siggeirr. 'She keeps me happy, and I don't care if she keeps me trim. Better for me if she does.'

'And why's that?' asked Ogmundr.

'Because if these boats are as bad as Alfarr claims, when we're out at sea and Tostig starts throwing heavy loads overboard to stop it sinking, you two lumps will be tossed over long before me. I look forward to waving you goodbye and toasting my hot Hilde as you two are going under the waves for the final time.'

'If it's a choice between drowning or being crushed between Hilde's thighs as her sweaty tits slap round my face I think I'd rather drown,' laughed Alfarr.

Siggeirr flipped Alfarr and Ogmundr the bird, but the talk of drowning brought them back to reality with sickening inevitability.

'You really don't think these will make it?' Ogmundr asked again.

'No. That cob is about the only thing here big enough to carry us all, but I wouldn't risk taking it beyond the lee of the shore on a winter sea. It'll ice up quick, become top heavy, wallow, and roll over. She'll not get us home.'

Siggeirr and Ogmundr shared an unhappy glance. Alfarr was the very epitome of Norse doom and gloom. If the world proceeded to give him lemons and the written instructions on how to make lemonade, he would still find a way to turn it into the most bitter lemon concoction imaginable. Some people are glass-half-full types, whereas Alfarr barely had a glass, but what both Siggeirr and Ogmundr understood was that Alfarr knew his ships, and if he said it wouldn't make it then it wouldn't make it.

'Do we know where we are anyway? How far away is home?' Siggeirr asked.

Alfarr looked up into the cloudless sky to see the first stars beginning to glimmer in the heavens and pointing, said, 'That's east; that's north. I think the Celts call this land Sealtainn, so home is that way, and that's many days' sailing. And that won't make it, not this time of year.'

'Shit!' Ogmundr cursed. 'Agnew isn't going to want to hear that.'

Alfarr shot him a fierce glance and together they shouted, 'Bagsy not me!'

'Fuck that,' said Siggeirr, 'I'm not telling him.'

'You have to, Siggy,' said Ogmundr solemnly. 'We said bagsy. You're it.'

'Piss off.'

'Them's the rules – you have to.' Alfarr grinned.

'Don't.'

'Do.'

'I'm not doing it.'

'You can't go back on a bagsy.'

Siggeirr looked at them both then cursed. 'Shit! Do I have to?'

'Yes.'

'But why can't we just stay here? At least till the spring?' Siggeirr implored.

'We're on a mission for a goddess; I don't think she'll wait,' Alfarr answered grimly.

'But we don't have a boat, and it's winter. No one sails in the winter.'

'We did,' said Ogmundr.

'And we sank.' Alfarr scowled.

Undeterred, Siggeirr continued, 'But even Hel can't want us dead, or we can't finish the job.'

'You think so? Remember the dwarf asked her for help and she sent the Midgard Serpent? What next? Fenrir himself? The bloody wolf would snack on us all. Sod Hel – we're stuck,' Alfarr replied morosely.

'Nah, it ain't that bad. You're just looking at this the wrong way round,' Siggeirr said chirpily.

'Really? The wrong way round,' Ogmundr scoffed. 'You're insane, Siggy.'

'We have no ship, at least not fit for this time of year. But we do have a village full of women. Women who are now lacking men. So, we winter here, let the women keep us warm, then we'll go do the quest come the spring.'

'You're an idiot,' snapped Alfarr.

'It's a great idea.'

'The only reason those women have no menfolk is because we just slaughtered them.'

'So, to the victor the spoils. Besides, they'll soon want a bit of hot Viking inside them.'

'Yeah, course they will.' Alfarr laughed sarcastically.

'They're not going to want anything to do with us.' Ogmundr shook his head.

'Course they will. Their men came up short: most are now dead; the rest are bound and gagged. Give it a week and they'll be clamouring to get with us, you just watch. I tell you now, in a week's time you'll have all the women you need to get through a long winter.'

'What about Hilde?' asked Ogmundr.

'She knows I only have eyes for her,' Siggeirr answered sincerely, 'but she knows my cock needs regular work. She won't begrudge me a bit of Celt whilst I'm away. She knows when I'm home I'm all hers.'

Alfarr shook his head and said, 'Even if Hilde doesn't cut your balls off the moment you let it slip you've been banging a Celt, which you will because you never shut up, you'll be long dead. You won't last the winter.'

'Course we will – who's going to challenge us? Not what's left of their men.'

Alfarr smiled coldly. 'You've never come across Celts before. Their blood runs with fire to match the colour of their hair, and that's just the women. Their gods demand blood sacrifice. They may play nice for a day, a week, maybe even a month, but at some point, one of those red-haired witches is going to be licking your dick, Siggy, and just when you are at your most vulnerable, she's going to clamp her teeth down hard and bite your cock off. Then when you're lying there screaming as you bleed out, she'll beat you round your chops with your own severed dick.'

'Damn, Alfarr, that's dark, even for you.'

'We'll not last the winter. One way or another those women will kill us.'

'Fuck me, Alfarr, can you never see the bright side in anything?' groaned Siggeirr.

'There's no bright side here, only pain and misery. Now stop dreaming of red-haired Celtic bints and go tell Agnew the news.'

Siggeirr's shoulders slumped as he turned to head back to the small village, which was barely visible now night had fallen, leaving only a faint glow of hearth fires leaching out from under doors to guide them back to shelter.

As the three headed back to what passed as the main hall, already inside, Agnew and the rest spread out across several long tables and benches while the village women nervously served up mead, fish, and platters of smoked meat. There was an undeniable sense of tension. At the head of the hall, on a raised platform, the lord of the village's chair and table remained empty, Agnew choosing to sit with Tostig, Delling, and a few others at one of the general benches.

As the women bustled carefully about the hall trying not to grab the eye of any of the invading Norsemen, Morag took a jug of ale off one of the younger girls and quietly told her to take herself off back to her own home. Carrying the jug over to Agnew's table herself, she began refilling their tankards.

Agnew watched her carefully as she topped up his drink. 'Thank you.'

'My chief,' Morag replied deferentially, 'will ye not sit at the chief's seat?' she said, indicating the vacant chair at the head of the hall.

'I'm not your chief; that's not my chair.'

'You have taken our village, killed our chief. It is yours by right of conquest.'

'As I said, I'm not your lord. We're just passing through. With luck we'll be gone tomorrow and out of your hair.'

Morag stared down at Agnew with a look of frustration.

'Something wrong?' asked Agnew, not looking up.

'You have taken our village. If you dinnae want it, why raid us?'

'I never intended to raid you. If your men hadn't turned up and attacked, I would have traded instead.'

'You're Norse; we know what the Norse do when ye show up. We would have to be reet numpties to not attack first, dee ye ken?'

'Really?' said Agnew, turning around on the bench to look Morag squarely in the eye, who held his gaze with a steely one of her own, which, although he would not tell her, Agnew rather admired. 'What have you heard of the Norse?'

'Ye dinnae trade. Ye turn up to plunder, rape, and pillage. Isnae any wonder our men attacked first?'

'Sounds like we aren't the first to arrive at your shore, and you know our language, so if some have taught you our words, I can only assume not all have simply ravaged your land.'

'Aye. The first of your countrymen who visited traded, but that was a long time ago. We were willing to trade with more recent visitors, but they dinnae want ta know. They just wanted blood.'

'I can't speak for those who came before me, but know I had no intention of plundering, raping, or pillaging your village. I just wanted to repair my ship and be gone. But if you'd rather we plunder, rape, and pillage just say, and I'll turn my men loose. I'd hate for us not to live up to expectations.'

Morag visibly blanched at Agnew's cold delivery, but something in her refused to back down. 'You're the chief; ye can do as ye wish. I only ask ye to spare the bairns.'

Agnew was about to reply that provided Morag kept her village in line, young and old would be safe, when an icy gust of air blew through the hall, causing fires and candles to flicker brightly as Alfarr and Ogmundr followed Siggeirr inside. Everyone turned to face the three as they entered to watch Siggeirr falter, only to receive a firm push in the back from Alfarr, causing him to stagger forward.

Already sensing bad news, Agnew asked, 'What is it, Siggy?'

'The boats are crap,' Siggeirr replied in a small voice.

'What?'

'The boats – they are rubbish,' he continued to mumble.

'Siggy, spit it out. I can't hear you.'

'The boats, Agnew, in the bay – they're useless!' Siggeirr shouted, then wished he had somewhere better to be, like maybe fighting an ice giant or a cave troll, anywhere but stood there under Agnew's withering stare.

'How so?' Agnew shot back. 'Explain.'

Siggeirr stood, dumbstruck and unsure how to answer. He looked at Agnew with a mounting sense of dread as Agnew stood up from the table, hand straying to the sword hilt strapped to his side, when Alfarr stepped in front of Siggy and replied, 'None of the boats this village possesses are suitable for the crossing to our homeland.'

Agnew stared darkly at Alfarr, Alfarr stared calmly back, and nearly everyone else in the hall paused, holding their breath, wondering what fury Agnew was going to bring down upon the bearers of such bad news. Some of the younger village girls quietly began to sob, fearing the worst.

Agnew's hands clenched tightly, his jaw tightened, and a dangerous tick started by his right eye. 'ARRRRRRRRRRRRRRRGH!'

he roared, throwing his head back furiously before hammering on the tabletop with his fists. 'Tell me, gods, what have I done to deserve THIS? YOU...' He pointed at Delling.

'Me?' The dwarf shuffled away, terrified, almost falling off the bench.

'YES, YOU! HEL DID THIS! HOW IS SHE GOING TO RIGHT IT?'

'Er?'

'Er? ER? WHAT FUCKING GOOD IS ER? I WANT ANSWERS!'

'I... I don't know what to say?' replied Delling, truly terrified, and given that he worked for Hel, that was quite something. 'Hel would just assume you would find a way to get the job done.'

'She wrecked my ship!'

'To be fair, it was wrecked when she rescued you,' Delling answered honestly, se immediately wishing he hadn't as an incandescent Agnew turned puce.

'I'll FUCKING DO YOU!' Agnew stepped towards Delling, spittle speckling his chin, his face an angry red, and with death in his eyes he ripped his sword free, took one further step then went down hard, his face smashing into the table as he dropped. Slowly, Agnew slid unconscious into a heap on the floor.

All eyes turned to Morag, who stood over Agnew's incapacitated body, holding what was left of the shattered ale jug she had used to smash over his head.

'See,' said Alfarr to Siggeirr, 'Celts – they'll have you first chance they get.' Everyone else sat in stunned silence.

Morag stared back defiantly, though she could feel her stomach knotting with fear and her knees begin to wobble, expecting this savage crew to kill her where she stood for daring to hurt their leader. As if to confirm her worst fears, the huge Viking who seemed to be Agnew's second loomed over her like some avenging monster. She felt herself shrink back from the ferocious spectre as he delicately took the remains of the jug from her trembling hand and pressed his own full drinking mug into hers.

'Drink, girl,' the monster said. 'You've earned it.'

Shaking, she took a stiff drink then made to hand it back.

'No – finish it.'

'Thank ye,' she replied softly, necked the rest of the ale and slammed the mug down on the table to be met by raucous cheers from Agnew's warriors.

'Tell me,' said the looming monster, 'ever considered becoming a shield maiden?'

Interlude

If this were the 1950s then we would flip to a black-and-white shot of someone working at a potter's wheel or something equally mundane to make one feel bored, so when the main feature restarted anything would seem exciting and brilliant in comparison, even if before the break you were thinking, this is the biggest pile of poop I have ever had the misfortune to sit through. But you are not about to be made to sit through fifteen minutes of black-and-white vaguely arty stuff. Nope, this is far worse, as we are going to take you for a quick bit of religious education. Stick with it – this may turn out to be fun and mildly educational. And no, you don't have to take notes, as we won't be asking questions at the end.

So, where does our lesson start? Well, we should consider the established so-called great religions of the world: Christianity, Judaism, Islam, Hinduism, Scientology, etcetera. Okay, so one of them isn't great, but I will let you decide which. Oh, come on – it's Scientology. Seriously, that shit makes even hardcore Catholicism seem rational. But ignoring Scientology, and who wouldn't, what the others have in common is that the god they purport to worship is quite clearly some kind of nutter, most likely a voyeur, and bored, very, very bored.

'What?' I hear you cry.

'Heresy!' I hear some of you scream.

'Yeah, fair point,' I hear some of you agree under your breath, hoping your god doesn't notice, but trust me, if the monotheist God is actually out there, then he/she/it is a voyeur, sees everything, hears everything, so you are doomed. You might as well just give up the good fight and go enjoy yourself instead.

'But you also said bored?' the more observant of you point out, and yes, I did say bored. Why bored? Well, I will tell you. Only a supreme being with more time on its hands than it knows what to do with and with nothing to occupy its mind would come up with some of the daft rules it imposes on its followers. For instance, why are Orthodox Jews only allowed to dress in severe black and white? And what's with the silly dangling hair ringlets on the men? How bored must a god have been to have issued that command to its worshippers? Did it have a hangover? Could it not cope with bright colours that day? So, bang, suddenly you get the godly decree that all of you must wear black and white only; anything else and you will be smitten with divine fury.

And don't the rest of you laugh. What about Islam, which insists men must have beards. Why? Did Allah have an accident with a razor at some point and think, 'Bugger that for a game of Jihad, I will spare my worshippers the risk and just forbid them to shave'?

And it is no less daft within Christianity. Choose any period in history, any denomination and you will find lunacy. Take the Puritans, for example, the most joyless bunch ever to walk the earth. And why, why were they so grim? Apparently, God forbade them to have any fun, at all, or find any pleasure in anything. Again, why? Why would a god do that unless it was a petty, small-minded creature who thought, 'Let's see just how far I can push these idiot humans'? Did the god sit there going, 'I wonder just how much shit they'll take? I know, I will tell them that everything is a sin and that they are consigned to hell unless they are never happy and wear buckles on their hats. Ha-ha-ha, they will never go for it. Hey, Gabriel, fancy a bet? I've just told the humans they must be miserable to enter heaven. I don't reckon they'll go for it.'

The Angel Gabriel ponders the proposition deeply then with astute observation replies, 'Nah, they're morons. When you flooded the joint and killed most of them on the basis that it was for their own good, they just went, "Okay, you're the boss" and continued to worship you. I reckon they'll take misery to whole new depths just to please you and punish anyone who so much as cracks a smile.'

'No, they won't. They can't, can they?'

'I'm telling you, God, they'll just fall straight in line.'

'Seriously? Okay, what you willing to bet?'

'Hmmmmmm, okay, I bet you that if they go for it you have to unleash an actual plague on them.'

'Oh, that's cruel.' God winces. 'What did they ever do to you? But okay, you're on!'

A few years later, or in God time, about six minutes, 'Well, blow me down with a heretic's kipper, they only bloody went for it.'

'Told you,' says Gabriel smugly. 'Some of them even banned Christmas. I told you, God, they're morons. So go on then.'

'Go on, what?'

'Plague – send it down.'

'Aww, do I have to, Gabriel? They're already miserable.'

'Do it. You lost, so let's wipe out Northern Europe.'

'Damn, you're hard-faced, and they think you angels are on their side.'

'More fool them.' Gabriel grins coldly as he and God stroll off for a pint and a pie, laughing maniacally as they let the Black Death loose to ravage the world.

Yes folks, gods are, by and large, nutters.

You may be wondering what the point of this is. Well, it is to put into context the way the organised big religions work compared to the Pagan gods. Back in the days of Agnew, the Norse gods did not have what we would consider organised churches, rituals, or set times for prayer. They also didn't set dumb rules about clothing, what language a prayer book was supposed to be in or whether they should hold coffee mornings, etcetera. Nope, the Norse just kind of worshipped on an individualistic basis. The head of a town, a farm, or an individual dwelling would generally lead whatever worship needed to take place in whatever way they saw fit. So, a farmer may sacrifice a horse if he thought it would please Eostre the Goddess of Spring, so she would look kindly over his patch. Or someone might decide before going to lay with his new bride to stroke the erect phallus on the statue of Frey and hope the god's fertility and rampant sexual prowess would be passed down to him for the night.

Yes, for the Norse worship was a fairly private affair performed and observed in ad hoc and oft creative ways to call on the blessing of whichever deity seemed most appropriate to the circumstance. Obviously, some got called on more than others. Being a warrior race, the warrior gods were more frequently favoured, but Frey and Freya, being the god and goddess of fertility and sex, would also be worshipped regularly. Hey, if you are going to spend your time worshipping a goddess, why not choose the smoking-hot redhead with liberal attitudes towards threesomes and toys?

All this of course meant that the gods and goddesses were not too prescriptive in what they desired from their worshippers and generally let the humans get on with things without too much external interference or instruction, which made for a much happier bunch of worshippers than those of just about every other religion which has followed, especially the monotheisms where the singular god is nothing more than a glorified control freak.

This of course did mean that Odin's instruction to his select band of fellow gods to talk to their seers, oracles, and witches to find out what Hel was up to was proving a harder task than one may have thought. None of them had a strict cabal of clerics spreading their word and instruction. More generally they just had some tormented souls driven half-mad by a god's occasional whispering in their ear, telling them whatever nonsense was on their mind at the time, hence most sat out in dark, gloomy forests or in dank caves throwing bones, smearing themselves in blood, and getting high on mushrooms whilst reading signs of what the gods wanted in whatever fevered manner took their fancy. Besides, who needs a two-thousand-year-old book to tell you what your god wants when you can just go straight for the mind-altering drugs?

As with all things, some were better at this and were more in tune with their gods than others. So, as Thor, Frey, Forseti, Heimdall, and the rest went about their intelligence gathering, things were not going all that successfully. Frey got lost for a week in an orgy given in his name. Forseti got bogged down in some theological minutiae, and Heimdall found himself in a bar getting pissed with a bunch of warriors recently returned from pillaging Southern Spain. Thor by contrast wasn't bothering with his worshippers. Even he knew better than to ask the freaks who represented him. Most were just drug addicts who didn't know what day it was or even what they were. He had at least one so-called wise man who thought he was a duck. No, Thor decided his best bet was to call on his old mate, Loki, so donning human form, he travelled down to Midgard and wandered the lands visiting every ale house and den of iniquity until he found him.

When he did finally locate him, it was in a place that even for the Dark Ages was considered rough. Inside, Thor didn't have to look too hard to find Loki. To the humans in the place, Loki looked like a dark-headed man of indeterminate age, with a charming smile, quick eyes, a ready laugh, and long, nimble fingers, who was currently fleecing all comers at a gambling table. Everyone to a man knew he must be cheating but not one could work out how, and the tension was rising, dangerously.

'Mind if I join the game?' Thor said, sitting down on the bench facing Loki across the gaming table.

Loki gave Thor a sardonic smile and said, 'Sure. The more the merrier.'

Thor looked about at those playing and losing against Loki and replied, 'I don't see much merriment here.'

'I don't know, I'm feeling pretty merry.' Loki laughed cheerfully. The comment elicited some dangerous growls from his opponents, who were feeling quite the opposite.

'Fancy a bet?' asked Thor.

'Sure, if you are feeling lucky.'

Thor just smiled and said, 'Let's play.'

'Okay,' said Loki, 'what we playing for? Money? Drink? Women?'

'Information.'

Loki nodded sagely then replied, 'Okay, and if I win?'

'Name your price,' Thor replied confidently.

Loki leant back and gave Thor an appraising look. 'Okay. I'd like a date with Þrúðr.'

Thor cocked his head and laughed ruefully. 'Seriously, you want to date my daughter?'

'I want your permission to date her. I won't force her, obviously.'

'Ha! Like you could. She'd have your balls in a jar before even you could charm her.'

'And that's the challenge.' Loki smiled wickedly.

'Okay, you win. I'll let you ask her out," Thor replied graciously, 'though if it gets to that, you may just wish you'd lost instead.'

'I can barely wait.'

'Just throw the dice.'

Loki laughed and with a deft flick of the wrist sent the pair of dice skittering across the playing board.

But ladies and gentlemen, this is just an intermission, so we shall leave Thor and Loki here to play out their game and pick up on the aftermath later, for now the main players of our saga are back from their fag break, have been to the toilet and quite possibly had a joke with the roadies, so now it is time to get this show back on the road.

15

Back to re-join our hero. Agnew was currently waking with a banging headache, beneath a heavy fur blanket on a comfortable bed. The room was dark, but not pitch-black, lit as it was by several candles bathing the room in a sallow glow.

Agnew sat up, carefully, and ran his hand through his hair, which even in bed-head mode instantly fell into place in a way which said windswept and interesting. Don't you just hate people like that? But if his hair was playing nice, his tongue was not. It felt as though it had been sandpapered dry then rubbed on a badger's arse – what the badger may have thought of this no one has bothered to ask. Disorientated – this was clearly not his room; it was sort of, well, girly – he tried to recollect his thoughts as he looked for some clue as to where he was and how he got there. He was, under the covers, naked, but it did not look like he had been doing anything remotely fun, so regardless of whomsoever this bed belonged to, he had either stolen it, crashed there in a blind stupor, or been dumped.

Agnew threw the covers off and stood, a touch unsteadily. His hand involuntarily went to his head, and he winced as his hand brushed across a sizeable lump at the back of his head. Wondering just what in Thor's name he had been doing last night he spied a water bowl, a jug containing more water, and a leather mug by its side. Placing his hands either side of the large bowl, he dunked his face in it, letting the cool water shock away a little of the fug clouding his brain. Still dripping, he grabbed the water jug, lifted it to his lips and began to gulp the water fast, ignoring the mug entirely as he tried to bring some life back to his mouth and remove the offending taste of badger.

Thirst sated, temporarily, he pushed aside the heavy drape which curtained the sleeping room from whatever was behind it and still naked, stepped through. As he stood there in all his glory, he suddenly found himself confronted by some red-haired woman, whose name he couldn't instantly place, and Tostig.

'About time,' said Tostig. 'I didn't think you'd ever get your lazy arse up.'

'Whaaaaa?' was all Agnew could manage.

'Forgotten something?' the redhead said, giving him an appraising stare.

Agnew's brow furrowed with confusion then remembering he was naked, he stammered, 'Clothes?' though he did nothing to cover himself, which, judging by the look on the redhead's face, was highly appreciated.

'Morag, can you get his stuff?' Tostig asked the redhead, who put down what she was darning and with a last sideways glance at the dazed and nude Agnew got up and brushed by him with a giggle to return moments later with Agnew's clothes.

'I'll leave you two alone,' said Morag, exiting the hut.

Agnew looked at the clothes handed to him and tried to focus on what was different about them. They felt... soft... they felt... 'These are clean,' he remarked, as though this were the most surprising thing in the world.

Tostig laughed. 'The girl felt so bad for whacking you over the head she thought she could at least clean your clothes. I think she fancies the arse off you, though only the gods know why. You have terrorised her village, had her chief killed and went crazy. I really thought you would kill the dwarf.'

'Err? Dwarf? What the hell are you... oh... Shit!' Agnew sat heavily on the stool vacated by Morag, clothes still in hand as snippets of the previous day started to crawl out from whatever memory hidey hole they had been lurking in.

'Get dressed. I'll be in the hall when you're ready.'

'Tostig, what happened?'

'Siggy and Alfarr told you the boats were no good and you lost it.'

'How bad was it?'

'For a moment it was as though your father stood before us.'

Agnew palmed his face in distress. 'Tostig, you can't let me go down that path. Did I do anything...?'

'No, it never got to that. Your face turned bright red; I thought your head was going to explode. Then Morag smashed a jug over your nut and put you down. We dumped you into bed. After that, everything settled down.'

'Morag?'

'The redhead.'

'Oh. How long have I been out?'

'Most of the day.'

'A day?'

'Aye. Now, stop asking dumb questions, get dressed, get over to the hall and get some food inside you,' Tostig ordered.

'Okay, I'll be over in a bit. And Tostig?'

'Yes?'

'If that Morag floored me, how come no one did the same to her?'

'Because if she hadn't hit you, I would have.'

'Odin's beard – was I really that bad?'

'Worse,' said Tostig, then he left the room, leaving Agnew to his thoughts, clothes, and aching head.

A little later, dressed in clean, sweet-smelling clothes – his men were never going to let him forget this – Agnew made his way to the largest building in the settlement, which was just about large enough to be called a hall. It wasn't hard to find, seeing as it was the only building which could hold more than five people comfortably at any one time. Thankfully, as he crossed the ground to the hall, he did not pass any of his crew, though he did pass some of the village girls, who bowed deferentially before going on their way, giggling much as Morag had. *Well, so much for instilling fear in them*, he thought gloomily.

Inside the hall it was cool but not unpleasantly so. Contrary to what you may have been led to believe at school, the halls of many Dark Age peoples were not overly stuffy cramped spaces so full of smoke you could barely see your hand in front of your face. Halls were, by and large, quite airy. Sure, they were dark. Open fires, braziers, and candles, whilst throwing out light do tend to cast long shadows, but during daylight hours often the doors would be open and the shutters thrown wide over windows high in the sides to let light and air in. Today, and despite this being winter, the hall was open to let fresh air blow throughout. At a bench sat Tostig, alone. A couple of the local women waited in attendance but not with any sign of fear. Rather, they seemed to be discussing the giant warrior and throwing him lustful glances.

Agnew sighed; it had always been thus. Tostig's sheer size and rippling muscles usually had women falling over themselves to grab his attention, not that Agnew was without his admirers, but Tostig always grabbed the attention first and generally walked off with the prettiest girl, quite often the two prettiest girls at the same time, and then of course there was that time in Viborg when he disappeared with the four best-looking girls, and neither Tostig nor the four girls surfaced for a week. That almost caused a riot. The Jarl of Viborg was not quite so happy, as his daughter was one of the girls whom Tostig was playing with.

Agnew wondered if they were welcome back there yet or whether the threat of grim, bloody death should they ever set foot anywhere in the Jarl's territory again was still in place. Shame, really. Agnew had quite fallen for a shield maiden of Viborg – Eydís – lovely girl, lithe, strong, legs you just wanted to wrap around your face like a scarf. Agnew felt the pang of a lost opportunity then brushed it aside as he sat by his friend. Tostig immediately called for a drink to be brought to Agnew and some food. Clearly both girls were trying to impress Tostig, as a bowl of stew and a jug of honey mead were placed before Agnew almost immediately. Tostig winked at one and gave the other a friendly pat on the bum as the girls removed themselves, all aflutter.

'I don't know how you do it,' said Agnew honestly as he dipped into the stew with some crusty bread.

'What can I say? The girls love me,' Tostig replied with a huge grin. 'How do you feel?'

'Like someone bashed me over the head with a jug of ale.'

'Good. Now eat up.'

Agnew replied with a non-committal grunt and tucked into the stew. It was not the best he had ever had; the meat was chewy and the stew watery, but right now it was doing the job. Damn, he was hungry. 'Where is everybody?'

'Repairing the ship,' Tostig replied brightly.

Touching the bump on his head carefully, Agnew stared at Tostig doubtfully. 'But it was as good as wrecked.'

'It is – was.'

'What?'

'It's being fixed. It will take a while, but the lads are on it.'

Agnew's eyes narrowed suspiciously. Seeing Agnew's unrest, Tostig filled him in.

'It was Erik's idea.'

'What was? And how is he?'

'What?'

'Erik,' said Agnew, 'how is he? Last time he had a bright idea he lost some of his fingers. What did this idea cost him? A foot? Some teeth? Maybe he got his cock cut off.'

'Sometimes I don't think you have much faith in us,' Tostig replied with wounded pride.

Agnew raised his eyebrows with a look which said, 'Faith, my faith has been crushed, burned, and the ashes blown to the four winds.'

'Get ready to be surprised.' Tostig rallied with genuine enthusiasm.

Agnew ran his hand through his hair, which fell with a manly bounce to his shoulders and which did not go unnoticed by the Celtic girls watching on from the shadows, eliciting at least one lustful sigh, if not two. 'Okay, surprise me,' said Agnew wearily.

'Great! You'll love this.'

'Just get on with it.'

'Our ship's wrecked, the villagers' boats are of no use to us, and this place has no trees which are good enough to patch up our ship.'

'Okay, tell me something I don't know.'

'Right. Erik said, what if we use the villagers' ships to fix ours?'

'Say that again?'

'Erik asked why we couldn't break their boats to fix ours? Alfarr said there was no reason. No, that's not right. First he argued for most of the night, telling us why we couldn't, but we ground him down till he admitted it was possible.'

'How?'

'We just beach their ships, start cutting out the good wood to splice into our own, and...'

'No, how did you grind Alfarr down?'

'Mead.'

'Mead?'

'Yes, mead. We got him drunk, and when he was more –'

'Off his face?'

'Yeah – he said we could,' Tostig finished happily.

'So, and stop me if I've got this wrong, you talked a drunk man into thinking he could repair our ship. A ship which has been sunk, broken, and torn into pieces by the Midgard Serpent. And you think simply cutting bits out of other boats, which he had already said were not seaworthy, will work just because once he was drunk, he said it would.'

'Err... yes.'

'The gods help us all. Are you mad?'

'Wh...?'

'You've put our lives into the hands of a drunk.'

'He isn't drunk now.'

'But he was when he agreed to this. How many times have we done something we thought was great when we were pissed?'

'Loads.'

'And how often did they go right?'

'Um?'

'I'll tell you – almost never. We have taken beatings, almost drowned, there was that time you got set on fire, and remember the bear?'

'Never mention the bear,' Tostig said with a shudder.

'Exactly. So why, in all that is holy, have you gone along with this?'

Tostig gave his leader a resigned shrug and answered with complete honesty, 'It's the only idea we've got.'

16

While Agnew sorts out his head, his men, and whatever the Celts may or may not throw at him, it is a good time to revisit the winter camp of Asa. For the most part the camp was happy. They had taken a place with solid buildings, had plenty of food stored and enough ale to keep even the most hardened drinker satisfied.

Of course, there were tensions. Where you get a bunch of warriors together in one place whose main occupation is fighting, then it is inevitable that fights will break out between them. Again, this is not necessarily a bad thing: it gives those not fighting a chance to bet on the outcome, though that in turn can lead to further fights if some take losing badly. But generally, post-fight the combatants often pick themselves up and, in some cases, go off for a drink together. At other times the loser limps off to lick his wounds and very rarely a dead body is dragged away, but generally no real harm outside of broken noses, ribs and pride is suffered.

You may also think in such hard and dangerous times the women servicing Asa's camp would be suffering abuses on an almost hourly basis, but no such thing. This was not a war of conquest, so the town where Asa had halted her winter campaign was seen by Asa, her Jarls, and the rest of the men as part of their rightful territory and not something taken from an enemy. Therefore, the town and its inhabitants were treated as home, so any abuse was punished quickly and brutally.

So, with one exception, the town was happy, and that one exception was Guthrun Doombringer, who was the black cloud hanging over Asa's camp. Aware that Guthrun was the cause of most of the unwanted tension, Asa had decided to do something about it. At a hut on the fringes of the town Asa pushed opened the door and stepped out of the cold into more cold. Apart from a single candle glowing feebly in a far corner there was no light and no heat. In the middle of this inhospitality sat Guthrun nursing a jug of mead, bare-chested and scowling. 'What do you want?' he asked gruffly.

'Are you not cold?' said Asa, pulling her cloak around her tightly. She would swear it was warmer outside than in.

'Always. Are you?'

'There are graves warmer than this.' Asa shivered.

Guthrun gave her a cold smile, which, given the heat in the room was at least in keeping with the general atmosphere, and gestured to the one other chair in the place.

Asa smiled but refused. 'I didn't come here to talk. I came here to get you. I would say get dressed, as you will freeze where we are going, but I think that won't be a problem for you. But please dress as though you feel Skadi's bite. I already hear unrest when your name is mentioned. Some say you are a skin shifter, others a troll, and you walking around half-naked, untouched by ice or snow fuels their suspicions. I don't need such suspicions filling the camp.'

'And you, what do you think?' Guthrun asked, leaning forward menacingly.

'I think you are my best warrior. You are also a man I have promised to help retrieve that which he has lost,' Asa replied calmly.

'Do you not fear me?'

'No.'

'I could kill you.'

'So could most of the men outside this hut. I do not fear them either. Why should I treat you any differently?'

Guthrun shrugged, relaxing slightly.

'Thought so,' said Asa, standing. 'Get dressed; meet me outside.'

Outside it was snowing, hard, but Asa waited patiently for Guthrun to appear. When he did, she was pleased to see he was back in his familiar black-wolf pelts, the ever-present rake slung across his back, axe lashed loosely at his hip. 'Is that necessary?' she asked, pointing at the rake.

'It goes where I go.'

'Suit yourself. Follow me.'

'Where are we going?'

'Into the mountains. There is someone you need to meet.'

'The mountains? Now? But it will be dark before long.'

'Yes, it will, so stop talking and let us get on.'

'Where is your guard?' asked Guthrun.

'You are my guard.'

'What if your enemies have spies out there watching for you?'

'Then you'll have someone to kill.'

'Or wolves?'

'The same.'

'Bears?'

'Probably already hibernating if they have any sense,' replied Asa, turning away from Guthrun and striding out.

Guthrun watched her go, walking confidently, and had to admire her fortitude. If she had been a man, he would have considered her someone worthy to fight and kill. *Oh, for an opponent like her*, he thought wistfully.

They left the town behind, walking into the wilderness, snow flurrying around them, the wind battling them every step, yet they pressed on. Even though Guthrun wasn't feeling any of the effects of the cold, though it must surely be afflicting Asa, for the first time since he had re-joined the living, he felt a pang of fear. It was fleeting but it was there, a momentary worry that he was being led out to freeze to death again and be cursed to an afterlife in Hel's Underworld. Suddenly what had been a momentary concern bit deep, causing him to pause. Ahead Asa pressed on, apparently unaware he had faltered. He felt heavy, his legs like iron, solid and unbending, his breath coming in short gasps – he felt true fear. He'd not felt like this since just before his first battle.

Asa, maybe realising she was suddenly alone, stopped and turned around to find Guthrun some thirty paces back, stock-still. 'What is it? Is there a problem?' she shouted over the howl of the wind. Guthrun didn't answer, lost in his own terror. 'GUTHRUN DOOMBRINGER,' she yelled as hard as she could, 'WHAT IS THE PROBLEM?'

Guthrun, his eyes locked on the floor before him, felt rather than heard Asa's voice, but it was enough to allow him to break fear's grip. Wrenching his eyes away from the ground he stared at where Asa was stood. Asa gestured for him to catch up. With a harsh grunt to himself he began walking once more. Seeing him heading unhurriedly towards her, Asa felt her own panic subside. She'd assumed he'd heard something threatening and was waiting to spot the danger. However, his calm trek towards her put her mind at ease that no such danger, bar the weather itself, was coming for them. With no idea of the torment in Guthrun's mind, Asa returned to her course and began trudging up the mountainside.

They walked in silence, lost in their own thoughts with only the crunch of their feet through the snow and the sounds of their own laboured breathing breaking through the sound of the wind. They walked like this for an hour, until Asa led them into a gully some way up the mountain. Instantly the shelter provided caused the constant buffeting of the wind to drop. The gully was deeply shadowed; what little of the day's sun remained did not penetrate this dark place. Guthrun unlashed the axe, taking it into his hands, weary and ready to strike at whatever foul thing may seek to turn them into its dinner. Carefully and unperturbed, Asa led them deeper and deeper until the pathway ended in a bluff mountain face towering up above them.

'Why have you brought us here?' asked Guthrun.

'Wait,' she said. With little option, Guthrun waited as Asa turned about on the spot, staring hard into the ever-growing darkness.

'What are you looking for?'

'That,' said Asa, pointing at a faint glow in the mountain face.

'What? I don't see...'

'Just there,' said Asa. 'Follow me.'

'I don't see... aaaah.' Guthrun's eyes picked out the same flickering. 'Lead on,' he said. Asa set off confidently, heading towards the intermittent light which pierced the dark at the base of the bluff. As they got closer, he could see the top of a cave opening and smell wood smoke.

'Who's in there?' asked Guthrun suspiciously.

'Someone who can give you answers.'

'Answers to what?'

'Only you know that,' she answered cryptically.

Guthrun, for the second time that day, felt an uneasiness in his gut but this time did not let fear halt him and followed Asa into the cave. It wound a short way down. Bones and feathers of dead creatures were bound together, hung from twine fixed into small fissures in the cave roof. As dwellings go it would be considered creepy with a touch of filth, but at least it was fully sheltered from the wind and once a few paces inside, the wind's howl had abated to a faint whine in the distance.

A few small fires burned, illuminating the way until they reached heavy pelts blocking the way. Asa didn't stand on ceremony but pushed them aside and stepped through, beckoning Guthrun to follow, who did so reluctantly. Behind the furs a large fire blazed in a stone-ringed pit, and behind it a slight figure crouched. Despite the fire obscuring his view he could make out scrawny arms poking out from beneath furs. A bony hand pointed at Asa to flick her away. Immediately Asa stepped back behind the hanging pelts. The bony hand then pointed at Guthrun and a strangely husky voice, which did not entirely mask its old age, told him to sit.

Something in the tone commanded obedience and Guthrun, not accustomed to simply acquiescing to orders, did so without so much as a murmur. He sat cross-legged upon a fur which was either incredibly old or had come off an animal which had been old. If one can, imagine an incredibly old incontinent dog which had been out in the rain and rolling in fox poo, for this was the smell which was assaulting Guthrun's nostrils. Even the smoke from the fire couldn't disguise the stench. Beyond the fire the hunched creature sat straighter, the furs falling away from the bony shoulders of a naked woman so old and wizened she looked like she had probably died but death had simply forgotten to claim her and left her behind.

'Give me your hand,' she ordered. Guthrun held out his left arm, which she grabbed about the wrist, turning his hand palm up. Guthrun almost recoiled at her touch, which was warm and clammy, though he would have struggled to pull away, as she held him with a vice-like grip. With her free hand she picked up a sharpened piece of bone and slashed it across his palm, slicing the flesh, blood instantly oozing from the wound. 'Clench,' she said and twisted his wrist, so his hand turned side on above a wooden bowl, which caught the blood dripping from his wound. Once satisfied she'd collected enough, she released his wrist, spat in the bowl and using the same bone she'd used to slice his hand, mixed her saliva with the blood.

Guthrun watched with disgusted fascination as she dipped her finger in the bowl and smeared some of the congealing mixture across her tongue and then over her brow. Dismissively she pointed to another bowl resting on a stone ledge. 'Clean your wound,' she said then, ignoring him completely, placed the bowl with his blood on a hot stone by the fire, watching it intently. When something within changed to her liking she picked up the bowl and cast the mix of blood, bone, and saliva on the floor before her.

Watching with mounting revulsion, Guthrun hadn't moved, at which the woman admonished him with a curt warning. 'I told you to clean the wound, or would you rather it be poisoned?'

'No.'

'Then wash it,' she snapped.

Guthrun rose from his place and went to the other bowl. It contained clear, cold water. He dunked his hand, his blood staining the water red. He held it under until the blood flow slowed. The crone pointed at some rags lying across another stone. 'Wrap the wound. Good. Now, sit, Guthrun Doombringer.'

'How do you know my name?'

'I know many things; names are not that special,' she replied enigmatically. 'Now sit.'

Guthrun, almost despite himself, sat and for the first time the crone looked him straight in the eye. He felt himself shrivel under her scrutiny, as though it were he who was naked, rather than her. 'Tell me, Doombringer, how does it feel to be a plaything of the gods?'

'I'm nobody's plaything, least of all the gods',' he spat contemptuously.

The crone cackled mirthlessly. 'But you are. They take a great interest in you. One is chasing you, two are using you, and another holds your fate in the balance.'

'Speak plainly, lest you want me to cleave your ugly head from your neck,' Guthrun growled, feeling his anger rise as his fear of the woman began to recede.

'Kill me if you like,' she answered without any hint of concern, 'it will not change your fate. But listen to me and you may yet get that which you crave.'

'My soul?'

Again, she cackled. 'Is that what you really crave?'

'Yes.'

'Liar.'

'What?' growled Guthrun.

'I called you LIAR!' She pointed an accusing finger.

'And what would you know, crone?'

'Everything which matters,' she snarled.

'How? Tell me who has been speaking of me and I will end them.'

The old woman laughed dismissively. 'You could no more end them than I could. No, Doombringer, your fate has been woven. There are but a few loose strands to tie up, and depending on how they are tied will determine your fate. So again, I ask you what you crave?'

'Valhalla.' He spoke quietly.

'Louder.'

'Valhalla.'

'LOUDER!'

'VALHALLA! I WANT TO ENTER VALHALLA!'

The crone laughed gleefully. 'That is the first honest thing you have uttered since your return from the Underworld. Heed me and heed me well, and I can help you get what you want.'

Guthrun was shaken. How had she known? How did she know he'd escaped the Underworld? Who was this crazy creature, and what power did she wield? Guthrun felt completely out of his depth and in total thrall to the old naked harridan before him.

'Guthrun Doombringer,' she started.

'Yes?'

'You will continue to serve Asa, faithfully and truthfully.'

'I will?'

'Yes, you will! Your fates are bound. Betray her and Valhalla will be forever denied you.'

'Then I will serve her.'

'A man is coming for you.'

'Many men come for me.'

'Not like this one. He is like you, but not. He serves a goddess yet holds her and the rest of them in contempt.'

'How will I know him?'

'He travels with a giant warrior and a dwarf. But you will know him for his hair – he has magnificent hair.'

'Hair?' Guthrun replied disbelievingly. 'Not because he carries some great sword, or has an army of trolls behind him, but his hair?'

'You will know him; all will become clear.'

'He sounds like a girl – his hair.' Guthrun began to laugh. 'I will chop this fool's head from his shoulders and tie it to a tree by his magical hair for all to see. I will destroy this man.'

'Do not take him lightly,' the crone warned darkly. 'He is favoured by the one whose rake you stole.'

'Hel?'

'The same.'

'Hel sent him for me?'

'She has. She wants her rake; she wants you.'

'I am never going back to that dank and miserable place. I deserve Valhalla. I am a warrior, not some farmer or fisherman. My place is by the All-father's side, fighting the Ice Giants. This champion of Hel will not take me. I swear, I will hack him down and any who oppose me.'

'Good, good,' said the crone, 'for if Hel retrieves her rake before Asa has her revenge, Valhalla will be forever denied you.'

'What must I do?'.

'Help Asa defeat Gudrød the Hunter and take his throne. You must defeat Hel's champion. Then and only then will you be able to bargain with the gods and demand your place in Valhalla. Fail and the Underworld beckons.'

Guthrun rocked back on his haunches and stared deep into the fire, considering the crone's instruction. 'Tell me,' he said after a while, 'why is helping Asa so important? Why should I not just wait for Hel's man and kill him? Asa has plenty of men; she can do this without me.'

The crone gave Guthrun a grudging nod of respect. 'Good question. Not many would question me so. The answer, Guthrun Doombringer, is that you need reputation. You need your name burned into the minds of the gods. It was Odin's will that Asa's family be slaughtered and her taken as wife against her will. It is Odin's will that Gudrød now rules.'

'Then if I serve Asa I am against Odin?'

'Yes.'

'How does being against Odin get me into Valhalla?'

'Another god has issue with Odin's actions against Asa. Serve Asa and that god will support your cause for Valhalla. Odin has no regard for you whether you fight for or against him. To him you are already the property of Hel. You need the favour of another to overturn that. You serve Asa, you serve the god. But you must be at the head of her army; you must be the warrior you declare yourself to be. Only the blood of Asa's enemies soaked into the ground beneath the feet of warriors led by you will prove your worth. Does that answer your question?'

Guthrun stared her in the eye and answered solemnly, 'I will do all this. I will carve such a bloody path through Asa's foes that my name will be spoken with so much fear that none will dare challenge Asa while I serve her. I will win her war; I will support her revenge, I will earn my place in Valhalla.'

The crone fixed him with a steely glare, which softened into a crooked toothless. 'Good, good. It is good to see such fire burn inside a man. You will both stay here tonight. You cannot go back into the storm, or the darker creatures will have you. Despite the rake, you are not invulnerable, Doombringer. There are furs at the back of the cave. You and Asa may bed down. Now, go back out front. You will find some meat hanging. Bring it here and we shall eat.'

The look of revulsion on Guthrun's face at the thought of staying in this cave of filth let alone eating here should tell you all you need to know about his views on having to spend a single second more in the company of the crone, but even Guthrun was wise enough to heed the warning that leaving the cave now would encourage a violent end lacking any glory, so despite his skin crawling at the thought of remaining, he rose to retrieve the meat.

17

We shall leave Guthrun and Asa behind for now, so cast your mind back a while and you should remember we left a bar where two gods were about to go head-to-head in a game of chance. For those of you unfamiliar with the two respective gods' work, here is a quick breakdown.

One is Thor, son of Odin, brave, bold, a warrior's warrior. He likes drinking, fighting, and chasing women, not necessarily in that order, and basically sending thunder and lightning crashing over the lands of Midgard. He also likes to expound the virtues of honour, though his actual views on honour are pretty much limited to honour on the battlefield. Everything else is fair game for possibly the biggest spoilt brat in the entire Norse pantheon.

Then we have Loki, a god who is known as the Trickster, a god whose primary talents are mischief and deception. Like Thor he too likes drinking and chasing women – actually, let's just say sex rather than chasing women. Loki will chase sex with almost anything – he's not overly choosy or discriminating. As for his thoughts on honour, well, that's just something to be manipulated and taken advantage of and not something to be taken too seriously. As far as a moral compass goes, Loki's spins wildly and fixes in no set position, and as such he tends to be free of guilt and remorse and just gets on with enjoying himself at the expense of, well, everyone, really.

Given two such diverse characters you would have thought these two would be the least likely of friends and yet, somehow, amongst all the gods this is probably the strongest friendship of them all. Thor genuinely likes Loki and will forgive him his most heinous transgressions, and Loki for his part truly values his friendship with Thor and is possibly the only god he respects. There is no malice in Thor, and Loki can respect that which he himself does not possess. It is due to this unlikely friendship that we find our two gods leaving the bar, chatting amiably despite a certain trickster god having just won the right to approach his friend's daughter for a date. Yes, that may sound creepy, but these are Norse gods, and the dating rules and ages of consent are different from ours.

'So, what does Þrúðr like?' asked Loki. 'Flowers? Gold jewellery wrought into fantastical shapes by dwarven smiths, or perhaps the heads of her enemies presented on a spike?'

'I agreed you could date her,' said Thor. 'I didn't say I'd help you win her over.'

'No need to be like that. Besides, I'd be a great son-in-law.' Loki smirked.

'Ha! Like that will ever happen.'

'You never know. You know how charming I can be.' Loki winked mischievously, which is kind of his standard response to most things, really. Just about everything he says and does is done mischievously. The time to be worried is when he does something sincerely, because it means he's just nicked your wallet, slept with your wife, and probably arranged to sell one of your kidneys to the Chinese underworld.

'I'm not worried. Þrúðr knows you too well. There isn't a bloody thing you can say or do which would impress her.'

'Not even my –'

'Especially not that.'

'Are you sure? Because it usually knocks the girls bandy.'

'Loki, if you approach Þrúðr in nothing but your chainmail posing pouch, once she stops laughing, she may just test how much protection the mail affords, with her axe.'

'Ouch!' Loki winced.

'Exactly, and, aww, now what?' said Thor glumly as four exceptionally large men stepped out of the shadows to surround them.

'Your friend,' the largest of the four pointed at Loki, 'he cheated us.'

'Can you prove that?' asked Thor.

'No, but no one has that much luck. He cheated, so hand him over, friend – this isn't your fight. We'll just take him round back and teach him a lesson he won't forget.'

Thor sighed and turned to Loki. 'Did you cheat them?'

'Of course I did,' replied Loki honestly. 'I mean, look at them. It was too easy. I wouldn't have been able to look myself in the mirror if I hadn't.'

On hearing Loki's blatant admission, the four men stepped forward, fists clenching.

'That isn't helping,' said Thor.

Loki merely shrugged and said, 'Fellas, be on your way and take this as a life lesson. If you think you've been cheated and can't tell how, just quit. Now get out of our way or my friend here will be forced to beat you to a pulp.'

'What?' said Thor.

'Is that right?' said the biggest of the cheated party.

'Hey, this isn't my fight.' Thor held up his hands to signal he had no part in this.

'Well, he says that now,' said Loki as the focus stayed fixed on Thor, 'but he does really think you're a bunch of pussies.'

'Pussies?'

'Yeah, pussies, and you on the right, yeah, you with the black eye, while we were in the inn, he was laughing at you, saying your woman must be a right battle-axe to give you that.'

'What?' growled the man sporting the black eye.

'Aye, reckons your woman is probably three times the size of you and twice the man. Does she shave?'

'Shave?'

'Yeah, shave. My mate placed a wager with me that your woman probably has a beard. But I said –'

Loki never finished his taunt, as the offended warrior threw himself at Thor with a ferocious battle cry, quickly joined by the other three.

To say the fight didn't last that long is a bit of an understatement. In fact, as understatements go it's right up there with a store in London which had been partially damaged, and by partially, I mean the roof had been blown off and it was missing a wall, during the Blitz in World War Two, which put up a sign declaring itself 'More open than usual'.

In a way, we shouldn't be surprised that four mortals were no match for a god, especially one well versed in warfare and known for his prodigious strength. Even so, Loki had been impressed by his friend's efficient and restrained handling of the scrap, and as he watched the two fellows just about still on their feet drag their other two very battered comrades away from the scene of their defeat and humiliation, he felt it only right to applaud. 'Good fight, well done. I particularly liked the way you let them feel they had the upper hand for a whole second, maybe even two – very sporting,' he acknowledged drily.

'They didn't know I was a god; didn't seem fair to just lay into them with my full might,' replied Thor, feeling a mite embarrassed.

'You're too soft. They were quite willing to gang up on you four-to-one when they thought you were human. I'd have just given them a straight godly kicking and been done with it. Teach them not to pick on the little guy.'

'They didn't pick on me; they picked on you because you'd cheated.'

'Minor detail. Anyway, they were quite prepared to go four-on-one on me – hardly seems fair. No, you were way too gentle on them, but I can appreciate where you were coming from.'

'Whatever.' Thor dismissed Loki's words grumpily. 'And how come you just kept out of it? You could have stepped in and helped, you know.'

'What, and ruin all your fun? Hardly, besides, you had it totally in hand. Now, if it had been some Ice Giant, that would have been different.'

'So, you would have helped me if it had been a giant?'

'Are you insane? No, I would have run away. They've a bloody nasty temper.'

'Your children are from you and an Ice Giantess.'

'Exactly, so I know what I am talking about, and what an angry bitch she could be, which is why I would run. Besides, I really don't want to have to get into a fight with my in-laws. They never liked me, and I don't think they'd go easy.'

'You're incredible.'

'Why, thank you.'

'That wasn't a compliment.'

'Says you. Anyway, why are you here?'

'What?'

'You didn't just fancy a bit of card time with little old me, so why did you come?'

'I need information. Remember, that was the bet.'

'Ah yes, of course. Did you really think you'd win that bet?' Thor just glowered. 'From me, seriously?'

'Yes, seriously.'

'I thought your father banned you from having anything to do with me.'

'He did, has. I really shouldn't be talking to you at all.'

'Yet here you are.'

'I am.'

'Okay, so what do you want?'

'You'll give me information?'

'Maybe.'

'But I lost the bet.'

'Okay, here's the deal. As well as giving me permission to date Þrúðr, you have to put in a good word with her first on my behalf.'

'Really? What are you, twelve?' sniped Thor.

Loki ignored Thor's taunt and asked, 'Do we have a deal?'

Thor sighed. 'Sure.'

'Okay, so what do you want to know?'

'I want to know what your daughter is up to.'

'Hel?'

'You have more than one?'

'No, maybe, I don't know. Okay, let's say yes, one, Hel. You want to know about Hel?'

'Yes.'

'Let me see. Last time I saw her she was sulking, skulking, running the Underworld, probably redecorating her bedroom all in black. I really hoped she would have grown out of that phase. It's all well and good when you're young and rebellious, but she really should have got beyond that stage by now.'

'That's it?'

'Well, it's embarrassing. How is she ever expected to meet a boy and get laid with that kind of black doom thing going on? It's hardly sexy.'

'I don't mean her decorating; I mean, is that all she's doing?'

'What?'

'Running the Underworld.'

'Last time I called in.'

'She isn't, well, you know...?'

'Know what?'

'Maybe overstepping her bounds?'

Loki scrunched his face in confusion. 'What are you talking about?' he asked, befuddled.

'Is she, your daughter, Hel, trying to bring about an early Ragnarök and collect more warrior souls than she has a right to? There, I've said it. What's she up to?'

'Hel?'

'Yes.'

'My Hel?'

'Yes.'

'My Hel, you know, play-by-the-rules, account-for-everything, sign-for-every-soul-in-triplicate Hel?'

'YES.'

'Nah, she wouldn't do that.' Loki dismissed the idea confidently.

'Are you sure?'

'Course I'm sure. She'd rather die than break the rules, just to spite me.'

'She can't be that bad?'

'I'm telling you she is. That whole painting her room black – that's a rebellion against her mother. Playing by the rules – that's a rebellion against me. She'd die in a ditch before she'd go against the rules just to make me angry. Sometimes I despair. Kids today – no respect for their fathers.'

'That's hardly a surprise.'

'Why'd you say that?'

'Because you're her father.'

'That hurts.' Thor raised an accusing eyebrow as Loki huffed and puffed as he looked at his feet then conceded, 'Okay, so maybe I'm not the best father.' Thor coughed theatrically. 'Okay, I've been a rubbish father, but it really wasn't my fault.'

'How was it not your fault?'

'Well, their mum kinda didn't want me around so I thought, sod it, they'd be better off with her, at least until they were old enough to drink...'

'Or fetch a stick.'

'Oi, Fenris is a good kid, if a little furry.'

'He's a fucking wolf.'

'Okay, so my kids are a bit...'

'Freaky?'

'I was going to say special, but yeah, you're right, they're freaks. Especially Jörmungandr. How screwing an Ice Giantess gets you a serpent for a son beats me, but hey, such is life. I suppose I shouldn't be so hard on Hel. Compared to the other two she's practically normal.'

'Normal?'

'Admittedly she never liked the sparkly shit most girls go for, and she's no looker – let's face it, see her in the wrong light and you'll die screaming – but she's a good girl at heart, very diligent, a good organiser. Keeps the Underworld in check – that's gotta count for something,' Loki finished, unable to disguise a smile which hinted at fatherly pride.

'So, what's she up to?' Thor asked again.

'As far as I know, nothing,' said Loki. 'I went to see her a little while ago, you know, show some fatherly interest, drink her beer, play with her dog, the usual stuff. She didn't mention any nefarious plans to bring about Ragnarök. I'll be honest, I don't think she's keen on the whole end-of-the-world-as-we-know-it bit. She'll put that off as long as possible.'

'You're sure?'

'Yes.'

'Totally sure?'

'YES!'

'Then who's wiping out town after town with plague?' Thor asked, concerned. 'Is there someone new around we don't know of?'

'Doubt it,' said Loki. 'We'd have known, sensed something.'

'What about that Christian bunch?'

'I wouldn't worry about them. They're all about forgiveness and not hurting things and stuff. Not a backbone amongst them,' replied Loki with disdain.

'If not the Christians, then who?'

'Damned if I know,' said Loki, 'but then again, plague, you say?'

'Yes. Why? What do you know?'

'It's probably nothing.'

'What is?'

'Nah, I must be wrong. Forget I even mentioned it,' said Loki enigmatically.

'Forget what? You haven't told me anything.'

'Haven't I?'

'No.'

'Oh, well, it's just that when I visited Hel last time it wasn't there.'

'What wasn't there?'

'The rake, of course. Come on, keep up.'

'Keep up? How can anyone keep up with your mad ramblings? Just tell it straight.'

'Right, well, last time I saw Hel her rake wasn't there. I didn't pay too much attention to it, though it did seem a bit strange, but then she gave me a beer and I sort of forgot.'

'Forgot what?'

'I told you, her rake.'

'What about her rake?' asked a thoroughly bewildered Thor.

'She didn't have it with her, and she always has it with her. It's usually in a wooden rack by the door, but it wasn't, and I couldn't help noticing, because that's like you without your hammer, or Odin without his spear, or Freya without her hawk and smoking red hair or Farbauti without his lawyer's supercilious "I'm better than you" smugness. You know, some things are just always present, and it wasn't, which I noticed. But like I say, it's probably nothing. She'd probably sent it away for a clean. Anyway, that's all I know. Now come on, spill – what does Þrúðr like doing of an evening?'

18

Leaving our two mismatched gods behind, let's once again shower our attentions on our ubiquitous hero, Agnew, and his bunch of murderous though basically well-intentioned men. Well, when I say well-intentioned, what I mean is hard-working and focused, and when I say focused, I mean focused on fighting, fornicating, and drinking, not necessarily in that order. But for once their focus was on working hard and repairing their ship.

Under the watchful eye of Alfarr, Agnew and the men had beached the villagers' cob, and at least two of the smaller boats, broken them down and salvaged the better wood from them. They had then lugged the wood across the island to the beach where their own wrecked ship lay and began an extensive restoration. They had also taken the time to explore the island itself and had discovered it was just one of several islands clustered together, though they seemed to be on the more north-eastern tip of the archipelago. According to Morag, other strands of the tribe occupied the other islands, but at this time of year, due to the winter seas, very few risked the crossing. Even so, Agnew placed men on watch during the day to ensure no bunch of heavily armed cousins appeared wondering why the men from this island had failed to show up at some prearranged piss-up the island's women were not aware of.

Less concerning to Agnew, but of more use to his men, they had found a few trees dotted around the island. It was this which had nearly caused the breakdown in cooperation between Agnew and the women of the island. Even though the ship began to look vaguely whole again, if not yet seaworthy, due to the short winter days progress had been slow, and what Agnew had hoped would take days to complete was stretching into weeks. You would have thought Agnew and his crew's continued presence in the village would have led to tensions which by now should have hit breaking point. With the village's men of fighting age still chained up and the women living in fear for their own lives it is a natural assumption to make. However, the mood, at least between the Norse and the women, had eased.

Agnew's men had followed his orders, and not one had tried to force himself upon any of the women and had treated them as they would their own women back home. As a result, the younger girls of the village especially and those who were already single before the Vikings had turned up had warmed to these rough raiders. So once fear had subsided, lust and nature had inevitably taken their course. All was going well until they'd chopped down some of the trees.

Seriously, I hear you ask, the murder of their chief and subjugation of the village they let pass, but cut down a few trees and it all kicks off? What the hell's wrong with these people? In many ways, it's a simple matter of perspective. The trees were rowan, and although Alfarr stated that the wood was tough but not that durable, it could still be used to help patch parts of the ship and would last long enough to get them where they were going. Unfortunately, while the Norsemen were happily taking an axe to the rowan, to the Celts this was pure sacrilege. For the Celts, the rowan was sacred, like the cow to Hindus or whiskey to Catholic priests. If their druids found out they would go mental. It is worth noting that today we tend to think of druids as ageing hippies with bad facial hair and a desire to run around Stonehenge naked on Midsummer's and being no more dangerous than a nasty lasting image of a pale, naked, out-of-shape fifty-something burned onto your retinas – I will never unsee that. However, back in Agnew's time, well, they were something rather different and not adverse to murder and blood sacrifice to keep their gods happy.

Upsetting the druids was not something to take lightly. Luckily, the nearest druid was on one of the other islands and not likely to find out about the desecration until Agnew and his men had gone. Mind you, this didn't placate the women, who until now had adapted to the new law in town remarkably well. In fact, some had even decided getting up close and personal with a big, strong Norse warrior was something to be valued and enjoyed. Even so, all knew that at some point the invaders would be leaving and the fallout once they left would be visited upon them.

With the rowan-felling incident threatening to unbalance the delicate peace they had managed to forge, Agnew demonstrated his more considerate side. Speaking through Morag, whom he had come to rely upon, he convinced the women to speak with one voice to lay the blame of the desecration on the inability of their own menfolk to guard the village, guard their women, and guard the sacred trees and not to waver from this regardless of what the druids may ask or threaten. Unsurprisingly, all the women jumped aboard this idea with an enthusiasm usually reserved for jewellery. I think it is fair to say that they were going to properly stitch up their own remaining menfolk with the blame for everything, not just the rowans, which had transpired since Agnew had turned up.

I don't know about you, but I'm glad I'm not one of those fellas, because if they thought they had it bad now, chained up in a cold barn as they were, they were at least being fed and watered and were currently safe, but it was only going to get worse for them once the Norse left. You can see it now. As the men are released their women will instantly lay into them. 'Oh, so you think you can start lording it over us again, do you? Who do you think kept you alive while they had you shackled? And who do you think kept this village going? Do you know how many times I had to sleep with a Viking, with his rough hands all over me? Putting up with his rampant, lustful desires and that huge throbbing cock pounding me day after day after day...' Yeah, we know this isn't going to end well, don't we?

Still, leaving aside the religious desecration and the impending cuckolding of the village's men, the general mood on the island was currently one of happy industry. All worked hard, including Agnew. He wasn't one for sitting back and letting his men do all the graft, something his men appreciated him for. There was one though who, despite how happy Agnew, his men, and some of the island's women may be right now, was not happy with the progress or lack of it being made.

'What do you mean, another two weeks before the ship is finished?' The image of Hel scowled angrily at Delling through the water in the scrying bowl.

Delling had been prepared for this, not that being prepared made him feel any happier or more secure in his position, but at least it gave him a fighting chance to keep his composure, which was about all that was left to him.

'It can't be helped, mistress. The Norsemen's ship was heavily damaged when Jörmungandr dumped them on the beach.'

'Trust me, I will be having words with my brother,' Hel growled menacingly, 'but it does not explain why it takes so long to repair a boat.'

'Ship,' corrected Delling.

'What?'

'Ship.' Delling winced as he said it, but hey, in for a copper penny, in for a silver piece. 'The Norsemen call it a ship. They get terribly angry when you call it a boat.'

'Do I look like I care? Boat, ship, plank – it is all the same to me. Fix it!'

'Easy for you to say, but you aren't the one having to sail in it,' Delling replied sulkily.

'Delling...'

'Yes, mistress?'

'I suggest you change your tone lest you want me to tear your tongue from your throat.' Hel's voice had dipped to little more than a whisper, a sure sign she was thoroughly angry.

'Sorry, mistress, but it is different when you are upon the sea. It is a wretched existence – cold, tiring, and wet. I do not know what possesses men to take to it. But I do understand the affection and trust they put in their ship,' Delling explained simply. 'It is all which separates life from a watery death.'

'And what is that to me?'

'It is the reason it is taking them so long to repair their ship. They need to have confidence that it won't simply break apart and drown them, otherwise they simply won't sail. There is a lot of work to do. The ship was a wreck before Jörmungandr ever got to it. His dropping it on the beach just finished it off. Please, have patience. Agnew and his men are resourceful; they are doing their best.'

'You sound almost impressed.'

'I am.'

'Don't be. I didn't rescue them from their first death so they could stop off to indulge in the pleasures of the flesh. I rescued them so they could get my rake back.'

'Mistress, they are working hard.'

'They are also playing with the women there, yes?' snorted Hel derisively.

'Well, yes. They're men, and they are driven by their needs.'

'I know full well what drives men, Delling – usually the baser elements of their being. Maybe I should strike down all the women. If there are none to distract, they can better focus on the task in hand,' Hel suggested with no hint that this was an idle threat.

Delling could feel Hel's animosity radiating from the scrying pool with a malevolence which terrified him, but forcing himself not to look away from the goddess' angry countenance, he swallowed heavily and pleaded for mercy for the women. 'Do not kill them; they have done naught wrong. Also, I do not know how their gods may react. Do you need some other gods getting in the way of you getting your rake back?'

'I am HEL, Queen of the Underworld. Why would I fear a god, any god, especially those excuses for gods the Celts cling to? They are a spent force; they are nothing to me...' Hel's voice became shrill.

'Yes, yes, I am sure they are nothing compared to your ghastly magnificence,' Delling flattered desperately. The last thing he needed was for Hel to go on one of her rants. They never ended well, usually involving a lot of pain and distress for anyone in her eyeline, which right now was him and only him, and tended to cloud the issue until she'd calmed down, which could take days. 'But they are not the issue, my Queen. The only issue we have is that this island is short of wood, at least wood suitable for mending Agnew's ship. They are stripping the islanders' own boats...'

'So, the islanders only have boats, do they?' Hel laughed sarcastically.

Bloody gods, they're worse than children, Delling thought to himself. 'In this case, with one exception they are boats, which are not giving up much wood,' Delling pressed on, 'but Agnew's crew are salvaging what is available. It is, by all accounts, more complicated than it sounds. If the wood was cut in the wrong direction to what the Norsemen need then it is next to useless. Once out at sea, the swell of the ocean will simply snap the reclaimed planks. The ship will break, and they will sink. But they are getting there – two weeks and all will be ready...' Delling could feel a slight dimming of the anger emanating from Hel and so steadied himself to deliver the piece of news which was really going to blow her top. 'But getting the ship fixed isn't the problem.'

'What do you mean?' In the pool, Hel's reflected eyes narrowed dangerously like a cat fixing its prey before pouncing.

'Even when the ship is ready, they will not be able to sail on this winter sea,' admitted Delling. 'They will have to sit out the winter here and wait for spring. To do anything else would-be suicide.' *And not just for them but for me too*, he thought.

Delling had expected Hel to explode with rage at that revelation. Instead all he got back from the reflected image was a long, thoughtful pause. Eventually Hel replied calmly, 'I hadn't considered that. Leave that with me.'

'What?'

'I said leave that with me. Inform Agnew I am unhappy with the progress he is making. I want him to have the ship ready to sail by ten sunrises from today.'

Delling winced at the demand and felt the same sinking feeling every engineer has felt when a programme manager who doesn't understand what a task involves puts a star on a progress chart indicating the due date, which is in no way achievable.

Bravely, some may even say stupidly, and regardless of godly wrath, Delling haggled. 'Make it twelve sunrises and you're on.'

Again, Hel surprised him. With a barely noticeable nod she granted his demand, after which the vision of Hel disappeared, leaving nothing but a basin of cold water reflecting Delling's own face back at him.

In the hall of Elivdnir, Hel stalked away from her scrying mirror and took up a fidgety repose upon her throne of bones. Despite the fact her throne was mainly bones it was quite comfortable, giving good support to the lower lumbar and promoting good posture. Today though Hel could find little comfort in it. She'd foolishly made a promise to Delling, telling him not to worry about the sea and that it would be okay. Unfortunately that was going to cost her, and in the first instance that cost was that she was going to have to talk to Ràn.

Hel found it difficult enough to deal with the gods of the Aesir and Vanir, but Ràn was a giantess like her, and it seldom ended well when two giantesses came together. Female giantesses tended to be fickle, malicious, petty, and vindictive, and that was just the pleasant ones. They'd all mastered the art of backstabbing two-faced bitchiness with a side order of bullying and body shaming which would put a U.S. sorority cheerleader to shame, and in such things, Hel was completely out of her depth. Add to that the fact that Hel and Ràn both vied for the souls of the dead. It also made them rivals, which didn't exactly make them easy allies. Still, needs must when some bastard has stolen your rake. Hel summoned one of her many minions and instructed it to go to Ràn's realm and arrange a meeting. Unable to get comfortable, Hel got up and went for a good stalk about her lands, much to the dismay of the souls residing there. It was bad enough being dead, but no one needed an angry goddess showing up poking their nose into your business.

Time passed for Delling, Agnew, and the rest. After twelve more days the ship was looking, well, not good, good is not the word, let's say functional, and we are probably being a bit kind here, but it at least looked like it could put to sea without sinking immediately. Spirits were high. For Hel, brooding by the side of a secluded fjord, her spirits were anything but. Perched on a flat rock, her cloak wrapped tightly about her with her hood pulled low across her face so only her chin was visible, she waited at the place Ràn had agreed to meet her, the very picture of sullen misery.

She'd been waiting for what felt like a long time and was about to give up when from out of the cold, still waters of the fjord strode a woman wearing nothing but what looked like a net. *Show-off*, thought Hel none too graciously, but if we take a moment to lavish our gaze on this woman, we can see she has a lot to be proud of, and probably most women would be proud to show it off also if they were put together like Ràn. Her skin was pale and glimmered under the weak rays of the winter sun with a silvery hue. Her hair was dark and fell past her shoulders in soft waves. Her eyes were an aquamarine, seemingly calm and inviting, though look closely and a storm raged in their depths. As she walked out of the sea her body swayed in rhythm with the tide, gentle, soft, yet belying an inner strength which was terrifying to be... Okay, let's quit with the angry sea metaphor, shall we. What you have here is a woman who was a perfect ten. This was a girl who didn't so much turn heads as screw them from their necks. She was hot, sultry, like an incoming storm and worse still, she knew it.

As Ràn approached it was all Hel could do not to attack her and claw at her perfect features, the jealousy burning deeply, but she kept it together, just, and said icily, 'Ràn, so good to see you.'

Ràn reached Hel and pulled her close, hugging her tightly. 'Hello, dear, so nice of you to call. We really should do this more often,' Ràn replied, equally frosty. She ended the embrace and stepped back.

'I see you are still favouring the whole net look,' said Hel as she shook out her cloak, now damp from being pressed against the soaking sea goddess, who was slowly drip-drying upon the shore.

'What can I say?' said Ràn. 'It's just so... me. And you, that cloak, that hood – very... enigmatic.'

'What, this old thing?' Hel tried to rally. 'It was just the first thing I came to,' she lied. She'd spent hours desperately trying to choose an outfit which would make her look as menacing, and, let's be honest, cool as she could possibly conjure up, but she'd be damned if she'd let on to Ràn that she'd tried.

Ràn cast her eyes about the shore, and seeing no other option came and sat on the large slab of stone Hel had been using as a seat.

'Lovely setting,' Hel observed honestly.

'Really? You think?'

'Yes, so desolate. I find it very calming.'

'I never thought of it like that myself,' said Ràn, 'but I can see what you mean.'

And then the talk dried up, leaving the two goddesses sat in awkward silence with neither wishing to be first to break the deadlock. In the end Hel swallowed her pride and spoke first. 'I need a favour.'

Ràn gave her a sidelong glance and with the merest hint of a smile replied, 'You require my help?'

'Yes.'

'The Queen of the Underworld requires MY help.'

' Yes.'

Ràn basked in the deliciousness of the situation as she stared across the icy fjord.

'Well?' said Hel impatiently.

'Well, what?'

'Will you help me?'

'I don't know. You haven't told me what you want yet.'

Hel had rather hoped Ràn would simply agree to help before knowing what she wanted and would simply be happy knowing Hel was in her debt, but Ràn was not about to let her off so easily.

'What do you want of me and why?' Ràn asked, giving Hel no way out.

'I need you to calm the sea between Shetland and Norway.'

'For how long?'

'Long enough for a ship to make safe passage.'

'And why ask that of me? Why do those wishing to sail not simply wait for a naturally calm sea?'

'Because it is winter, the sea is naturally rough, and I need them to sail now.'

Ràn sat silently, pretending to consider the request, though it was as much about making Hel sweat on her answer. 'So, the ship,' Ràn enquired eventually, 'what ship? Who sails it?'

'Agnew, son of Grimor the Furious, and his men.'

'Agnew, son of Grimor the Furious? Never heard of him.'

'He is oft known as Agnew the Miffed.'

'Why do I know that name?' asked Ràn suspiciously.

Damn, thought Hel. She had been hoping this wouldn't come up, however she answered innocently, 'No idea. I do not think he is anything to you.'

'No, no, I definitely know that –'

'Even if you do, it is of no consequence, but to me he is –'

'You BITCH!' Ràn suddenly turned on Hel, her voice thundering like waves against a rocky shore. 'He and his were mine!'

'Technically they were still alive.'

'They were fated to drown; they were my souls to claim.'

'You should have been quicker then,' Hel snapped.

'You crossed a line. You claimed souls not rightfully yours.'

'I have claimed no souls,' Hel answered truthfully. 'I answered a prayer, something you could have done. I was not obliged to wait for the sea to deliver them to you.'

Ràn laughed bitterly. 'So that is how it is now? The Queen of the Underworld thinks she is above our laws.'

'I have broken no law. I have taken nothing not due to me. If you were not so capricious, they could have been yours; not my fault you choose to toy with those who sail atop your realm before you strike. You're worse than a cat.'

'Careful, Hel, or I may strike you down where you sit.' Ràn's words carried the threat of a tempest on the wind. Ràn sprang to her feet, her hair whipping wildly as harsh winds suddenly howled down from the north, breaking the tranquillity of the fjord, the waters swirling angrily, lashed into a frenzy by the rising wind.

Hel stood angrily, the ground turning to ice beneath her feet, the lichen which clung to the stone seat withering to dust as her baleful influence pulsed from her. Ràn stared back, all about her seeming in storm, and Hel hated her for it, for even Ràn's anger held beauty, a terrible beauty perhaps but one which Hel couldn't help but admire. Years of jealousy and insecurity whenever she found herself in Ràn's presence came rushing back. Hel threw off her hood, revealing her terrible visage. All around, any living thing within sight suddenly felt its blood freeze and heart stop. From vole to hawk, all succumbed to Hel's corruption. She lifted her hand to strike as Ràn raised her arms ready to bring down the tempest upon her foe. The goddesses clashed!

19

When last we left Guthrun Doombringer he was in a filthy cave about to share meat with Asa and a worryingly naked crone. He is still in said cave, but the hour is late, the fire is but a smouldering heap, and all is quiet. But what is this? We see Guthrun wake and although it is dark – to be honest, the cave is pretty much pitch-dark, bar some last glowing embers – Guthrun can see. To him the cave is bathed in light as though the fire were raging. If I didn't know better, I'd say there be magic afoot this night. But forget the lighting – it's no different to any bedroom scene in any film where supposedly all lights are off and yet the hero and heroine are lying together in the warm glow of post adventure coitus, both lit by a strange blue glow. You know the scene: he is naked from the waist down and lying flat and yet the heroine is sat up, further up the bed with the sheet pulled up high on her chest, which begs the question, where does all that blue light come from and who makes L-shaped blankets for just such a moment as this, and why do only people in films possess these sheets?

Actually, forget the sheets, forget the blue light and instead let's look through Guthrun's eyes. So, what does he, sorry, do you, see? You're on your back, lying upon soft furs; you are naked from the waist up. The cave is bathed in a warm orange glow as the fire burns brightly between you and the cave mouth, casting long flickering shadows, yet that is not what catches your gaze but the silhouette standing above you. For a moment you feel a cold fear grip your stomach. You have been caught asleep and now you're at this unknown enemy's mercy, but before you can react, the light from the fire illuminates the figure more clearly. It isn't some tooled-up warrior about to shove a spear through your chest but a woman. A tall, athletic woman. A very, very naked woman with ripe breasts, flat stomach and a light mound of blonde hair doing just enough to conceal her sex.

She drops to her knees, straddling you. You notice her face for the first time, which stops you muttering 'Asa', for this is not Asa but someone else, grey-eyed, slim yet inviting mouth, high cheekbones, long neck and the blondest of blonde hair. The sort of blonde you can't get out of a packet, it is the most natural of Scandinavian blonde – fine, full, resting atop her breasts and practically glowing in the firelight. Your throat feels dry; you swallow but it doesn't help. Your pulse races and you feel that familiar stirring, the fire in your loins as the woman's hand reaches for your belt and starts to help you out of your trousers.

It's a dream, it must be a dream, but hey, this is such a dream you don't want to wake, you can't wake, and then she releases your member. It stands proud and erect, and you watch with barely contained excitement as she slides up your lap, rises slowly on her knees then sinks herself down upon you, her hot wetness enveloping your throbbing... and I think that's just about enough of that. I don't know about you, but I suddenly feel a bit dirty and in need of a cold shower. What, you want more? No, come on, give the man a break. He deserves some privacy.

So, let's leave Guthrun for a bit and instead move time on and watch as he wakes, much later. The cave is cold and dark, he can barely see anything, but he can tell he is naked. He didn't go to bed naked, but he is clearly naked. He reaches down under the furs, where his hands run through the cold, sticky patch upon him and the furs. For a moment he feels a pang of guilt. He hasn't done that in his sleep since before he barely became a man. But, and this is the strange thing, in his dream he had felt, properly felt, everything. Every touch, every sense, every emotion – it was like he had been not just alive but more alive than he'd ever felt, and now he can feel the sensation dwindling away like a barely remembered half-dream as the numbness begins to take hold once more. He wants the feelings back, but they will not come, leaving him feeling empty. He should feel angry but instead a sense of calm satisfaction falls over him. He'd felt, he could feel again – perhaps this was a sign from the gods. Keep his word to the crone and serve Asa and all life's pleasures could be his once again. Ignoring the sticky patch, Guthrun pulls the wolf pelts tight around him and drifts back off to sleep.

'Guthrun.' A voice sidled into his mind. 'Guthrun.' There it went again. 'GUTHRUN!' The voice pierced his consciousness as something heavy thumped his side. With a start, Guthrun awoke to find a fully clothed Asa kicking him in the side and bawling his name. 'Finally – I was beginning to think you'd died,' she snapped tetchily.

Guthrun sat up, rubbing the sleep from his eyes. Despite the rude awakening he felt refreshed. 'What time is it?'

'Almost noon. If we don't set off soon, we won't make it back before nightfall.'

Guthrun noted the slight warble of concern in her voice. 'Where's the crone?'

'No sign of her. It's like she was never here.' Asa cast her gaze about the very empty cave.

'Fuck it,' said Guthrun, getting up, ignoring his nakedness. 'It's time to get off this mountain.'

In quick time, Guthrun dressed and with weapons at the ready the pair of them exited the cave. The sun was about as high as it was going to get, which wasn't very, but the sky was clear, the air icy sharp but thankfully there was no wind. Wrapping their furs about them, not that Guthrun felt the cold, they began the trudge off the mountain. The journey was hard-going, the snow was deep, and every step caused each to sink up to their calves and sometime knees but was otherwise it was uneventful. Even so, night had long fallen by the time Asa and Guthrun finally reached the outskirts of Kaupangen Borgund. As they approached a voice called out sharply, challenging them, only to turn into sounds of relief as Asa announced herself. As the town's gates began to open, Asa turned to Guthrun. 'Did you get what you needed up there?'

Guthrun stared at the would-be queen and nodded solemnly. 'I did. Thank you.'

'Good,' said Asa with a faint smile.

Guthrun thought about saying something else but before he could frame the words, men with burning torches streamed towards them. Asa laid a hand upon Guthrun's forearm and gave it a gentle squeeze then turned away, leaving Guthrun to head towards her men coming towards her. Leaving Asa to the mounting clamour Guthrun slipped away, avoiding the others, taking himself back to his own dwelling. Despite being in sopping-wet clothes he wasn't feeling cold, he wasn't feeling hungry, and he had to admit that despite what had transpired in the cave, nothing much seemed to have changed. Despite this he was prepared to believe that if he kept his promise things would change for him and that was in his own hands, which if not exactly making him happy at least made him grimly determined.

Over the coming days Asa's camp settled back into the normal life of a Norse town during winter. For the most part folks stayed indoors and came together in the evening for drinking, eating, and the telling of tall tales of imagined heroic deeds, stories of the gods and their misadventures and of course quite a bit of sex. Those Norse folks certainly knew how to make those long winter nights fly by. So, all normal then, well, almost normal, as now the dark brooding cloud which had been casting an exceptionally long shadow over all attempts at levity, namely Guthrun Doombringer, had, since his return from the mountain, lifted, albeit slightly. Okay, so he wasn't the equivalent of small blue Disney birds adding a light-hearted cheeping to cleaning the kitchen, but he was no longer a mood black hole sucking up and crushing every happy moment which came within his orbit. If he were a Dulux colour chart he would have gone from black to dirty grey, which may not sound great, but the effect it had on everyone else was immense. But the person most uplifted by it all was Asa herself, who began to draw Guthrun back into gatherings of the inner circle rather than just meeting with him in private.

For his part, Guthrun began to take more of an interest in what else was happening in Kaupangen Borgund. He began to organise training fights to keep the warriors conditioned, he stopped simply drinking alone and occasionally attended Asa's hall to drink with her most favoured, and he even began to talk to others in a manner which didn't immediately say, 'I'm going to bite your throat out and shit down your neck,' which for Guthrun was a major step forward. All in all, the mood in the town lightened as it headed for midwinter, and they geared up to face the darkest period of the year.

Humans, especially pagans, have from the dawn of time faced midwinter with a party to help banish their fears. A pagan party then, even with its religious overtones, was in all respects just like any other party. The host would spend ages getting the place clean and tidy even though by the end of the night it would look like a bomb had hit it. There would be too much food, someone wouldn't bring enough drink of their own and nick someone else's, singletons would hope to meet someone and get laid, and those with kids would just be glad that they had managed to get a sitter and planned to get wasted as though they were twenty again, only now they were forty, out of practice and would get drunk off half a cider and then spend the rest of the night fretting about whether the kids had behaved, not killed the cat or worse the sitter, and that the sitter was in fact not watching the kids but humping her boyfriend on their bed. And of course, it wouldn't be a party until some girl was crying sat on the stairs. Add in blood sacrifice, more beards than you could shake a stick at, axe-throwing competitions and copious amounts of sex and you had the Dark Ages pagan version of the above.

The party was going well. Spirits were high. No one had killed anyone else and at least a few babies had been conceived. Even Guthrun had been enjoying himself. Beer and a large-busted wench had been keeping him amused, when for some reason the wench whispered in his ear, 'Protect Asa.'

Before Guthrun could say, 'What?' she had got off his lap and slipped away into the crowd. If this had been old Guthrun he would have ignored such stuff, but now a sense of unease settled upon him. Cursing, he put down his tankard, grabbed the small throwing axe he had with him and climbed up on the bench to look across the many heads in the hall, trying to spot Asa. Nothing. Guthrun jumped down and pushed his way through the revellers towards the back of the hall and Asa's private chambers. After a brief search it became apparent she wasn't there. With a mounting sense of urgency he rushed back to the hall, grabbing the first person he came across. 'Where's Asa?'

'Don't know,' came the reply.

Barging his way towards the front of the hall he accosted others, asking the same question, but none knew of Asa's whereabouts. It was only as he reached the far end of the hall, almost outside, grabbing one of Asa's serving maids that he finally got an answer.

'She went off with Torsten.'

'Who?'

'Torsten Wildhair.'

'Who is Torsten Wildhair?' Guthrun grabbed the girl roughly, dragging her outside so he could better hear her.

The girl quivered in terror and stared, horrified, at Guthrun.

'Where has he taken her?'

'I... I don't know.'

'What?'

'I don't knoooooow,' she wailed pitifully. 'Please don't kill meeeeeeee.'

'I am not going to... grrrrrr – where does Torsten stay here?' The girl looked at him blankly. 'Torsten Wildhair – where is his dwelling?'

'Be-... behind the blacksmith's.'

Guthrun let go the girl and ran for the blacksmith's as best he could across snow-covered paths. He didn't pass many revellers, as most were inside. The few he did pass had not seen anything of Asa or Torsten. Fearing the worst, he reached the blacksmith's place, which was in darkness. Everywhere was in darkness. The sky was sat beneath a blanket of cloud so thick even light from the moon had been denied him. He moved around the back of the blacksmith's, desperately trying to catch a glimpse of light or sound which would show him Torsten's place among the many huts, but there was nothing, nothing until a muffled crash and stifled scream from a place just off to his left caught his attention.

Without thinking, Guthrun hurled himself at the building's door, bursting through into a dimly lit space, where he was just in time to see Torsten wrestling with Asa. Torsten grabbed her hair, forcing her head back painfully as a dagger's blade, held high, reflected the single candle's light dully. For a heart's beat there was a pause, as Guthrun's unexpected entrance had stilted Torsten's downward strike, which would have ended Asa's life, which gave Guthrun the second he needed to hurl his axe at Torsten. The axe buried itself deep into Torsten's face, the impact sending him stumbling backwards and over. Still clutching Asa's hair, he dragged her upon him, his dagger dropping from twitching fingers.

Guthrun strode over to where Torsten and Asa had fallen, Asa twisting and tugging to release her hair from the grip Torsten still had upon her. Guthrun stood over them, reached down and ripped his axe from Torsten's face. Still alive, Torsten reached weakly for his dagger just as Asa finally tore herself free and rolled away as Guthrun brought his axe down into Torsten's face again and again and again, blood, bone, and brain covering Guthrun in a gruesome shower until Torsten was no longer recognisable as the man he'd once been – hell, you'd be hard pressed after Guthrun's frenzied attack to recognise the bloody pulp as ever having been human at all.

Panting, Guthrun rose from his kneeling position to face Asa, who was sat, back to the bed, knees pulled up to her chest. 'You okay?'

Asa looked up at Guthrun with barely a hint of recognition. Slowly the shock in her eyes dwindled, replaced by anger and fury. Spitting obscenities, Asa got to her feet to kick and stamp on the corpse of Torsten.

'Fucking bastard! Cowardly fucking bastard! Pissing excuse for a man!'

'He's dead,' said Guthrun dispassionately as Asa continued to pummel the corpse. 'Asa, leave it. Stop. I said stop!' Asa paused as her anger began to abate. Guthrun stepped forward, took her firmly by the shoulders, pulled her away from the dead Torsten and sat her on the bed. 'Why did Torsten want to kill you?' he asked.

'He was an assassin sent to kill me by my so-called husband, the cowardly whoreson!' she spat.

'That's good,' said Guthrun.

'How is that good?'

'It means he's scared. Too scared to face us directly so he sent an assassin. Men like that panic and make mistakes.'

'What, so I am to just accept this, this, this insult!'

'Accept it and use it. Let everyone here know what has happened. Let everyone know Gudrød is too scared to fight, an excuse of a man. Let everyone know that you, his ex-wife, are more a warrior than he is. Let all know and that you are coming for him. And your battle is already half-won.'

Asa straightened her back and stared defiantly at Guthrun, smiling angrily. 'When we finally meet, he is mine.'

'As you wish,' agreed Guthrun, standing. 'We should leave. This is no place for you.'

'Take me back to the hall. I want a drink.'

'As you command,' replied Guthrun, offering his arm, which she took gratefully and without a backwards glance at the dead Torsten, blood-spattered and grim, headed back to the hall and festivities.

20

Welcome back to the fjord side. If you remember when you were last here, this was a place of wild yet calm beauty: crystal water, clear sky, nature doing nature's thing. Now, however, it is a scene of devastation. Trees are torn asunder, scorch marks blackening the once silvery bark. Fish float belly-up, dead, the water murky from the mud churned up from its bed. Even an otter lies by the shoreline with one paw outstretched, the other across its eyes, forever frozen in a dramatic death pose worthy of an Oscar. This little fella went down with style.

Sat on the large boulder, amidst the carnage sat our two goddesses, battered, bruised, and panting like dogs in a heatwave. They had literally fought each other to a standstill. Now, without the energy left to skulk away to lick their respective wounds they shared the boulder, clearly with some unspoken truce between them keeping the peace.

Hel took a deep breath, straightened her back, set her shoulders and turned slightly to face Ràn. 'Can we start again?' she asked wearily.

Grimacing, Ràn slapped Hel weakly on the shoulder. 'There, will that do?'

'I don't mean fight, I mean talk.'

'Isn't that what caused this?' Ràn replied, casting a guilty eye across the tattered landscape.

'Just hear me out. If you don't like it, we can part ways and never speak of this again.'

Ràn sighed and stretching painfully said, 'Go on.'

'I didn't snatch Agnew from you to spite you. I know your claim on him and his men was greater than mine. But he called for assistance, and I had a need for him.'

'Honey, with your looks I don't doubt it, but really, stealing a soul from me just so you can get laid? That's low. But I get it – he's a good-looking man, bit short for my tastes, but beggars can't be choosers.'

Hel bit her tongue and let the sleight pass. 'That isn't why I wanted him. I needed someone willing to undertake a quest.'

'Really?'

'Yes. No one willingly offers to go on quests for the Queen of the Underworld. I needed leverage.'

'So...'

'So, promising to save his men from a watery death gave me that leverage. I did not do this lightly. I know the rules.'

'You've always been a stickler for the rules, haven't you,' Ràn observed drily, 'that's why no one really warms to you. No one likes a goody two shoes.'

'And there was me thinking it was because I look like a skeletal crone.' Hel laughed coldly.

'Ah, you're not so bad.' Ràn mellowed. 'You just make folks uneasy. Nothing personal, but you remind us that our time is not infinite. It's like someone telling you what date you will die when you're only twenty – it darkens the mood.'

'Like Odin, then.'

'Yeah, killjoy!' Ràn swore viciously, which triggered a bout of giggling as they temporarily parked their animosity towards each other in favour of their shared animosity towards Odin. 'What do you need from me?' asked Ràn once they had got themselves back under control. 'You've already saved them. I no longer have a claim on them, so what do you want?'

'I need them to make up time. They are currently stranded on an island fixing their boat – I mean ship – damn you, Delling...'

'Who's Delling?'

'Just my dwarf on the inside. He is very insistent I don't call their boat a boat. Don't ask me why – it floats on water, so it's a boat, but for some reason everyone gets annoyed when I call it such.' Ràn looked at Hel as though she were having a breakdown. 'But don't worry about that,' said Hel, getting herself back on track. 'The thing is, they will have it repaired and ready to sail for their homeland in a few days' time.'

'Seriously?'

'Yes.'

'No, I mean are they seriously going to brave the seas at this time of the year? They must be mad. You may as well have left them to me first time around, because if they sail now, they will surely sink and be back with me in a heartbeat.'

'Which is why I have come to you,' said Hel seriously. 'I need you to give them a calm passage.'

'I don't understand.'

'I need you to let them make it north across the sea.'

Ràn's brow furrowed, as though deep in thought. 'What you are asking is no small matter.'

'I know.'

'It is sure to get Odin's attention.'

'I know.'

'He won't be happy with this kind of meddling.'

'I know.'

'In truth, he will be raging.'

'I know.'

'Then I'm in.' Ràn smiled.

'I kno – What?'

'I said, I'm in. I don't know what the quest is you have this lot on and nor do I really care, but if this is something which is going to upset the All-father then I'm in.'

'Are you sure?'

'Damn right. He's never really liked me, always making snide jokes about me being a giantess to my hubby when he thinks I'm out of earshot. Yeah, I've heard what he's called me, the sexist bastard.'

'What, seriously? He doesn't think you're good enough! But you're gorgeous.' Hel conceded, surprising herself with her own honesty. 'Why would he slag you off? Me, I get, but you...'

'I just think he really doesn't like us giantesses; thinks his precious Aesir can do better.'

'Like he's one to talk,' Hel snarled. 'One of these days one of those young humans he's always seducing is going to see right through his disguise and send him packing.'

'Yeah, and have you noticed how he always goes for the same type?' said Ràn, warming to her topic.

'You mean about eighteen, slim, big boobs, and blonde?'

'That's it.'

'To be fair, he also goes for brunettes and redheads.'

'Yeah, okay, yeah, but they all have big tits and hair down to their arse, and a waist I could put one hand around.'

'He's just a dirty perv.'

'You know he's always trying it on with Freya.'

'Doesn't surprise me. How does Frigg take that? I know she turns a blind eye to the humans – well, they don't last long, and he gets bored quickly – but Freya, she's a goddess; surely Frigg doesn't like that?'

'I think he's as popular as elk shit right about now.'

'I don't know why she stays with him,' said Hel in the tone of every woman ever who has marvelled at how some bright, attractive young thing could possibly want to be with the crinkly old multi-millionaire. Yep, even female goddesses are still female and therefore jealous of the younger prettier model even if it is just using its youthful charms to snag a sugar daddy.

'Guess she doesn't want to give up being queen.' Ràn acknowledged the obvious. 'When do you need the sea calm?'

'If everything goes to plan, two days from now.'

Ràn smiled wickedly and stood. 'Call me – it will be done,' she said, swaying her way to the water's edge. 'We should do this more often, you know. It's been fun.'

'I'm not sure the land would cope,' replied Hel, taking in the destruction the pair of them had wrought.

'Hahahaha! Nonsense – it's been a blast. I'll see you later.' Ràn blew Hel a playful kiss then dived beneath the waters of the fjord.

'Oh no, what have I started?' Hel muttered beneath her breath. She waited a while as the sun began to dip behind the mountains, casting the fjord in a pre-night dusk, which was quite captivating, before heading back to her own domain, which despite being a goddess was actually more arduous than one might assume, but we won't bother you with the Queen of the Underworld's route map. Instead we shall ignore the next few days and join the queen as she stared at the face of Delling in her scrying pool.

'Are you ready?'

'Yes, my Queen.'

'Are Agnew and his men ready?'

'Honestly? No. The waves are high, the air is full of snow, so given the choice between an angry sea and a bed filled with a warm woman, they are going with the woman every time.'

'Men,' Hel hissed icily. 'I don't care if they are being entertained by Freya herself. Get them up, get them ready. Tell Agnew he is to sail today.'

'But the seas?'

'They will be calm.'

'They don't look calm. They look bloody angry,' said the face of Delling, looking nervously over his shoulder to something in the distance.

'Delling... DELLING!'

'Yes, Miss?'

'The seas will be CALM!'

'If you say so, Miss.'

'I do. Now, raise Agnew and get that ship in the water.'

'Awwwwww, you called it a ship.' Delling's face smiled broadly.

Hel cursed herself and swept her hand over the scrying pool, instantly erasing Delling's grinning image. Swiping her hand back, she pulled up another view into which the face of Ràn appeared, looking, if it were even possible, more radiant than before. Hel instantly felt the sisterly détente, which had existed between them since their fight, almost evaporate there and then on seeing Ràn's beautiful countenance. Her old jealousies and insecurities threatening to overtake her again, but keeping her voice cordial, Hel said, 'Are you still willing to do this?'

'Of course.'

'Then I thank you. They leave today.'

'Have no fear; I will make sure they make it. Just one thing...'

Ah, thought Hel, *here comes the debt.* 'Yes?'

'Agnew?'

'What about him?'

'You don't actually have any designs on him…?'

'I don't know what you mean?' Hel replied innocently.

'I mean, he's not yours now, is he? I know you saved him, but you haven't claimed anything else?'

'What? No, I, I don't think of him like that. That isn't why I did… no!' Hel blustered.

'So, you don't mind if when this is all done I…?'

Hel felt herself flush, and it was like a hand had gripped her insides and given them a damn good squeeze. She suddenly felt incredibly angry and very, very threatened but in a strangled voice managed to squeak, 'No.'

'Good, because, well, I really want to know what he does with his hair. It's gorgeous.'

Hel suddenly felt her spirits lift. This was a very strange sensation for her. Oh no – she wasn't falling for a bloody human, was she, was what was racing through her mind, but outwardly she stayed looking calm and replied, 'Ask him everything you want.'

'Cheers, hun,' said Ràn, and then by way of a parting shot she threw in mischievously, 'Then after that, if you don't mind, I'm going to fuck his brains out,' and closed off the scrying from her side.

Faced with nothing but a cold pool of dark water in which only her own tortured reflection stared back, an emotionally hurt Hel screamed, 'ARRRRRRRRRRRRRRGGGGHHHHH!'

21

We have been spending too much time of late with gods and goddesses, so it seems only right we once more head back to a small settlement on the northern tip of a bunch of islands perched in the icy North Atlantic. The ground is blanketed beneath snow and a heavy frost, and smoke trails from the various dwellings rise in the air, only to be blown south-westwards by a strong, sharp wind howling in from Scandinavia as soon as they get above rooftop height. This is winter in all its harsh glory. Pretty, isn't it?

Someone who it is safe to say wasn't taking the time to look about him and revel in the icy formations hanging from the few stunted trees or stopping to admire the swirling ice mist thrown up by the wind was a dwarf with frost in his beard, who was running hard from the sheltered spot out in the countryside back to the village. This was no mean feat. It is hard to run through snow at the best of times, but when you only have short legs it becomes even harder, but with the determination of a Jack Russell trying to keep up with a longer-legged hound, Delling pounded on.

Ignoring the outlying buildings, he made straight for what passed as the hall. Inside he stomped to a room at the back. Tearing aside the animal pelts, he stepped into a smallish room where the fug of two warm bodies and the smell of leather and fur greeted him.

'Agnew! AGNEW!' he cried urgently. 'It's time. C'mon, wake UP!' He shook the sleeping Viking awake roughly.

Agnew, cosy, rested, and for once in his recent life relaxed, took a moment to react to Delling's insistent braying.

'Agnew, get UP! She's calling.'

Agnew sat up and rubbing his eyes, forehead, and cheeks slowly came to. Morag was laid beside him. She turned over, pulling the disturbed furs closer to her.

'What is it?' asked Agnew.

'It's today,' said Delling.

'What is?'

'It's today we set sail. We need to rouse the men and get going.'

Agnew stared at the dwarf like he was mad and said, 'Hear that?' pointing above him.

'Hear what?'

'That howling wind?'

'Well, yes, obviously. What about it?'

'We can't sail in that. Go away; come back when it's calm.'

'But –'

'No buts. Leave me alone. Come back when it's not blowing a gale,' Agnew said sleepily as he lay back down, sliding back beneath the covers and snuggling up to Morag's back.

Delling, still breathing hard after the exertions of his run, stared angrily at the back of Agnew's head. He grabbed the top of the furs and tore them off the sleeping couple savagely.

'What the...?' Agnew reacted angrily, sitting up.

Morag squealed as she was exposed to the cold air and turned over sharply, only to see Delling stood there gripping the cover. Seeing the naked Morag, Delling felt himself flush with embarrassment. He mumbled something incoherently, threw the blanket back over Morag, turned away then said, 'Hel commands it. Be dressed and meet me in the hall, quickly.' Then he stomped away, leaving a bemused Agnew and Morag trying to cope with the rude awakening.

If this were a tale set in the modern world, we could show Delling stomping about, frustrated, staring periodically at a clock to show you how much time passed between him waking Agnew and stepping out to leave him to get dressed, but it isn't, so we can't, so for the sake of argument let's say five minutes pass before Agnew appears, and for someone who has only just climbed out of bed and hasn't had the advantage of a shower, shave and chance to blow-dry his hair, he is looking salon-ready. How does he do that? If that were me, I would be looking rougher than a badger's arse.

However, enough ruminating on Agnew's natural good looks – though I really do hate him for it right now, seriously, I do – let's get back to the actual story and see how things pan out.

'What's all the fuss, Delling? And you'd better make this good.'

'Hel has commanded we sail today. There can be no more delays, so rouse your men, ready the ship, and let us depart.'

'Is she mad? We can't sail in this weather. We'll not get past the breakers before being smashed to pieces. We can't complete her quest if we're dead.'

'Well, that's not strictly true,' replied Delling a little worryingly.

'What?'

'What? Oh, you could still work for Hel even if you were dead. But if you do as she says and sail today that won't need to happen.'

Agnew sat heavily upon one of the wooden benches, pallid and suddenly unsure. Even at the darkest of moments since taking this crazy quest he'd always assumed Hel needed him alive. This suddenly put a whole different slant on things.

'So, you're telling me she could kill us and still have us doing her dirty work for her?'

'Yes. She is the Goddess of Death – it's kind of her thing.'

'Shit!'

'Why? What did you...? Do any of you ever listen to your own mythology? Goddess of Death and the Underworld, Ragnarök, end of days and lo, the army of the dead shall rise and be carried upon monstrous ships to do battle with Odin and his cohorts as the sun is swallowed and all the lands be plunged into darkness ready for the last battle. What do you think an army of the dead is? How is it you lot are still alive?' Delling asked sarcastically.

'You tell me – you work for her.'

'And so do you, Agnew the Miffed. Now get your men together. Today we sail.'

'Why? So she can drown us and send our corpses to do her bidding?'

'No. Do as she commands and it won't come to that.'

'How can you be so sure?' asked Agnew, staring at Delling suspiciously. 'Because believe it or not she believes in playing by the rules. She told me you will be fine. I trust her, so now you need to trust me.'

'Give me one good reason why I should trust you.'

'Because I am going to be on that bloody ship with you, so if it goes down, I go down with it along with you.'

Agnew scratched his chin thoughtfully. 'Okay, I believe you.'

'No, you don't.'

'You're right, I don't,' said Agnew honestly, 'but it doesn't seem I have any choice, so we'll do it Hel's way and hope she's somehow going to see us through this. I'll gather the men. While I am doing that, get the womenfolk up and get them preparing whatever provisions they can spare us to see us through a few days at sea.'

Delling scurried away, leaving a dispirited Agnew, running his hand through his luxurious hair, to say, 'I take it you heard that?' to Morag, who was standing in the shadows, wrapped in furs.

'I did.'

'Seems I have to go.'

'So, it does.'

'We both knew this day was coming.'

'Aye.'

'If I could stay, I would.'

'Dinnae lie. You stayed because you had to.'

'I bloody hate farewells.' Agnew kicked at the ground, wanting to avoid the accusing look he was sure he would see in Morag's eyes.

'You dinnae hang aroond long enough to get to know your victims, do ye?' Morag accused him shrewdly.

'Not if I can help it,' Agnew answered honestly.

'So, what noo?' she asked, her voice catching.

'I sail off into the sunrise, hope I don't drown, go kill a man for a goddess, retrieve her rake and if she and the other gods be willing, come back for you.'

'Yer aff yer heid.'

'Aye, probably.'

'Dee ye really want that?'

'Truthfully?'

'Aye.'

'No. What I want is to jump back into bed and fuck till it hurts, but Hel has called, so...'

'Then git going, ye dunderheid,' she said, moving to him. 'Do your thing, get yerrself back to me, and we'll fook each other till we're puggled, dee ye ken?'

Agnew put his hand round the back of Morag's neck, pulling her to him. They kissed passionately for not nearly long enough before moving apart. Morag slid her hand out from beneath the furs and rubbed the bulge in his pants. 'Now fuck off,' she said, let go and, still wrapped in the furs, walked away, leaving him standing breathless, aroused and definitely miffed in the shadows.

From there on things moved quickly. Agnew's men were roused from their slumber, provisions were prepared, the ship was stocked, some men took their chance for a last goodbye from a willing woman, and others looked tentatively at a storm-tossed sea and wondered on the madness which commanded them to set sail in that. But through it all, Agnew moved with a grim determination, cajoling, encouraging, and in a couple of instances threatening, but one way or another by midday they were almost ready to go.

Tostig, ever the loyal number two, informed Agnew that they were ready to set off as soon as he gave the command. Actually, what he said was, 'The men are scared shitless thinking they're about to drown, so if we're going we'd best go now before they tell us to fuck off and refuse to shift.'

Agnew looked at the heavy sea before them, said a silent prayer to Hel that she wasn't about to just send them to a watery doom as some kind of sick joke, and instructed Tostig to set the men to position and that he would join them shortly. He just had one final thing to do.

Morag had kept herself on the fringes as Agnew had prepared to leave. Now he made his way to her. 'I need to speak to your menfolk; will you accompany me?'

'Aye,' she agreed and followed him to the barn where they had kept the menfolk chained since that first fateful day on the island. Inside, on seeing Agnew, there was a murmur among the men. Some shuffled backwards nervously, others kept their eyes downcast, but a few dared to stare in his direction.

'When we leave, who here will be chief?' Agnew enquired of Morag.

Morag pointed at a heavily built young man with red hair, pale skin, and a calculating look which belied his young years.

'What's your name, boy?' asked Agnew.

'Dowie.'

'Morag here has pointed you out as the new chief. I don't care why she has pointed to you. I don't care why you have more right to lead than the rest in here, but if she says you're the new chief then new chief you are.'

Dowie said nothing.

'I am leaving now. Once we have gone, Morag has been instructed to free you all. I want you to keep something in mind. The only reason any of you still live is because your women have kept you alive by following our instructions. Everything they have done is so I wouldn't have to kill you. So, when I go, and you are set free, do not take out your anger and shame upon them. Understand?'

'Wha's it to ye wha we do wi our women?' asked Dowie sharply.

Agnew crouched down so he could look Dowie straight in the eye. 'Remember, you attacked us. Everything which has happened since is on you. You being chained here is on you. What has happened to your women is on you. The only reason you're not already dead and suffering the shame in front of your ancestors is because of your women.'

Dowie shifted uncomfortably but held Agnew's gaze.

'More than that, I like this one,' said Agnew, pointing back at Morag, 'and when the raiding season comes round again I'm coming back for her, and with more men than I have this time, so if you don't want us to put you all to the sword and take ALL your women when we return, Morag and the rest had better be in good health.'

'What if Morag dinnae wanna go wi you when you return? Wha' if she finds a man here?' asked Dowie.

Agnew turned to look at Morag and contemplated her refusing his invite. He didn't like it, not one bit, but Agnew was a practical man and not one given over to sentiment and he knew he could be dead within the day. He might never make it back. Reluctantly he turned back to Dowie and lowered his voice. 'She's her own woman; she can take whom she wants. I won't have a problem with that. If she wants to stay, she stays. Just make sure she's happy and not battered or I will bring Ragnarök down upon this island.'

Dowie looked at Agnew with, if not respect, then at least some shared understanding. 'She'll be alreet.'

Something in Dowie's tone made Agnew believe him. 'Good. Then I'm off. You'll be released once our ship has sailed from view. Make a better job of leading your men than your last chief did.'

Agnew got up and left the building, Morag behind him.

'Will you not take me wi you now?' asked Morag. It wasn't pleading, it wasn't even in that way a girl will ask you to call after a one-night stand even though you both know that isn't going to happen. It was just a straight question to which she waited calmly for the answer.

'I can't. I'm not even sure we'll make it a mile out to sea without sinking. I won't risk you on this goddess's errand. It is my quest, not yours.'

'Then ya best go. Yer men are waiting,' she said sadly, gave him one last kiss and walked away, not even coming to see them off.

Agnew returned to the ship and climbed in, where the pensive faces of his men looked back at him. 'Okay, let's go,' he commanded without fanfare.

'Okay, lads, put your backs into it,' Tostig shouted, and as one the crew lowered the oars and pulled strongly. Slowly the ship pulled away from the shoreline. Some of the women had stayed to watch. Some waved, some even cried, and some turned away, glad to see the backs of the Norsemen. Almost all turned with trepidation to face the barn, where their own men were held, unsure of what retribution may befall them once they had been released. After all, collateral damage is nothing new.

Back on the ship, it moved out further into the still waters of the sheltered bay, though any who cared to look could see that outside the bay the waves were a broiling mess which promised nothing but destruction to those foolish enough to venture out upon them. Upfront, stood at the prow, Agnew suddenly felt his stomach churn. He quickly grabbed the side of the ship and leaned over, where he threw up heroically.

At the stern, Delling stood with Tostig. On seeing Agnew chucking his guts up, he asked, 'Why do you follow him?'

'Because he always does what's best for us.'

'I thought the Norse followed strong, brave men like you. Not someone who throws up on the flat bits.'

Tostig laughed. 'Don't worry yourself. He'll be all right soon. He always throws up when he gets back on the water, doesn't matter how calm it is. He's a rotten sailor.'

'And still, you follow him. Why? I don't understand.'

'He thinks, Delling, sometimes too much, but he thinks of things the rest of us don't. He sees ways round problems the rest of us couldn't, and in battle you know he will stand with you and not falter no matter the odds. That's why we follow him.'

'Didn't he get you into this mess in the first place?' Delling continued to pick at the mental sore which had been nagging him from the start.

'Maybe, but he also got us out of it. And what could be more heroic than going on a quest for a goddess?'

'You do know that goddess is Hel, don't you?'

'Still a goddess,' replied Tostig matter-of-factly.

Delling was about to say something else when the ship lurched suddenly as it neared the start of the angry sea, and the roar of the waves and the howl of the wind hit him like a hammer blow as the shipped moved out of the lee of the land. The pair stared wide-eyed and afraid as the shipped plunged into a trough between giant waves, which threatened to fall and swamp the ship. 'Hel, protect us!' Delling called out desperately. Upfront, on seeing what was about to befall them, Agnew forgot his seasickness, grimly gripped the side of the ship and said quietly, 'Whatever it is you are going to do, Hel, you'd best do it now.'

As the bow carved into the maelstrom it heaved savagely upwards, and the ship heaved alarmingly over on its side only to suddenly right itself then pitch down at a scary angle. Inside the ship everyone was flung about. Almost no one kept a grip of their oars. Those standing lost their footing. Alarm spread through the crew, as all immediately thought they would definitely drown this time, when the violent motion ceased and the ship rested upon calm waters, though all around still raged. Agnew pulled himself to his feet just as a gorgeous woman, dressed in naught but a net, hopped over the side from the sea to drop lightly into the ship.

'Hello, boys,' said the heavenly vision, 'are you pleased to see me?'

22

We shall come back to how Agnew and his men suddenly deal with having a wet, naked goddess stood in their ship and instead briefly switch our attention to a god, to be accurate not just any god but The God, Odin, the King, Top Dog, Head Honcho, Da Man of the Norse pantheon. Right now, we find him a little conflicted and struggling to deal with what he's feeling.

On one hand, he was feeling powerful, energised, as someone somewhere had just done a very elaborate and powerful blood sacrifice in his name, which always gave him a massive boost. Let's be honest, it is the godly equivalent of having a line of the purest cocaine – that shit will give you a buzz like no other, and that was what Odin was running on now. It also tended to make him extremely horny. Unfortunately, his wife, Frigg, Queen of the Gods, was having nothing to do with him and warned Odin that if he came anywhere near her with his Rod of Power, as he liked to call his penis, she'd break it in two. Even Odin knew that being both king and husband would get you only so far and today that wouldn't get him Frigg, so he'd done what all chastised husbands do in this situation and slunk off with his tail between his legs. Unfortunately, he couldn't just put his erection between his legs so instead it pressed angrily against his armoured codpiece.

Any sensible husband finding themselves in this situation would simply find some quiet place to rub one out and get rid of the pent-up frustration. They certainly wouldn't go on the prowl for another woman, but that's exactly what Odin did, turning up at Freya's door trying to look all kingly and irresistibly sexy. Maybe if he'd taken a moment to think about what he was doing he would have realised why Frigg was angry with him, but although in most things Odin was wise, he wasn't when his little head took charge of his body, not that it came to aught this time, as Freya rebuffed him with nothing more than an arched eyebrow and a condescending pout which seemed to say, 'Come back when you have something more impressive to show me, old man.'

Curses – does no one respect the position of the king any more, thought Odin petulantly. With a huff he considered visiting Midgard to look for some buxom serving wench with loose morals to see if he could find what he was looking for, but it was while contemplating the wisdom of this action that his ravens, Huginn and Muninn, showed up and crowed in his ear, dragging his attention to things unfolding on Midgard, and this was the real reason he was feeling conflicted and confused.

If you are unfamiliar with Huginn and Muninn, let me enlighten you. Odin has two ravens of the aforementioned names. For the uninitiated, ravens are the cleverest birds out there. Yeah, eagles may be noble, swifts speedy and penguins cute, but compared to ravens all the rest are mere simpletons. If they were humans, Huginn would be Stephen Hawking and Muninn would be Sir Isaac Newton. There used to be a third one, but Geoff proved to be a bit of a disappointment, as he was the raven equivalent of a breakfast radio DJ. Sadly every species has its village idiot. Huginn and Muninn tended to swoop around Midgard keeping a beady eye on things. Well, they are ravens – of course their eyes would be beady. They would swoop about, steal bread, beat up on magpies, and occasionally return to Odin's side to report on what was happening in the world of the Norse. I suppose they were a bit like a Dark Ages Skippy, but unlike the pesky Aussie bush kangaroo they didn't give a damn about annoying blonde kids falling down wells. No – you got yourself down there, you can get yourself out again – don't look to ravens for help, not least of all because they were smart enough to know if you died in the well, they could fly down and peck out your nice, tasty, squishy eyes. Hey, it's a hard world out there, and ravens have to scrape out a living just like the rest of us.

That isn't really the point though. The point is they had just told Odin about a certain sea goddess directly helping humans and more worryingly the reason why he was buzzing from a massive blood sacrifice. The news worried him and angered him in equal measure and effectively dampened his ardour quicker than Frigg armed with a pair of wickedly sharp garden shears. With a furrowed brow and a feeling of disquiet seeping into his very core, Odin commanded Huginn and Muninn to summon the boys. The birds wheeled into the air, their harsh crowing receding as they flew off to carry out Odin's summons. Once out of sight, Odin turned on his heel and stalked back to Valhalla a very troubled god.

23

We last left Agnew just as it seemed he was about to be sunk, again – I really am beginning to wonder if he is really suited to being a sailor – when the Goddess Ràn turned up in his ship, instantly the sea beneath their hull becoming calm and benign, though off to either side the sea was still a maelstrom.

'Hello, boys, are you pleased to see me?' Ràn announced herself flirtatiously with a flick of her luxurious hair.

Agnew stood at the prow of his now steady ship momentarily stunned, as much by the sudden calmness of the sea as by having a wet, naked goddess sat in his ship.

'Cat got your tongue, Agnew?'

'You know me?' Agnew finally found his voice.

'Aww, sweet.' Ràn patted him on the cheek before she rested back against the side of the ship, her hair lapping against it like gentle waves caressing a beach. 'Of course I know who you are. You're all Hel talks about these days. It's all quite boring really.'

'Hel talks of me?' Agnew said with horror.

'She certainly does, but don't worry,' she said, catching his look of horrified surprise, 'only to her friends. And I have you to thank for bringing us girls closer together. Between you and me, I think she is rather short on friends, especially girlfriends, and the giants know a girl needs a friend from time to time.'

'I... sorry, what?'

Ràn didn't seem to be listening to Agnew. Instead she let her gaze run down the length of the ship and over the faces of Agnew's crew, who looked back at her with a mix of awe, fear, and lust. She moved from the side to stand with her back against the ship's dragon-headed prow in the sort of pose which would be painted on the side of American World War Two bombers over a thousand years later. Just about every man on board gulped, throats suddenly dry and heart rates up. No one moved. Everyone just stared while Ràn drip-dried provocatively upfront, with one exception.

Delling, used to being in the presence of goddesses, left Tostig's side and made his way forward to come to stand by Agnew.

Delling bowed deeply to the goddess and turned to Agnew and in a voice loud enough to be heard by everyone, even above the roar of the storm surrounding their calm stretch of water, said, 'Agnew may I present Ràn, Goddess of the Seas.'

'Ràn?' said Agnew, bewildered.

'At your service,' Ràn replied graciously before addressing Delling. 'I have something for you, but first I need to converse with Agnew.'

'Of course, mistress,' Delling replied respectfully.

On hearing Delling announce Ràn's name, the rest of the crew started to murmur amongst themselves.

'Is that really Ràn?'

'The dwarf seems to think so.'

'Doesn't she drown those at sea and claim their souls?'

'Have you seen her? She can drown me any time.'

'But you'll be dead.'

'Yeah, but if it means I get to look at that every day till Ragnarök, count me in.'

'Drowning might not be so bad after all.'

'I'm surprised she can actually go underwater. You'd think she'd just float.'

'I know she's a goddess and all, but is it wrong to just want to put my head between her tits and go brrrrrrrrrrrrrrrrrrrrrrrr.'

'And look at that arse. I would follow that down to the darkest depths.'

'Like she'd want you staring at her bum.'

Ràn, seemingly oblivious to what the men were saying about her, continued to address Delling. 'You'd best ask the others to get on with sailing this thing; we can't just bob about here all day, you know. Well, go. GO,' she commanded, waving him away. 'Now, Agnew, let's have a chat. Will here do, or would you rather I take you somewhere more... cosy?'

Agnew swallowed hard and squeaked, 'Here,' then coughed and started again in more manly tones. 'Here will do.'

'Shame. Okay, take a seat,' she said, lowering herself onto one of the sea chests, shuffling sideways and patting its top. 'Sit beside me.'

Agnew sat next to the goddess, who wriggled playfully closer, pressing up against him, her heat pervading his being. 'So, tell me, how do you keep your hair so clean and full of body out here? Do you use a conditioner?' Ràn laughed mischievously. 'I'm only kidding,' she slapped him playfully, 'but no, really, do you? No, tell me later.'

'Err?'

'Don't worry about it,' she said, placing her hand on his thigh. 'Oooh, now I see what the fuss is all about.' She gave his leg a squeeze. 'Where you heading, Agnew?'

Agnew tried to ignore the over-familiar touch and said, 'Norway.'

'Obviously, but where? North? South? The middle? It might help if I knew.'

'I never really gave it much thought,' Agnew replied honestly. 'I didn't think we were going to make it, so I thought we'd just set off and hope we hit land somewhere.'

'How wonderfully calm and fatalistic. I approve your choice. Well, there's this little bay I know – quiet, secluded, with a fabulous waterfall – where you can just fool around, if you know what I mean.' Her dark eyes sparkled like the sea under a summer sun.

'That sounds... just fine,' Agnew answered, trying to ignore the sweat running down his back and desperately looking Ràn in the face, as in his head he repeated, *look at her face, not her tits, look at her face, not her... oh, by the...*

To be fair, this was an unfair struggle and not helped by the fact Ràn was playfully stroking his thigh, and a little too high up it to be decent. She gave it one final squeeze then stood and stretched languidly, which elicited a shared groan from amongst the crew, who were not rowing as ordered but were all turned, watching her.

'Take a moment,' she said to Agnew. 'I just need to have word with Hel's dwarf then I'll be right back.'

'Okay.' Agnew panted and sat staring at her peachy bottom as it wiggled its way up the length of the ship, causing a Mexican wave of Norse heads as she passed each line of rowers, whose heads snapped around to watch her as she passed. If she minded, Ràn gave no indication.

Agnew, sweating and breathing hard, screwed his eyes tight shut, took a few deep breaths and forced himself to calm down and ignore the thoughts which were surging through his head. He stood and with a bellow commanded the men to row. It took him a few shouts and a few slaps to get them to wrest their attention from Ràn and concentrate on rowing the ship, but eventually he got them, if not pulling entirely in unison, at least rowing with enough co-ordination to have the ship vaguely underway. Although he was interested in what Ràn was saying to Delling, he was wise enough to know the calm seas she was blessing them with might not last for long, so the more sea they covered whilst the sea was favourable the better. As he waited for the return of Ràn, he did his best to ignore looking out to either side, for although directly in front of the ship it was calm, everywhere else was a raging storm. It wasn't worth contemplating what would happen to them if they found themselves back amidst those waves again. They would surely be doomed.

With whatever message Ràn had for Delling delivered, she sashayed back to Agnew accompanied by groans, the clattering of oars, and some swearing as the crew succumbed to her distractions. Luckily, Tostig was on hand to help them refocus and after a couple of aborted starts the men got themselves rowing together once more.

Seemingly oblivious to the mental devastation she wrought, Ràn draped an arm around Agnew and stared out to sea with him, though for Agnew it was more of a desperate attempt to keep his wits about him.

'You know,' she said, 'the winds will be favourable for you, so if you want to put up your sail thingy and spare your men trying to row all the way to Norway, you can.'

'Really?'

'Yes. I have it all sorted.'

Agnew allowed himself to turn to the goddess. 'Thanks.'

'Beautiful, isn't it?'

'Yes, you are.'

'Oooh, aren't you the cheeky one,' she gave him a squeeze, 'but I meant the sea.'

'What? Oh shit, sorry, I didn't mean, but, well, err, damn, you're just the...'

'Yes, I guess I am.' Ràn winked, cutting off his stuttering sentence.

Agnew didn't respond. All he could think about was her soft curves, her lips, wet and inviting, the twinkle in her eye.

'Tell me, is that a dagger in your pocket or are you just pleased to see me?' she asked, looking down at the bulge in his crotch.

Agnew looked down and suddenly very self-conscious, shoved his hands over the tell-tale bulge. 'I'm sorry, I didn't mean to be... I should be more in control and...'

'Don't be shy,' she said. 'It's rather flattering.'

Agnew could feel himself blushing hard and if he weren't at sea would be wishing the ground would just open up and swallow him whole.

'Tell you what,' she said, 'go put the sail up, let your men sit back, then you and I can discuss... terms.'

'Terms?'

'Yes. Don't worry, it will just determine how quickly and smoothly you get to Norway. Does that seem fair?' she purred in the way a tiger purrs, in other words growls happily just as it has made a kill.

'Hmm-mmm.' Agnew nodded and, adjusting himself so his arousal wasn't too obvious, left the side of Ràn to organise getting the sail up. While he did so, Delling took a moment to have a quiet word in his ear, well, once he'd got Agnew to crouch down to him, otherwise it would have been a quiet word to his chest. Sometimes short folks forget that those quite a bit taller than them can't hear them unless they get them to come down to their level.

'Agnew, has Ràn requested anything of you yet?'

'No, not yet, but she wants to discuss terms.'

'Okay, well, listen, and listen good. She isn't doing this for you. She is doing this for Hel. You, therefore, don't have to agree to anything.'

'Okay,' said Agnew suspiciously.

'But if I were you, short of being asked to commit suicide or kill your crew if you want to survive this voyage, give her whatever she wants.'

'Seriously?'

'Yes.'

'Won't Hel be pissed with you telling me this?' asked Agnew shrewdly.

'Oh yes. I will most likely be tortured for aeons but I'd rather that than drowning out here.' The look of terror on Delling's face as he cast a terrified eye at the raging sea in the distance told Agnew he was serious. 'Whatever she asks, whatever she wants, just give it to her or we're all doomed.'

Agnew said nothing but nodded and gave Delling a reassuring pat on the shoulder then left the dwarf to ensure the sail was hoisted correctly, directed Tostig where to steer, told the men to rest and then made his way back to the waiting goddess.

'So, terms,' he said. 'What did you have in mind?'

'How direct; how wonderfully refreshing.' Ràn's eyes lit up and she clicked her fingers, and all about them time slowed for all but her and Agnew.

'What did you do?' he asked, alarmed.

'Don't worry – I just took us out of your time. To your crew, everything is the same, but for us, well, we now have lots of time to play with.'

'Okay, so what do you want to do with this time?'

'Why, play, of course.' She giggled and grabbed him by his shirt and dove over the side, taking Agnew with her.

As he hit the water, Agnew felt panic like he'd never felt before and thrashed desperately against the rush downwards to the ocean's icy depths, only for Ràn to take him in a warming embrace, and through the gloom she gave him a wink which miraculously calmed him. Strangely able to breath and not feeling the effects of the cold, Agnew resigned himself to his fate and let the goddess drag him to the goddess knew where. After what seemed an age down amongst the strange sea creatures on the ocean floor, a magnificent Norse hall made of whalebones and shells appeared before them, a warming glow coming from within. Ràn swam in through the open hall doors and swam up till they breached the surface of a pool. Ràn helped Agnew out, who despite being soaked to the skin didn't feel cold. Even so, Ràn turned to Agnew and said, 'I would remove your clothes if I were you, or you'll catch your death,' and as if to confirm the point, she lifted her own net dress from her and dumped it by the pool.

'Come,' she said, taking him by the hand, 'there is much to… discuss.' She led him to a vast sumptuous room dominated by a large bed, which she threw him upon.

'Um, won't your husband, the god, be home soon?' Agnew said nervously as he crawled backwards up the bed as Ràn crawled upon her knees towards him.

'I do hope so,' she said, 'he does so love a threesome.'

24

All in all, it is probably time we had a quick recap of where each of our chief protagonists is up to before re-introducing you to the final player in this tale of derring-do, revenge, and godly meddling.

As we know, Agnew's men are taking a rest as the wind takes the strain and fills their sails. Delling maintains a watchful eye on behalf of Hel, who, it has to be said, is feeling a little more content with things now Agnew is moving again. With contentment comes a little less obsessing about her stolen rake, allowing Hel time to concentrate on those pesky jobs she'd been ignoring, like organising the cleaning of the tattered souls from the swirling blades of the Slidr.

Our hero, Agnew, as you have probably surmised, is currently being used as the sexual plaything of a goddess with a killer body and dubious morals, the lucky bugger. Some guys get all the luck. I doubt his men will be so willing to get back to rowing their ship with as much gusto as before should the wind drop if they realise that while they are getting breathless and sweaty hauling on an oar, Agnew is achieving the same condition but between soft thighs and voluptuous breasts. Maybe we should tell them. Yeah, then see how this plays out for... what? We can't? We are contractually obliged to keep the story going? Well, that's just no bloody fun, is it? Okay, whatever, if you say so. Really, sometimes I wonder why I bother.

Right, moving on and ignoring Ràn's depravities, let talk about Asa. Post the failed assassination upon her life she has become a little colder and even more hardened in her approach to revenge. Let's face it, she hasn't taken assassination well, seeing it as a personal sleight. If Gudrød had turned up and challenged her to a one-on-one fight she would have been okay with that, but sending someone to slit her throat like some farm girl being robbed on the road, well, that just showed no respect, and she wasn't about to take that lying down. In response, she'd embarked on a rampage of terror, bringing destruction to those places which had willingly sided with Gudrød when he'd usurped her father. With both Guthrun and Hel's rake at her disposal she'd sent them out to lay waste to every village which was within a week's ride of Kaupangen with an insidious plague, which, given the terrible winter conditions, meant anywhere within a ten-mile radius. For his part, Guthrun had ceased to view this as a blight on his warrior's honour. Instead he was treating it as merely gardening. By pruning the weak he was removing the obstacles which sat between Asa and her getting to Gudrød and him getting his soul back.

That leaves us with Odin and his inner circle of gods, whom he had commanded to attend him following the news brought by his ravens. What before had been an item of concern was rapidly becoming a full-on crisis. The word Ragnarök had even been mentioned, and that was enough to frighten even the toughest Norse warrior god. No one is ever truly ready to go into a fight knowing full well it is to be their end. As such the mood in Valhalla was a little strained, but we will come back to that later.

So, now you know where everyone is it is time to visit the last major player. The man who in many ways was the catalyst for at least some of this. A man who even by Norse standards is a bit of a rotter. Yes, let's go see Gudrød the Hunter, usurper, rapist, murderer and by all accounts nasty to kittens. Yes, this man is a bad 'un.

We find him, midday, drunk and sexually abusing one of slave girls. Luckily for her he is so drunk his sexual prowess amounts to pushing rope. The girl is letting him go through the motions and thanking her lucky stars he isn't up to the job. Red-faced and sweaty, Gudrød continues to pound away when one of his Jarls appears in his room, grim-faced and impatient. The drunk king takes a moment to realise he is being interrupted before turning angrily to face his man.

'You'd better have a good reason for coming in here.'

'Send her away,' the Jarl replied unflinchingly. 'We have news from Kaupangen.'

'Kaupangen?' Gudrød said hazily.

The Jarl looked at his king with contempt, which, given the king was stood with his trousers round his ankles and limp dick on full display, was hardly surprising. The slave girl had remained stood with her arms against the wall, her skirts lifted and bottom on show for all the world to see, not daring to move. With a sigh, the Jarl barged past his king, pulled the girl's skirts down and told her to leave. With a nod of thanks, she scampered out, relieved to be away from Gudrød.

'Why d'you send her away? I didn't command it!' growled Gudrød.

'There is time for pussy later. You need to come and see what has been sent here.'

Gudrød snorted derisively but grabbed his trousers and hauled them up. 'You over-step, Egil.'

Egil ignored Gudrød's put-down and walked away, saying, 'I am not your problem.'

Gudrød watched Egil's departing back and wondered if he should just bury an axe in it, but even drunk, Gudrød knew Egil was too good a warrior to waste in such a manner. No, he would find other ways to put Egil in his place. For now he would find out what fuss had got in the way of him and his slave.

Gudrød entered his hall, sat himself down on his throne, called for ale and waited until he had the flagon in hand, despite the angry and anxious faces of his warriors looking back at him. With a show of utter contempt for their presence Gudrød downed the beer, burped, and threw the flagon behind him, calling for more before he finally deigned to give his men his attention. 'Well?' he asked sharply.

Egil stepped forward, a large hessian bag gripped in his fist. 'This was nailed to the outer wall.'

Gudrød leant forward, unease creeping into his beer-fuddled brain. 'What's in it?'

Egil upturned the bag, letting the severed and mangled head of Torsten Wildhair drop at Gudrød's feet just as a serving girl passed another beer to him.

'Fuck!' Gudrød cursed as the serving girl screamed and dropped the flagon of beer over Gudrød and one of the large hounds which was lying by the throne. The dog leapt up and spun around, growling in shock. Gudrød ignored the soaking. Bending down, he lifted the head by its blood-matted hair, regarding it coldly. 'Who sent this?'

'No one saw.'

'You let whoever did this get away?'

'No one saw him come. The bag was nailed to the outside of the palisade.'

'No one noticed?'

'No.'

'Fuck, fuck, FUCK!'

'There is one other thing,' said Egil.

Gudrød drop-kicked the head across the hall, the beer-sodden dog chasing after it. 'What?'

'This was also in the bag,' Egil said, passing him a blood-stained piece of parchment.

Gudrød took it, looked at it, struggled to focus and passed it back to Egil. 'What does it say?'

'It is the rune of death.'

Gudrød threw his head back and cursed wildly, kicking out at the throne and throwing a punch at one of the cowering slave girls. Oblivious to his anger, the hound returned with Torsten's head and dropped it at Gudrød's feet, looking up expectantly. 'ARGH!' screamed Gudrød and kicked the head viciously, which skidded across the floor, the dog in happy pursuit.

'The fucking bitch! Why couldn't she just fucking die? Where is she now?'

'Who? What bitch?'

'Asa.'

'Asa?'

'Yes, that bitch, daughter of Harald Granraude.'

'Your wife?'

'Yes, that Asa, my fucking wife.'

'How do you know that's from Asa?'

'Because I sent Torsten to kill her and now his useless ginger head's here. So, where is she?'

'Last I heard, in Kaupangen.'

The dog returned with the head, dropping it at its master's feet once more, who, taking a perverse pleasure from it, kicked the head down the hall for the dog to chase. Laughing evilly, Gudrød addressed his gathered warriors. 'Gather the men. We march for Kaupangen, where we'll slaughter the cow.'

On hearing that order, a slight weasel of a man stepped forward and whispered in Gudrød's ear. The others couldn't hear what was said but Gudrød turned on the man. 'You're not scared of a woman, are you?' Gudrød stared nastily at the weaselly fellow, who stared right back, unflinching.

'Our spies tell us she has raised a sizeable force of her own,' the weasel replied.

'What is going on?' asked Egil.

Gudrød fixed his bleary eyes back on Egil. 'Rangvaldr had heard rumour Asa was moving against me. Me, a king, and she, the cast of dregs of a man not fit to bloody the end of my sword – how dare she! Fucking bitch, fucking, fucking cunt!'

Gudrød continued to rant. Knowing it was pointless trying to interrupt, Egil waited for his king to blow his anger out. Finally, with his king quiet and breathing heavily, Egil asked, 'So, what does it matter? She is nothing. What warrior of worth is going to follow a woman?'

'It would seem many," Said Rangvaldr.

'Egil, I want to crush her. I want her head on a spike and her cunt nailed to her lips.'

Egil wasn't entirely sure about that last bit, but he was sure about something else. 'If we march our men to Kaupangen in this weather, by the time we get there they'll be too weary to fight. Asa's men, however many she has, will be fresh. I will not lead our men to certain slaughter.'

'Coward! You're no warrior of Odin.' Gudrød cursed his man.

Egil stepped forward, gripping the haft of his axe. 'Face me if you think so.'

Gudrød's hand moved to his side where his own axe should have been only to realise he was unarmed, forgetting to bring his weapon in his drunken state. Luckily for Gudrød, who'd taken a nervous step back, his dog ran between him and Egil, blocking Egil's way, dropping the mangled and dog-slavered head of Torsten Wildhair at Gudrød's feet. Gudrød used the momentary distraction to break the tension. 'Use that if you dare, Egil, but it would be better used cutting down Asa's men. But I agree; we'll wait for spring,' he said, levelling his tone. He stooped to pick up Torsten's head, holding it up for all to see. 'We will bide our time and wait for them to come to us. Plan for battle. We will meet them on ground of our choosing. But let it be known that there will be a substantial reward for any man who brings me Asa's head before then. I want it for my dog.' He laughed vilely and threw Wildhair's battered head across the room for his dog to chase. 'It's going to need a new toy.'

25

Out on what seems a strangely calm stretch of sea when all about is surrounded by a churning, raging tempest, a battered patched-up Norse longship sails on serenely. The crew are starting to relax, stretching out tired muscles and taking a moment to breathe in heavy lungfuls of sea air. At the helm, a mountain of a man with a salt-encrusted beard, bare-armed, muscles gleaming with sea spray, stands majestically, keeping the ship sailing straight and true. Beside him a dwarf is staring at the monstrous waves magically being held back by some invisible force and praying hard that a certain Norse adventurer with salon-prepared hair and a short temper is keeping a sea goddess happy.

To all but the dwarf the sail had only been hoisted minutes ago. Delling, who was a magical creature in his own right but also the Goddess of the Underworld's right-hand minion, was immune to the sea goddess's twisting of time and was fully aware that she'd had Agnew away for hours. *Just keep her happy a little longer*, he was thinking, when a sudden geyser of water spouted high above the ship's prow and dumped a soaking Agnew into the prow of the ship. For all on board, time snapped back to where it should be, causing a moment's confusion among the crew as suddenly the ship went from sailing in daylight, albeit weak winter sunlight, to the gloom of day's last rays of light slipping beneath the waves.

Fear, consternation, and panic tore through the crew with the exception of Delling, who, telling the men to be calm as he went, moved down the length of the ship to the heavily breathing Agnew. Just before he reached him, he heard a female voice say, 'Call me,' then there was nothing left but the sound of the wind and the sea slapping against the ship's hull.

Delling reached Agnew, who feebly propped himself up against the hull. 'Are you okay?' he asked worriedly.

Agnew took a moment, allowed himself a tired smile and a steadying breath and replied, 'Yes. I'm good.'

'You don't look it. You look –'

'Drained,' said the voice of Olsen, who'd been the first to reach Agnew after Delling.

'Trust me, I'm okay.'

'Are you?' asked Delling. 'Olsen is right – you have no colour. What did Ràn do to you?'

'Huh? What didn't she do? I swear tha...' But Agnew never finished, as other members of the crew had left their seats to gather around their crumpled leader. Only Tostig remained aft at his post, keeping the ship on course.

'By the gods – Ràn has taken Agnew's soul,' cried Ogmundr, who had joined the throng and didn't want to be left out of the drama.

'No, seriously, she...' Agnew held up his hand, trying to calm his men as others jostled each other to get a better look.

'Is he dying?'

'Ràn really has claimed his soul.'

'Is Ràn a succubus?'

'Well, there was some sucking involved but I wouldn't call her a –' Agnew began, but his voice was drowned out by the panicked mewling of his men.

'Give him some air! GIVE HIM SOME AIR!' commanded Olsen.

'Oh, for...' Agnew pulled himself wearily to his feet. 'I'm okay!'

'You don't look it,' said Delling honestly.

'So everyone keeps telling me. I'm just a bit tired, and... ow, well, okay, I'm a bit sore down...' Agnew fiddled with the crotch of his trousers, 'and I need a drink. And... why are you all looking at me like that?' Agnew finally registered the genuine looks of fear and concern in his men's faces. 'What's wrong with me?' he asked fearfully.

'Just sit there,' said Delling calmly. 'I'll be back in a moment, and someone get this man a drink!'

Olsen grabbed a water skin and passed it to Agnew, who drained it greedily. Delling returned quickly with the burnished metal dish he used for scrying. 'Here,' he said, holding up the polished face in front of Agnew, who took one look and shied away fearfully.

'What has she done to me?' he cried as a face barely recognisable as his own stared back. His skin was drawn tight, grey and ashen, his lips thin, eyes sunken, even his usually magnificent hair hung damp upon his brow, though even in this incredibly weakened state it still held a certain lustre, not unlike a movie star in a gym scene where their hair is made to look like they've been working out for hours with a type of sexy sweat which can't be achieved by hours of exercise but is applied by a makeup girl and lit by a 1000-watt bulb. You know how it is – the actor throws a towel around their neck, pants huskily, a perfect V of sweat formed on the front of their tee shirt, which clings to perfectly formed pecs and abs. Yep, that was Agnew's hair, even if the rest of him looked like he'd barely survived mummification.

Delling sat down by Agnew and put an arm around his shoulders.

'Ow,' winced Agnew pathetically.

'You will be weak for a while, but don't worry; it's normal,' said Delling with a reassuring calm. 'This is what happens when mortals spend too long with a goddess.'

'Really?'

'Yes. It doesn't happen often. Gods usually go in for a quick shag with a human of their choice, then before the mortal has had a chance to clean themselves up the god or goddess is making their excuses about how Fenrir needs to be taken for a walk, or they simply have to get back for that work appointment with the Ice Giants and are up and out of the door quicker than you can say a raven is calling.'

'What happened to me?'

'Ràn's got a sex drive which puts Odin to shame, and judging by where the sun is and that smudge on the horizon, I reckon she's been fucking you for a day and a half.'

'A day and a half?' said Olsen, amazed. 'You were with her for a day and a half! You lucky, lucky bastard!'

'Still, that's some performance,' said Delling, impressed. 'A day with Ràn would kill most men. You must have some stamina.'

'Don't big him up,' said Siggeirr tetchily, who'd been listening in. 'While we've been sailing this thing he's been balls deep in a goddess.'

'Oh please, for you lot he's only been gone a couple of minutes. You lot haven't done any work yet.' Delling started to defend Agnew, but the men's mood was already turning.

'Yeah, why does he get all the good shit?'

'Yeah.'

'We should make him row the rest of the way by himself.'

'Aye.'

'Bastard.'

'How come he keeps having all the fun?'

'Yeah, why doesn't that happen to me?'

'Because you look like the back end of a cow, Siggy,' said Olsen as the rest of the men sniggered.

'Fuck off, Olsen, or I'll turn that baby face into something only a mother could love.'

'Like yours then.'

'Fuck you!'

'You wish.'

'Yeah?'

'YEAH!'

'Stop,' Agnew said weakly.

'Come on, Siggy, let's see what you've got. I'll throw you over the side before you land a blow.'

'I said stop...' Agnew tried again.

'At least I've been blown. Who's ever touched your cock, Olsen?'

'For the last time...'

'Your mum.'

'WHAT!'

'You heard – your mother wrapped those old lips of hers round my cock and sucked me –'

'You take that back.'

'That's what she said.'

'ARGH!' Siggeirr lunged towards Olsen, who sidestepped with impeccable timing, causing Siggeirr to overreach and topple forward. Raging, Siggeirr scrambled to his feet, grasping for the first sharp object in reach – one of the boat hooks, heavy, pointy, and lethal.

'I said...'

Swinging wildly, Siggeirr came at Olsen, who danced back and away but found himself suddenly pressed up against the ship's prow with nowhere to go. Siggeirr brought the boat hook down towards Olsen only for a hand to grab the haft and stop it before the iron hook could strike Olsen's unprotected head.

Agnew, arm aloft, hand wrapped around the hook's shaft, stared sternly at Siggeirr. 'I said STOP!'

Siggeirr glared at Agnew and back at Olsen and then back at Agnew, who was beginning to buckle at the knees with the exertion. 'Shit, Agnew, I didn't – fuck!' he swore, letting go of the boat hook.

Agnew, who still had hold of the sharp end, let it lower to the deck carefully, and despite the exhaustion he was feeling he remained stood as best he could. Behind him, still pressed against the prow, Olsen took a relieved breath.

Agnew cast an angry eye about his crew. 'Ràn almost killed me. Admittedly in the most pleasurable of ways, but I was still in mortal danger, and I did it for you,' he said, staring pointedly at Siggeirr. 'And you,' he said, turning to Olsen. 'And all of you bastards.' He glared at the rest, who shuffled back, suddenly feeling shamed. 'Everything I have done of late is to keep you alive and from perishing out here on the waves. None of you had to spend time with Hel. I bloody did, and it's terrifying.'

The crew murmured, embarrassedly thanking Agnew.

'What was that?'

'Thanks, Agnew,' they chorused feebly.

'I can't hear you. WHAT?'

'THANKS, AGNEW.'

'Better. See that?' he said, pointing to the smudge on the horizon. 'That is home. So, stop fighting each other and sail to that. You will all have battles soon enough.'

'Yes, Agnew.'

'Sure, Agnew.'

'Okay, Agnew.'

'I still don't see why it's always him who gets to shag the goddesses.'

'Shut it, Siggy.'

'Whatever.'

'Right, if you've all done whining, I'm going to get some sleep,' Agnew grumbled weakly. Pushing past his men and making his way aft, he grabbed some furs, wrapped himself up in them and curled up against the sternpost.

'Better now?' asked Tostig, who hadn't left the steering board throughout the crew's altercation with their leader.

'Yes. Sometimes that lot –'

'Do not worry,' said Tostig cheerfully. 'They're all idiots.'

'Don't I know it.'

'But they're loyal idiots. And brave.'

'Yes,' Agnew conceded with a sigh, 'they're all right. They mean well.'

'They will calm down once we get back on land. This crazy sea is enough to give anyone the willies.'

'You're not wrong.'

'So,' said Tostig with a wry grin, 'just how dirty was Ràn?'

26

While we leave Agnew to get back his strength and replenish the bodily fluids drained from him by Ran – eeeuwww, do we really have to dwell on all that sweating and panting and thrust…? No, no we don't. Instead let us take time to consider the gods. This of course is something quite often done by those of a more theological bent, forever musing on what does God want? What's his plan? Why is the world as messed up as it is, etcetera? It doesn't help that there is more than one God or possibly that they are all manifestations of the same being or maybe they are competing entities vying for our devotion. Sheesh, this is making my head hurt.

Anyway, what that means is it's very hard to come up with an answer, as there is no one answer. Maybe if the god or gods just got off the pot and in a big booming voice declared, 'Oi, you lot, I want my prayers to be understood by all. I want you to sing like the evangelists. Stop praying to me five times a day – trust me, that shit gets dull after the second time – and you can all wear what the hell you like, except the Jews – you lot still have to just wear black and white. Why? Because I said so, that's why. Hey, who's the god around here? Now, go do my bidding!' At least we'd all know.

Of course, not everyone cares what the gods want. Those with, let us say, a more megalomaniacal leaning don't really care what the gods want. They pretty much spend their time dreaming about being a god themselves and of what they would do with such power. Strangely, it never seems about feeding the five thousand but rather seeing how much wealth they can steal and how many people they have under their thumb. I guess megalomaniacs, when all is said and done, don't really have that much imagination. A bit like the gods really. However, and to get back on track with our story, if both the theologians and megalomaniacs were to look at Odin right now, they would first off be entirely clear about what was on his mind and what he wanted and secondly may realise that even when you are an all-powerful all-knowing deity, there are still those beneath you who have a habit of mucking it all up and causing you nothing but stress. So, let's put the theologians out of a job and just go and listen to an angry Odin as he berates his godly underlings, and we'll let the megalomaniacs sympathise with Odin's position as they, better than anyone, know how hard it is to get good, competent, loyal staff.

'What do you mean, it's not Hel doing this!' Odin ranted while stomping back and forth angrily. 'There are villages being laid waste and the dead are going straight to Niflheim and we're not getting our cut. That is not part of the deal with Hel. I want her brought before me. I want her on her knees begging my forgiveness. I want my quota BACK!'

Thor, for once keeping his bravado in check, held up a calming hand and said, 'Father, it's not Hel's doing. She's lost her rake.'

'So what? Tell her to go get a new one. The old one will turn up eventually, I'm sure. It will be behind a pile of bones somewhere, or her dog will be using it as a chew stick. It still doesn't give her the right to claim so many souls.'

'No, Father, you're not listening. Someone has taken her rake, stolen it, and is now using it down on Midgard for their own purposes.'

'That's rubbish. No one gets out of Niflheim alive.'

'That's because they're already dead,' said Frey with ill-timed humour.

Odin turned angrily on Frey, poking him with the point of his spear. 'You think this is funny?'

'Well, yes, it sort of is.'

'You think the onset of Ragnarök is funny? Really? Do you?' Odin poked him again, harder, causing Frey to wince.

'No, I didn't mean –'

'No, you never mean anything, do you?'

'That isn't what I –'

'No? Isn't it?'

'No, what I meant is –'

Odin poked him again. 'Go on, what did you mean, Frey? What possible insight could you have about this? Go on, enlighten us with your wisdom.'

Frey, like a rabbit caught in the headlights, stood gawping, unable to respond. The other gods stood around, partly in relief that Odin's anger was aimed at Frey rather than them and partly with perverse pleasure in seeing one of their rivals being torn off a strip. Yes, boys and girls, the gods that make up the numbers beneath the supreme God, whether that be Odin, Jupiter, or a Zeus, all tend to behave like a big corporation's middle management. A mix of sycophants and yes-men ready to stab their fellow managers/gods in the back as they climb that greasy pole to the top. However, it is at times like these, when the guy at the top has lost it a bit, that one of the middlemen needs to step forward, put his neck on the line and tell it like it is to bring everything back to an even keel and allow the company to sort itself out. Today Thor was, uncharacteristically, that middleman.

'Alive or dead, someone has escaped Hel's realm and taken her rake. It's the truth.'

Odin turned angrily on his son. 'How did you come by this information?'

Thor swallowed hard. This was the bit he'd been dreading. 'Loki,' he said quietly.

'What?'

'Loki. Loki told me.'

'Loki?'

'Yes. He said he'd visited Hel and, well, he thought it strange at the time that she didn't have it with her. She always has it with her, but this time it was missing, but he didn't pay it any more attention than that. He only really thought about it when I asked him what Hel was up to. He was adamant it wasn't Hel, because that would be breaking the rules, which she won't do. I think he is quite hurt by his daughter's law-abiding ways. Anyway, he reckons someone else must have stolen it.'

Odin, incandescent, turned the point of his spear towards his son. 'Loki is a snake. He will ruin us all and you expect us to take his word for the trouble we find ourselves in? How do we know this isn't just Loki trying to kick-start Ragnarök early?'

'Because...' Thor started as Odin took a dangerous step forward, spear still pointing directly at Thor's chest, 'because why would he? He loves life too much. He doesn't want Ragnarök any more than we do. He probably wants it less. Loki just wants to drink, gamble and have sex with as many things as he can.'

'Don't you mean have sex with as many women as he can?' chipped in Frey, who had shaken off the headlights.

'No, I mean with as many things as possible – women, men, Ice Giants, goddesses. I think if he came across a good-looking goat, he'd give it a go,' Thor answered honestly.

'He really is a sick and twisted bunny, isn't he?' said Frey.

'You can hardly talk; you're always off shagging,' said Thor, feeling the need to defend his friend.

'Yeah, but only with women.'

'Really?'

'Sure. You know me – I'm a tit man.'

'Well, you're a tit, I'll give you that.'

'Fuck you!'

'Not while there is breath left in my body.'

'Knock it off!' snarled Odin. 'Give me one good reason why I should believe Loki.'

'Because he had no reason to lie.'

'No reason? He always has a reason.'

'Okay, so maybe he does have a reason to lie,' conceded Thor. Well, there was only so much he could do to defend Loki's reputation. Sometimes you just have to accept a friend's shortcomings. 'But in this case I believe him. It wasn't like he had the rake with him when I found him. He wasn't hiding it and he wasn't expecting to see me. He was at a gambling table, fleecing humans, which is more his style than laying waste to village after village.'

'Well...'

'And I asked him for the information, which is what you wanted us to go out and get; he didn't just offer this up. If I hadn't asked him, it wouldn't have crossed his mind. He didn't try and conceal it. He wasn't gloating.'

'He wasn't?'

'No, and we all know he loves to gloat when he's up to something. It's what always gives him away.'

'No gloating?'

'Not even a smirk.'

'FUCK, FUCK, FUCK!' Odin cursed the sky, causing Huginn and Muninn to wheel about their master's head, crowing balefully.

'I thought that would have pleased you, knowing it's not Loki,' said Thor.

Odin threw down his spear in disgust, cursed vehemently as the Asgard skies roiled angrily above, turned towards his gods, who all, bar Thor, took a step backwards, raised his fists as though to strike, teeth gritted in anger, then like a ball bitten by a dog, Odin deflated. His shoulders slumped and he let out a big, anguished sigh. 'If not Loki then who? And why? At least if it were Loki, we'd know how to sort him out. If this is someone else then we have no idea.'

'C'mon, Dad,' said Thor calmly, 'we'll figure it out. We're gods; it's what we do.'

'What if...' Odin said with a catch in his throat, 'what if this is Ragnarök?'

'Then we go down fighting,' replied Thor with steel in his voice.

Odin looked at his son with something akin to pride, which didn't happen all that often, grabbed Thor's shoulder and gave it a paternal squeeze. 'And what of the rest of you?' he asked, turning to the others.

'I've never shirked a fight yet; I'm not going to start now,' said Frey seriously.

'Heimdall?'

'My sword is yours to command, Sire.'

'Týr?'

'Fucking bring it!'

'Forseti?'

Forseti shrugged despondently. 'Like I have a choice. It's pretty much contractual. Count me in.'

'Wow,' said Thor, 'you really are a walking downer, aren't you?'

'I said I'm in, didn't I?'

'Yeah, but for fuck's sake, Forseti, couldn't you at least put some oomph behind it? You know – energy, power, belief, something?'

'Okay, quiet down, the lot of you,' said Odin firmly, once more feeling like he was in control. 'If Hel isn't behind this and neither is Loki then we need to find out who is. Fenrir hasn't devoured the sun, so maybe this isn't Ragnarök, so let's try and keep it that way. Thor, Týr, go and pay the Ice Giants a visit, make sure they aren't up to anything. Forseti, go check the runes, make sure there isn't something in the Ragnarök prophecy I've missed. Heimdall, cast your eyes over Midgard. Find out who has that bloody rake. Well? What are you all standing about for? GO!'

27

Now that Odin has got his rage and fear under control, there is little point spending any further time with him, at least for now. Trust me, it doesn't make for interesting reading when all one can write is reams and reams about impatient pacing, which is pretty much all Odin is doing, and nobody wants to read that. Instead let us refocus our attention on the hero of the piece and see what Agnew and his crew are up to. Hopefully it will be something exciting and maybe a little racy. Or possibly undeniably dangerous, something to get the heart pounding with fear and anxiety. Yeah, that would be... Oh, they're making landfall, in a quiet inlet, up some fjord. Well, okay, maybe something exciting will happen later.

Right then, so what have we got? Typical fjord scenery – crystal-clear water, a small rocky beach. High-sided cliffs flanking both sides, with a flatter snow-covered piece of land running between the beach and the cliffs. There isn't much else to see except a few hardy tufts of vegetation poking out from under the white blanket here and there, which is nice. The men have dragged the ship ashore and have tethered it down, so that isn't going anywhere any time soon, though looking at the battered thing I'm not sure it is up to going anywhere ever again. If that ship were a dog you'd put it down; it would be the kindest thing. Seriously, there are fewer holes in my socks.

The men seemed quite jovial, clearly glad to be back on land and back in Norway even if they were not a hundred percent certain where in Norway they were. They also didn't seem overly perturbed being stood on a barren beach in the middle of winter. With little commotion and just friendly banter, each man was readying themselves for a hike, gathering their gear and packing it in such a way to make it as easy to carry as possible. Only the essential things were being taken: armour, weapons, food. Non-essentials were being left in the ship.

While the men prepared themselves, Agnew, Tostig, and Delling stood off to one side, deep in conversation.

'Do we know what direction Hel's rake is from here?' asked Agnew.

'No,' replied Delling honestly.

'Could we ask Hel?'

'You really want to do that? You know what happened last time.'

'All we need is a direction.'

'Yes, true,' Delling conceded thoughtfully then added gloomily, 'but she's just as likely to send a troll down here to point the way using an arm torn from one of your men.'

'She'd do that?'

'She's a goddess with no sense of humour. What do you think?'

'Sod that,' said Tostig. 'No trolls, no serpents, definitely no Ice giants. Let's just go.'

Agnew scratched his chin, which now sported a few days' growth, which gave him a sort of rough-and-ready look which male models in the twenty-first century tend to have when modelling outdoor gear. If one looks a little closer, beyond the beard and his hair, which is being ruffled gently by the breeze, you can see that Agnew is still not fully recovered from his bedroom tryst with Ràn. There are still black rings beneath his eyes, his cheeks are a little hollow, and occasionally, as he moves he winces as his sore nether regions rub against his clothes. But he no longer looks like the walking dead, which is good.

'Well then,' he said after a moment's contemplation, 'let's head inland and see what we can find.'

With no better suggestion and a shared unwillingness to ask for Hel's guidance, Tostig and Delling simply replied, 'Okay.' A short time later, with Tostig and Agnew at their head, the crew began a hard trudge through the deep snow and into the Norwegian hinterland. The going was hard. The snow was a struggle to wade through, laden down as they were with armour, weapons, and heavy packs. The icy air burned their lungs, and as hardy and fit as they were the going was slow.

'This is going to take us forever,' said Agnew.

Tostig just grunted.

From the beach the land had risen sharply and now they paused, as before them the land became yet more cliffs. Their only option was to turn and follow the line of the fjord. They trudged on, occasionally the path dropping them back to the water's edge before rising again. At no point was there any clear way of heading inland. The third time they were about to be taken back down to the water's side, Tostig pulled them to a halt and gestured for the men to kneel.

'Look, down there,' he said, pointing at yet another beach, this one a little less snow-covered than the rest.

'What?'

'There.'

'There what? What are we looking at?' asked Agnew.

'Ponies.'

'What?'

'Fjord ponies, there.'

Agnew followed the line of Tostig's finger, and sure enough at the far end of the beach a herd of hardy dun-coloured ponies grazed on what little vegetation was available.

'No,' said Agnew, shaking his head vigorously.

'Yes,' said Tostig.

'We can't.'

'I'm not walking any further if we can ride.'

'I am not riding a horse.'

'Agnew, we're hardly moving. On foot we won't catch up with Hel's rake till summer. But those beauties could help us get out of here much faster.'

'No.'

'Yes. We just need to catch them.'

'How will we do that? We are not horsemen.'

'Olsen is; so are Sven and Henrik.'

'This is a bad idea,' argued Agnew. 'We should just press on. We could waste the rest of today trying to catch them.'

'We've got to try. Olsen!' Tostig summoned Olsen to them. 'What do you think?' he asked after he'd pointed out the ponies.

Olsen had a quiet word with Sven and Henrik and after a short conversation hunkered down by Tostig and Agnew. 'We can get them if we get that one,' he said, pointing to a mare with a two-tone mane. 'Rope her; the others will fall into line.'

'You sure?'

'No.'

'No? Well, that's just great.' Agnew huffed.

'Don't listen to him,' said Tostig. 'Can you three rope it?'

'We'll give it a go.'

'Do you need us to do anything?'

'Sit here and be quiet. We'll signal you to come down when we need you.'

Tostig nodded and gestured for the rest of the men, including a grumbling Agnew, to move further away from the lip of the rise overlooking the beach, leaving him to settle back to watch Olsen, Sven, and Henrik do their stuff.

The three men moved with careful purpose, staying downwind of the horses for as long as possible so as not to spook them. When they were within a hundred yards of the herd they split, with Olsen and Henrik looping round to the left, skirting along the tree line which separated the beach from inland, leaving Sven to follow the water's edge.

Much to their amazement, the horses remained calm as Olsen and Henrik drew near. Given the heavy snow and hard going if the horses bolted, they knew they would never catch them. Quietly they crouched behind a fallen tree and readied the ropes they carried. They would probably get one chance at this, and that relied upon Sven launching himself from the water's edge to drive them towards Olsen and Henrik. Time seemed to pause as they watched Sven prepare himself to run out. Olsen cast a final glance towards the herd, noticing some of the horses were showing signs they were aware something wasn't quite right. Some had stopped eating, ears were pricked, some snorted the air. *It's now or never*, thought Olsen. He raised his hand, made sure Sven was ready for his signal and counted down beneath his breath, three, two...

SNAP!

Olsen and Henrik spun around suddenly at the sound from immediately behind them, dropping ropes and instantly reaching for their weapons just as a young girl stepped out of the woods carrying an armful of twigs and branches, singing merrily just as Olsen and Henrik seemed to rear up out of the snow before her. Startled, the girl screamed, dropped her branches and turned to flee back into the trees.

On the opposite side of the horses, Sven, waiting for Olsen's signal, heard the scream. Unsure what had happened, he stood and reached for his axe only to find the now startled horses break and bolt right towards him. Suddenly faced with tons of frightened horseflesh barrelling towards him he turned and stumbled back towards the lake. Unfortunately for Sven, fFjord ponies in full flight are faster than humans. If the ground had been hard and firm, he may just have made it, but through knee-deep snow he didn't stand a chance, and before he could make it to the relative safety of the water he was trampled into the snow as the horses ran over him in their bid to escape from whatever terror had caused the scream.

Up on the small hill Tostig cursed and called for the men to rally to him. Agnew, first to him asked, 'What is it?'

'The horses – they're bolting. C'mon.'

'And do what?'

'Catch them, Agnew. Just catch them.'

Tostig was already turning to run down the hill towards the wheeling horses when Agnew placed a hand upon his shoulder and shook his head, no.

'Agnew, we...'

'Look at them,' said Agnew. 'We'll never catch them now, not through that snow.'

'Fuck, fuck, fuck, fuck!'

'It was a good idea.'

'You hated the idea,' snapped Tostig.

'No, I hate horses, but your idea was good.'

Tostig glowered but said nothing.

'Let's go down and find out what's happened to the others. Draw your weapons,' Agnew commanded and started down the hill cautiously. Behind him his men swung shields off shoulders, hefted a mix of axes, hammers, spears, and swords, following him down to the beach. Of the fjord ponies there was no sign, the ponies having galloped away and around a narrow headland at the far end of the beach.

With Tostig at his side the men formed a raggedy line and waded through the snow. Tostig split away, leading half to where he'd last seen Sven, while Agnew and the rest made their way to Olsen and Henrik. As they got closer it was obvious they had another person with them, who turned out to be a slight girl of no more than ten looking frightened, and if it weren't for the fact Henrik had her held firmly by the back of her shawl she would have fled.

Seeing no obvious threat and judging Olsen's relaxed demeanour, Agnew sheathed his sword and signalled his men to lower their weapons.

'Who's this?' Agnew asked.

'Says her name is Adi,' replied Olsen.

'Hello, Adi, what brings you out here?'

The girl wriggled weakly in Henrik's grip but said nothing.

'If I get Henrik to let go of you, will you promise not to run?'

Adi looked at Agnew then craned her head to look up at Henrik, who glared down at her.

'Well?' Agnew asked and watched Adi take a moment to reflect further on her position. Clearly realising she was trapped, she nodded a reluctant yes. 'Good. Let her go, Henrik.'

Henrik released his grip upon Adi. Agnew, watching her closely, could see that for one mad second she considered running before defeat took over and her shoulders slumped, leaving her stood there staring glumly at her feet.

'That's good, Adi,' said Agnew calmly. 'So what brought you here?'

'I was to feed the horses and collect firewood,' she said, not looking up.

'Just you by yourself? Isn't it dangerous to be out here alone?'

'I wasn't alone. I had the ponies.'

'True,' said Agnew, 'but what if wolves had come, or a bear?'

'I would have run. They wouldn't get all of us.'

'Us?' said Agnew, who look pointedly at Olsen and Henrik.

'There's no one here but the girl, Agnew,' answered Olsen.

Agnew frowned thoughtfully. 'Who do you mean by us, Adi?'

'Me and the ponies.'

'The ponies?'

'I look after them, they look after me – us.' Adi looked up from her feet and stared at Agnew as though he were stupid.

'Well, obviously,' Agnew agreed seriously, 'but where are they now?'

'Don't know.'

'You don't know?'

'Not right now, but they will come back.'

'Will they?'

'Yes, for me.'

'And why will they do that?'

'I will call them, and they will come,' said the girl, puffing herself up importantly.

Agnew looked at Olsen. 'It's possible,' he agreed.

'Okay. So why don't you call them?' said Agnew.

'Won't.'

'Why not?'

'Cos you're here.'

'So?'

'So, I protect them,' said the girl seriously. 'If I call them, you'll hurt them. I won't let you hurt them,' she said, giving Agnew a defiant glare.

'What if I promise you I won't?'

'My mother told me never to trust strange men with swords.'

'Your mother is a wise woman,' Agnew replied sagely, 'but she couldn't have meant us – we're not strange.'

'Then what about that?' Adi said, pointing at Delling.

Without missing a beat Agnew replied, 'It's okay; he's not a man so doesn't count.'

'Oi!' said Delling, but no one was listening to him.

'Mmmmmm,' said Adi, unconvinced.

'He's a dwarf. It's a totally different thing.'

'O-kay,' said Adi thoughtfully, 'but what about that one?' this time pointing at Siggeirr.

Agnew pulled a defeated face, looked at the girl and said honestly, 'Yeah, I'll give you that one. Siggy is strange.'

'Hey!' Siggeirr squeaked indignantly.

'But the rest of us aren't, I promise.'

'Then who are you?'

Agnew had to admire the girl's courage. Even Norse children, when confronted by a band of large heavily armed warriors, would normally shy away from directly questioning such men.

'I'm Agnew,' said Agnew, 'and we are a bit lost, so maybe you could tell us where we are?'

'Lost?'

'Yes. We have crossed the sea and are trying to get home, but we're not sure which way to go.'

'Then why were you after the horses?'

'Well...' began Agnew just as Tostig and the others joined the group.

'Agnew,' said Tostig.

'Just a moment; I'm talking to Adi,' Agnew replied, still on his haunches, looking Adi directly in the eye.

'It's Sven,' said Tostig, not to be put off. 'He's dead.'

'What?' said Agnew, turning to look at Tostig.

'The ponies trampled him. Didn't stand a chance.'

Agnew hung his head, staring hard at the snow beneath him. Feeling his anger rise, he thrust his hands deep in the snow and crunched it hard between his fingers, letting the cold of the snow bite his senses. When it became painful, he let go, pulled his hands free and stood up. Agnew brushed the snow from his knees and dried his hands on his cloak. 'Dig Sven a grave and build a cairn over it.'

'Shouldn't we burn him, send his spirit to the gods?'

'We don't have time,' Agnew answered brusquely. 'It will be night very soon and we need to find shelter. If we stay to build a pyre for Sven then more of us could pass in the night.'

'But he was one of us. He didn't die in battle. He won't get to Valhalla if we don't at least give him a warrior's funeral.'

'If we do that none of us will die a warrior. We will all just freeze to death by the lake, and all this will have been for nothing, as Hel will get us all after all.'

Tostig glared at Agnew, torn between doing right by Sven and the risk to the rest.

'Tostig! Bury Sven... now!' Agnew commanded sternly as the tension grew thick between them.

Tostig opened his mouth to speak, thought better of it and cursed, 'FUCK! FUCK! FUCK! FUCK!'

Agnew stood implacably on as his friend cursed all before him. He waited until Tostig had cursed himself hoarse and just stood breathing hard, then he said firmly, 'Be quick, but do him as good a cairn as you can. The wolves must not have him.'

Tostig, fuming, growled, 'I promise they won't,' and pushing three of the men before him he stomped angrily back through the snow to the trampled corpse that until recently had been Sven.

Grim-faced, Agnew turned back to Adi, who had wisely decided not to move so much as an inch during the tense stand-off between the giant angry Norseman and Agnew. 'Adi, do you live near here?'

The girl nodded.

'How far?'

Adi looked nervously at Agnew and gently shook her head, fear etched in every feature.

Agnew forced his tone to be more conciliatory and said, 'We don't want to hurt anyone in your village. We just need a place to stay for the night. Somewhere out of the cold. Could we stay the night at your village, please?'

'You promise you won't hurt anyone?'

'I promise. We are not here to kill. We just need a place to stay and directions on where to head in the morning. Maybe we can even buy some ponies from you to help us on our way.'

'You'd pay?' the girl asked, clearly not believing a word Agnew was saying. 'You'd just take them. Your sort always just takes them.'

'Adi!' Agnew snapped sharply. 'I swear that if we steal your horses, Hel herself can claim me. I promise we will not just take them.'

The girl looked about her nervously and despite being clearly unconvinced by Agnew's plea said quietly, 'Okay.'

'Thank you.'

'But first I need to get the ponies.'

'Okay.'

'And I need to gather wood. Can you gather wood?'

Agnew smiled, relieved. 'That we can.' Agnew set the rest of his men to gather as much wood as each could carry. 'Will you call the ponies now?'

For the first time since her encounter with the scary men, Adi broke into a wide, toothy grin, put her fingers to her lips and let out a loud piercing whistle, which was answered by the distant rumble of hooves.

28

Given the sheer breadth of locations and characters now involved in Agnew's saga – okay, so when I say breadth, we're hardly talking a Tolkienesque level quest here, but there is still more than one group to keep track of so you will, by now, have got used to the endless skipping from group to group with a frequency akin to a bored teen channel-surfing the TV. But this time we're going to stick with Agnew. The story is about to pick up its pace, so let's not waste time describing the trek from the beach to Adi's village. And yes, while it is true some readers get their kicks from immersing themselves in highly descriptive passages about the flora and fauna through which a story's hero passes, let's be honest – those sort of passages are just there to demonstrate to you, the reader, that the author has done his or her homework and researched every nook and cranny of the world the story inhabits, but does it really add to the story? Does it aid the plot? I shall wait a while; let you ponder the answer.

Okay – time's up pondering and the honest answer is no, no, it really, really doesn't. That is unless you are describing one member of the group hiving off from the main band to take a pee behind a tree. Seriously, the only time anyone ever takes time to describe someone going to the toilet is so something bad can happen to them. It's a tried and tested trope to have a character when literally at their most vulnerable have something large, angry and with more teeth than is strictly necessary spring from the undergrowth and tear the poor unsuspecting urinating person limb from limb, leaving nothing but a forlorn hand holding a severed cock lying in a pool of yellow-and-red stained snow. Fair sends a shiver down your spine, scenes like that – nasty.

Luckily for you, we're not subjecting you to such things, so instead let's re-join Agnew and the rest, okay, not Sven, obviously, he was left buried back on the beach, and not the ones eaten by the serpent a few chapters back, but all the rest have made it to Adi's village... alive.

By now it is dark, in fact it has been dark for some time, which makes you wonder why no one from the village had been sent out to search for Adi and the ponies, but it didn't seem anyone had, and when she turns up no one seems overly surprised. The bunch of heavily armed, angry-looking men she has acquired on the way, by contrast, has raised rather more eyebrows, so much so that on seeing them walking into the village, those few people who were moving about outside all flee from sight.

'Warm welcome,' Delling whispered to Agnew.

'Hardly surprising. We're not a friendly sight.'

'So, what now?'

'We get Adi to take us to the elder or chief or whoever leads here and ask for shelter.'

'Can we make it sooner rather than later? My balls are frozen.'

'Your balls?'

'My legs are a lot shorter than yours,' Delling winced jealously as he tried to rub some life back into his groin, 'and my balls have been dragging through the snow since we landed.'

'From anyone else that would be a boast.' Agnew laughed sarcastically, to which Delling grumbled with displeasure.

'Can you go fetch whoever is in charge?' Agnew asked of Adi, ignoring Delling's discomfort.

The girl nodded and handed the rope rein of the mare she was leading to Olsen. 'Wait here,' she said and skipped off into the heart of the village, leaving the men standing cold and on edge, waiting in the dark.

'I don't like this,' hissed Tostig.

'It'll be fine.'

'No. Something isn't right about this place.'

'That's probably what the villagers are saying about us right now.'

'Don't you feel it?'

'Feel what?'

'Something... unnatural.'

Agnew looked at his friend, concerned. For all his warrior bravura Tostig was quite sensitive to his surroundings, in the same way dogs are, which is why if Tostig said he felt uneasy you didn't take it lightly, just as you wouldn't take it lightly if a dog shoved its tail between its legs and snarled at something unseen in the darkness. Actually, thinking about it, most people do ignore dogs when they do that, bloody idiots. Agnew, bucking the idiot trend, had learned long ago to trust Tostig's instincts, so quietly and with minimum fuss he instructed those nearest to draw their weapons and pass it on. Within seconds Agnew and his men had gone from shivering grumbling men to shivering grimly alert men hefting weapons, which was the sight which greeted Adi when she returned with a small delegation of one old man, one old woman, and a couple of other men in their middle age. Wide-eyed and suddenly afraid Adi wailed, 'You promised you weren't here to hurt anyone.'

'We're not,' replied Agnew.

'Then why are you all holding weapons?' She pointed accusingly.

'Err, we thought we heard… something,' Agnew said weakly, to which Adi gave him a stare which said she didn't believe a word of it. Agnew laughed feebly as he stared at the less-than-threatening delegation. 'I think we were wrong,' he said, turning to face his men. 'Put your weapons away.'

'Agnew?' Tostig warned.

'It's okay; weapons away,' Agnew commanded, so maybe not so wise after all.

The men paused, looking between Agnew and Tostig for some clear sense of direction, gripping their respective swords and axes nervously.

'Tostig.' Agnew stared meaningfully at the axe in Tostig's hand. Tostig gave a worried, almost imperceptible shake of his head to Agnew, who only returned his stare more wide-eyed and meaningful than before, beneath which Tostig crumbled first and lowered his axe. This was greeted by an almost collective breath of relief by Agnew's men, Adi, and her village elders as the tension abated.

'Sorry,' Agnew addressed the elders, 'we've had a bit of a Hel-ish time of late, and we're all a bit...'

The aldermen stepped forward, non-threatening, hands outstretched, palms up. 'Adi tells us you are travellers who are lost. Is this true?'

'It is.'

'Then you must stay here tonight. We will find room for you, provide food and drink. But please tell your men to not worry and put their weapons away. They will be safe here.'

Agnew sheathed his sword and indicated that the rest should do the same. 'Thank you,' he said. 'I am Agnew.'

'You are welcome, Agnew. As are your men. Please, come.' The alderman waved them to follow. 'Adi, stable the horses.'

'Would you like a hand?' Olsen asked Adi as she took the rope from his hand.

'No, I can manage.' Adi pouted. 'Go with the chief.'

Despite Tostig's fears, the night passed without incident. The villagers found places for each man to rest. They were fed, well, sur-prisingly, and Agnew had to wonder if the village had used more of its winter store than was wise to ensure his and his men's hunger were properly satiated. It made sense – better to risk a hard win-ter and some starvation of the weak and infirm than risk a bunch of hungry, angry men killing everyone and taking it all anyway.

The following morning, Agnew held a tense conversation with the village alderman, at the end of which the alderman left Agnew alone to talk in private with Tostig and Delling.

'Can we leave now?' asked Tostig, his eyes darting nervously to the shadows, looking for unspecified treachery.

'Honestly?' said Agnew.

'Yes.'

'Then no.'

'Why not?'

'Because with the winter snows we are probably a couple of weeks' hike away from where we need to be. And that's if we could make it at all. There isn't going to be much in the way of food out there to sustain us.'

'Two weeks? Hel isn't going to like that.' Delling grimaced.

'We're miles away from wherever her rake is. There's no way we're getting there any time soon walking.'

'We have to,' said Delling. 'Hel isn't going to accept excuses.'

'Well, if you have a suggestion as to how we can go faster without you having to wade balls deep through the snow I'd like to hear it.'

Delling's hand went involuntarily to his crotch.

'That's what I thought.'

'I may have a suggestion,' said the village alderman, appearing as if from thin air.

Tostig turned sharply at the sudden reappearance, reaching for his axe, only for Agnew to place a reassuring hand upon his arm. 'You do?'

'We are horse traders. We have horses, the ones you helped Adi bring in yesterday. I can trade you those horses. They will carry you and your men to where you want to go easily and much quicker than you can go by foot.'

'And what price would you ask for enough horses to carry all my men?'

'We require firewood. Fell us enough trees to see us through the hardest months and you will have your horses.'

'Firewood?'

'We are short of young, fit men. Felling a tree at this time of year is hard and dangerous. The forest is full of hungry wolves. But your men are fit, strong and have the weapons to keep wolves at bay.'

'And you will give me the horses I need, for firewood? Just firewood? No coin, no gold?'

'Gold and coin cannot keep you warm. You cannot cook with gold and coin. Gold and coin will not scare off wolves. Wood will, fire will. The winter came early. It has been harsh. Extra wood felled now will help see us through till spring. That is my price.'

'Fair enough. You have a deal.'

'The best trees are just to the south of here. Adi can lead you.'

'There are trees closer; what of those we came through?'

'They are sacred to us. They shield us from the ice which blows in from the fFjord. We leave those alone. Only take from the south.'

'We can do that.'

'Agnew, this is a bad idea. We should leave now,' Tostig pleaded.

Agnew paused. Tostig's fear was infectious and Agnew could feel a shiver of disquiet run through his body. For a second he almost caved and gave the order to pack up and leave, but somewhere in Agnew's mind his practical self grabbed his superstitious self, gave it a kicking and stuffed it away in the dark recesses of his mind, under the stairs behind old books, children's toys, and all those bits of wire, screws, nuts, bolts, and bits of random metal men tend to collect because they may be useful someday but never are.

'It's just firewood, Tostig, that's all they are asking for. Between us all we can get this done quickly. The sooner we get that wood, the sooner we can leave. We won't stay a day longer.'

Tostig grumbled something incoherent but put his own misgivings on hold, realising he wasn't going to win this argument. When Agnew's mind was made up, he wasn't for shifting. Decision made, the three of them got up to gather the others from the various dwellings they had been placed in and head to the forest to gather wood.

In the end, it took the best part of a week of back-breaking hand-blistering tree felling and wood chopping. Only cutting in the places indicated by Adi, Agnew, Tostig, and the rest put their backs into it, and apart from a run-in with a couple of wolves, nothing untoward, save biting cold gnawing at their hands and feet, beset them. On the sixth day, as the sun rose weakly above the horizon, casting long shadows, barely giving out any warmth, they gathered at the village boundary. There, good to their word, the village presented each man with a horse, saddled and harnessed. With mixed success each man mounted his steed. Even Agnew, whose impatience to be back on with the quest outweighed his antipathy towards horses, climbed on, itching to be away.

Adi had led each horse out and carefully selected each one for each rider like it was a solemn ceremony. Finally she brought out the lead mare they'd originally wanted to rein and presented this one to Olsen.

'Are you sure?' he asked. 'Isn't this one the leader of your herd?'

'She is, but another will take her place.'

'Does she have a name?'

'I call her Små Triks.' Adi petted the horse's snout. 'Be careful – this one's devious and will have you off first chance she gets if she doesn't feel respected.'

Olsen patted the mare's flanks. 'I will take good care of her," Said Olsen.

'You promise?' said Adi, giving him a searching look, holding the reins away.

Olsen knelt, bringing him level with Adi. 'I swear I will look after Små Triks as though she belonged to the Valkyries themselves,' he answered solemnly.

Satisfied with his answer, Adi tentatively handed the reins to Olsen and whispered something to the horse Olsen couldn't quite catch. Adi smiled and stated with a conviction which belied her young age, 'She will look after you, Olsen Thormarsson.' It was only later that Olsen would realise he'd never told Adi his last name, and by then it was too late.

In a line two abreast, led out by Agnew with Olsen by his side, the troop filed out of the village and headed south towards the area where they'd cut the trees. Slowly, in pairs, they entered the manmade clearing before plunging into the darkness of the forest proper. It was now, riding at the back of the procession that Tostig craned his neck to look back towards the village from whence they came and for the first time noticed what had been bugging him all along but which he hadn't been able to put his finger on.

'There's no smoke,' he said to himself, as he realised there should have been columns of smoke drifting up into the winter sky from the various hearth fires in the village, but there was nothing. The sky was just a clear, icy blue. 'Agnew, STOP! There's NO SMOKE!' Tostig called out urgently, but it was too late as his horse followed the others, carrying him into the forest.

29

Some people, usually hippies who live in cities and only ever visit those parts of the countryside which have been tamed and managed, like to view nature as a benign and caring thing, when in reality it is cruel, cold, full of sharp teeth and grasping claws riven with blood and death, where the only rule is don't be the small squeaky thing. In the Dark Ages, where more brutal gods, goddesses, and wild spirits held sway, nature wasn't just cruel, it was bloody psychotic, and the forest into which Agnew and his men had just entered was out for blood.

If this were a movie, which it isn't, but if it were then you know the warriors in Agnew's crew, who have never been given a name or talking part, other than an occasional gripe, would now be toast. They are the Star Trek red-shirts, there to die horribly so the main cast can go on. But this is the Dark Ages, full of vengeful gods and creatures which really like to do bad, nasty, painful things to humans, so let's just say before we go any further, don't expect everyone, even those with a name and talking part, to get out of this unscathed. So, sit back, take a sip of your favourite tipple to fortify your nerves, and at the end of this we'll see who made it and who didn't. And just to help you keep score as they enter the forest, the number currently alive, including Agnew, is thirty-seven.

As each man entered the forest, almost immediately the trees seemed to close around them, blocking each from his nearest companion, turning them into just so much shadow moving vaguely along with them. As they travelled deeper, the shadows appeared less frequently, but if pressed they would have sworn the other shadows moving along either in front or just off to the side must have been the rest of the crew, ignoring the obvious fact that they were, in fact, alone. Each man pressed on, following what to them looked like a path of sorts, a path which even the snow had not managed to totally eradicate. Possibly this should have been their first warning, but ignoring the obvious question, 'What made the path?' the fjord ponies carried Agnew's men into the heart of the forest, where the trees became thicker and the foliage turned into nothing but twisted thorn-laden bracken, until each man's path became a thing more of imagined fantasy than something tangible.

Upfront, at least he thought he was upfront, Agnew pulled on the reins of his pony and turned to call a halt and summon all to him to make camp for the night, but looking about him, not a single member of the crew was in sight. Sat atop his pony, scanning all about for signs of his men, all he could see was a wall of shadow and trees. Agnew felt his skin prickle, and the hairs on his arms and the back of his neck stood on end, his pulse suddenly racing. He was alone, exposed, and lost. Through the trees a sharp wind rushed through, cold, biting, and with it, buried within the sound as it whooshed by, he could have sworn he heard a manic laugh. Agnew's hand fell to the hilt of his sword and as the last of the day's rays seemed to melt away he thought, *damn this ain't good*.

It wasn't just Agnew who was having trouble. The entire crew was beginning to experience the forest's malevolence, and it wasn't just unnerving the men; the horses were also becoming skittish. Magnus, a slim, athletic member of Agnew's crew with a bald tattooed skull, crooked teeth, and a generally devil-may-care attitude suddenly found himself no longer sat atop a docile pony but a bucking galloping terrified mare fleeing from some unseen terror. It was all he could do to stay atop the beast. He should have let go and fallen from the animal, for as it charged along a path visible only to itself, it galloped beneath a wicked-looking branch which was in its path. Unfortunately for Magnus atop the pony, the branch was at chest height and point-on, which he hit with enough force to drive it through his sternum leaving him impaled, feet dangling in the air as his pony continued on unscathed as he gurgled his last.

Number left: thirty-six.

Lost, disorientated, unable to see the stars through the tree foliage, Olaf, a hardened sailor, who loved the open spaces of the sea, feeling hemmed in and trapped dismounted his horse, which, as soon as it felt Olaf's weight leave kicked out and trotted off into the night, leaving Olaf stranded. Stood knee-deep in snow, his eyes darting from side to side, trying desperately to pierce the pitch dark of the forest, it was as though the trees were crowding in upon him, forcing him to his knees. Overcome with extreme claustrophobia, Olaf lay down where he was, curled up, eyes screwed shut, hoping to make it to daybreak. Unmoving and uncovered, hypothermia would claim him. Thirty-five.

Lost, alone, but aware that thrashing around a forest in the dark of night was a recipe for disaster, Erik took the time to tie his pony to a tree. Secure in the knowledge his mount wasn't going anywhere, Erik fashioned a torch. With the light from the torch helping him to pierce the gloom he carefully unhitched the horse and led it on foot through the forest, looking for shelter. After what seemed and age, torch burning low, Erik stepped into a clearing. Almost immediately his pony reared, ears flat, hauling against the reins in panic and pulling him over. Erik, unable to stop himself, let go of the reins and could only listen as the horse disappeared back into the forest. Lying face down, Erik pushed up onto his knees then tried to stand, but as he did so his foot slipped from beneath him, causing him to crash back to the ground, dropping the torch as his arms flailed out.

The torch hit the snow and with a sad fizzle went out. Blanketed in darkness, Erik got onto his knees again, hoping his eyes would acclimatise to the gloom but before they had chance, he heard the growl. It sounded close, it sounded large, it sounded hungry. Desperately he reached for his axe, but the troll's club found him first. Unconscious but not dead, over the next few days Erik would wish he'd died under that first blow as the troll proceeded to devour him, limb by limb, before finally getting to his guts and finishing him off. Men left: thirty-four.

A hard man of few words, Dag, fell to wolves. Knott was taken down by a bear which should have been hibernating. Enar's horse stumbled when crossing a fast-flowing stream and punted

Enar off, who bashed his head on a viciously sharp stone and passed out, face down in the stream and drowned. Thirty-one.

Gunther was mobbed by goblins, the only plus side being the goblins used every part of him. He became chops, a stew, and at least one bone was turned into a flute, which would be found a thousand years later and confound archaeologists as to what type of human would make a flute out of a man's femur. Goblins, that's who. Thirty.

The brothers Magnuson would each mistake the other for a monster in the dark as the forest played tricks on them and die on each other's blade. Twenty-eight.

Mortenson would make it out alive, but during his nightmare time he saw many dark and fearsome shapes flitting about, seeming to come right for him. In desperation he would shoot his bow until his quiver was empty. Three of his shipmates would die by his arrows unbeknownst to him. Twenty-five.

Strangely, despite all its malevolent power, the one pairing that the forest hadn't been able to split up was Ogmundr and Siggeirr. They'd ridden side by side into the forest, chatting away, seemingly oblivious to their surroundings. Neither had heard Tostig's anguished call and neither had been paying any attention to Agnew or the rest of their shipmates. So wrapped up were they in their own little world that it took some time before the forest could make its presence felt.

'What happened?' asked Ogmundr. 'How did you escape the smith?'

'Ah that's the best bit,' laughed Siggeirr. 'When he burst in, all man mountain and angry-like, and waving this fucking huge hammer about like it was nothing, I thought, this is it; I was gonna die right there and then. No heroic death on the battlefield for ole Siggy, I thought, just beaten to death while naked and in the bed of the smith's woman. I almost crapped meself.'

'But you're not dead, so...'

'As I said, in he came all fucking angry, looking for blood, when his woman jumped up, naked as the day she was born, covered in nowt but the sweat and juices from our lovemaking, and told him to put the bloody hammer down. Well, I thought for a moment he was going to hit her with it first before he came and used it on me.'

'But?'

'But she walked right up to him, tits jiggling, and grabbed him by his crotch. "Stop mucking about," she told him, "and get your fucking clothes off and join us." And there was me thinking I wasn't sure I was in the mood for that kind of kinky shit...'

'You're always in the mood for that kind of kinky... Siggy, where are the others?' Ogmundr asked, suddenly aware they were alone.

'What?'

'Everyone else – where are they?' he asked, pulling his pony to a halt. He stood up in his stirrups and looked all around, but all he could see was the rapidly darkening forest. 'Shit, we must have wandered off the path.'

'What path?'

'The path the horses were following.'

'The horses were following a path?'

'Of course they were, otherwise how did they know where to go?'

'Dunno. I just thought they followed each other.'

'Horses aren't daft. They don't just wander around blindly.'

Siggeirr took a moment to also check on their surroundings.

'Well?' asked Ogmundr.

'Well, what?'

'Well, what do we do now?'

'Dunno. Why you asking me? Anyways, as I was saying, there I was with the smith's woman and now the great big bastard was stripping off as I lay on his bed, my dick still wet with his –'

'Siggy, not now.'

'But we're just getting to the best bit.'

'It'll have to wait. We need to find the others.'

'Why? They'll be fine. We can find them in the morning.'

'No, we need to find them now!'

'Okay,' Siggeirr replied easily and then at the top of his lungs began to shout, 'ALFARR! AGNEW! TOSTIG!'

'What the fuck are you doing?'

'Calling for them.'

'Are you mad?'

'No – how else do you expect to find them? ALFARR!'

'By the gods, be quiet, or do you want to bring every wolf down upon us?'

'Wolves?'

'Yes.'

'There are wolves?'

'Of course there are wolves,' Ogmundr snapped just as a mournful howling split the night, followed by answering howls seemingly from all around them. 'See?'

Beneath them their mounts began to spin nervously, heads shaking in alarm, but surprisingly both Ogmundr and Siggeirr were comfortable in the saddle and quickly brought them to heel.

'We should go,' said Siggeirr, suddenly serious.

Carefully the pair let the horses wheel to a direction they seemed happiest to go when another noise caught their attention.

'Ogmundr! Siggy!'

'Did you hear that?'

'Um...'

'Ogmundr! Siggy! Is that you?'

'Is that...?'

'Alfarr. Yes, I think it –'

'Ogmundr! Siggy! HELP!'

This time there was no mistaking Alfarr's voice or the terror in it. Ignoring the wolves' howling they turned their horses once more and headed towards their friend's cries. Kicking and cajoling their steeds forward they made for the sounds of a struggle, which were becoming clearer by the second. Like Erik before them, Ogmundr and Siggeirr broke into a clearing to find a nightmarish scene unfolding before them. Bathed in nothing but moonlight, Alfarr, down on one knee, an arrow shaft protruding from his right shoulder, brandished his shield and axe. His horse lay dead or dying by his feet as three dark shapes sat atop giant wolves circled him.

With a blood-curdling howl two of the wolves and their riders launched themselves at Alfarr, who parried the first sword blow with his shield and lashed out painfully with his axe at the second of his tormentors, only to scream in pain as the second wolf rider's blade severed his axe hand at the wrist.

The third rider, who'd been holding back slightly, raised its bow and took aim at the floundering Norseman. Just as its fingers released the string to send the arrow on its way, there was a soft whirring noise as an axe tumbled head-over-shaft to strike the bowman in the chest, sending it falling backwards off its wolf, the arrow which was to finish Alfarr shooting harmlessly up into the air. The wolf, unsettled by having its rider fall from it, failed to react as an angry Siggeirr pounded across the clearing with his other axe in hand and leapt mightily to bring it crunching down on the wolf's skull. The wolf squealed hideously as it collapsed beneath Siggeirr's blow, which he followed up with two more.

Ogmundr had also charged into the fray with a little more caution but no less intent and faced off against the two other wolf riders. Grimly he set himself behind his shield and hefted his axe.

With a shriek of anger, the two riders spun their wolves to face him and charged, dark curved blades raised to strike. As they closed the short distance Ogmundr threw himself forward, placing his shield on the ground and rolling over it shoulder first to move his line of attack to the flank of the wolf on the left. Unable to change its direction, Ogmundr rolled back up to his feet and with a determined swing buried the blade into the side of the beast, sending it crashing to the floor, upending its rider. Before the rider could regain its footing, Ogmundr was upon it, bringing the edge of his shield down on the back of its neck. The rider hissed in pain and desperately rolled over to try and stab up at Ogmundr with its sword, only to get Ogmundr's axe in its face.

Seeing its two companions slain, the last of the wolf riders fled from the clearing, leaving Ogmundr and Siggeirr to cautiously make their way to Alfarr, who, knelt in the snow, was cradling his mangled wrist in his good hand.

'Thanks, lads. I knew you'd come.' He breathed raggedly.

Neither said anything, but Ogmundr carefully took stock of Alfarr's wound. 'We need a fire,' he said.

'What? No!' said Alfarr, wide-eyed.

'We have to seal the wound.'

'No, not fire.'

'Siggy, get the fire going.'

Siggeirr did as he was told as Alfarr fearfully watched flames spring into life and Siggeirr hold the blade of a dagger in the flames. 'It's ready,' Siggeirr declared once the blade glowed red hot.

'Alfarr, hold out your wrist,' commanded Ogmundr.

'No.'

'Alfarr.'

'I'd rather die.'

Siggeirr nodded to Ogmundr, who moved sharply around Alfarr, gripping him in a bear hug and holding him steady so he couldn't move. Siggeirr grabbed Alfarr's injured arm and before Alfarr could resist placed the burning blade against his wound. The forest was suddenly filled with the smell of cooking meat and a pained scream from Alfarr, followed by a cooling hiss as Siggy forced Alfarr's burnt wrist into the snow.

Ogmundr felt his friend go limp in his arms as Alfarr passed out. Carefully he laid him down. Siggeirr inspected the arrow in Alfarr's shoulder. Luckily his armour had stopped it piercing his flesh, though it was clear Alfarr was going to have a hell of a bruise the next day. Siggeirr removed the offending item.

'Well,' said Ogmundr, 'Alfarr finally got to battle his dark elves after all.' He pointed at the dead creature on the other side of the fire.

'Bet he wishes he hadn't. So, anyway, before I was interrupted,' said Siggeirr as between them they hefted Alfarr across the back of one of their horses, 'there I was with the smith's wife, only now the smith was stood there staring at me with this raging boner and...'

Still twenty-five.

Of all the Norsemen who had entered the forest, only Tostig had realised something was amiss. Admittedly Ogmundr and Siggeirr had been too ignorant of their surroundings to realise anything was up at all, but the rest, as we have seen, had been having problems. Tostig, immediately on entering the forest, had dismounted from his pony, hefted his axe and walked steadily forward, prepared for whatever madness the forest was going to throw at him. As a child, his mother had told him tales of changelings, enchanted forests, and of all the mad, bad, and evil things which lived therein. Tostig was ready to face whatever came out of the dark to get him – be it a troll, ogre, or wood nymph, it was going to feel the bite of his axe.

Maybe it was because he was ready. Maybe it was because he was aware he was in a magical realm which was just waiting to have a go that nothing did. Maybe the forest realised it was being watched too closely by the big Norseman and so felt less inclined to attack. Besides, what tree doesn't fear an axe the size of Tostig's? Whatever the reason, come the morning after a long, cold, hard trek Tostig exited the forest, tired but unscathed, and there he waited for others to arrive.

Twenty-five.

Agnew had, on hearing the manic laugh, stomped about the forest trying to find his men, though the more he searched, the more distant became their voices until alone and disoriented he stood next to his horse, utterly lost and angry. Angry with himself that he'd failed his men, angry that he'd been lumbered with a horse when he absolutely hated horses and anything to do with riding, and angry that yet again it seemed Hel was happy to let him struggle on when she could have just plonked him and the crew down somewhere near where they needed to be. Ever since they'd found themselves back in the land of the living it had seemed they were having to go through extraordinary efforts to get anywhere, and that was just bloody infuriating. And then there was that manic laugh. Well, whoever was doing that could bloody well stop right now.

'Show yourself, you cowardly bastard!' he called out into the forest. 'Come on, be a man and face me!'

'What makes you think I'm a man?' whispered a voice right behind his ear. Agnew spun around sharply but no one was there. 'What you going to do, Agnew?' the voice whispered again.

'How d'you know my name?' he shouted as he turned again. Still no one was present. 'Delling, if that's you...'

'Leave the dwarf out of it,' said the voice.

'Screw you.'

'I don't think so; you're not my type,' the voice whispered again, only this time when Agnew turned, he was confronted by a silver-haired woman clothed in wolf pelts and leather, carrying a bow and a quiver of silver-flighted arrows upon her back.

Agnew, who was starting to become an old hand at this, let out a discontented sigh and said, 'Oh, for f... so, which goddess are you?'

The goddess nodded appreciatively. 'You're smart. I can see why Hel chose you.'

'You know, you look sort of familiar.'

'Do I?'

'Yes. You remind me of...' Agnew rubbed his chin thoughtfully. 'Adi? You're like a grown-up Adi... aaaaaaaaah – bollocks!'

The goddess laughed warmly. 'So you are smarter than you look, Agnew, son of Grimor the Furious.'

'Adi, short for Skadi?'

The goddess bowed.

'Just tell me what you want.'

'What makes you think I want anything?'

'Because so far every goddess I have met has wanted something, so what do you want?'

'I want you to stop.'

'Stop what?'

'Your quest.'

'Why?'

'You don't need to know why.'

'Then I cannot stop. I made a deal with Hel, and she's scarier than you, so I think I'll just keep going.'

'You dare to defy me?'

'Yes,' Agnew answered honestly. 'Yes, I do.'

The goddess's face hardened, and her voice cooled. 'Call off your quest, and you and your men can leave the forest alive.'

'Or?'

'Or you don't leave it alive – your choice.'

'Do your worst, Skadi,' Agnew growled, his anger getting in the way of common sense. He was angry and tired of being the gods' plaything. It was about time they saw he wasn't someone they could just toy with.

Skadi, in one languid movement, slid the bow from her shoulder and knocked an arrow, drawing the bowstring back, her thumb resting lightly aside her chin. 'Give me your word to quit this quest or die here, now!'

Agnew stiffened but stared the goddess in the eye. 'Best shoot me now. I'm not quitting.'

'So be it,' said the goddess just as a short barrel-shaped figure came crashing out of the undergrowth.

'NOOOOOOOOOOOOOOOOOO!' yelled Delling as he slipped and fell unceremoniously at the goddess's feet. 'You can't shoot him, Skadi. This one is owned by Hel.'

'You dare tell me what I can and cannot do, dwarf?'

'Yes, Miss... I mean, no, Miss... I mean... ah, damn it. You just can't. You know the rules.'

Skadi regarded Delling with open hostility.

'Don't do it, Miss. Do you really want to go to war with Hel?'

'I do not care for your cursed mistress, dwarf.'

'Nor she you, but I ask again, do you really want a battle between you and her?'

Skadi continued to sight down the arrow at Agnew's chest.

'Skadi!'

The goddess let out an angry screech, easing the pressure on the bow, lowering the arrow's point. Agnew let out a breath of relief but said nothing, leaving instead Hel's minion and loyal dwarf to fight his corner against the goddess of the hunt.

'You know it makes sense, Miss. Let him go.'

The goddess knelt in the snow to look Delling in the eye. 'Okay, dwarf, I won't touch a hair on his head, but I cannot speak for the forest. It is angry and answers to no goddess, even yours.'

'Understood.'

'Farewell, Agnew, son of Grimor the Furious. Hopefully we shall never meet again.'

'Suits me,' said Agnew, though the goddess had already gone. 'How does she do that?'

'Do what?' asked Delling nervously.

'The whole disappearing thing. It's very clever.'

'She's a goddess; they have powers beyond your mortal ken.'

'Guess so.'

'We have to go,' said Delling urgently.

'But my men?'

'They're on their own. They'll either make it or they won't, but if we don't get going, we certainly won't.'

'Okay, but which way is out?'

'That way.' The dwarf pointed into the darkest deepest recesses of the forest.

'You sure?'

'Yes.'

'How do you know that for sure?'

'I just do.'

'But how?'

'I'm magic. I'm not from Midgard, and I shouldn't even be here, but here I am. So, are you going to stand there and argue about whether I know my stuff or are you going to trust me?'

Agnew looked down at Delling and saw in the dwarf a sense of urgency which was hard to ignore. 'Okay, lead on.'

Delling set his shoulders, paused as he steadied his nerves. He really, really didn't like forests, any forests, especially magically psychotic ones, but with no other choice he led Agnew deeper in. After what would feel like a night which lasted days and not a single night, Delling would lead the pair of them plus horses unscathed from the clutches of the wooded monster.

Slowly, over the course of the day, those who had made it would all arrive at a similar point, where they would gather and tell tales of their encounters. Alfarr was in a bad way. The crew's berserk Thom arrived naked, skin a lacerated mess and gibbering incoherently. Johansson would crawl out, minus his horse, his mind a shattered wreck which would take time to recover. Finally, of Olsen there was no sign. He would not re-join the crew.

Final number: twenty-four.

30

While Agnew's men take a moment to mourn their dead, let's jump back to the hall of King Gudrød, who wasn't having a good time. Every day, news was leaking back to Gudrød of how village after village within his kingdom was coming down with plague, a curse which was always preceded by an ultimatum issued by Asa of 'join her or die'. It seemed no one had been taking her curse seriously, but even in winter bad news travels fast, and it wouldn't be long before villages currently loyal to him would start to fold and turn themselves over to Asa if it was a choice between that or plague.

It is at times like these when being king isn't a position to crave. Gudrød's man, Egil, had been right when he'd said that to march on Asa at this time of year would be suicide and better to let her expend the energy coming to them, but as king he could hardly let his villages fall to Asa without answer. A sensible king is one thing but a weak indecisive one is no king at all. Feeling his hand was being forced, Gudrød decided to do what most Norse kings would do at a time like this – consult the gods. Yeah, it may seem silly to us in our enlightened times but back then the gods were seen as the key to everything. And how does one consult the gods? Well, you drag in your nearest sage, priest, wise woman, or whatever unsavoury unwashed creature which dwells in the woods living off berries, carrion, and the occasional fricassee rat and demand they divulge what the gods want you to know. It's the equivalent of a modern government calling in their intelligence services to brief them with relevant information, information which, sadly even today, is about as reliable as the woodland nutter spitting on the bones he's just chucked in a bowl and declaring that the gods want you to slaughter a goat and have sex with its carcass. Crazy but true.

This is why we are now inside a dark, smoky hall as Gudrød and his men watch a strange, wizened creature, wearing what looks like a coat of badly stitched-together otters, prancing about the room, muttering incomprehensibly and occasionally sneaking meat from a warrior's plate. Hey, even nut-job sages need to grab the chance of a good meal when they can, before throwing the bones into a bowl – see, told you – and spitting on them. After moaning for a bit, rubbing his chin, and casually waving his cock in the face of the younger prettier maids, so maybe not mad more just a pervert, he made his announcement.

'Gudrød, you must march on Asa!'

'This is Odin's will?' Gudrød enquired, wanting to be in no doubt.

'Odin demands it.'

'Then it is settled. In three dawns' time we march. Egil, get the men ready.'

'Gudrød, are you sure?'

'Are you questioning me?'

'No, but –'

'Or perhaps you question Odin?'

'Perhaps I do. This is madness.'

'And who set you above Odin?'

'How do we know this is what Odin wants?'

'You've seen the bones. You've seen the signs.'

'No, I've seen a crazy old man waving his cock in the air, which does not mean he is Odin's messenger.'

'Enough! Odin has spoken. Who are we to refuse the Allfather's call to arms? If it's blood in battle he wants, it is blood in battle we shall give.'

All about them the hall erupted into wild chants and the banging of horns, knives, and anything vaguely hard and bashy on the wooden tables as the men rallied to their king's war cry. Only Egil stayed silent, feeling a sense of unease grip his soul.

'We march in three days,' Gudrød declared.

Despite his misgivings, Egil answered firmly, 'Yes, my King.'

Three days later, based on nothing more than dodgy advice from his intelligence service – sorry, I mean wise old seer – and the need to be seen to be doing something, Gudrød led his army off in the direction of Kaupangen. Word had been sent by carrier birds to his vassal villages along the way, ensuring that as he progressed his war-band would be swelled with more fighting men.

Gudrød, it has to be said, wasn't the first leader to act on dubious information or be driven by a need to react to his opponent's actions, nor would he be the last. History is littered with kings, emperors, dictators, generals, and politicians who have made similar bad decisions based on dodgy dossiers and a desire to get stuck in. Harald Godwinson took his Saxon army, tired and depleted from its recent battle at Stamford Bridge to face William Duke of Normandy at Hastings. He could have waited. He could have taken the time to amass more warriors and let those recently returned from battle get their strength back. He didn't, and William Duke of Normandy beat him and became King William I of England, known as the Conqueror as a result.

Or what about Guy of Lusignan, King of the Crusader State of Jerusalem, who ignored sensible counsel and instead let himself be guided by those with personal scores to settle into marching out into the desert to find and battle Saladin? Dehydrated from marching beneath a summer desert sun in full armour they were massacred by the fresh, well-watered troops of Saladin, which helped end the Crusader presence in the Holy Land. And who could forget the many failed invasions by the Daleks, who never bothered to find out if the Doctor was about first? Bad information and impatience are not a warlord's friend, and what else isn't a warlord's friend is winter, which Gudrød was also having to combat. All in all, his decision to march on Asa was looking ever more stupid with every passing snow drift.

In the summer, Gudrød could have expected to have marched his men to Kaupangen in four days, and if he wanted them fully fighting fit maybe take a day extra so as not to push them. In the depths of a Nordic winter, with the temperatures in the minus twenties, four days was looking like turning into twelve and even that was proving hard. There were very good reasons why armies didn't campaign in the winter.

None of this was helping Gudrød's mood. Also not helping was that as they got closer to Asa, fewer and fewer fighting men joined them from the villages on the way. It seemed word had already got out about what happened to those who refused Asa's ultimatum and the men had chosen to join her instead. Gudrød may have been a nasty piece of work, but he wasn't a complete idiot, and he was coming round to Egil's viewpoint that this wasn't going to end well. Yet each night he got his sage to implore the gods for favourable signs and each night the gods gave him cause to go on.

Ten weary days in, the men, cold and wet, hunkered down at yet another village. This one had provided no fighting men. It was a place caught between the threat of plague and having their angry king demanding fighting men it could not provide. The sense of fear here was thick. The only thing saving the village from Gudrød's wrath was that he was too tired to give in to petty feelings and violent retribution. Instead he settled for eating and drinking anything the villagers could put before him.

That night, as with every night so far on this horror march, Gudrød and his Jarls sat in a cramped hall as the sage theatrically implored the gods for another sign. The man whirled, cursed, spat, a lot, and finally chucking his bones into a bowl, he took a dagger off Gudrød, held up his own hand and sliced his palm, letting his blood fall into the dish. With yet more spit he stuck his fingers in the mess and swirled it about before grabbing the bowl and holding it aloft.

'Well?' demanded Gudrød.

'The gods promise you shall be victorious.'

'You're sure?'

'Do you doubt the gods? For doubt can make them angry. They're capricious and can take away their good will in a heartbeat.' The sage cackled for dramatic effect.

'No, I do not doubt the gods. Odin be PRAISED!' Gudrød held his drinking horn high, his men joining his toast to Odin, downing honey mead as one. All, that is, except Egil, who was determined to keep a clear head.

The evening passed into night, and one by one Gudrød and his tired warriors passed out either from drink, exhaustion, or both. Egil also looked to all the world to have succumbed to slumber, but as the hall torches burned low, he kept a watchful eye on Gudrød's sage. Finally, and desperately fighting back his own need for sleep he saw the sage stand and make for the outdoors. No longer stooped and wizened, the sage stood tall and moved lightly and with speed. Egil gave him a moment to exit the hall before he too stood, grabbed his sword and carefully picked his way past the sleeping men strewn about the floor and stepped into the bitter cold of the night. Snow was falling and visibility was almost non-existent, but just ahead a flame flickered and danced as it moved through the village. Egil followed as best he could, safe in the knowledge that as he hadn't brought a torch he wouldn't been seen.

The sage moved through the blizzard with impressive speed, leaving the village behind. It was all Egil could do to keep sight of the torch's flame. A few times he'd felt he'd lost the trail, only to catch a sudden glimpse of a faint glow away in the distance. Doubling his efforts, Egil pushed on, trying to keep up.

Beneath him Egil could feel the ground rising. A little way further he followed the torch light into forest, where at least the snow abated. The closely packed trees made it almost impossible to keep the sage's light in sight, yet every now and then he caught just enough of a glimpse to keep on, never catching up until, with his lungs burning and his legs feeling leaden from the effort, the flickering light suddenly grew closer. The sage was finally slowing, allowing Egil to close the gap. With a last push he came to the edge of the forest, which thinned out as it neared the top of a hill, with the ground beginning to slope down again. Some hundred yards ahead Egil could make out the sage who'd stopped and seemed to be waiting for something.

Carefully Egil left the cover of the trees and as quietly as possible edged forward, hoping to see or hear what the sage was up to. Unfortunately, the snow had ceased falling and the wind had dropped, leaving him dangerously exposed out on the snow-covered hillside, the light of a waning moon occasionally breaking through the clouds, illuminating him with a weak silvery glow. Despite this the sage failed to spot Egil stalking closer. When fifty yards or so from his quarry, he was sure he could hear more than just the one voice and straining his eyes could make out another figure. Egil gripped his sword and made to stride forward to confront the sage and whomever he was in talks with, convinced it would be a spy for Asa.

'I have you now, spy,' Egil announced accusingly, drawing near. The sage turned to look at him. Worryingly for Egil, he didn't seem at all surprised to see him. The sinking feeling of unease he'd felt back in Gudrød's hall before they had set out on this mad escapade hit him again. Something was very, very wrong. It was then that he saw the woman as she stepped out from behind the sage. She had silver hair and was wrapped in hunting furs. She raised her bow, knocking an arrow and let it fly. It flew straight and true, taking Egil full in the throat, pitching him backwards.

Shocked by the sudden violence wrought upon him, Egil lay on the snow staining red with his blood, desperately trying to catch a breath but only able to manage a bubbling gurgle from his ruptured throat.

'Who is he?' Egil heard the woman ask.

'Gudrød's right hand.'

'You were careless. What if others had followed?'

'None have. This is the only bright one amongst them.'

'Shame,' replied the woman, 'he would have been the only one worth sparing.'

'Bit late for that now,' replied the sage.

Vision dimming, lungs filling with blood, drowning Egil where he lay, the last thing he heard was the woman declare, 'At least this one will have passage to Valhalla.' Coughing his last, Egil died happy.

31

We've been spending time of late with human and God, who haven't been in the best of spirits. Not that this is surprising given the Norse propensity, in both human and God, for a gloomy outlook on life. If you don't believe me, watch any Scandi thriller and you'll see what I mean. It's all washed-out colours and staring moodily into the middle distance waiting for something bad to happen. Really gets you down. It is therefore time for a change, something a little more upbeat and cheerier, and where shall we find such levity, I hear you ask? Unbelievably with Asa and Guthrun Doombringer. Who'd have thought?

The first thing to notice is that despite the heavy winter weather the mood in Kaupangen is quite cheery. Sure, once the sun goes down, at approximately three p.m. in the afternoon, the tales of things that go GRRRRR, ROAWR, and EEE EEE EEEE in the night drag them back to their more typically superstitious selves but while the sun is, I was going to say up but that's maybe pushing it a bit, so let's just go with lurking above the horizon, everyone is happy. Asa is feeling good – you can almost hear Nina Simone playing in the background. Yes, Asa has got over the recent assassination attempt. She no longer feels violated and belittled but strong and powerful, and that's making her feel sexy, because let's face it, when you're feeling good, you look good, because make no mistake, confidence is attractive.

Even now after a tumultuous night with a stable hand and one of her serving maids, both who were still in her bed, she was sat at a table, wrapped in a single fur pelt with bed hair, puffy eyes, and some dubious crusty bits on her upper thigh, and still all the men gathered about her were thinking, *oh yeah, I so would*. Asa for her part was completely aware of the affect she was having on the men and was both flattered and dismayed at how obvious and easy they were. But more than anything she was feeling in command, for despite their lustful thoughts, each man was treating her with the deference and respect she expected as their queen. Rewarding as that was, it wasn't why she was out of her bed. The reason for that was because a snow-covered scout, shivering by the open fire, his wet clothes steaming as he heated up, had news.

'You say Gudrød is just two villages away?' Asa requested confirmation.

'Yes.'

'He's really marched his men to us, now, at this time of year?'

'Yes. I watched as his army entered Brekka.'

Asa's smile could have lit up the room by itself. 'I have you now, you bastard.'

The men surrounding her, feeding off her excitement and itching for the distraction of battle, all suggested they march on Brekka and face Gudrød immediately. Asa, impatient for victory and to see Gudrød's head parted from his shoulders, all but jumped up to give the order to march there and then, when a strong voice hushed them.

'No,' said Guthrun, who till now had remained quiet.

'What? Why? We have them.'

'So why rush?'

Asa looked at him suspiciously. 'Are you afraid?'

'No.'

'Then why not face Gudrød now and finish him while he is weak and tired? Or are you secretly allied to him?' Asa stared accusingly.

Guthrun paused, not rising to the sleight, and for a moment wondered why he, of all people, should counsel caution when he was still Guthrun the Berserk. He didn't know what caution was. He'd been known to run into battle naked and weapon-less. To be fair, that had almost got him killed, the livid scar across his abdomen a constant reminder that sometimes one can be brave to the point of idiocy.

'Well?' Asa pressed.

'Let him march another day. He'll find naught at his next stop but death and pestilence. We've laid waste to the last place he can make camp before facing us.'

239

'I don't want him to die of pestilence. I want him to die with a sword through the gut and my dagger lopping off his cock.'

'He won't die of pestilence; the curse has lifted. But the village is still full of the dead, rats, and rotting food. He'll find no comfort or sustenance there. It will make for a depressing night before battle for him and his men. Some will no doubt desert. His numbers will dwindle. All will sleep badly. Come the morning they will be in such a rush to be away from the cursed place they'll leave without proper preparation, tired, weak, and already with the mark of death upon them. You'll be able to smell their fear as they approach. The only thing to ask is, do you want to kill him or do you want to make him suffer? Do you want to humiliate him?'

'Humiliate him. Shame him. Break him. I want him to cower before me.'

Guthrun grinned evilly. 'Then this is what we'll do...'

By the end of the war council all had fallen in behind Guthrun's plan. Satisfied all was in order, he left the others to drink and carouse and headed back to the house commandeered as his own. Despite being of better mood of late, drink still had no effect on him and he only partook for the look of the thing and to build a bond with the men. Women held only a little more interest. He could still admire an attractive woman, but despite his best efforts to reconnect with the living world, since that night in the witch's cave, physically he still felt nothing. He could get hard but there was no feeling in his cock. He could pound away for hours, much to the discomfort of the woman beneath him, but feel only the smallest of delights and certainly nothing to bring the sex to a successful conclusion. Knowing this after a few fruitless unfulfilled tries, he'd steered clear of sex. The only thing which gave him any real pleasure was planning Asa's war strategy and upcoming battles. Working out the tactics, risks, and logistics got his mind firing in ways he'd never imagined before his first death. With his mind awash with all the possible outcomes and options, over the past weeks, to the casual observer Guthrun had become less intense, less aggressive, less dangerous, which is probably why, as he neared his place, four armoured men stepped out of the lengthening shadows to surround him.

'Are you the Doombringer?' the one in front asked.

Guthrun stopped and took a moment to consider the man before him and those around him. The speaker was tall, not particularly heavily built but long-limbed. Braided hair fell from a top knot upon an otherwise bald head, and grey piercing eyes looked out from a face which had just enough scars to declare this wasn't a man who shirked a fight. The other three were of mixed heights and builds, but all had the stance of men accustomed to battle.

'Who wants to know?'

'It's him,' declared the one standing immediately behind him. 'He carries the rake.'

'What, this thing?' Guthrun said amiably as he casually reached over his shoulder to release the binding which held the rake in place on the specially made baldric he had fashioned to carry it.

As he flicked the rake lightly between his hands, two of the men took uneasy steps back, but Grey Eyes in front stayed resolutely still.

'You do not deny you're the Doombringer?'

'Why should I? I've killed many to earn the title.' Guthrun smiled, though there was no warmth in it.

'Bastard!' the one behind spat and took a step forward, shifting the grip on his axe, ready for striking.

Guthrun twirled the rake and widened his stance and with a contemptuous sigh said, 'Do what you have to.'

The man behind made to attack first with a clumsy lunge forward, axe swinging to strike Guthrun in the small of the back only to be met by the haft tip of Hel's rake in the throat. Coughing and struggling for breath, the warrior staggered away. Before the others could react, Guthrun adjusted his grip and swept the rake around low and fast, catching the man to his right on the back of the knees, dropping him with a pained yelp. Letting go of the rake's head, Guthrun spun it one-handed to grip it like a spear and jabbed the rake's metal tip savagely into the fallen man's right eye, which exploded with a squishy popping sound. With an agonised scream the fallen Norseman rolled away, clutching his ruined eye.

Guthrun, with the rake shaft gripped once again in both hands, stood poised and ready to strike the next unfortunate to step within its range, beckoned to his two remaining opponents. If he'd expected Grey Eyes or the other to have fled at this point, he was mistaken. In fact, Grey Eyes merely smiled, and Guthrun recognised a fellow warrior relishing the fight. Guthrun grinned and waited for the onslaught. The fight was savage. Grey Eyes was experienced, moved forcefully and with purpose, was skilled with the axe he wielded. The other man was also skilled, not given to over-committing, waiting for the right moment to strike, usually when Guthrun's attention was given over to the flight of Grey Eyes' axe. Guthrun used the rake to parry blow after blow, carefully using its momentum to keep the others just far enough away that their weapons repeatedly missed their mark. Moving smoothly despite the icy conditions beneath his feet, Guthrun kept both men in front of him. Even so, he was having to concede ground. Even with Hel's rake in his hands he didn't think it would save him from an axe to the head.

Despite being nothing more than a glorified piece of gardening equipment, Hel's rake was still a warrior goddess' piece of gardening equipment and was beautifully balanced and as good as any quarterstaff, which in the hands of a fighter with Guthrun's prowess was devastating. Yet skilled as he was the rake could not, in a fight, contend with two well-managed axes, and he felt himself losing the fight. It was surely only a matter of time before one would land a telling blow. Guthrun was trying to edge closer to one of the many houses, to give himself something to put his back to and avoid being outflanked, but each time he tried to move the fight to where he wanted, one of the others would ensure that his route was blocked, and only a desperate dodge on his part avoided him receiving a mortal blow.

Sensing Guthrun was on the back foot, Grey Eyes pushed forward, forcefully chopping down with a strike aimed at splitting Guthrun's head in two. Guthrun raised the rake's shaft above his head, only just stopping the axe's downward trajectory in time, catching it in the angle between the haft and head. Guthrun shifted his weight, stepping back, hauling the rake with him as he went, dragging the hooked axe forward and with a twist forced the axe down, causing Grey Eyes to stumble forward into a vicious headbutt to the crown of his nose. Grey Eyes staggered back under the impact, giving Guthrun the chance to release the pressure on the axe head and swipe the haft round with all his might into the side of Grey Eyes' chin, breaking his jaw. Swinging wildly, Grey Eyes stumbled backwards, howling in pain, the whirling axe preventing Guthrun getting in a killing blow, but so intent was he on Grey Eyes, he'd lost concentration on his other opponent, who, seeing his chance came in from the side with a killing blow, or at least it would have been if he hadn't pulled up suddenly with a scream before toppling forward with a spear in his back.

Guthrun paused, unsure of what was happening when two axes whirled out of the gloom to crunch with deadly accuracy into the back of the still staggering Grey Eyes, who slumped to his knees, pain, anger, and shock all encompassed in a split second in those eyes before he keeled over, dead.

A bunch of men swarmed out of the night to circle Guthrun protectively while others made sure all Guthrun's antagonists were dead. The lead man Guthrun recognised as Bjarke, which in Norse meant bear, and to look at him, he couldn't have been more aptly named, given he was a huge, hulking, heavily bearded brute of a man.

'Are you okay?' Bjarke asked with genuine concern.

Guthrun, a bit taken aback by the question, simply nodded.

'That is good. Halvor thought he had seen you being followed and so thought it wise to fetch us. It looks like he was right.'

Guthrun looked to Halvor, who tapped his chest with his axe when he saw Guthrun looking at him.

'Are there any more out there?' asked Bjarke.

Finding his voice, Guthrun replied, 'No. It was just these. Who are they?'

'They arrived in Kaupangen a week or so back. They said they were from Tønsberg.'

'Why would men from Tønsberg come for me?'

'Perhaps Gudrød sent them to kill you?'

'Perhaps,' Guthrun conceded, 'but something about this felt more...' Guthrun searched for the word, 'personal.'

'Whatever; they did not succeed.' Bjarke slapped Guthrun heartily on the back, grinning happily. 'Anyone else wishes to try we will kill them also.'

'I'm in your debt,' Guthrun said solemnly, 'to you all.'

'Brothers do not owe debts.' Bjarke waved away Guthrun's gratitude. 'Come, let's drink. These can be thrown to the beasts in the morning.'

It had been a long time since anyone had called Guthrun brother. Surprised, he realised he'd missed that type of camaraderie. With all thoughts of sleep gone, Guthrun holstered the rake and joined his newfound brotherhood as they traipsed back to the drinking hall, leaving the corpses of Grey Eyes and his men to stiffen in the cold night air.

32

I think we can best sum up what we have witnessed of late as being Guthrun finally finding some sense of comradeship, Gudrød and his men being put through the ringer, and we've spent time with the gods, some who have been surly, some panicky, and at least a couple up to something dodgy, so pretty much normal behaviour for a Dark Age Norse Tuesday. It would seem only right and proper then that we turn our attention back to the hero of our tale, the man of the hour, the front-cover hunk, the most stylish Viking as voted for in the 813 A.D. edition runes of Trondheim. Yes, we're back with Agnew.

Throughout this quest we have seen Agnew miffed, angry, and bloody furious, and it is that constant fire of anger which drives him forward, confident of pulling off Hel's task through little more than belligerent bloody-mindedness. Sadly, the loss of so many of his crew to what the surviving members are calling, quite unimaginatively, 'the Cursed Forest' has knocked the spark out of him. It's as though Agnew's anger has been quenched, replaced with nothing but numbness. This is most evident when you consider Agnew's crew are sat upon snowy rocks, cold, shivering but not willing to move, a dangerous stupor wrapping itself about them. Normally we'd find Agnew dragging his men to their feet, cajoling them forwards towards the end of the quest, where glory and honour awaits, like a true rip-roaring hero of old. Instead, we find him sitting on a rock, staring morosely back at the cursed forest. Worrying times indeed.

A little way away, Tostig, Agnew's long-standing friend, right-hand man, warrior, and occasional magic mischief diviner, stood next to Hel's minion, the dwarf, Delling, watching Agnew with mounting concern.

'I've never seen him like this,' Tostig confided, worried.

'What, never?'

'No. I've never seen him... beat.'

'That's bad. Seriously bad. Hel won't take kindly to him giving up.'

'She won't?'

'She's Hel. What do you think?'

Tostig looked at the dwarf despairingly. 'Then what do you suggest?'

'Could you lead?' asked Delling seriously. 'You know, if he can't, or won't.'

'Not while Agnew breathes.'

'Don't balls this up because of some misplaced loyalty to Agnew. Hel won't care who leads so long as someone does. Take up the mantle.'

'Mantle?'

'Okay, the crown.'

'There is no crown. He's not a king.'

'Well, whatever it takes to lead, pick it up and lead.'

'I cannot.'

'Why? Agnew is just sat there doing nothing.' Delling threw his hands up hopelessly. 'Take charge, damn it!'

'I cannot, not while Agnew still breathes.'

'Okay, so, you know...'

'No.'

'You have to.'

'I won't.'

'Tostig, you know what needs to be done.' Delling cocked his head meaningfully towards Tostig's axe and then at the sitting Agnew.

Tostig looked at the dwarf with contempt. 'I am no murderer, dwarf. I fight with honour; I will not just kill my leader.'

'Why not? You killed the chief of the Celts' village without a moment's hesitation. Where was the honour in that?'

'He had already been vanquished on the field of battle.'

'He was an unarmed prisoner.'

'That was different.'

'How was that any different?'

'He was not one of us.'

'But we can't wait here, waiting for Agnew to become Agnew.'

246

'We can and we will.'

'Even if it means you all die?'

'Even that, yes.'

'By Odin's beard, you're all mad. His inaction is leading you to your doom.'

'We go when Agnew says we go.'

'And nothing will shift you?'

'No, not after the forest. We will not separate again.'

'Bloody Skadi!' Delling cursed.

'What?'

'Nothing.'

'Can't Hel do anything?' asked Tostig.

'I'd say we're in enough trouble already. Let's not go... then again...' Delling paused, staring into the middle distance, lips pursed, a look of deep concentration upon his face.

'What are you thinking?'

'Um, what?'

'You went silent.'

'Did I?'

'Yes.'

'Oh, well, that doesn't matter. What does matter is that I know what to do.'

'You do?'

'Yes, I just need to... well, you don't need to know what I need to do; best you don't know.'

'Are you calling up something else which will eat us?' Tostig asked suspiciously.

'No, nothing like that, but, well, just leave me to it. I will return.'

'Return? Where are you going?'

'Back in there.' Delling turned and pointed at the cursed forest.

'Are you mad?'

'No, maybe, yes, but I am a dwarf, and trees do not frighten me,' he lied.

'There is dark magic at work in there.' Tostig shuddered as he stared back at the brooding forest.

'Yes, and it will be mine.' Delling smiled grimly.

Tostig looked at the dwarf, who seemed suddenly to radiate confidence.

'I'll be back.'

'And what do we do till then?'

'See that wood down there?' Delling pointed at a small clump of fir trees about half a mile away. 'Get the men there. I will join you later.'

'And how do I get the men there?'

Exasperated, Delling snapped, 'Do I have to think of everything? Work it out. Be the big, scary Norseman you are.'

Tostig continued to eye the dwarf with suspicion. 'If you mean to trick us, dwarf, I will –'

'Yeah, yeah, I know, you'll track me down and split me head to groin with your axe.'

'And feed your gizzards to the crows.'

'Well, at least something will get a meal.'

Tostig grunted then relented. 'Do you need someone to go with you?'

'Yes. Agnew.'

'What? Why?'

'I just do.'

'He won't follow you in there. Look at him.'

Delling took a moment to take stock of the subdued Agnew, shrugged and said, 'We'll see,' and left an utterly bewildered Tostig behind as he made his way to stand in front of Agnew. 'I need you to come with me,' he said.

Agnew looked up at Delling but without really seeing him.

'Agnew, get up,' the dwarf tried again.

'Huh?' Agnew grunted, a faraway look in his eyes.

'Agnew!' Delling said again. Agnew remained unresponsive. Delling gave him a ringing slap across the face. 'Agnew! Move!'

The crew saw the slap, which they greeted with a collective gasp. To a man they expected Agnew to strike Delling down where he stood, but Agnew just rubbed his cheek and said, 'Go away.'

'Agnew,' Delling looked him squarely in the eye, 'I need you to come with me. We need to talk to Hel.'

'Why? What good will that do?'

'She needs to know of Skadi's part in this.'

'Hel, Skadi, like I care. They can fight whatever this is out between themselves. I'm done.'

'You're quitting? Hel will be displeased.'

'Then let her be displeased. I've had it with her, Skadi, and the rest. We shall be a toy for the gods no more.'

'That is dangerous talk, Agnew. The gods do not like to be ignored.'

'Well, fuck 'em.'

'You think you're the first human to be a god's plaything?'

'No, but if any speak to me like that again it will be the last thing they do, as I will take my axe and –'

'Oh, not you as well. Yeah, yeah, I know – axe, split, gizzards, all very theatrical. What are gizzards anyway?'

Agnew stared at Delling blankly.

'Gizzards – I asked what they were.'

'Does it matter?'

'I am sure it matters to whoever's you are hacking out with an axe.'

Agnew refused to bite and simply turned away from the dwarf, who was having none of it, stepping around the boulder upon which Agnew was sat to continue the conversation. 'We must go, Agnew. You have to go.'

'Give me one bloody good reason why.'

'You made a deal with the goddess of the dead; did you think that would be easy?'

'No.'

'Do you think she gives a damn about you or your men?'

'Of course not, but –'

'Do you think any of us really matter to the gods?'

'Not any more, but –'

'There is no but.' Delling shut Agnew down coldly. 'They only care about themselves and their own petty arguments with each other. They're children, admittedly very powerful children, but still children. All Hel wants is her rake back. She let you live so she can get it back; that's it. Not because she likes you, not because she admires you, certainly not because she thought you were worth saving. You're just a tool to her.'

'If this is meant to be making me feel better, it's not working.'

'I'm not here to make you feel better. I'm just being honest, so you understand your place in the pecking order.'

'Really?'

'Aye. You're nothing but a goddess' tool to be used however she sees fit. Your only reason for being is to get that rake. Nothing else matters. Fail to get it and she will react in the only way an overly powerful child knows – with petulant fury, which she will take out on you and your remaining men. If you care about your crew, if you want to give them the fighting chance they deserve, come with me, now!'

Agnew glared daggers at Delling, who, to his credit, didn't back down from Agnew's steely-eyed death stare. 'If I go with you, what then?'

'I'm not sure, but I think, maybe, I can get Hel to play dirty for once.'

'And all I need do is come with you?'

'Yes.'

'Back in there.' Agnew stared fearfully at the forest.

'Yes.'

'Fuck,' Agnew swore, dejected.

'Agnew...'

Agnew, still staring at the forest, blew out his cheeks, pushed his hands through his hair and surrendered to his fate. 'Okay, I get it. Just don't expect me to like it.' Agnew grimaced, standing stiffly. He brushed the snow from his legs and rubbed his hands to generate some feeling back in his fingers. 'Do the others have to follow us back in... there?'

'No, it will just be me and you. I have tasked Tostig to get the men to shelter. We'll join them later.'

Agnew spent a moment taking in the sorry state of his crew, wounded physically and mentally, tired, cold, hungry, and with all the fight beaten out of them. Only Tostig, cajoling them to their feet, displayed any of their bravado.

'Do you see them, Agnew?'

'Yes.'

'That's how you look.'

'Seriously?'

'Yes.'

'But they look defeated.'

'Yes. Is that how you want this quest to end for them? Beaten by a forest?'

'No.'

'Then find your fight, Agnew, and come with me, now.'

'But the men, they'll –'

'They'll be fine. Tostig will look after them. Come, Agnew, it is time.' Delling turned his back on Agnew and began making for the Cursed Forest.

Further away and out of earshot, Tostig watched Delling turn away from Agnew and stride, well, more like plough, through the snow back towards the forest. Moments later, a reluctant Agnew squared his shoulders and followed in his wake. Tostig was unsure if this was a good or bad thing but decided it wasn't his problem. His problem was persuading the surviving crew to follow him into yet another forest. Firstly, he had to contend with the crew watching their leader going back into the place of devilment. Already he could hear the wild speculation.

'Where's Agnew going?'

'He's going back in?'

'Is he mad?'

'Nah, he must be looking for the others.'

'He won't find them – they're dead.'

'You don't know that.'

'That place is cursed; it wants us dead.'

'Can't be that bad if Agnew is going back in.'

'We'll not see him again. The forest won't let him escape again.'

'ENOUGH!' Tostig bellowed. All eyes turned to him. Suddenly the centre of attention, Tostig's mind went blank, wondering what to do next. For a moment it looked like he was about to lose their attention, then Siggeirr opened his mouth, which triggered an immediate response in Tostig, who shut him down instantly. 'Say nothing, Siggy.'

'I was just –'

'You were just nothing. All of you, to your feet, now!'

'Why?' Siggeirr challenged.

'Because I say so.'

'You're not our leader. He's just gone back in there.'

'Shut it, Siggeirr.'

'But Agnew?'

'Agnew and Delling are going to...' Tostig froze. He had no idea what they were doing, but he rallied, as all good number twos throughout history have done and simply ignored the question, and merely using implied knowledge of the leader's mind he retorted, 'Why am I telling you anything? You do not need to know. All you need to do is what Agnew ordered and that is to move to that wood.' Tostig pointed. 'Agnew and the dwarf will meet us there later.'

'Why not stay here?'

'Because you'll freeze. Is that how you want to meet the All-father, as ice, not worthy of anything other than something to cool his beer?'

'Fuck no.'

'Screw that.'

'No fffff-ing way.'

Tostig held up his hand, silencing the crew. 'Then get off your fat arses and shift to the wood.'

'I can't go,' a voice weak and wobbly with pain said quietly.

'Who said that?'

'I did,' said Alfarr.

The crew turned to their ship builder who, sat upon the cold, hard ground, back against a snow-covered rock, pallid, sweating, cradled his tattered wrist.

'We're not leaving you.'

'I can't make it.'

'Yes, you can.'

'No,' Alfarr smiled weakly, 'the wound, it is poisoned. I feel the poison working its way through me. I am done. Just leave me a blade and I will finish the job so that I may at least ascend to Valhalla.'

'Valhalla be damned. I swore I would get you to that wood and so I will.'

'You can't save me, Tostig. I can't walk. Leave me.'

'I will carry you if needs be.'

'No,' chipped in Ogmundr. 'Me and Siggy will carry him.'

'We will?' questioned Siggeirr.

'Yes.'

'Okay.' Siggeirr shrugged compliantly.

'No!' Alfarr protested. 'Leave me.'

'We didn't pull you out of that forest for you to just die here,' Ogmundr responded sharply. 'I can sort the poison once we get to the wood. So we're taking you.'

'How?' Tostig asked. He was beginning to think Alfarr may be right, given the hue of his skin and his short rasping breaths.

'Easy – we'll pick him up and carry him.'

'No, how will you save him?'

'Oh, I see. I can concoct a compound of leek and garlic.'

'What?'

'Garlic and leek, boiled with wine in a copper pan; it draws out the poison and helps dull the pain. Works wonders.'

Tostig shook his head sadly and said, 'Ogmundr, we would if we could, but we don't have any of that stuff with us. We won't find leek or garlic at this time of year. The ground is dead. As we will be if we don't move now. So, all of you get going, and I will honour our brave brother by sending him to the golden halls myself.' Tostig laid a reassuring hand on Alfarr's shoulder as he pulled his axe free with his other.

'Thank you.' Alfarr smiled gratefully.

'But I have leek and garlic,' Ogmundr said, rummaging through his pack, 'and some salt, some pepper, bit of honey. All good for wounds. Alfarr, I can fix this.'

'How have you got all that?' Tostig asked suspiciously.

'Why wouldn't I?'

'I said to only take the essentials when we left the ship.'

'These are essential.'

'How is any of that essential?'

'If we catch a boar or a deer you will want something to season the meat and bring out the flavour.'

'The flavour?'

'And the leeks add a nice touch on the side, boiled in wine – it's lovely. And you can always coat the meat with honey to give it a lovely sweetness. Tell me that isn't essential...' Ogmundr tailed off as he realised everyone was looking at him like he was talking a different language, or in the case of Siggeirr, positively salivating.

'When the fuck were you going to tell us you had that stuff?'

'Or share it?'

'Were you keeping that to yourself?'

'You have wine? Where did you get wine?'

The accusations came thick and fast, which, to Ogmundr's credit, he answered calmly and honestly. 'When we caught something to cook. Of course I would share it. When have I ever kept anything to myself? The village, of course. They had loads, so I filled a couple of skins with wine. Didn't you?'

The others could only answer, 'Um, err, well...' and things along those lines until Tostig cut to the point. 'So, you can make a poultice?'

'Of course.'

'Then why are we still talking? Grab Alfarr and let's go. Sorry, Alfarr, there will be no Valhalla for you today.'

'You bastards! Aaaaaaaarrrrrgggggghhhhh!' Alfarr cried out in pain as Ogmundr and Siggeirr hauled him to his feet.

'Don't be such a girl.' Siggeirr laughed. 'We're not letting you off so easily.'

'Fuck you!'

'You should be so lucky.'

And so, slowly, the remaining crew got themselves together and followed Tostig to the wood, dragging a cursing Alfarr with them.

33

For now, we can leave Tostig and the others behind. Don't worry, they will make it to the wood, though by the time they get there Alfarr will have passed out from the pain, not to mention from the fever which is burning through him. Well, what did you expect? He's had his hand lopped off and the stump burned to seal it. The wound wasn't even washed. God knows what bacteria they've sealed into his mangled wrist. Needless to say, poultice or no, Alfarr is about to have a bad time of it. But as I say, they will all make it to the wood, where they will set up camp and await Agnew's return. So, rather than watching a bunch of unwashed, weary, wounded, and generally knackered Norsemen and their remaining ponies resting in some wood, let's instead follow Agnew following Delling into the cursed forest.

To begin with, all seems fine. Delling doesn't even pause at the forest edge but plunges straight in, apparently oblivious to the whispering of angry things lurking in the gloom. Agnew, who, let's be honest, is doing this more out of shamed resignation than any burning desire to enter the cursed place, follows behind but with a feeling of dread settling upon him which gets heavier with each passing step until no more than twenty steps in, he halts.

'We have to go on,' Delling stated bluntly.

Agnew heard Delling's words and knew them to be true, but his feet were having none of it and he remained rooted to the spot.

'Agnew, we must go on.'

'Yes, go, sure. Let's go then.'

'You're not moving.'

'What?'

'You are stood still.'

'No, I'm fine, promise. We'll just, you know, keep going till you say stop.'

'Okay then. Let's go.' Delling turned and made to move deeper into the trees. He didn't get far before he stopped and turned to see Agnew still in the exact same spot. 'Well?'

'Well, what?'

'Are you coming?'

'Yes,' Agnew answered.

'So...'

Agnew looked at the dwarf, looked at the trees, looked to his feet, which were still where they'd been the moment he'd stopped walking. 'Shit.'

'Agnew?'

'Shit, fuck, shit, bollocks, fuck!' Agnew cursed but still did not move. 'Why can't I move?'

Delling, frowning, trudged back to the frozen Viking. 'Are you okay?'

'No.'

'What's wrong?'

'I can't move.'

'Your mouth's moving.'

'I mean my legs. My legs won't move. I want to move but they are not obeying. Why is that?' Agnew looked to the dwarf, clearly stressed.

'How do you feel?'

'Cold.'

'No, not how do you feel, but how do you feel?'

'I told you, cold.'

'You're not...' Delling took a deep breath, smiled patiently and said, 'I mean, how do you –'

'If you say feel I'm going to hit you.'

'Good, that's what I mean – are you feeling angry, furious, tired, what? And don't say cold.'

'I feel... I feel...'

'Yes?'

'Hot.'

'What?'

'No not hot; sweaty. And I can't catch my breath. My chest feels tight, and my fucking feet won't fucking move.'

Delling placed a comradely hand upon Agnew's wrist. 'Relax, Agnew, it's normal.'

'There is nothing normal about this place,' Agnew replied, casting furtive glances to his left and right.

'I mean you feel scared, and this forest is cursed, so that's normal.'

'I'm not scared,' Agnew snapped.

'No, of course you're not, just rooted to the spot for no bloody reason.'

'NO, I'm not scared. I'm... I'm terrified.' As soon as he'd uttered his confession of terror, a wave of shame washed over him and he slowly folded at the knees till he was knelt in the snow before Delling. 'What's become of me?'

'Err...'

'I'm not fit to be called a warrior. I'm not fit to be considered for the hall of fallen heroes. I am naught but a frightened child. No, not even that – a child would run away. I cannot even bring myself to do that. I disgust myself,' Agnew cried. 'End me, Delling. End me now. It's all I deserve.'

'Fuck. Agnew, it's not real.'

'My shame is. The All-father will turn his gaze from me.'

'I think that happened the moment you threw your lot in with Hel, but –'

'I'm not worthy. I'm a coward and deserve to die. Finish me,' Agnew implored bleakly, slowly getting to his feet, arms spread wide, a willing target for Delling's axe.

'Agnew, it's Skadi's dread. It's magical, not real. It's something Skadi puts on forests occasionally. Fight it; fight the feeling.'

'No, I need to die. I need to be cut away. I'm not fit to still be – Uuuuuuugh! Why did... you... do...' Agnew slowly crumpled back to his knees, hands cupping his testicles, where Delling had punched him.

A few minutes went by as Agnew lay prone on the ground, fighting the fire in his groin and the feeling of sickness which sat high in his gullet. Slowly the pain ebbed away, though the feeling of sickness did not. Slowly Agnew regained his feet. Bent over, hands on his knees he panted, trying to get the sickness under control.

'Better?' asked Delling.

'No, my balls are on fire, you little shit.'

'But do you still feel terrified?'

'No. I feel sick, and as soon as I can stand properly, I'm coming over there to... no, wait, the terror...'

'Yes?'

'It's... it's gone.'

'Yeah, a punch to the happy sacks usually works.'

'You've done this before?'

'Well, no, not as such, but it's well known that Skadi's influence only works if it gets hold. But if it does then it's all you can think of and then you're screwed. But kick a man in the balls and suddenly that pain is all he can think of – spell broken. Works like a charm.'

'You could have warned me.'

'What, and miss the fun?' Delling gave a twisted little laugh. 'But if you're quite done maybe we can get going now.'

Agnew spat on the floor, stood upright, took a deep breath of the cold winter air and shook himself like a wet dog. 'Okay,' he huffed. 'Let's do this,' he said with some of his old vigour, the feeling of dread which had plagued him dropping away like a discarded toy.

'About time. Well, don't just stand there; follow me,' Delling ordered and set off again, only this time Agnew kept up. As they travelled into the ever-thickening forest, Agnew got a sense it was trying to split him and Delling up, but now the lingering ache in his groin seemed to make him immune to whatever dark magic was prevalent in the forest. Eventually Delling led them into a ravine, where at its end a waterfall cascaded into a clear, icy pool from the cliff face above.

Ordering Agnew to collect some wood and to build fires in places he marked out, Delling set about preparing himself for the ritual to come. Agnew followed Delling's instructions and soon had fires blazing where directed. Once all were lit, they formed a protective ring between them and the forest and leaving a clear path to the pool. Satisfied all was ready, Delling pulled some rune stones from his pocket and began to chant. With the runes held aloft he cast them from him towards the water's edge. Agnew watched quietly as Delling paced about like an agitated animal cooped up against its will, chanting in the strange arcane language which had summoned the Midgard Serpent upon them weeks before. Agnew could feel the hairs on the back of his neck rise and his skin grow itchy as the air became charged with power, so thick he swore he could taste it. Transfixed, he saw Delling slice his own hand upon his axe blade and, moving to where each rune had landed when he had tossed them at the start of the ritual, allowed his blood to fall upon the ground.

The dwarf, moving jerkily, twisted and spun, approaching the pool. Now oblivious to all but the words swirling in his head and issuing forth from his mouth, he reached the water's edge and held his hand aloft, allowing his blood to drip into the water. Holding his axe in his other hand, Delling used it to cut intricate swirls in the surface of the pool, still chanting, still bleeding. Although Agnew did not understand the words, he could feel power emanate from Delling with each utterance. As the chanting grew louder, Agnew felt the charged air grow colder until his breath was forming ice clouds before him. Beyond the fires Agnew could see the trees turning brown, shedding pine needles at a great rate as though death were running its fingers through the very foliage.

Delling's voice grew louder and stronger, the rhythm of the chant hitting a constant beat. Finally, when it seemed he could chant no louder, Delling raised his axe above his head and brought it down upon the pool as though he were trying to slice the very water in two. There was a loud crack as the water in the pool flash-froze around his axe head then spread with icy blue tendrils across the water until all was frozen solid. Even the water plume where it hit the pool caught the freeze. The waterfall suddenly turned into a solid blue crystal rod.

Delling, breathing heavily, gripped the axe with both hands, shoulders rippling. He heaved it from where it was stuck in the surface of the pool, leaving behind a slim scar. For a moment nothing happened, then the ice cracked apart along the scar and with a terrible rendering a deep fissure formed across the pool, out of which stepped the goddess of the Underworld.

'This had better be good,' grumbled Hel. 'You know, I was in the middle of... oh, hello, Agnew, I hadn't expected to see you here.' Hel almost smiled on seeing Agnew. Delling, tired, sweaty, and spent, looking at his mistress would have sworn she twiddled her hair slightly.

'Hel,' Agnew said, barely acknowledging the goddess.

'Mistress, I need you to know –' began Delling, panting, but Hel completely ignored him.

'How do you fare, Agnew?'

Did she just blush? thought Delling. *No, surely not. No, hang on, she just flicked her hair... did she... oh, by the smiths of Niflheim, she just did.*

'I am... quite well,' Agnew responded, 'in part thanks to your servant, Delling.'

'Really?'

'Yes. I doubt I would have made it from this forest if not for Delling,' Agnew answered honestly.

'Is this true, Delling?' Hel pulled her attention away from Agnew to focus upon her servant. Delling, unused to praise of any sort, mumbled something self-deprecating into his beard. 'I thank you for your loyal service, Delling.'

'Thank you, Mistress.'

'Now, why did you summon me?'

Delling decided honesty was the best policy and just poured it all out. 'Skadi lured Agnew and his men here and demanded Agnew cease his quest for you.'

'What?'

'Skadi, Mistress, she wants Agnew to stop. She was all for killing him when he refused her request.'

Hel once again looked to Agnew. This time Delling was sure she blushed. He also noticed her hand fly to her throat in a clumsy feigned attempt at looking shocked and vulnerable. 'You did that for me?'

Agnew also was struggling to gauge this new seemingly more approachable Hel and wasn't sure he liked it. 'I gave you my word. I will serve you in this quest or die trying.'

Yeah, right, you weren't saying that a little while ago, thought the dwarf but kept that thought to himself. Hel however seemed totally entranced by Agnew's pledge and stepping forward touched Agnew's arm with a smile Delling was sure she thought was playful but which was strangely twisted and terrifying, as though the idea of playful was something she'd heard about but never tried and had totally missed the point of. If Delling was having problems with this, Agnew was doing his best not to recoil in horror. He was sure the goddess was flirting with him, but it was quite possibly the scariest thing he'd ever seen, and how does one rebuff a flirty goddess, especially the Goddess of Death? Agnew smiled weakly and was rewarded by a rictus grin, which Hel thought was charming but made Agnew's skin crawl.

Sensing Agnew's unease, not least of all because it mirrored his own, Delling tried to get Hel to refocus on the situation with Skadi. 'Mistress, if Skadi is working against us, against you, what would you have us do?'

Hel continued to smile at Agnew, ignoring Delling, until the dwarf's incessant questioning broke her concentration. Angrily she asked, 'Did Skadi say why she wanted you to stop?'

'No,' said Agnew.

'Is it not fair to assume,' said Delling, 'that if Skadi is blocking us, Mistress, she may be aiding those with your rake?'

'It is possible,' Hel conceded frostily.

'Agnew and his men suffered greatly at her hand, or at least at this forest's. Is there nothing we can do to level things up?'

'What do you suggest, Delling?'

'The rake imbues the holder with immunity from death.'

'It does what?' Agnew looked alarmed.

'So how do we expect Agnew to retrieve it, especially if the holder also has Skadi's protection?' Delling ignored Agnew.

'Hang on; no one told me about this.'

'Sssh, Agnew. Delling and I are talking.' Hel brushed aside Agnew's concerns.

'But...?'

'Ignore him, Delling. Go on.'

'Mistress, we need aid, something to counter the power of your rake.'

'What do you suggest?'

'My cousin, Eskil, he makes weapons and armour. Ask him to bring Seethe.'

'Seethe?'

'Have Eskil present it to you, then curse it, Mistress. Then return to us and gift it to Agnew – he will need it.'

'You want me to have a cursed sword?' Agnew's voice quavered.

'No.'

'Well, that's all right then.' Agnew huffed.

'It's far worse than a mere sword.'

'What?'

'Consider it done, Delling.' Hel ignored Agnew's protestations.

'Thank you, Mistress.'

'I don't want a cursed... cursed whatever it is.'

'Trust me, Agnew, you're going to need it,' Delling replied darkly.

'But I...'

Hel stepped forward and placed a cold hand upon Agnew with something approaching tenderness, though she couldn't disguise the icy touch of death which seeped through Agnew's clothes and armour, which he bravely withstood. 'You are questing for me, Agnew. Despite what you may think of me, unlike some of my fellow gods I do not forsake those loyal to me. You have earned an honoured place in my realm, you and all your men. I know that isn't what you want to hear. I know you will all want Valhalla, but should that be denied any of you, I will give you a place where your heroism will not go unrewarded.'

Agnew wasn't sure if that was a good thing or a bad thing, or maybe just a useful thing, but he was nothing if not open to new ideas. The possibility of a fall-back plan, even in death, was not to be sniffed at. 'You do me a great honour, Hel.' Agnew thanked the goddess of the Underworld sincerely. 'We will get your rake back or die in the attempt.'

'The dead are wearisome,' Hel replied dismissively. 'I'd rather you live and burn brightly, at least for a few years yet. Get the rake; don't die.'

'O-kay?'

'Good, then that is settled. Delling, take this.' Hel handed a rune to the dwarf. 'Return to the others. Set the rune; it will do the rest.'

'Yes, mistress.' Delling bowed solemnly.

Hel twiddled her hair, which was the one part of her which radiated genuine life and allure in the same way Lily Munster's raven hair, with its silver streak, throbbed with the sex appeal of life and death intertwined. 'I have chosen well,' she said, more to herself than to her servant and champion, who watched her step back onto the frozen pool and down into the open fissure, which closed over her, leaving them stood alone in a dark, foreboding, cursed forest.

'You know, I was rather hoping she would have just magicked us back to the others,' said Delling, disappointed.

'She can do that?'

'Yes.'

'Then why didn't she?'

'I think she forgets that she can. Also, she has no concept of distance. She is death; she is everywhere. Moving about isn't really an issue for her.'

'Then, what now?' asked Agnew.

'Um, well, we go back.'

'Okay.'

'Through the forest.'

'Okay.'

'Which is starting to feel angrier by the moment and I think is out for blood.'

'Really? Whose?'

'Ours.'

'Oh. Seriously?'

'Can't you feel it?' the dwarf asked nervously.

Agnew stopped and tried to shake the disturbing notion that Hel had been flirting with him, and sure enough, as he banished Hel's hair-twiddling from his mind, he felt the sense of dread lurking in the dark shadows of the forest, which seemed to be growing closer as each fire started to burn out. 'That's not good.'

'No.'

'You're not going to punch me in the balls again, are you?'

'Do I have to?'

'No, I'm good, but let's go.'

'Great, never did like forests anyway. Give me a good solid cave any day.'

'You dwarves really are strange, aren't you?'

'What makes you say that?'

'Caves are dark, damp, cold places, unless you light a fire, in which case they become shadowy, smoky places where you struggle to breathe. Also, they tend to be home to bears, and they don't like to share.'

'Clearly you've never been to a dwarf cave.'

'Let me guess – more smoke and endless noise of hammers bashing on anvils.'

'When did you visit my mum?'

Agnew and Delling's voices began to fade into the distance as they disappeared back into the forest, the dread failing to get a hold, much to the anger of a goddess in silver furs, who watched them coldly from the darkness. Despite her anger, she chose not to follow but to let them go. She didn't need a confrontation with Hel right now; that was a distraction which could wait for another time. With other things on her mind, Skadi changed form and loped off back into the forest, a silver she-wolf, on the prowl. If she'd been paying attention, she may have noticed the god of mischief who'd been watching her, watching them. Grinning broadly, Loki waited till everyone had gone. Unlike Skadi, Loki checked no one was watching him then sauntered off, whistling merrily while thinking proudly, *I didn't know you had it in you, daughter*

34

Maybe we should have stayed with Loki for a while, if for no other reason than that interesting things tend to happen around him, which he would claim is just coincidence, but if this sorry tale has taught us anything, nothing happens by coincidence. However, much more seems to be happening to Agnew and his crew right now, so it would seem silly to step away from them just now. Look, no one is paying us for this so we can do what we damn well like. Get used to it. So, if you are sitting comfortably, maybe with your favourite drink in hand, possibly sat by a roaring fire, let's take in the view.

It's dark. Mind you, it's winter in Norway so it's pretty much dark for ninety percent of the day. However, this night is particularly dark. The moon, such as it is, has been obscured by thick cloud for hours; it's like it can't be bothered. There is sleet in the air, not much but enough to obscure visibility, clogging up the sky as it does. Even the snow upon the ground, with little light to reflect from it, is grey and uninviting. Again, it's a Norse winter, of course the sky is foreboding, it can't help itself. If you could ask it what it is doing it would tell you it's boding; it's kinda what I do.

Despite the oppressive dark there is a pinprick of light, more a flicker, in the distance, partially hidden by trees clustered tight together, but even they cannot hide the warm glow of a fire entirely. Moving closer, maybe staying up in the trees, next to the owl, if you look down you will find Agnew and his men. It is a couple of days after his and Delling's foray into the cursed forest, and they really haven't progressed any further. What has progressed further is Alfarr's sickness. The fever has taken hold proper, his skin is ashen, his eyes sunken, lips blue, and he is mumbling incessant nonsense in the throes of his physical decline.

'Will he make it?' asked Agnew.

'I've done all I can. It's in the hands of the gods now,' Ogmundr replied bitterly.

Agnew felt like saying that if it was down to the gods then Alfarr was screwed, but that didn't seem helpful, so he didn't.

'Maybe we should bleed him again,' suggested Siggeirr.

'What is it with you and wanting to bleed him?' snapped Ogmundr. 'It didn't help the first time, or the second, or the tenth time you tried it. It's just making him weaker. No more bleeding.'

'But my old man always used to say –'

'Siggy, your father said lots of things, all of them nonsense,' said Agnew. 'I think we should spare Alfarr any more of your father's wisdom.' Before Siggeirr could come to his father's defence Agnew asked, 'Anyone else got any ideas?'

'Put a sword in his hand and let us dispatch him,' said Tostig.

'No.'

'But we would be sending him to Valhalla.'

'No.'

'He'll like it.'

'I'm sure he would, but I'd rather keep him alive.'

'Why? He's suffering.'

'I know but...'

'We should ease his passage to the next life, to wenches and fighting and mead and more wenches and more mead and fighting and, and –'

'More wenches?'

'Yeah, wenches.'

'No. Besides, you know what Alfarr's like. Hardly seems fair to the wenches; he'll just bore them with talk of ship building.' Agnew smiled weakly.

'Maybe, but...'

'I think we can spare the wenches the pleasure of his company a little while longer.'

The others laughed, briefly lifting the mood. 'So, how do we break this fever?'

'If you let me kill him his fever would be gone.'

'Tostig, no!'

'You're no fun.' Tostig sulked.

'You worry me sometimes.'

266

'Only sometimes?' smirked Ogmundr.

'Well...'

'Sod off!' Tostig prodded the fire sulkily.

'You have to admit you are a bit stabby,' said Agnew.

'Stabby?'

'Yeah, your first reaction to any situation is to stab something.'

'That's not true.'

'Yes, it is.'

'Like when?'

'Delling,' said Agnew, 'is or is not Tostig stabby?'

Delling, sat a little detached from the group, was a bit taken aback by the question. Until recently he'd tended to sit away from the group, where he listened with amusement and a little jealousy at how easy the crew were in each other's company, envying that bond. But something had changed; he'd become one of them. He wasn't sure when or why, but he felt accepted, and the inclusion in the banter was the final sign that he was if not truly one of them then at least a trusted travelling companion. 'I wouldn't say stabby,' Delling answered.

'See,' said Tostig, 'Delling doesn't think I'm stabby.'

'No, he's more, choppy.'

'What the... You cheeky bast...'

Delling smiled happily as the rest of the group laughed at his joke while Tostig blustered with self-righteous indignation. The banter continued, as much to ward off evil spirits which might be gathering outside the reach of the fire's glow as to keep away the unpalatable truth that despite Ogmundr's best efforts, Alfarr was dying. Maybe it was because they were all distracted, maybe it was because even though the fire blazed they were still cold, maybe it was because they were hungry that they never heard the approaching footsteps crunching through the snow or the clank of metal on metal, but when a bunch of dwarves stepped out of the darkness into the light of the fire they caught everyone off-guard.

Momentarily panicked, the men jumped to their feet, desperately reaching for their weapons, knowing it was already too late. They'd been caught cold, but instead of the dwarves falling on them with whirring axes bringing bloody death, the dwarf at the front dropped the stuff he was carrying and said, 'Al-reet, Delling, ha's it hanging, son?'

Delling, who'd also been caught in the moment's panic, paused and said, 'Eskil?'

'Aye, lad? Why thas all jumping about like a bunch of frightened lasses? Seat theesell daan, lads, tha's nay danger 'ere.'

Agnew, who had been one of the faster off the mark and had managed to draw his sword, turned to Delling and asked, 'You know him?'

'Aye, I mean, yes, he's my cousin. Put your weapons down.' Delling laid his axe down, encouraging the others to do the same. 'These are friends.'

Wearily and with just a hint of relief, Agnew's men relaxed and withdrew hands from axe, spear, and sword.

'I tak' it this long streak o' piss is the one Hel's got errself all bandy abaaht?'

'What did he say?' asked Agnew.

'He is,' Delling answered Eskil. 'How did you know?'

'The hair, lad, the hair. Yer boss lady fair got al in a tizzy when describing who all this lot's fer. Couldn't stop going on abaaht 'is hair. I can see why now; them some luscious locks. How does he keep 'em so clean aht here?'

'Beats me. It's like some kind of magic.'

'Aye, well I can see why yon lass has gone all dewy o'er this one an' no mistake.'

'DELLING!'

'Yes, Agnew.'

'Who is this? Why are they here?'

'Ah, yes, well, as I said, this is my cousin, Eskil and, and, and yeah, Eskil, why are you here?'

'Oh, aye, well, his boss lady.' Eskil pointed at Delling.

'You mean Hel?'

'Aye, the freetning one. I don't know how you work as her right hand, Delling; she's terrifying.'

268

'Ah, she's not so bad when you get to know her.'

'Delling?' Agnew snapped impatiently.

'Go on, Eskil.'

'Aye, well, as I were saying, t' Death Queen approached me and said she needed some special stuff like super urgent for yon fancy bugger wi' the flowing locks. I told her it would take a week or so. She said I 'ad a couple o' days, so I got all t' lads on it and 'ere I am.'

'What have you brought?' asked Delling.

'Oh, yer gonna luv this stuff. Some o' my finer work, well, not the rushed stuff – that's a bit shite if I'm honest. I mean, two days – nah one can make quality stuff that quick.'

'ESKIL!'

'Wha'?'

'What have you brought?'

Eskil smiled proudly and said, 'Gather araand, lads, and take a butcher's.' He beckoned the other dwarves to lay out the bundles they were carrying. Each rolled them out on the ground to reveal a selection of weapons and armour, though no one paid any of them any attention, as all eyes were fixed on the piece in the centre of it all. Unlike all the others it was not made of metal. It was a wooden staff made of intricately woven wooden strands, each as thick as a man's thumb, which formed a single piece six foot tall and three inches thick, with a solid bulbous club-like end at one extremity and a sharpened point at the other.

'Is that...?' Delling began.

'Aye, lad, feast yer eyes on Laevateinn.'

'I thought that was just a myth.'

'Nay, lad, it's reel enough. It'll kill... anything.'

'But I didn't ask for this. I asked for Seethe.'

'Aye, well, t'boss decided you was gonna need something more special than Seethe, so she sent that.'

'Can I touch it?'

'Yer can swing it around yer 'ead if yer like, just don't whack anyone wi' it, or you know what'll 'appen.'

Delling reverentially ran his fingers down the wooden shaft and was instantly filled with a sense of grief and anger. He pulled his fingers away sharply to be greeted by a cold laugh from his cousin.

'I don't understand it, it...'

'It remembers,' replied Eskil cryptically.

'Remembers what?' asked Agnew.

Delling looked at Agnew, sadness cracking his deep baritone. 'The death of Balder.'

'What?'

'This is Laevateinn, made from that which killed Balder, the best of the gods. It knows what it did, and it feels the grief of the gods, understands the loss the living suffered when Balder died and feels the guilt and shame for the life taken and the anger at being blamed for something beyond its control,' Delling explained. 'Hel has sent it here for you.'

'That?'

'Yes. You need something to combat the effect of her rake. This is that.'

Agnew eyed the staff warily.

'Pick it up... carefully.'

'I'm not sure I should.'

Eskil patted Agnew on the back kindly. 'Don't worry, lad, t' deathly one's 'ad a word; it'll not bite thee. It'll do thee reet.'

Agnew looked to Delling. 'I don't understand a word he just said.'

'He said Hel's made sure it will be all right with you. Take it, Agnew, you're going to need it.'

Agnew looked about him to see the faces of his crew staring back at him with trepidation. To hold that which had killed a god was of no small consequence. Agnew ran his hands through his hair, which Delling had come to recognise as a sign Agnew was nervous, and rightly so for once. Agnew, his pulse racing, reached out for Laevateinn. He wrapped his fingers about the shaft and lifted it from the ground.

'I don't know what all the fuss was about. It's just a...'

A collective gasp left the assembled Norsemen. Those standing took a step backwards; those still sat on logs fell backwards in their desperation to scramble away. Delling stood rooted to the spot, transfixed by what he saw. Agnew's face contorted into a rictus grimace, and from deep inside he let forth an anguished cry as though the pain of the world were being torn from his soul. From Laevateinn tendrils of wood sprouted from the shaft, wrapping about Agnew's wrist, arm, and hand. Vicious barbs sliced into any exposed flesh, and then, as if its hunger were satiated by Agnew's blood, the tendrils and barbs withdrew, leaving Agnew holding the staff briefly before it fell from his twitching fingers.

All remained in place, unmoving, only the crackle of the fire making a sound until Eskil spoke, breaking the spell. 'Fookin 'ell, I adn't seen that comin.'

Tostig took a tentative step forward, laying a cautious hand on Agnew's shaking arm. 'You all right?'

'I felt it all,' Agnew said, as though speaking in a daze.

'Felt what?'

'The grief, all of it, of everything.'

'Grief, what grief?'

'The gods, Midgard, and, and Laevateinn itself, when it knew what it had done. The regret, it was... everything.'

'I think we heard its cry,' said Tostig.

'Cry?'

'You, Agnew, you cried out like nothing we'd ever heard,' said Delling. 'I think you just gave voice to Laevateinn's pain.'

'It wants to make amends,' said Agnew, reaching down for the staff once more.

'Nooooooooooooooooooooooooooo!' Tostig tried to bat his hand away but too late, as Agnew's fingers once again gripped the staff, only this time as his men prepared to move yet further away this time nothing happened. It simply remained an intricately woven staff.

'Well, looks like Queenie were reet after all. He is okay,' Eskil said, impressed.

'Seriously? That was Hel's gift? She's given Agnew a weapon with emotional issues?' Delling fumed.

'Don't sweat it, lad; yer know them goddesses ain't reet in the 'ead. Bet she thought she was doing reet by t'lad.'

'I don't know what she's thinking any more.'

'It's okay,' Agnew said calmly, 'she's given a great gift.'

Delling and the men all stared at him suspiciously.

'What?'

'Say something else,' said Tostig.

'Why?'

'Just do it.'

'Okay, I said she's given me a great gift.'

'His voice has changed,' said Siggeirr. 'It's become all...'

'Weighty,' said Delling.

'Aye, weighty, that's it.' Siggeirr nodded.

'What?'

'Your voice, Agnew, it has timbre,' said Delling.

'Timbre?'

'He means yer voice has got deeper and gravellier,' Eskil answered. 'The lasses will love that.'

'I don't understand.'

'Don't fight it, lad,' said Eskil, 'just go wi' it. Now, I guess we'd best sort the rest of you out.' The dwarf turned away from Agnew to start doling out new armoured wrist braces to all the men. 'Replace your leather bracers wi' this stuff and you'll be able to deflect all manner of blades trying to lop your arms off,' he said cheerfully as he handed a pair of dark-blue metal wrist bracers to Siggeirr.

'Cor, cheers.'

With the promise of new better gear, the men forgot about Agnew and Laevateinn, all except Tostig and Delling, who asked him, 'How you feeling?'

'Purged,' said Agnew brusquely, then he brushed them away, telling them to see Eskil and get whatever he was passing out.

Hours passed, by the end of which all of Agnew's men had either received new pieces of armour or in some cases new axes, spears, or swords. When everyone was finally kitted out, the dwarf turned his attention to Alfarr, who'd been lying quietly as his life slowly drained from him. 'Delling, is this the one who's nearly 'ad it?'

'Yes.'

'Then Hel's sent something for him.'

'Really? How did she know Alfarr was in trouble?'

'C'mon, lad, she's Queen o' t' Dead. She felt his shade, but she doesn't want 'im dead, not now at any rate.'

'So, what's she sent?'

'Just this,' said Eskil, pulling out a pouch containing a foul-smelling paste. 'She said put this on his wound morning, noon, and night taemorra and the next day. He'll be reet as rain on t'day after that. Then when he feels better, gi' 'im this.' Eskil clicked his fingers, prompting one of the other dwarves to roll out the only bundle not so far unwrapped. Within was a copper cap which looked like a wrist-sized thimble with a socket to stick on one's wrist and stout leather bands to go around the wearer's forearm to keep it secure. On the outer face of the cap was a wicked-looking blade a foot long, with a hardened tip and a serrated leading edge.

Agnew, who had finally lain down Laevateinn, asked, 'Hel believes that paste will cure Alfarr?'

'She does, lad. She wouldn't 'ave had me bring the wrist cap if she din't.'

'Then tell her, thanks.'

'Yer can thank 'er yerself next time yer see her, and yer will.' Eskil winked slyly, which caused Agnew to shudder faintly. 'Reet, I can't 'ang about here any longer freezin me nads off. Me an t'lads will be off. Remember to apply the paste to yer injured man morning, noon, and night and he'll be up and kicking in a day or two. Reet, that's me done. Good t'see yer again, Delling. Don't be a stranger next time yer in Niflheim.'

'Thanks, Eskil.'

'Oh, one last thing.'

'Yes?'

'Once you are ready to leave, head that way,' said the dwarf, pointing east. 'That's where t'death goddess wants yer to be. And get a crack on, 'cos you don't 'ave that much time.' And with that, Eskil had his dwarves gather up the oilskins and with a comradely wave walked out of the light of the camp fires, disappearing back into the night.

35

And so, things are finally moving apace, well apace as much as deep winter snow and sub-zero temperatures will allow, and currently watching over proceedings on behalf of Odin were Huginn and Muninn, the Norse raven equivalent of a Predator drone. Soaring over the winter landscape, watching things unfold, the birds took note that to the south, Asa and her army were calmly readying themselves to leave the town within which they had been wintering. To the north, Gudrød the Hunter and his far more ragged and worn army were trudging south towards Asa. This pleased the ravens, for several reasons. First off, humans were messy creatures, forever dropping food, which made a tasty snack for the conscientious raven about Midgard. Secondly, a moving army tended to churn up the ground, even when it was wallowing beneath a Nordic winter, which made getting at some tasty worms far easier. Thirdly, when two armies meet you get death, blood, and corpses, all of which a hungry raven just loves to feed on. But given that the armies were not yet in fighting range, the birds decided to stay with the ready-made mobile all-you-can-eat buffet that was Gudrød's war-band.

The going for Gudrød was hard and slow, and it wasn't long before Odin's ravens had stuffed their birdy faces with all manner of tasty morsels which Gudrød's army had dropped or kicked up. Appetites satisfied, the ravens took to the air for a last look about and to torment some robins on the way, just because they could, before flying back to Odin. It was as they made a final wheel west that they noticed another much smaller band of humans heading on what looked like a collision course with the other two armies. Now, that was something the birds hadn't expected to see but was worth reporting. With a final flap of their wings Huginn and Muninn made for Asgard.

How long it takes Huginn and Muninn to reach Odin is open to speculation, but given that these birds are Odin's own messengers, it is fair to say that it doesn't take them that long to arrive. Somehow their apparent velocity compared with ground covered doesn't quite tally up – it would give a physicist a major headache, but where gods are involved, normal rules don't apply.

Odin, as you may have already discerned earlier in this tale, isn't always the most attentive listener, however the one thing he does listen to is his ravens, though even the All-father can get a bit weary of their endless tales of eating and where to find the best crumbs. Today though, the news is definitely more interesting than crumbs and worms. Once the birds had cawed their piece and flapped off, what we're left with is Odin stood outside his hall looking angry. He says just one word – bugger – before stomping back inside.

Some gods are rash, some impatient, some are nutters, and some can barely tie their own shoelaces, but Odin was nothing if not wise. Okay, his wisdom tended to fly out of the window when confronted by something female, pert, and nubile, but today he barely paid attention to his pretty serving maid, paused just long enough to grab a horn of mead before sitting himself down in his favourite chair by a large roaring fire, pet wolf curled at his feet, and took time to think. Alternately stroking his beard and wolf between sipping mouthfuls of mead, Odin contemplated what he had seen and heard since things had started to go awry. He knew what Ragnarök looked like, and this didn't look anything like that. None of the portents of the end of the gods had manifested themselves. He'd even been to check on Fenrir to make sure the giant wolf was still bound and hadn't eaten the sun, which he was, so it was probably safe to assume it wasn't that.

Even so, things still felt very wrong. Given the last meeting, Odin was loath to call on his council, but needs must. He sent messengers on their way to gather the council together. While he waited he sat back, closed his one eye and dozed by the fire like any other ageing grandparent. See, the gods aren't that much different to us. Next time one demands homage, worship, or some kind of tribute, just remember they all still need to poo.

Makes you think, doesn't it, like, maybe they're not all that special and maybe not worth the reverence they demand, definitely worth considering next time some bug-eyed priest preaching hell and damnation demands your fealty.

However, such philosophical discussion is for another time. For now, let's get back to Odin kipping on his chair. In what seems the blink of a human eye, but probably at least half a day in Asgard, Odin's council turned up. None of them were looking particularly thrilled about this, but after each had been fed a few meaty snacks, played with the wolf, except Forseti, who was more of a cat man, and had downed some mead, they gathered at the large table which dominated the main space in Odin's hall.

'Right, which of you lot wants to start?' Odin threw down the challenge to his subordinates.

'Start what?' asked Frey, still petting the wolf.

'Start explaining why Gudrød is marching his army south during the winter.'

'Gudrød?'

'Who's Gudrød?'

'Is he the plumber?'

'No, that's Din O' the Rod.'

'Really? I would have sworn it was Gudrød.'

'It isn't.'

'Then I have no idea.'

'Nor me.'

'Never heard of him – why?'

Glaring angrily, Odin replied, 'He is my chosen for kingship of Midgard.'

'Is he?'

'How come I've never heard of him?'

'Are you sure?'

'Doesn't sound very kingly to me.'

'Seriously? Are you telling me not one of you, not one, knows who Gudrød is?' asked an increasingly incredulous Odin.

The gods looked to each other for a clue, but none was forthcoming.

'You lot are useless.' Odin slapped his face into his palm. 'Frey, you made sure that his mother got pregnant by his father.'

'I did?'

'Thor, you helped him win his first battle.'

'Really? Because I don't remember...'

'Forseti, YOU made sure I was within my rights to ensure he became king when he killed Harald Granraude.'

'Err, I don't think I would have given such advice, but if you say so, then...'

'I do say so. How is it none of you remember him? Why have none of you taken any interest in ensuring my man thrives? How is it none of you are aware that he seems to be marching an army in the depths of winter to attack what seems to be a well-armed well-fed well-led army?'

Each god displayed different versions of bemusement, but none provided an answer.

'Surely before such an endeavour he would have called on one of you, any of you, to bless his action? To guarantee him victory in battle? No? Not one of you?'

'No one's called on me,' said Thor.

'Or me,' replied Frey, 'at least not for battle. It's the winter; this is time for hot lovin' while the nights are dark, and beds are warm. Oh yeah.'

Odin turned away from Frey, slightly disturbed. 'Heimdall, surely you were aware of this?'

'Humans wandering the snows like idiots? Yeah, I saw them but thought if they're daft enough to do that then they don't deserve my attention.'

'You didn't think it warranted your attention?'

'No. Watching for Ice Giants seemed more important.'

'With everything going on, you didn't think this was worth mentioning?' Odin's voice had become little more than gravel, causing Heimdall to think carefully before he gave his next answer.

'No?' he replied cautiously.

'You're a fucking moron. You're all fucking morons.' The king of the gods thumped the table angrily. 'Even my ravens knew this was something strange to be reported, yet you lot have failed to see it or simply ignored it. What's wrong with you?'

'To be fair, Dad,' said Thor, 'you never asked us to look into Gudrød or any marching armies. You had us looking into Hel, Ice Giants and Ragnarök in general.'

'And...?'

'This doesn't seem to be any of them.'

'No?'

'No. Me and Tyr went to check on the giants.'

'And?'

'They were quite chilled. Weren't looking for a fight. In fact, they invited us in for a drink.'

'A drink?' said Odin, unable to believe his ears.

'Aye,' replied Tyr. 'We had a right old party. My head's still banging from it, and that was days ago. How's yours, Thor?'

'I swear my tongue still feels like it has a dead badger living on it. What was in that blue stuff?'

'I don't even want to think about the blue stuff.' Tyr shuddered.

'SHUT UP!' Odin banged his fist on the table. 'Midgard's going to Hel, and –'

'It's not Hel, Dad, we already told you that.'

'ARGH! I know, we all know it's not Hel. So, who the fuck is it? Who's behind this monumental shit storm?'

'Skadi.' The answer rang out from the end of the hall.

All turned to look. Only Odin spoke. 'Loki?'

36

Just what Loki says to Odin and the rest or they to him is subject to a godly blackout. No one has so much as leaked a thing, damn them. Don't they know the people have a right to know? No? What? They say they're gods and can do what they want? Bugger; they always have a get-out clause, don't they? Ah well, we can hardly hang about for an 'unnamed source' to give the game away, so instead let's skip time on a little. Imagine, if you will, a clock spinning, or pages from a calendar being ripped away and fluttering to the ground, but seeing that this is a time before such things, instead just imagine the sun going down and coming up a few times – yes, that works. Okay, once all that's done, what we can see laid out before us is the preamble to a battle.

If this were a movie, which it clearly isn't, but if it were, then right now with two armies facing off and Agnew's plucky but depleted band a further way out, waiting to get stuck in, there would be potential for a great musical score to set the tone for the forthcoming violence. Think something by John Barry – orchestral, capturing the mood of each group with an instantly memorable hook. Or if this were *The Lord of the Rings*, think some swooping epic piece full of rousing majesty juxtaposed with impending bloody threat. However, given our budget, this will probably be more akin to an eighties B movie with some strange over-synthesised tune with too many bleeps, whistles, and pings, or maybe a pop song of the day, meant to be rousing but with lyrics entirely out of place for what is potentially a bloody and brutally violent set piece climax to our tale. Anyway, I invite you to choose your own musical backdrop for the montage of watching each army prepare for battle, though no modern or experimental jazz. If a band can't play something which at least approximates a coherent tune, then they can't call it music and it certainly has no place here.

Okay, so you have your music ready to hand... good, then let's go. As the drums kick in, we'll take you on a raven's-eye view of each group. Below, Asa is standing on a raised piece of ground which overlooks her army forming up under the direction of Guthrun Doombringer. Flanked by a couple of her larger men, she has the stance of a warrior queen – straight-backed, proud, swathed in furs, her dark hair whipping dramatically in the wind. She cuts an imposing figure.

Guthrun Doombringer is no less impressive, oozing confidence, his black armour and dark-grey wolf pelts contrasting sharply with the white of the snow laying thickly about. He is stood atop a small hillock between Asa and the main body of the army, surrounded by those who have become his most trusted, loyal and dangerous men. Below them, forming up in a shield wall, Asa's army are strung out in three blocks, each up to six men deep and thirty men across. Five hundred and forty men in total, which for an early ninth century Viking army in the depth of winter is a huge testament to Asa's power of persuasion. They command the high ground, the solid ground. They are well fed, wide awake and lusting after the fight.

Some two hundred metres away, across an expanse of open land covered in deep snow and below Asa's army is Gudrød's army. Due to the time of year, illness and desertion could only muster around three hundred and fifty men, all of whom are tired, hungry, and cold. Common sense would have you think that Gudrød, on seeing what confronted him, would merely slink away and not engage, but bravery and honour outweighs common sense plus the very real belief that Odin is on his side gives him an inflated sense of his own importance and what he is fated to achieve, so he stands, raises his banner and prepares to fight.

To the side of all this, stood in the treeline of the forest which flanks the western edge of the battlefield, we can see Agnew and his twenty-three men. For now, they are merely watching and waiting. We shall come back to them shortly, for there is something far more interesting to witness watching over the battlefield, and the only reason we can see them is because the ravens can.

The other protagonists are, for now at least, blissfully unaware of their presence. Yes, the gods and at least two goddesses have shown up for the match. Standing behind Asa's band is Skadi. She is staring at Odin, revenge on her mind. Odin and his council are standing off to the side of the battlefield, opposite effectively to Agnew, whom Odin has already noticed and discounted as a non-entity. Well, what can twenty-four men do to affect a battle to be fought by nigh on nine hundred? Odin is angry. Odin is standing stock still and glaring at Skadi with ill-concealed contempt and at the same time desperately trying to work out how to turn things in favour of his man without breaking the godly code of non-interference in human affairs, something he hasn't been very good at doing in the past.

Unnoticed by all, Hel has also taken up a position to watch the battle, well, unnoticed by all but Loki, who ambles up to her from who knows where. 'Morning, lovely day for it,' he greeted his daughter warmly.

'What are you doing here?'

'Just watching. Thought I'd keep you company. Who are you backing here?'

'None of them.'

'Oh, so you're just here in a professional capacity then?'

'What?'

'You know, to claim anyone who dies a coward in the battle.'

'Well, yes, but no, no, that isn't why I am here.'

'Oh, okay, because you do know as the Queen of the Underworld you don't have to do the donkey work? You can just send your minions to come and collect that which is owed you.'

'Not for this,' Hel said quietly.

'What?'

Hel turned to her father. 'Do you really want to know why I'm here?'

'Only if you want to tell me. No pressure.'

'And if I don't say anything, don't tell you anything, you won't sulk?'

'I never sulk.'

'You always sulk.'

'I find that very insulting.'

'Like I care,' Hel replied, breezily turning back to regard the amassed armies and ignoring her father, leaving the pair stood in silence until Loki could stand it no more. 'Oh, for pity's sake, go on, tell me why you're here. Please.'

'You're pouting.'

'No, I'm not.'

'Yes. You are. You always do when you don't get what you want.'

'Oh, so I pout. What of it? Are you going to tell me or not?'

Hel allowed herself a small smile. 'The rake.'

'Rake?'

'Yes, my rake. The rake that one stole from me,' she said, pointing to the figure of Guthrun, who was issuing orders to his men. 'I want it back.'

'Then just go take it.'

'I can't.'

'Course you can. You're a goddess; just tootle over there and get it.'

'Ha! You know the rules. I can no more wander over and take it than Odin over there can wander into the army and personally slaughter all those who oppose his man.'

'Mmmmmm. I wouldn't put it past him.'

'No, not even Odin would – will he? No, surely not.'

'You don't know him like I do,' said Loki ruefully. 'All rules apply until it doesn't suit him, then they don't. You just watch.'

'I intend to.'

'If you are not going to grab it, how do you intend to get your rake? Wait till everyone dies and then just take it out of his cold dead hands?'

'While he holds it, he won't die.'

'Of course he will. An axe to the head will pretty much end anyone. Even us, and we're gods.'

'No; he's already dead. He just doesn't realise it.'

'He looks pretty alive to me. The whole walking and talking kind of gives it away, wouldn't you say?'

'No, he's dead. The rake is just affording him life over death for now. Unfortunately, while he has it, he is indestructible.'

'Really? Who came up with that loophole?'

'It was never a consideration, until now.'

'So, if you can't, or won't, take it and no one can kill him, how are you getting it back?'

'Them.' Hel pointed at Agnew's war-band lurking in the trees.

'What, them?'

'Yes.'

'There are only a couple of dozen of them.'

'I know.'

'They look like they have been dragged through your realm backwards.'

'True. They have had a hard time of it but have proved their mettle.'

'Even so, you are asking them to battle through hundreds of men then take the rake off an invincible man. This doesn't sound like much of a plan.'

'You're forgetting I'm your daughter; don't think I haven't picked up a few tricks from you down the years.'

'What are you up to?'

Hel laughed menacingly. 'Nothing much, just protecting that which is mine. Other than that, I couldn't care less about who wins the battle. If you really want to know what's going on, I suggest you go listen in on what Odin and Skadi are saying to each other.'

'What?'

'Over there, look; see, they're having a meet.'

'Damn!' Loki cursed, realising he'd allowed himself to be distracted by his daughter and was missing out on the key event, which is where, unlike Loki, we shall go and listen in.

The king of the gods and goddess of winter and hunting strode forward to meet in the no-man's-land between the two armies. For any normal person that would be a stupid place to stand, but with a click of his fingers Odin had paused time, allowing him and Skadi to meet, unseen by the armies, but very much in the thick of it.

'My king.' Skadi gave a contemptuous bow.

'What are you up to, Skadi?' Odin got straight to the point.

'Revenge,' she answered simply.

'Really? You are doing all this just for Harald Granraude's daughter?'

'You know that?'

'I have my sources.'

'Then why ask?'

'I wanted to be sure my source was telling the truth.'

'Well, now you know.'

'You're really going to defy me?'

'I am.'

'If you go ahead with this, there will be consequences, and not just for you.'

'You think I care about your threats? You have played fast and loose with the rules too long. You started this. This is on you.'

'I had my reasons.'

'Pah!'

'You don't understand, Skadi. There is more at play here than you can imagine. Go back to looking after nature and leave the world of men to me.'

'That's your argument? That I don't understand? Why, because I'm a woman?'

'Yes.'

'You're pathetic.'

'I'm not the one being all emotional.'

'If you think this is emotion, you haven't seen anything yet.'

'I am giving you an out, Skadi. Walk away. Let me correct your misguided attempt to thwart that which I have put in place.'

'No. I am going to watch my carefully, painstakingly and calmly raised forces wipe yours from the battlefield.'

'Watch yourself, Skadi. I can cut you down where you stand.'

'No, you won't. You can't. You've seen Ragnarök; you know I'm there. You can't touch me.'

'Try me,' Odin growled. 'I can always make an exception.'

'Don't you want to know why?'

'Why what?'

'Why this.'

'Go on, if you must. Embarrass yourself, girl, but when I school you in your misplaced schemes of revenge, I will expect your total and complete supplication, here, now, before the others.'

'You wanted Asa for yourself,' announced Skadi.

'Sorry, what?' Odin recoiled like he'd been slapped.

'Asa – you wanted her.'

'That's a lie. I never... I wouldn't stoop so low as to...'

'You wanted her. You thought you could seduce her in Gudrød's form.'

'Lies. All lies.'

'I know you, Odin. What's more, I watched you try. Shame Gudrød's such a bastard. He'd fucked up your chances with her before you ever got a chance to work your... magic.' Skadi grinned coldly, revelling in Odin's discomfort as he realised he'd been caught out.

'That wasn't it at all. It was all part of ensuring a lasting human kingdom that...'

'Sex.'

'No, not sex...'

'Sex, Odin. That's all this was ever about. Just you and the fact you can't keep it in your pants. You're nothing but a colossal pervert with a hankering for human women, especially strapping ones with dark hair. What is it with you and dark hair?'

'It's different. Nearly everyone else is blonde, and I like a bit of dark fur around the... oh, balls.'

'And there we have it,' Skadi gloated, 'the All-father's confession. Everything happening here is on you and your pathetic fetish for dark hair.'

'So? I like dark-haired girls – that's hardly a crime. I'm their god; most would willingly give themselves to me. Why do you care, anyway? What is it about this one? It's not like she's your daughter.'

'Maybe not, but she was, is, under my care. You ignored that back then. You will not ignore that today.'

'You will stand your army down, Skadi,' Odin roared, trying to regain the initiative, but Skadi was not for being bullied.

'Or what? Want me to tell your men over there the reason for this? Or maybe I should tell Frigg?'

Odin squirmed uncomfortably. 'You wouldn't.'

'Try me.' She mimicked Odin.

'I am giving you one last chance.'

'You're in no position to offer me anything. But I am giving you a chance,' Skadi goaded. 'Go back to your little boys' club, say nothing of this and watch as my side destroys yours and puts Asa on the throne. You will do nothing. You will interfere with nothing. You will just accept the inevitable. Do this and I will consider the sleight against Asa and therefore me forgiven. This conversation will go no further. What say you, my king?'

'So be it,' Odin said, deflated, 'but on one condition.'

'Which is?'

'You can no more interfere in the battle than I.'

'Is this a trick?'

'No trick. We let the humans decide this.'

Skadi took a moment to compare the strengths of the opposing forces, looking for anything she may have missed which would hand victory to the weaker smaller force of Odin's man but seeing none she smiled coldly. 'Very well. I accept the terms.'

'Then we're agreed,' Odin growled angrily, 'but try something like this again...'

Skadi dismissed Odin with a contemptuous wave and walked away. Odin turned away furiously, thumping the haft of his great spear Gungnir into the ground, causing the air to thunder and time to snap back in. On the battlefield, the roll of thunder acts like the crack from a starter's pistol. So, with the last bars of your music of choice fading into the background, it's time to step back and watch as all hell is about to be let loose.

37

As the final peal of thunder dissipated a roar of defiance went up from Gudrød the Hunter, which his men returned tenfold. With axe held high, Gudrød led his men in a charge across the open expanse of land to the foot of the hill upon which Asa's army was waiting. The move was as bold as it was reckless, and for all his faults you at least had to admire Gudrød's bravery as he led the charge. Stood off in the tree line, Agnew, Tostig, Delling, and the rest watched this with a mix of disbelief and admiration.

'Is he mad?' asked Agnew.

'Mad? He's bloody furious,' replied Delling with a smirk.

'He is a brave man,' Tostig declared, impressed.

'He'll get his men killed,' said Agnew. 'They haven't made it to the shield wall and they're tiring.'

'Why would they charge through snow that deep?' asked Delling.

'Because they are warriors, and their king demands it,' replied Tostig.

'Then he's a loon.'

'That's no way to speak of the brave.'

'No, but it is the way to speak of a loon.'

'They're slowing,' observed Agnew as Gudrød's men fought against snow and hill. 'And here it comes.'

'Here what comes?' asked Delling.

'Arrows,' said Tostig as from the rear of Asa's army came a hail of deadly missiles which hit with a sickening thud against shield, skin, and bone with man after man falling under the barrage, the air about them turning red and thick, a mixture of blood mist and the exertion of a charging army's breath.

'He's still going.' Tostig pointed at the enraged figure of Gudrød still ploughing forward, his efforts galvanising his men to close the distance so they could get to grips with their enemy. Finally, with an almighty shudder, Gudrød's army crashed into the shield wall of Asa's army and battle was joined. The wall held the initial impact and with an answering roar from behind the shields, spears thrust through into unprotected bodies, axes cleaved down upon helms and shoulders, and an occasional sword sliced against arms and necks. Roars turned to screams, white snow turned red, wood splintered, metal buckled, bone shattered, and muscle and sinew was sliced and diced in a maelstrom of death.

'That's gotta hurt,' said Delling as he watched one of Gudrød's men take a spear to the face.

'Yes, but tonight he will feast in Valhalla,' Tostig answered proudly.

'You do know that you don't all go to Valhalla? Freya gets to claim half of the fallen. Well, I say half; if any die a coward, then my mistress gets them, but yes, about half go to Freya.'

'What?' Tostig looked down at the dwarf in disgust. 'How dare you cheapen their sacrifice and bravery.'

'No, it's true. Freya gets half of the fallen, who go to her hall, Fólkvangr. It's a nice place, very bright and airy, much better than Odin's hall in Valhalla, plus you get the added advantage of spending time with Freya.'

'How is that an advantage?'

'You haven't seen her.' The dwarf smiled longingly.

'If you two have finished, it's time to get ready.' Agnew hushed them, taking charge. 'Though not you, Delling.'

'What? Why?'

'I've seen you whirling that axe around, remember. You go out there and you'll be killed.'

'You can't stop me.'

'Do you really want to face Hel as a dead spirit?'

'I can do this. You need all the men you can get out there.'

'Delling, you're not a warrior.'

'I've been practising.'

'Really?'

'Yes. Ragna has been training me.'

'Ragna?'

'Yes.'

'But he's over six feet tall.'

'So?'

'His fighting style isn't going to suit you. You should have asked Audolf.'

'Why?'

'Because he's only just a foot taller than you and about as wide. His fighting style is much more... Anyway, doesn't matter; the answer is still no. You are to wait here.'

'You can't ask this. How can I look the others in the eye if I stay back?'

'Delling, you're more a danger to them if you are out there. They'll have to keep their eyes on you to keep you safe rather than concentrate on their own fight.'

'But Agnew...' Delling's voice pleaded, but Agnew was having none of it.

'Sorry, You are too important to lose out there. Stay put.' And with that, Agnew left Delling, crestfallen, who now could only stand back and watch the others prepare for battle.

As the men tightened wrist braces, ensured their mail sat evenly across their shoulders and checked their weapons, Agnew could see grim delight settling over them, all except maybe Ogmundr, who Agnew suspected shared some of his own doubts on the glories of heroic death, with the operative word being death. Agnew gave Ogmundr a singular nod of recognition, which Ogmundr returned with a lopsided smile and a tap of his axe to his chest. Well, whatever Ogmundr's thoughts on death in battle, Agnew didn't doubt his bravery and knew he would do his bit. Now he just had to get his own doubts under control. Taking a moment to compose himself, Agnew set his helm upon his head and steadied his shield before tentatively letting his fingers brush over the haft of Laevateinn before taking it in a firm grip, feeling a surge of remorse and shame before the feeling changed into something altogether darker.

Delling, who, with little else to do, was the only one taking any notice of this tiny war-band rather than Guthrun and the rake, felt a chill to his soul the moment Agnew took hold of

Laevateinn, as a shadow fall over Agnew. He quietly intoned, 'Mistress, what have you done?'

Oblivious to Delling's misgivings, Agnew kept his eyes fixed upon the battle, waiting for the moment to strike. To either side of him the crew were chomping at the bit, fired up by the roar of battle like racehorses in their stalls waiting for the off. Despite the restless energy surrounding him Agnew ignored it, instead concentrating solely on the battle unfolding before him. At first it was like watching an uncontrolled mob scrapping but with a practised eye the battle began to take a coherent form. Agnew could discern the battle lines, the formations in play, and for now he could see that Gudrød's men though not making any headway against Asa's army were at least holding their own. This status quo held for a while as the fight raged on until amazingly, the centre of Asa's army began to give against the ferocity of Gudrød's assault. Slowly, inexorably, Asa's men began to give ground, buckling under Gudrød's assault; at least that's how it looked. From his vantage point Agnew knew better. He could see Guthrun's battle plan developing. It was a trap expertly crafted.

Guthrun Doombringer stood impassively watching the battle, unflustered by the seemingly disastrous developments taking place in the centre of his lines. If Gudrød weren't stuck in the thick of it, trying to cleave his way through to Asa and finish things quickly, he may have observed Guthrun's lack of concern and taken a moment to take stock of his situation. As it was, he was too busy dodging yet another spear thrust which came in from the side. Ignoring the thrusting weapon, Gudrød kicked hard against the shield of the man directly before him, at the same time deflecting the axe strike which came from behind it, the combination momentarily exposing Gudrød's opponent to his counterstrike. Gudrød's axe bit viciously into the unprotected neck of his enemy, nearly severing the man's head from his body except for a small amount of skin and muscle, which kept it attached, flopping loosely to the side. Gudrød, blood-soaked, filled with battle lust, stepped over his dead opponent, axe swinging brutally against everything in his path. His men followed, using his momentum to fuel their own violent surge, sensing victory, the victory promised by the gods.

Unfortunately for Gudrød, those self-same gods, who hadn't promised anything of the sort, stood on watching the battle unfold and like Agnew spotted what Guthrun was planning. Despite the gains Gudrød was making, they could see that barring a miracle, or more likely some godly interference from them, Odin's man was about to get a bloody hiding. None of them spoke. All looked to Odin to see what he would do. Inexplicably, he didn't seem to be doing anything. He just watched, scowling, his right hand gripping Gungnir so tightly his knuckles had gone white.

Guthrun Doombringer, unlike Odin, was happily seeing the opening phases of the battle going exactly to plan. Casually, he said something to the bannerman stood next to him, who raised his banner high then lowered it to point at the bannerman at the rear of the centre troops. On seeing Guthrun's lowered banner, he too lowered his in answer. Instantly, throughout the centre formation a command rippled to the men at the front forming the shield wall, which held for a moment then gave more ground, more pronounced than before. Feeling the line give, Gudrød's men doubled their efforts, pressing forward with renewed vigour, failing to notice that every step forward cost them more men to the blades and spears which continued to slash and thrust at them from behind the intact bank of shields. The snow on the slopes was bloody red and slick with gore. The going becoming ever harder as each man had to step over, on, or through the bodies lying in their way.

Guthrun, for all the world standing as calmly as someone simply enjoying the view, continued to let the centre fall back until it looked like the centre must surely break, but before it gave way Guthrun again said something to the bannerman, who raised the banner high, whirling it in a circular motion. Immediately the lowered banner of the centre troops rose in answer to flutter proudly against the grey winter sky. Again, a ripple of command worked its way to the shield wall, stiffening its defence, feet dug into the snow. Men stepped forward to plug any gaps left by the fallen and exerted pressure outwards, halting Gudrød's army before they crested the incline up which they'd been fighting. Suddenly confronted by a resolute and unyielding shield wall, Gudrød's men felt the first pangs of doubt since their initial charge, and the attack faltered.

If Gudrød's men thought things had turned bad, they were about to get a whole lot worse. Guthrun's man signalled to the bannermen stood on the flanks of his army, each answering with vigorously waved banners. Guthrun allowed himself a self-satisfied smile as each flank wheeled inwards, pushing back against Gudrød's men, forcing them back down the hill and in towards their own men. Slowly, Guthrun's flanks began to envelop Gudrød's army, trapped within a horseshoe of wood and lethal iron, leaving only a single route of escape behind them but crushed together without the room to make a successful breakout for all except those at the very back, who were still trying to push forward, unaware of the impending doom facing their comrades towards the front. With their enemy trapped upon the slopes before them, Guthrun's men began the systematic massacre of Gudrød's army.

Still in the trees, sensing Guthrun's attention was focused on the battle, Agnew signalled his men to move. With Agnew at the fore, they moved out of the trees silently in a loose arrow formation. This was no headlong charge but a controlled advance as they spread out, stalking forward like a wolf pack, positioning themselves to separate Guthrun from the rest.

Like Gudrød and his army, Agnew's men were having to wade through the same deep snow but unlike Gudrød they had the advantage of being positioned above Guthrun. With the slope working in their favour they made rapid progress, with the sound of battle more than drowning out the crunch of snow beneath their feet. Agnew and his men moved within striking distance of Guthrun without being seen, that is, without being seen by human eyes. The various watching gods and goddesses had no such impediment. Cursing herself for discounting Agnew, Skadi was about to do something which would change the whole state of the battle.

Back in the human sphere of perception, with just fifteen or so feet to go, Agnew and his men prepared to fall upon Guthrun with extreme violence when in Guthrun's ear a female voice screamed, 'BEHIND YOU!' Assuming it was Asa, Guthrun turned. Shocked to see Agnew and his men descending upon him, he yelled a warning to his own men as he swung his axe into position, ready to fight.

With the element of surprise blown, Agnew yelled, 'For HEL!' and charged.

Agnew made straight for Guthrun, but before he reached him a large warrior wielding a two-handed axe stepped in front, hacking at Agnew's head. Agnew reacted quickly, raising his shield, deflecting the strike and thrusting Laevateinn forward beneath the rim of his raised shield. But he struck nothing, his opponent already side-stepping away the moment his attack failed, which allowed him to bring his axe round in a figure of eight for a second strike. Again, Agnew's shield deflected the axe. This time Agnew stepped back to open the distance and give himself a chance to counter, but the man was fast and stepped forward with a third strike, this one coming up from below and which Agnew only just parried in time. He lashed out with Laevateinn, not expecting to hit but just to give his opponent something to think about and slow his advance. It worked. Agnew steadied himself, set his guard and prepared to fight.

Around him, his own men engaged in life-and-death battles of their own, but they were no longer his concern. Agnew's world had boiled down to just him and the man before him with the two-handed axe. The man grinned as he swung the axe in lazy figure of eights, looking to intimidate Agnew. He oozed confidence. He was much larger than Agnew, and with a bigger weapon and longer reach he was a formidable opponent, which wasn't lost on Agnew. He was going to have to be crafty. Despite his size the big man was fast, suddenly lunging forward, his axe spinning through the air with dangerous speed, which Agnew only just dodged, forcing him backwards. Agnew's opponent continued to come forward, the axe a blur, unafraid of Agnew, maybe even a little dismissive. Seeing Agnew was armed with nothing more than a wooden staff, he moved in and out, looking for the opening to finish Agnew. The axe whistled by Agnew's head alarmingly. A couple of times Agnew deflected it with his rapidly splintering shield, each blow causing a shudder which ran through his wrist, arm, and shoulder. Agnew ignored the pain. He was too busy counting.

A couple more attacks came his way, then a third, which again Agnew took on his shield, only this time he stepped into the attack rather than back. The shield cracked alarmingly, taking the full brunt of the axe head, but it allowed Agnew to step inside his opponent's distance, knowing that as soon as he brought the axe down his opponent would take a half-step back and to Agnew's left, because he'd done that every time so far. Agnew was ready and stabbed Laevateinn up and left from below his shield into the warrior's gut, piercing the leather armour as easily as pushing a hot knife through butter. The man screamed a scream like no other. Hot blood gushed down Laevateinn onto Agnew's hand, wrist, and forearm, and in Agnew's head Laevateinn sang a song of blood and triumph as it devoured the warrior's soul. This one would not reach Valhalla, for there was no longer a soul left to claim. Laevateinn absorbed it all.

38

If we take a step back from the middle of the carnage, we can take stock of the battle, courtesy of the ravens. Looking down, we can see Gudrød's men surrounded on three sides and becoming tightly squeezed. There are also now signs that those at the rear of Gudrød's army have begun to realise that only disaster awaits them, and some men are starting to slink away from the fight. Yes, despite the myth that all Vikings sought a hero's death in battle, when confronted with imminent defeat and a death which was anything but heroic, Vikings would flee the field of battle the same as any other combatant.

Now we not only had numbers falling away from the main battle, we also had the arrival of Agnew's men into the fray, so that behind the main army a small separate but no less brutal fight had commenced, centred around Guthrun Doombringer, which just goes to show you that despite the best laid plans of mice and men, no plan survives the first five minutes of battle and something always crops up to stick a spanner in the works. For Guthrun, that spanner was Agnew and his crew.

The only folks not currently engaged in the fight were Delling, Asa, and her bodyguards and of course the gods and goddesses watching outside the view of the combatants.

Of those currently watching from the stands, so to speak, we'll pick up with Delling. The dwarf had at first felt a sense of shame at seeing Agnew's men leave the safety of the forest edge to stalk forward to attack the rake holder and his warriors. Yet as the two groups engaged in a clash of iron, wood, grunts, and screams, a treacherous feeling flittered through his mind, which secretly thanked Agnew for not letting him be part of the fight. He watched as Ragna ran some hapless man through with his spear before the other was close enough to even get a chance to attack the lanky Norseman, and Delling realised that Agnew was right; he would have been nothing but a liability and, probably by now, dead. Even so, it did not ease the sense of shame and cowardice he was feeling.

Delling remained transfixed by what he saw, that is until he heard the scream from Agnew's first victim and looking to where Agnew stood, he almost baulked in fear at the terrifying grin on Agnew's face. *This is not good*, he thought, and ignoring Agnew's orders he took a steadying breath, gripped his axe firmly and left the safety of the tree line and set off through the snow towards Agnew.

Out on the field, Agnew's men, although small in number, outnumbered Guthrun's bodyguard slaying them with brutal efficiency. Even so it wasn't all going the way of Agnew's crew. The first two to reach Guthrun were cut down without the Doombringer needing to break sweat. Guthrun's axe moved with a fluid precision which belied the power invested in each strike. Moreover, Guthrun was enjoying the fight. He felt alive again, and when a giant of a man with an expansive beard, huge axe and with a similar grin to his own confronted him, Guthrun roared a challenge, which Tostig roared back with gusto.

With the fight having broken up into small contests, Agnew found himself stood alone, looking for sight of the man in the dark-grey wolf pelts who held the rake, just in time to see him challenged by Tostig. Grimly, Agnew pushed through the snow to join the fight before Guthrun, protected by the rake's power, could kill his best friend.

Before he could get at Guthrun, his bannerman and another of the Heeth came at Agnew from either side. Agnew could feel Laevateinn quiver with excitement, and before the fight even started proper Agnew had rushed the bannerman and parried his spear thrust with Laevateinn and keeping the pressure against the spear's haft, he slid Laevateinn up its length to impale the bannerman under the arm. Like the axeman before him, the bannerman died with a scream to frighten the hardiest of souls. Agnew felt the surge within himself as Laevateinn absorbed the man's energy, only this time it transferred it to him. The second warrior, suddenly facing what looked like a man possessed by a demon, with a rictus grin and lurid green flames burning in his eyes, fell back in horror, broke and ran. The way to Guthrun was open.

While Agnew and his men engaged in battle, outside of the mortals' vision the gods and goddesses present at this shindig were now beginning to become more engaged in the proceedings. Skadi's unwitting breaking of the terms of no interference in the battle, which she'd agreed with Odin, by warning Guthrun Doombringer of Agnew's attack had been all the invitation Odin needed to intervene. Decreeing Skadi had broken the rules he had no compunction in ordering his godly retinue to stop standing and get stuck in and do something useful, or as he put it, 'Go help Gudrød win this battle!'

Skadi, for her part, had lost the plot. Raging, she screamed at Hel, who was still standing off quietly watching things unfold, 'Call your men off. You're ruining everything. They have no part in this. Stop them now! NOW! ARGH!'

'Why should I?'

'You are interfering in the lives of men.'

'Who, me?' Hel replied innocently.

'Yes, you. This is not your fight.'

'I'm not involved; I'm just watching,' Hel called back smugly. 'I think you'll find it is you who has meddled.'

'That's a lie.'

'Er, no. You meddled, not I.'

'I did not.'

'Yes, you did.'

'Didn't.'

'Uh-huh, you did. Think about it,' Hel gloated.

'What? No, I... did I? No...'

'You gave your man a warning. You spoke to him, Skadi, mid-battle. You helped.'

'That wasn't... it was within the rules, because you sent your men in and directed them personally.'

'I haven't said a word. The only person who has interfered is you, well, that was until Odin got involved just about... now.'

'What?'

'Look over there. Odin's mob are helping out the other side.'

'No, he wouldn't. We had an agreement.'

Hel didn't answer but merely pointed. Skadi, fuming, dragged her ire away from Hel to turn her attention back to the battle. 'NOOOOOOOOOO!' she screamed as she saw out on the battlefield Thor, Tyr, Heimdall, Frey, and even Forseti striding amongst Gudrød's men, imbuing them with temporary god-like strength, invulnerability, and amazing fighting skills. Suddenly the outcome of the battle was very much in doubt as Gudrød and his men with godly assistance started to overwhelm the shield wall in the centre. With every strike it began to splinter, the men forming it cut down, leaving large gaps on which Gudrød's warriors capitalised, stepping into the breaches to get at their tormentors, taking out their anger and frustrations upon them.

Skadi, incandesced, screamed again, turned to Hel, turned back to Odin, who was smirking maliciously, then back to Hel. 'You... you... you're ruining everything!'

Hel shrugged. She didn't care about Skadi's plan. She didn't care about Odin or his chosen human. Hel only cared about her rake and, strangely, Agnew. That was a bit of a disquieting feeling but nothing she couldn't park for now. Besides, Agnew seemed to be doing all right.

'Damn you, Hel. Well, if my man can't win, neither can yours,' Skadi raged, knocking a silver arrow to her bow and training it upon Agnew.

Hel's eyes widened with fear. Even she couldn't save Agnew from the huntress' arrow. She was simply too far away, and it was to be her turn to scream, 'NO!', when a saviour came from an unlikely source. Appearing at Skadi's side just as she made to loose the arrow, Loki calmly nudged the bow, forcing the arrow wide of its mark. Hel breathed a sigh of relief as Agnew's life was spared but almost instantly became concerned for her father, which was another unfamiliar sensation for Hel, who usually felt nothing but contempt for her dad. This whole experience with Agnew and the rake had awakened all sorts of feelings she was neither used to nor much cared for; she was finding they were getting in the way. But right there and then she found she didn't want Skadi to kill her father, which she expected was about to happen, given Skadi's long-running hatred of Loki.

Skadi, on being thwarted in her attempt to kill Agnew, rounded angrily upon the God of Mischief with death in her eyes. Dropping the bow she drew her hunting knife, ready to gut him where he stood. She wanted to see fear in his eyes, wanted to see terror, wanted to see some form of contrition. She got nothing of the sort. All she received was a charming grin and a wink. Skadi paused. That wasn't what she had expected, not even from Loki. Then he spoke. *Damn it, why did she let him speak*, a voice in the back of her head admonished her, but it was too late – silky-smooth, calming words issued forth from Loki. Hel, from across the field, watched in wonderment as the pair stood facing each other in what looked like a tense stand-off as Loki continued to speak, expecting at any moment Skadi to howl. She often howled when she was angry, out for blood, horny, or just hungry, come to think of it, but no, instead Skadi's whole body relaxed and she sheathed her knife.

Well, I wasn't expecting that, thought Hel. *How does he do that?* She looked at Loki as again tricky feelings washed over her, leaving her feeling confused as a surge of pride swelled inside her as she watched her father.

Skadi, who wouldn't have cared less for Hel's emotional turmoil, asked Loki, 'So, what now?'

'Who are you angry with, my daughter or Odin?'

'Odin.'

'So why not concentrate on beating Odin?'

'How? His lackeys are turning the tide of the battle. Gudrød will win; Asa will be done. This wasn't the plan. The day is lost!'

'Nah, you can turn this around. Your lot's army is still bigger than theirs; it's not too late.'

'How?'

'Easy – just undo what the lads are up to.' Loki grinned.

Skadi looked at Loki, head cocked like a dog trying to work out what its human wants. 'Your bow,' Loki prompted, and Skadi understood. She stooped, picked up her bow from where she'd dropped it, knocked an arrow and sighted down the shaft till it was aiming at one of the men Tyr had blessed and loosed. The arrow flew straight and true, striking its target with deadly accuracy. The arrow's unfortunate target was spun around with the force of the impact, falling dead into the warrior pressing up the slope behind him.

Skadi looked back over her shoulder at Loki. 'Thanks.'

'You're welcome.'

'I still hate you.'

'I know.'

Skadi graced Loki with the briefest of smiles, which sent a shiver of expectation straight to his groin and a little voice in his head said, *well, hello*, just as Skadi began to fire arrow after arrow into the god-touched warriors out on the battlefield, causing the little voice to moderate itself to, *well, maybe later*.

With Skadi's intervention, the battle once more hung in the balance. Asa, stood at her vantage point, could see all was not well, and a sinking feeling was beginning to engulf her. She couldn't lose to Gudrød, not now, not when they'd planned this so well, not when she had the better men, the rested men, more men. Gudrød's weary troops had no right to fight as they were, no right. She couldn't see the part being played out by the gods. She was a mortal, after all, but she wasn't just some farmer's wife either; she was the daughter of a king, a warlord, a man of violence and cunning and she'd picked up a thing or two as a little girl sat in her father's great hall as he talked war strategy with his men. The one thing she had learned, above all else, was that victory tended to go to the force which took the initiative – better to do than react.

Asa took a moment to weigh up all which was going on below her. She turned to her two guards. 'Bjarke, gather some men from the rear and go help Guthrun,' she commanded. 'Halvor, it is time for our flanks to break over them like an angry river. See to it.'

Neither man questioned her authority. Neither questioned the wisdom of leaving her alone and unprotected. Both grinned, hungry to be in the thick of the action and set off to carry out her commands without so much as a backwards glance.

Whether Guthrun would have been happy to know that Asa valued him highly enough to take men from the main battle to aid him, no one was likely to know, and for now Guthrun had other things on his mind, locked in battle with an opponent he actually deemed worthy. The man was much bigger than him, but unusually he hadn't rushed in, as so many did, expecting to swat Guthrun aside like an annoying fly, but instead was treating Guthrun with a fighter's respect. Guthrun, lighter on his feet, made fleeting darts at the big man, who, sunk deeper into the snow couldn't move as freely, but his greater reach and expertise with his axe was keeping Guthrun at bay and threatening to cleave him in two every time he darted forward. For the first time since the night in the cave, Guthrun could feel his heart pound, the blood thumping in his ears, his breath short and rasping. The excitement of battle and a life-and-death fight flooded his senses. He had never felt more alive than he did right now.

The pair fought hard, speed versus power, both equally cunning, honed by years of experience in the ways of battle, each one's strengths countered by the other's, each one's weaknesses suitably defended. In the end though, the rake began to play its part. The big man tired as each step was dragged at by the snow, eating into his energy. Slowly, the big man's blows lost some of their strength, which Guthrun felt every time they landed upon his shield. It formed a link to him which the rake exploited, taking a little bit of life force from the big man every time the two connected. Guthrun sensed his moment was coming.

Tostig had entered the fight with Guthrun knowing his opponent was magically protected, but his warrior's creed meant he could not shirk this fight. In fact, it practically demanded he accept the challenge. What could be braver and more worthy of Valhalla than tackling a man guarded by an implement radiating a goddess' magic? The fight had been good; he'd enjoyed the challenge. Even without Hel's rake this man would have been a worthy opponent, but now Tostig could feel himself weakening, and fast. It was like his energy was being torn from him at an alarming rate. It was – Tostig struggled for the comparison – no, he knew – it was like bleeding out. He had seen comrades go the same way in other fights, slowly succumbing to a number of cuts from where their precious blood flowed and with every drop lost so they became weaker, slower, dead men walking. Tostig could feel his time coming to an end. He stepped away, taking a huge lungful of air, his axe heavy in his hands, and planned on one last death-defying move in a bid to end the fight before it ended him. His last thought before he attacked was, *I hope Odin is watching.*

Agnew finally dispatched the last man who was blocking him from getting at Guthrun. He looked up to just in time to see Tostig launch his suicide strike. He had seen it before. Tostig had even used it against him when they trained. It could work; he hoped it would work; it usually didn't. Roaring, Agnew bolted forward, hoping against hope that he could get at Guthrun first, hoping Tostig would see him coming and would delay, but if he had it didn't stay him. Tostig feinted a tired slip, bringing Guthrun towards him, expecting to be able to catch the off-balance warrior cold, only to find the big man suddenly, remarkably shift his weight forward and leap from the snow, feet clear of the ground, axe raised above his head for the killing strike, intended to catch his opponent off-guard and render him frozen in fear at the sight of the big man and an axe bringing death from the sky.

Guthrun was not so easily intimidated, still fresh and thinking clearly. Agnew watched as the man in the black wolf pelts with a rake strapped to his back stepped sideways, avoiding Tostig's killing blow and struck up with all his might into Tostig's chest. Tostig howled in pain and hit the snow-covered floor with a grunt, his axe falling away from his hands.

Guthrun stood over his fallen opponent and admired how, even hideously wounded, the big man still reached for his lost axe and tried to stand. Fun as this had been it was time to end it and send him to Valhalla, where a place amongst the valiant fallen awaited this one. Guthrun placed a booted foot upon the big man's back, forcing him back into the snow, raised his axe above his head and brought it down towards his head, only for the strike to be parried away at the last second. With a growl of disappointment, Guthrun turned to face whoever had dared to spare his kill to find himself face to face with a man wielding what looked like a wooden staff and laughed.

'What's so funny?'

'You dare face me with a stick?'

'It is more than a match for you,' Agnew answered, his voice, deep, resonated with cold certainty, and in a moment of reckless bravura he pulled his helmet from his head, discarding it on the floor.

Guthrun suddenly felt sick to his stomach, as the man's hair, instead of being a sweaty plastered-down mess, sprung to life with movie-star perfection before his eyes, wind ruffling it playfully, and an old crone's voice in his head said, 'You'll know him for his magnificent hair.'

'Who are you, stick wielder?' Guthrun asked, as for the first time in as long as he could remember he felt fear, but like Tostig before him, he was not one to back out of a fight.

'I am Hel's retribution,' replied Agnew, and Guthrun could have sworn his eyes blazed with green fire.

'Bring it,' Guthrun challenged.

39

Battles are, by their very nature, chaotic. Even in ones where things go exactly as planned by one of the warring factions, mayhem still ensues, and there are always moments, tipping points if you like, where a battle can be won or lost. Sometimes a tipping point can be down to a single unwise decision; sometimes it's a build-up of small decisions which turn into one catastrophic clanger which loses the fight. Sometimes it can be down to bad intelligence – believing one side has more in reserve than you have left to counter with, and sometimes it can be down to a moment of inspired leadership. In this case, Asa's inciteful intervention was about to swing the day her way.

Asa's man, Halvor, had reached the right wing of her army. He took up the fallen banner from the dead grasp of the bannerman felled by one of the few of Gudrød's archers and waved the signal which would free Asa's army from the constraints of an ordered battle line to break over Gudrød's depleted army in a tsunami of whirling steel.

Tired, hemmed in, depleted in number, Gudrød's men were in no state to repel the onslaught. They held for a moment and then broke. Despite the gods' best efforts, they could not instil enough bravery and fight into enough men to hold the tide, also not helped by the fact that Skadi was cutting them down almost as fast as the gods could bless them. The gods desisted, returning to Odin's side.

'Sorry, Father; there is nothing we can do. The day is lost for your man,' Thor announced glumly. 'And who knew Skadi was such a great shot?' He cast an admiring glance at the huntress, who now stood resting, breathless and tired, against her bow.

Odin too looked to Skadi and seeing her momentarily distracted gave Thor one last order. 'Find Gudrød and get him away from here.'

'What?'

'Gudrød, get him out of here. Clear a path for him and his most loyal. They may not win today but nor are they dying.'

'Seriously, let it go, Dad. Skadi's humans have done a better job. Let them have the win.'

'No. I want to see the look on Skadi's face when she realises her prey has escaped. I want to see her fury. I want to hear her howl!'

Thor gave his dad a worried glance. 'O-kay. Well, you lot, with me!'

'Why? What are we doing now?' asked Frey.

'I'll tell you on the way.'

Skadi, her attention drawn to the last remaining fight of any consequence, namely Guthrun versus Agnew, failed to notice Thor and the others bundle Gudrød and his best away. Later, in a rage, a huge silver wolf would rampage across this winter land, slaughtering beast after beast which may have helped provide sustenance to Gudrød's loyal villages over the long, hard winter, causing many more to die than would normally have been the case. But for now, she watched as Guthrun Doombringer faced off against a warrior with amazing hair and carrying the mark of Hel – Agnew.

As well as the Agnew–Guthrun fight, Skadi witnessed Agnew's men turn to face a force which had detached itself from the main army and was streaming up the hill to tackle them. Hel's mob, as Skadi had come to refer to them, locked shields and hunkered down, ready to fight, but Skadi, ignoring that as a mere side show, gave her full attention to the Guthrun-and-Agnew showdown.

Guthrun Doombringer, normally so self-assured in battle, moved with a reticence no one had seen before. It was as though he were fighting for the first time, concerned he had something to lose. Agnew by contrast was moving with a cold focus which belied any doubts. What by all accounts should have been a monumental fight instead became a game of cat-and-mouse, with Agnew very much the cat, toying with its prey. A little nick here, a small slice there, bit of a cut under that – Guthrun was losing the fight by increments. Worse still for Guthrun, every time Laevateinn bit he felt the skeletal hand of Hel taking a grip once more, the rake powerless to protect him. In his opponent he only saw annihilation in green burning eyes looking back. Guthrun didn't know what he was fighting but it was no longer a man. It was something far worse.

Guthrun dropped back a few steps to buy himself a moment or two to think, to look for a weakness in Hel's champion which he could exploit. Worryingly, he could spot nothing, except that out of the corner of his eye he caught sight of men from his own army charging up the hill towards him. Those with Hel's champion formed a line to resist them, but the numbers were not on their side. Guthrun's men would simply overwhelm and burst through. Guthrun just had to hold out until they made it to him. He was prepared to die but not at the hands of this monster. He had earned a place in Valhalla, but all he could see with every strike from Agnew was the portal to Hel's realm opening up beneath him, and he knew with complete certainty that if this man killed him, he would be Hel's to torture until Ragnarök.

Fear drove Guthrun on. He fought with a tenacity and strength which would have normally beaten far better warriors than Agnew, but Agnew was now Laevateinn and Laevateinn was better than any human. The end, when it came, was sudden and strangely unclimactic. Tiring, not unlike Tostig before him, Guthrun took a desperate step away from a low swipe from Laevateinn when his ankle turned beneath him. Part stumble, part hop, Guthrun tried to move away, but he was too slow and Laevateinn simply kicked his good foot from under him. Guthrun landed on his back, the wind knocked from him. Laevateinn stepped over him. Guthrun tried to swing his axe from his prone position at Laevateinn's ankles, but the weak strike was brushed aside, leaving him exposed and undefended. He saw some of his own men sweeping around the shield wall to get to him as the others engaged Hel's troops, but he knew it was too late. Laevateinn pierced his heart, from which the magic from the rake, which had restarted and continued to keep pumping his heart since escaping Hel's domain, scattered to the four winds, leaving

Guthrun's body dead and empty on the ground. Guthrun's soul fell away into the depths of Niflheim, watching the world of the living close over him. An icy female voice whispered, 'Welcome back, Guthrun Doombringer,' and the soul of the great berserk let out a horrific wail of despair, which was answered by the wails of the doomed.

Back on Midgard, the warriors, led by Bjarke, who had swept around the shield wall formed by Agnew's men, saw Guthrun fall. They charged at the man stood over his body, determined to cut him down to avenge Guthrun, but as they came face to face with the demonic Laevateinn, Bjarke and the others' charge stalled. A feeling of terror took over them, and as one they turned and fled, the feeling transferring to those battling Agnew's men. As Bjarke and the others streamed past them, they too fled. Alone on the hillock Laevateinn stood, cold and imperious, over the body of Guthrun. Those who remained of Agnew's crew took a moment to catch their breath and look for where the next attack was likely to come. Delling, who'd ended up having to take a place as part of the shield wall after he'd finished his charge across the battlefield to reach Agnew, bloodied and weary, finally got the chance to approach what he thought of as Agnew.

'Agnew?'

Laevateinn looked down at him with an uncomprehending stare.

Delling took a tentative step closer. 'Agnew, it's me, Delling.'

'Delling?' the creature replied, its voice seeming to come from a far-off place.

'Yes, you know, Delling. Hel sent me to support you. Don't you remember? You threatened to kill me; I tried to kill you. I kicked you in the balls once.'

'Delling, Hel's minion?'

'I prefer the term aide.' A bit of the old Delling's pride surfaced, causing him to cringe the moment he replied, expecting to be cut down where he stood, but the creature made no move against him.

'What do you want, Delling, aide of Hel?'

'Um, well for starters it would be nice if you stopped talking as though you were miles away in a cave. And if you could stop the flaming green eye thing, that would also be good.'

'And why would I do that?'

'It's friendlier.'

'Is that important?' Laevateinn spoke with a voice like a tree's roots cracking a boulder.

'Yes,' said Delling, 'it's important to me.'

'Why?'

Delling paused.

'Well?'

'Because you're my friend, and I don't like seeing you like this.'

'Friend?'

'Yes, you're my friend. It's hard to have a friend who is bloody terrifying.'

The Laevateinn creature looked blankly at Delling.

'Dammit, Agnew, you're human, not demon. You need to come back. I need you. Your men need you. Tostig needs you,' he said, pointing at the prone figure of Tostig lying in the snow some way away. 'You need to come back.'

'I don't think I can.' The voice changed momentarily to that of Agnew's. 'I, we, are not what we were.'

'For fuck's sake, Agnew, pull yourself –' Delling shouted, when a cold hand rested upon his shoulder.

'Allow me,' said Hel, who carefully took hold of the wooden staff which was Laevateinn, which by now was fully entwined with Agnew's arm all the way to his shoulder, with further tendrils piercing him about the neck. Speaking in a tongue unknown to even Delling, she maintained her hold. Slowly, carefully, the tendrils piercing Agnew's skin withdrew from his body, only leaving pinpricks of blood to show they had been there at all, the thicker strands unwinding until eventually Laevateinn separated itself from Agnew, with only his own grip upon it keeping the two together. Hel whispered in his ear and planted a light kiss on his cheek and slowly Agnew's grip loosened upon the staff until, reverentially, Hel removed it from him entirely. As she did the green fires within his eyes flickered out and Agnew collapsed to the floor.

'Is he dead, Mistress?' Delling asked, concerned.

'No.'

'Are you sure?'

'I'm the Queen of the Dead. I think I would know.'

'Oh, sorry.'

'And so you should be.'

'Sorry, Mistress.'

'Now, if you really want to be my aide,' she grinned wickedly, 'go find something to wrap Laevateinn in.'

'Aide?'

'Yes. Why are you still stood here?'

'Yes, Mistress, sorry, Mistress.' Delling scurried off to find something to wrap Laevateinn in.

Still holding Laevateinn, Hel reached down to the body of Guthrun. Flipping the corpse on its side, she removed her precious rake from the holster which held it to the body. Instantly she felt a surge of power she had been missing since it had been taken and felt like her old self again. Hel stood tall, unseen by the mortals still doing battle. She saw, a short way from where Agnew's comatose body lay, the rag-tag band of Agnew's men, those still alive, starting to form another shield wall as another larger part of Asa's army came hurtling up the hill towards them.

'Enough!' she commanded, and time stopped for her. Hel walked along the line of Agnew's men, tapping each upon the shoulder, then walked through those who had fallen, touching each. Once she got to Tostig, the last to feel her touch, Hel chanted something and clicked her fingers. Time snapped back into place, leaving Asa's men to charge up the hill into a strange, cloying mist which appeared as if from nowhere, obscuring their view of all but those closest to them. Slowly the mist dispersed. Of their enemy there was no sign, only their own slain, Guthrun among them, lying upon the snow.

Behind the tree line from whence they had launched their attack, Agnew and his men, the living and fallen, rested in a protected bubble separated in time between the living and the space where the gods dwelt, leaving only Delling conscious in her presence.

'Mistress.' Delling offered up the cloth which had originally bound Laevateinn. The Queen of the Dead took it and carefully wrapped the staff within it once more.

'I have a job for you.'

'Yes?'

'Return this to your cousin.'

'What about them?' Delling pointed at Agnew and the crew.

'Leave that to me.'

'I would like to say goodbye, if I may.'

'Delling, go now. Don't make me tell you twice.'

'Yes, Mistress,' Delling replied sulkily, not moving.

'You're still here.'

'Just getting my things together,' said the dwarf reluctantly. He paused, hoping for a reprieve, but none was forthcoming, only a terrible stare, and Delling realised his wish to bid them farewell was not to be granted. Delling chanted the words which, while in the presence of Hel, would open a portal to Niflheim without the need for expansive and convoluted rituals, and stepped through.

Hel took in the moment of her victory; she had her staff back and it felt good. A small smile played across her lips until the sight of Agnew lying weak and washed out made her wonder if the price had been too high, then she shook herself of such stupid notions. She was a goddess – what was the plight of a single human to her? Then again... She was about to admonish herself when wild whooping carried across the winter sky along with the snorting of horses. 'Valkyries.' Hel huffed, leaving the trees and made her way out upon the battlefield, where the battle was all but done. Hel watched as Asa's army put to the sword those of Gudrød's army who had failed to break away and flee into the darkness of the rapidly falling night.

Hel placed her cowl upon her head, straightened her cloak and, as befit the Queen of the Underworld, stalked across the field of battle to where the immortals had gathered acrimoniously to divvy up the spoils. She asked sarcastically, 'So, how are we going to sort this mess out?'

40

The gods, goddesses, and other magical creatures which made up the Norse pantheon were, by and large, a lairy bunch that liked a good fight and tended to break their own rules like they were going out of fashion, but despite that, when something serious was to be sorted they all tended to fall back in line and looked to the King of the Gods to bring order. It is of little surprise then that over this bloody body-strewn battlefield, everyone who wasn't human was looking to Odin to speak first, in part out of deference to his rank and partly because no one else wanted the job of sorting out the current schism.

Odin, still bristling with anger, was doing his best not to smite Skadi where she stood. Skadi, while not exactly happy, because Odin had ensured Gudrød the Hunter had got away, was still feeling smug that her side had won the battle and rendered Gudrød a vastly weakened king. Confident Asa's force could deal with Gudrød later, Skadi glared triumphantly at Odin, which was not helping his mood.

Bright enough to realise an open confrontation with Skadi was not in his or the gods' best interests, Odin ignored the huntress to address Hel. 'Why are you here?'

'Just collecting what's mine,' Hel replied enigmatically.

'You have already collected far more than your due this winter.'

'True. More have come my way, but that was not of my doing.'

'You lost your rake.'

'It wasn't lost; it was stolen.'

'Same thing.'

'Hardly.'

'It still worked out in your favour. Why did you just not just take it back from the one who stole it? That would have been no effort for you.'

'Unlike some, I believe in following the rules.'

Odin growled at Hel's caustic reply. 'Careful, Hel, I am not in the mood to be lenient.' And in the world of men, the sky rumbled menacingly.

Hel's face hardened, and she was about to snipe back when Loki stepped between the two. 'I think all my daughter is trying to say, in her own cold less-than-diplomatic way, is that the rules forbade her to interfere directly with the human who stole her rake. It was not a slight at you, All-father.'

'Yes, it bloody –' Hel bristled, only to be cut short by her father.

'She merely applied the rules as best she could to retrieve that which is rightly hers, and as you can see, it is once again back in her ownership.'

'Why should I trust you, Loki? All this,' Odin gestured to the carnage lying across the field, 'has your mark upon it. If I find you had anything to do with any of this, I will ensure your last torture will seem but a pleasant distraction by comparison.'

'Whoa, there's no need for that,' Loki wheedled. 'I was minding my own business down on Midgard. It was Thor who dragged me into this.'

'And yet why don't I believe you?'

'Ummmmm?'

'He's right,' chipped in Thor, 'I brought him into this. This wasn't Loki's doing, it was hers,' he said, pointing accusingly at Skadi, though he couldn't help giving her a crafty wink, which only she, and of course Loki, noticed.

'I was within my rights to avenge the daughter of –'

'Yes, yes, I get it – you all had reasons.' Odin snorted irritably, not wanting Skadi to go into her reasons in front of everyone. 'You know, I think I'm beginning to see why that Christian god works alone.'

'Like you could do any of this alone,' Hel scoffed.

'Daughter...' Loki warned.

'Hallo.' A female voice spoke from above them. Each looked up to see a tanned blonde girl in her early twenties, sat atop a horse, wearing a winged helm and armour which looked like it had been fashioned more to accentuate her youthful, lithesome form than to provide any protection in battle. 'My sisters were wondering if we can claim our dead yet?'

'Not now, Hildr,' Odin snapped.

Hildr sighed heavily. 'Are you going to be long?'

'Why? Have you some other battle to be at?'

'No.'

'Then you can wait like everyone else.'

'But we have plans.'

'Dammit, Hildr, just wait. The dead aren't going anywhere.'

'But they are going off,' Hildr replied petulantly.

'Put your lip away; that doesn't work on me.'

'You're no fun.' Hildr pouted, wheeled her horse around and trotted to join a bunch of similarly attired young women sat atop magnificent steeds, looking bored.

'Right, perhaps the adults can continue. How about we all just claim our due, go our separate ways and never speak of this sorry affair ever again?' Odin suggested hopefully.

'Fine by me,' said Hel.

'Do we even need to be here?' Thor asked. 'Me and the lads were just wondering if we could, well, you know...'

'Can I come?' asked Loki, but his request was not met with enthusiasm by the male gods.

'What?'

'Surely not.'

'He can't, can he?'

'No, Thor, say no. Nothing good will come of this.'

'Awwwww, come on, lads, I've done my time away,' Loki pleaded. 'Thor, please? You know things are always more fun when I'm around.'

'Fun for whom?' said Frey. 'Certainly not us.'

'Really? Have you forgotten the time me and you partied with those wood nymphs?'

'Well...'

'And you, Heimdall, you can't tell me you've forgotten when we pranked Idun and swapped her apples for pears.'

'Seriously, you're bringing that up? That little trick nearly killed us all.' 'What, no, did it? I don't remember. Oh, hang on... shit, yes, that... fuck... sorry.'

Thor sighed. It was always fun with Loki around but he did have a habit of pushing things just a little too far. Still, this time he'd hoped enough time had passed for the other gods to let him back into the fold without too much persuading, so before Loki managed to talk the others out of letting him join, he threw a meaty arm around the trickster's shoulders and with a pointed stare at the others said, 'You can come, Loki, on one condition.'

'Which is?'

'You can only fleece them, not me.' The God of Thunder smiled, causing at least three of the Valkyries to have a bit of a moment.

'Agreed.' Loki smiled.

'What?'

'No!'

'No fair!' the others protested, but Thor was having none of it.

'He's coming. And that's the end of it.'

'YES!' Loki fist-pumped.

'Well, sod off then,' said Odin.

'One moment,' replied Thor. 'I've just got to have a word with my daughter.' And he wandered over to one of the Valkyries.

They spoke for some minutes as everyone else just sort of hung around not really saying much, as people who know each other too well but finding themselves in an unfamiliar setting tend to do. They all watched as Thor and the Valkyrie, another impossibly blonde, impossibly pretty girl with shoulders and toned arms an Olympic swimmer would kill for, spoke animatedly, both of them occasionally looking over at the main group. For a while the girl seemed determined to defy her father in whatever he was asking her to do until finally, with a peevish flick of her hair, she seemed to concede. Thor said one last thing and patted his daughter's horse. Ignoring the rest, he walked up to Loki.

'Well?' asked Loki.

'She said yes.'

Loki's face split into a beaming grin, and he gave Thor's daughter a wave, who said something to the Valkyrie to her right. They both looked at Loki, giggled and went back to whispering between them. 'What? What are they saying?' he asked.

'Search me, but you have a date.'

'Thanks, mate.' He clapped Thor heartily on the shoulder.

'Don't thank me yet. She's a holy terror.'

'Nah, thanks. It'll be fun.'

'I'll remind you of that when she's beaten you black and blue.'

'What?'

'Just don't come crying to me afterwards. Remember, I warned you.'

Loki looked to the whispering giggling Valkyrie, his smile wavering. 'What? No, it'll be fine,' he said, as much to reassure himself.

'Can we get on, please?' snapped Skadi.

'Just helping out a friend,' said Thor.

'What are you, twelve? Can he not ask the girl out himself?'

'Normally, yes, but Þrúðr, she can be difficult, and...'

'ARGH! Will you all shut UP!' Odin banged Gungnir on the ground. 'I don't fucking care about Loki's love life. Will you lot just fuck OFF!'

'Okay, okay, keep your hat on; we're going. C'mon, lads.' Thor gathered the men to him, ready to leave.

'Going somewhere? Not on account of me, surely.'

'Oh, for the love of...' Odin's shoulders fell. 'Might have guessed you'd show, Freya. What do you want?'

'Oh, you know me,' the goddess with fiery-red hair ran her hand playfully across Thor's chest, 'never one to miss a party,' she purred, and every one of the male gods felt a sudden stirring in their pants while the assembled goddesses and Valkyries alike felt just a twinge of jealousy. 'I believe you have some lovely warriors for me to pick out. Oooh, what about that one?' she said, eyeing the prone form of some strapping warrior whose body lay upon the snow where he'd fallen.

'You cannot just turn up and claim any you fancy!' Hel pronounced forcefully.

Freya looked at her as though she were only noticing her for the first time. 'Sorry, hun, didn't see you there. You want him, you have him,' she answered graciously. 'There's plenty to go around. Ooooh, that one looks like he could be a lot of fun,' she said, pointing out another muscle-bound hulk. Say what you like about Freya, but she definitely had a type.

'You lot, why are you still here?' Odin addressed Thor and the male gods.

'No reason,' said Thor.

'We were, just, you know,' replied Tyr vaguely.

'I think I dropped my axe. It's around here somewhere,' Heimdall stuttered.

'It's in your hand, Heimdall,' Frey slapped its haft, 'and stop leering at my sister.'

'I wasn't.'

'Was.'

'Was not.'

'Yes, you were.'

'I'm telling you, I don't leer.'

'I bloody was.' Loki grinned as Frey turned angrily towards him. 'Hey, I'm just a god who can't say no. You know that.'

'Thor, get out of here, and take that sorry bunch with you, then maybe the rest of us can finish here before Ragnarök starts.'

'Yes, Dad,' Thor replied apologetically and ushering the bickering gods away like a sheepdog marshalling its herd, they finally left the battlefield, leaving Odin, Hel, Skadi, Freya, and some bored-looking Valkyries to finish up.

'So, shall we get to it?' asked Hel.

Odin let out a heavy, tired breath. 'Yes, if you must.'

'Good. Those who died fleeing are mine.' Hel staked her claim.

'What of the one who served me?' asked Skadi.

'Whom do you mean?'

'The Doombringer.'

'He's mine,' Hel answered forcefully. 'He escaped me once, stole my rake and is now back where he belongs, languishing in my lands.'

'He fought and died bravely,' Skadi attested. 'He deserves better.'

'He deserves naught but torture, despair, and suffering.'

'For what, humiliating you?'

'There are other reasons,' Hel answered coldly.

Skadi turned to Odin. 'He fought bravely; he died bravely. He is a fearsome warrior. You will need such men at the end.'

'Why do you care?' asked Odin. 'For once, I agree with Hel. She has claim.'

Skadi squirmed on the spot, looking vexed.

'Speak now or I leave him with Hel.'

'I promised him.'

'You had no right,' spat Hel. 'He was already mine.'

'You lost him.'

'Temporarily, and now I have him back, and I intend to keep him. He has caused me much trouble.'

Odin grinned nastily. 'I defer to Hel.' He bowed disingenuously and walked away, leaving the goddesses to themselves.

'You have no place here,' Hel dismissed Skadi, walking away. 'What is to be done now is between me, Freya, and the Valkyries.'

'What will it take?' Skadi called after her.

Hel took another step then paused. Without looking back she asked, 'What do you offer?'

'A favour.'

'Ha! A favour from a wolf. You'll as soon tear my throat out as offer me your help.'

'Wolves are honest. They defend their pack. There is no duplicity between wolves. You allow the Doombringer to ascend to Valhalla, and I owe you a favour.'

Hel turned back to face Skadi. 'Why, Skadi? Why all this for him?'

'I didn't do it for him. I did it for her.' Skadi pointed at the figure of Asa, frozen in time, stood overlooking the battlefield.

'All this for a human female?'

'Why not a female?'

'I didn't think you leaned that way.'

'Does that matter?'

'Not to me.'

'Then, will you release the Doombringer?'

Hel leaned in close, took Skadi's face between both hands, pulled the huntress towards her and kissed her deeply. Hel could feel Skadi recoiling from her touch, but Hel ignored it and held Skadi hard against her. Slowly she released Skadi, their lips the last thing to disengage. 'Hmmm, not bad. Maybe there is something in this after all.' Hel smiled salaciously. 'Have him. But when I come for the favour, you will not deny me, whatever I ask.'

'Whatever you ask,' Skadi repeated, deflated.

'Know this: if you refuse me, I will drag his soul back to Niflheim, and on the last day he will fight for me.'

Skadi nodded.

'Then go, though you will have to retrieve him yourself; I have better things to do than scour my lands for one errant soul.' Hel waved the huntress away. Skadi paused briefly, fuming at how her victory had been so tarnished but accepted Hel's terms and begrudgingly sloped away.

'Finally,' said a statuesque Valkyrie with uncharacteristic short hair. 'Can we do this now?'

'Yes. Take your fill; the only ones you cannot take are those.' Hel pointed at Agnew and his men, still held in the protective bubble nestled within the trees.

'But those who died fought bravely. They deserve to feast in the halls of Valhalla.'

'They do, but I owe them a feast first.'

'You?' The Valkyrie raised a sceptical eyebrow.

'Yes.'

'But, they are heroes; they deserve –'

'Girls, girls, girls,' Freya swept into the middle of the group, 'let Hel have some of the good men for once. You have a play, darling, it'll be good for you.'

'What? No, that isn't –'

'And I just loved the way you put Skadi in her place – didn't know you had that in you.' Freya winked playfully. 'Any time you want to come up and... play, send a raven and we'll hook up.'

'I... I... I...'

'I'd love to know what freaky shit you dark girls get up to. Love the hair, by the way.'

Hel's hand strayed to her locks involuntarily and she felt herself blushing. 'I... but... it's just...'

'And just a suggestion – on your ebony side, try some ice-blue makeup on your eyelid, coupled with a blue lipstick,' Freya whispered conspiratorially, 'and have you ever considered a half-mask, made to look all mysterious, for your other side? Just think, your good side on display all made up, coupled with a sexy mask – trust me, it'll drive the boys wild, especially that nice warrior with the amazing hair I've seen you fawning over.' Freya stroked the ebony half of Hel's face. Then, as though she'd entirely forgotten what she had been saying, she spun around in the snow, laughing gaily. 'Oooooh, can I have that one?' S,he pointed at a strapping warrior pinned to the ground with a spear through his chest.

Hel looked to the Valkyries, who merely shrugged at the capricious Freya's behaviour.

'I will have him, and him, and oh yes, definitely him...' They could hear Freya's voice echoing across the field as she flittered from dead warrior to dead warrior. The Valkyries responded by kicking their horses into action to charge across the battlefield, selecting fallen warriors before Freya claimed all the hot ones.

Before she followed her sisters, the short-haired Valkyrie rode up alongside Hel and leant down in her saddle to whisper, 'Any time you want to borrow my lipstick, and lips, call me,' and then she was gone amongst the fallen, selecting warriors to take back to Asgard.

Hel, suddenly alone amongst the carnage, thought darkly, *seriously, kiss one girl and suddenly everyone wants to party with you. Why did no one tell me this before?*

41

I think it is time we left the gods, goddesses, and Valkyries squabbling over souls and instead take a trip back to the mortal plain where, true to form, humans were going about their usual business in the aftermath of battle: looking for fallen friends, putting the wounded enemy to the sword, robbing bodies of anything of note – you know, normal stuff. Not only that but ravens, crows, and other carrion opportunists were gathering to pick at the still warm and squishy flesh which littered the battlefield. Someone's loss is always something else's gain, so while an axe to the face may ruin your day, just remember, it's party time for magpies.

So, what of our various human protagonists? How were they dealing with the aftermath? Let's start with the living, shall we, and who shall we pick – um, eeny, meeny, miney, Asa. Yes, despite her convincing victory we find Asa feeling strangely deflated. Bjarke and Halvor had re-joined her, along with others of her trusted inner circle, ensuring no lurking Gudrød supporter wanted to make a name for himself by killing the woman who had brought down his king. At the final reckoning of the battle, it was the news of Guthrun's death she was finding the hardest to take. Even Gudrød's apparent escape from the killing field was causing her less distress.

'Who killed him?'

'We do not know. Before we reached those who took him down, a mist descended in which they disappeared like ghosts,' Halvor answered.

Asa looked to Bjarke, who was being surprisingly silent and looking a bit disturbed. 'Didn't you get to Guthrun first?'

'I did.'

'And?'

'Guthrun was already dead before we reached him.'

'Why did you not take revenge upon those who killed him and his men?'

Bjarke swallowed heavily as the image of Laevateinn staring at him sent a tremor of fear through him, almost causing him to break and run again.

'Bjarke? What is it?' asked Asa. 'You shake like a frightened woman.'

'I do not know what killed Guthrun, but it wasn't a man.'

'Surely you are mistaken?'

'No. It was...' Bjarke's voice tailed off.

'It's an evil omen.' Halvor shuddered as though the fear felt by Bjarke were contagious. 'The mist was not natural. It must be the work of the gods.'

'No, it was a demon,' Bjarke said quietly. He had been trying to come to terms with his encounter with Guthrun's killer and his own cowardice for not fighting it. He would say nothing of this, of course, but the fact he ran would eat away at him for years with disastrous consequences, but for now all he said was, 'I did reach Guthrun, but he was already slain. A strange demon stood over him. It had the build of a man, but one arm was of wood, its eyes glowed with a ghastly green fire, and... and...'

'And what?'

'Its hair. It had the most fantastic hair. Hair which moved as though blown by sweet Freya's kiss.'

The other Norsemen looked at Bjarke like he was mad and not a little suspect.

'You think I lie?' Bjarke bristled.

'No.'

'Then why do you look at me as though I am mad, Henrik?'

'It is nothing,' replied the warrior Henrik.

'You say "nothing", but your face says otherwise.'

'It is just I have never heard tale of such a demon.'

'It was a demon. It was, I tell you, it's true!'

Henrik looked to respond and not too nicely and most likely to allude that it was probably just some warrior whom Bjarke considered too pretty to kill – huh, nice hair, indeed – when Asa held up her hand, bidding them be silent. Asa had been convinced she'd felt the presence of something powerful and otherworldly ever since the death of her father, which had been guiding her hand, driving her belief that she would prevail and did not doubt for a second that if gods were on her side, other malevolent powers may not be. It stood to reason therefore that such powerful enemies may have chosen to rob her of Guthrun at her moment of victory. 'If Bjarke says a demon killed Guthrun, then a demon it was. Now, enough of such talk, for tonight we feast, celebrate our brave dead, and praise Skadi for our victory.'

'Skadi?' said Halvor, surprised. Skadi was not a goddess one normally thought of first when battle had been won. *Then again, Asa is a woman*, thought Halvor, *and they don't always think right*, but he was, despite everything else, wise enough to keep this thought to himself, for now.

'Yes, Skadi. She has been my guide throughout. Has she not brought us an amazing victory over the dog, Gudrød?'

'Well...'

'Skadi, Skadi, Skadi,' Asa started quietly, turning on the spot to face each of her retinue in turn, all the while her chant becoming ever more powerful. 'Skadi, Skadi, Skadi, SKADI!'

No Norseman worth his salt was about to bad-mouth a god or goddess, so even Halvor, despite his reservations, along with the others took up the chant 'Skadi, Skadi, Skadi', which went on for some time. Eventually, like a Mexican wave at a sporting event, the chant ran out of steam and died off. Satisfied her men were still with her, Asa ordered them to gather the troops together, collect their fallen and to head back to Kaupangen. Bjarke was commanded to take two other men and gather up Guthrun, charged with returning him to Kaupangen, ensuring no one was to rob his body on pain of death.

'What of Gudrød?' asked Halvor.

'Leave him.'

'We can send a party to chase him down. He won't have got far; we can still finish him.'

'No. Our men have done enough today. We will finish Gudrød later. Just gather the fallen and leave for home.'

'And the enemy fallen?'

'Leave them for the birds and wolves. The gods can decide if any among them are worth collecting.'

Without another word, each man went to carry out Asa's orders, only two staying by her side as guards. It would take time, and it would be late by the time the army arrived back in Kaupangen but arrive they did. For the next seven days there would be much celebration, which basically involved copious amounts of mead, meat, and sex, sometimes all at the same time. The dead were not forgotten. A mass of funeral pyres was built and lit, each pyre holding many fallen warriors. Only Guthrun was singled out with a pyre of his own and heralded as the hero amongst heroes of the battle. The mass funeral was, if anything, more of a party and celebration than the victory celebration itself. Here the Norse truly let rip as they praised and made sacrifice to the gods, in this case with Skadi the most exulted. Many looked on enviously at the funeral pyres, wishing that they too had fallen with their comrades, where they would join them in the feasting halls of Valhalla, but because they were still very much alive instead consoled themselves in the pleasures of drink and women.

If you are wondering what happened to Gudrød, in the days to come, after he skulked back to his own lands to see out the winter at Stivlesund, licking his wounds and swearing vengeance, he became, as we first found him, a drunken sot. Possessed of even darker and more violent moods than he'd displayed before, many looked to distance themselves from him. Yet those loyal to him knew their status came from the status for their lord, and so none dared depose him, and not only that but many of his men looked forward to the spring, when they could raise more troops and march on Asa again to wreak bloody revenge.

But it was not to be. One night, and while very drunk, having been carousing on one of his ships – why on a ship, who knows – maybe it was some Norse winter party boat thing like you would get in the summer at any Mediterranean party resort, though probably with fewer girls in bikinis because it's simply too fecking cold – Gudrød was staggering down the gangway to leave the ship when an assassin melted out of the night and thrust a spear through Gudrød. Tough as he was, Gudrød was no match for a spear through the chest and died where he fell. Gudrød's men instantly fell upon the assassin, killing him before he could escape. As it turned out, Gudrød's assassin was no trained ninja-esque special-ops type with years of assassinations under his belt but rather just Asa's page-boy, which is probably why he failed to escape, rather than fight his way out of a ring of steel presented by Gudrød's angry men, leaving a trail of corpses in his wake. Nope, being little more than a simple page-boy, he was simply hacked down where he stood with merciless fury. So, let that be a lesson to any would-be assassins out there encouraged to kill someone by a beautiful woman who is smiling seductively and playing coyly with their hair. It never ends well for you, EVER!

After the death of Gudrød and finally secure in her position, Asa returned to her father's lands and hall at Agder, where she raised her son, Halfdan, who in time would become Halfdan the Black, but that is another story.

With everyone else accounted for that just leaves us with the hero of this story and his brave if less-than-stellar crew. Last we saw of them, Agnew and the rest were held in Hel's protective bubble, either asleep or in some cases dead. Hel moved among them, touching each upon the brow, leaving Agnew till last. She stared at her sleeping champion and wondered why he awakened feelings in her no mortal should be able to. Pushing the treacherous emotions down and reminding herself that this was no way for the Queen of the Underworld to behave, she lay her ebony hand upon Agnew's brow and chanted softly. An icy-blue glow flowed out from her fingers to slowly envelop the sleeping Agnew. For a moment nothing happened, then his eyes flickered open, and the Viking sat bolt upright, teeth chattering, his hair almost frozen to the point where you could snap the ends off and cried out, 'AAAAAAARRRRGH! I'm f-f-f-f-fucking freezing!'

'Welcome back, warrior.'

'H-H-H-Hel?'

'You were expecting someone else?'

Agnew, shivering uncontrollably, couldn't answer. He felt literally cold to his very soul; it was as though ice ran in his veins. For a moment he wondered if he was now in fact dead. Was this what death was like? Just cold and a sense of emptiness?

'You are not dead,' Hel said, reading the concern upon his face.

'H-h-h-how do you know?'

'Really? This again? I am the Goddess of the Dead. I would – ah, forget it,' she cried, exasperated. 'Just trust me, Agnew, when I tell you, you are very much alive.'

'Th-th-th-then w-w-w-w-w-why am I so c-cold?'

'That will pass.'

'Before o-or after I d-d-d-die?'

Hel's eyes narrowed, and she placed her hand upon the shivering Agnew once more. She instantly recoiled as the cold bit deep into her fingers. 'What the...?'

'Th-that does n-n-n-not look good.'

'What is the last thing you remember?'

'G-g-get-t-t-t-t-ing ready f-f-f-f-for b-b-attle.'

'Do you remember the battle?'

Agnew scrunched his eyes and tried to pull back memories, but as he searched all he could see were two green glowing eyes staring back. Ghastly, green, and malevolent. Agnew tried to search past them. Hel, watching, saw his eyes close, brow furrowed in pain, his hands scrunching deep into his hair.

'Agnew, what do you see?' Hel asked.

Agnew couldn't hear, for in his head the green eyes had been joined by a green mouth which cackled and taunted, 'Did you think I would go so easily?'

'Who are you?'

'I am part you, son of Grimor the Furious, and also part Doombringer,' the voice bayed, and in Agnew's mind the visage of Guthrun Doombringer appeared, confused and angry.

'What is this?' asked the image of Guthrun.

'The pair of you are wedded to me. Your salvation lies in freeing me.'

'Who are you, demon?' the spirit of Guthrun growled.

'Ask him.' The green mouth laughed.

'Laevateinn,' Agnew whispered.

'What?' asked Guthrun.

'Play nice; set me free,' the voice of Laevateinn oozed.

'Or else?' Agnew's mind's eye stared defiantly back.

'Or else the pair of you will be cursed to limbo, where I shall torment you till the very stars wink out.'

'Ragnarök, then.' Guthrun's spirit huffed. 'Always fucking Ragnarök.'

'How?' asked Agnew. 'We killed him,' he said, pointing at the shade of Guthrun in his mind.

Laevateinn just laughed. 'Ask your goddess.'

'Goddess?' queried Guthrun.

'It means Hel.'

'Why would Hel help?'

'Long story; don't ask.'

'Best not hang about, Agnew. I give you till Midsummer.' The green eyes and mouth swirled angrily and lunged at Agnew, who threw up his arms to protect his face, only to be hit by what felt like a hundred sharp teeth piercing his skin, causing him to cry out in pain, and suddenly he was back awake, lying on the forest floor, staring up at an anxious-looking Hel.

Agnew sat up. He no longer felt cold, but his right forearm prickled. Agnew ripped off his bracer and rolled up his sleeve, only to see there on his forearm a ghastly green slightly luminescent tattoo of Laevateinn. Agnew looked at Hel, looked back at his arm, back at Hel, ran his hand through his hair and said, 'I think I have a problem.'

And here, folks, ends the first part of Agnew's saga. Will he do what Laevateinn wants? How is a dead Guthrun Doombringer involved? What of Tostig, Siggeirr, and the others? Now she has her rake back, will Hel care? Come to that, do you care? Does anyone care? All questions for another time. For now, it is time to leave these Nordic shores, leave the snow and blood behind and go get a warm brew and maybe a biscuit. Go on, you've earned it for sticking with this for so long. Until the next chapter of Agnew's saga, farewell and good health.

Epilogue

Olsen, sat atop Små Triks, had had a steady, uneventful journey through the forest. The fjord pony had, with an unwavering gait, carried Olsen along pathways it seemed totally comfortable with, finally bringing them out of the forest as the first light of dawn lit the sky. Of Agnew and the others there was no sign. Olsen dismounted and let Små Triks graze away at some tufts of grass which hadn't entirely been blanketed by snow.

Olsen waited and waited but none of the crew exited the forest. Assuming he'd taken a wrong turn somewhere, he assumed the others would come out some way further round the forest. Mounting the pony once more he began to skirt the forest edge, assuming he would meet back up with the men at whatever point they exited the forest. After the best part of a day and with the sun, which had never gotten particularly high, hanging low in the sky, casting long, weak shadows, Olsen knew he needed to find some form of shelter for the night and to gather some wood for a fire.

Something about the forest suggested he shouldn't seek shelter within, so he turned the pony's nose away and let it choose its own path. Små Triks carried them away from the forest, though every now and then, as they came out of a hollow and crested a rise, Olsen could see that the forest still flanked them on either side. He let this go on for a little while, aware that the forest seemed to be closing back around them, when as they trudged over yet another small hill, down below he could see a ramshackle – well, the first word which sprung to mind was hovel, but at second glance that may have been a bit unfair, so we'll stick with ramshackle – dwelling nestling near to the forest edge, which flanked each side bar the one he was approaching from. He could hear a stream babbling lazily away somewhere nearby, though he couldn't see it.

A faint glow pierced the sides of the dwelling from within and a thin plume of smoke drifted skywards in the still evening air. Not giving a moment's thought as to who may live in a place like this, Olsen nudged Små Triks down to the dwelling. Just as he reached it, the door swung open and a woman stepped out, wooden bucket in hand. She saw Olsen, screamed and dropped the bucket, spilling its contents on the hut's threshold as she fled back inside.

This wasn't a wholly new experience for Olsen. When heavily armed warriors turned up out of the blue, especially when day gave way to night, this was a fairly typical reaction, so not taking any offence at this apparent rudeness and perceived statement of his intent, Olsen calmly dismounted the pony, scooped the food waste back into the bucket, setting it down right way up, then knocked on the door.

'I don't have much,' the woman's voice called out fearfully from within. 'Please, take what you want and leave. Just don't kill me.'

'I have no intention of killing you,' Olsen replied in his most reassuring voice, which still sounded gruff and threatening. Oh, come on, he's a bloody Viking; they don't tend to sound anything but gruff and threatening, but to Olsen, he thought he sounded friendly, probably in the same way tigers don't purr but occasionally growl, friendly-like. 'I am lost. I have got separated from my friends. I just need somewhere for me and my pony to shelter for the night.'

Nothing happened. Olsen could feel heat coming from within just as on his back he could feel the temperature plunging drastically as the sun finally gave up the unequal struggle and gave in to the night.

'Please. I am just looking for shelter for the night and for my pony. I wish you no harm. We will leave in the morning as soon as day breaks.'

Still no response. Olsen was considering if he would actually have to force his way in, which he didn't want to do, but he was damned if he was going to freeze to death through a sense of politeness, when the door opened a crack and the woman peeked furtively out through the crack.

'Are you alone?' she asked.

'Yes.'

'How did you end up here?'

'I came through the forest.'

Suddenly the door opened wide, letting light and heat flood out, which only further reminded Olsen just how cold he was. 'The forest?'

'Yes,' said Olsen. Behind him his pony snorted impatiently and stuck its head in the bucket and began munching on what was within.

'She did it,' said the woman. 'She kept her promise.'

'Who did?'

'Skadi; she has provided.'

'Skadi? I don't think...'

'Please take the pony around the back. There is a shelter it can go in. There are some turnips there you can let it eat.'

'Okay.'

'Then please join me.'

'Okay. I am Olsen,' said Olsen, 'and thank you.'

'I am Kalda.'

Olsen took Små Triks to the lean-to around the back of the main dwelling and stabled her. The lean-to was surprisingly snug and well sheltered, and the pony seemed content being placed inside and even happier when presented with turnips to munch on. With the pony sorted Olsen returned to the front. Removing his weapons first, he entered Kalda's home.

Outside, stood at the top of the hill looking down upon Kalda's place, Skadi and Loki watched as Olsen entered.

'Do you think he will be quite so happy when he realises she's a witch?' Loki asked.

'She is more than just a witch,' said Skadi.

'And you think that will make him any more well disposed towards her?'

'She is pretty. She has given him shelter. She will feed him. Before morning breaks, he will be under her spell.'

'If you are doing this to get back at my daughter, I doubt she will care about this one.'

'This has nothing to do with Hel. Also, I wish him no harm. He was good to me and my pony. This is his reward.'

'Shacked up with a witch surrounded by a forest which wants to kill him? Some reward.'

'I did not ask you here to comment on what I have planned for these two. I just wanted to make sure we understand the nature of our alliance.'

'Sure, Skadi. I scratch your back and you don't rip my throat out when I'm not looking.' Loki smiled playfully in the dark.

'You joke, but if you cross me that is what I will do.'

'Chill, wolfie. I've got your back.'

Skadi glared at Loki with ill-concealed distaste. 'I am not happy that it is you I need to rely on.'

'I know.'

'And this changes nothing between us. I still hate you.'

'I know.'

'But I hate Odin more.'

'I know. And the enemy of my enemy...'

'Agreed.'

'And if it helps, I still think you're hot, and if you ever want to get it on –,'

'That's not going to happen.'

'Shame.'

The god and goddess stood in silence for a while, Skadi wondering if she could really trust the Trickster God, while Loki wondered how he would get her to let him bed her. With nothing left to say for the moment they parted ways, leaving a Viking and a witch getting to know each other. What could possibly go wrong?

The author

Lee Kite was born in Chiswick, London and attended Preston Polytechnic, now the University of Cen-
tral Lancashire. Lee lives in rural Lancashire with
his partner, Aimee, and their dog Milo. When not
working or walking Milo, Lee can be found either
attempting to write or more likely filling his time
with all things distracting, be it travelling, reading, watching movies, or hunting down new and
interesting bands. To make sure he does something
energetic, Lee also goes fencing, as he claims there
is something very therapeutic in stabbing someone
legally in swashbuckling ways.